THE OPERATOR

PRAISE FOR *THE OPERATOR*

'Gripping from the very first scene.'
Ann Cleeves, award-winning author of TV's *'Vera'*
and *'Shetland'* crime novels

'Intelligent, dark and shot through with sly comedy, Valerie
Laws is one of those writers who consistently satisfies.'
Alex Marwood, best-selling author of *The Wicked Girls*
and *The Killer Next Door*

'A terrific book. Laws has crafted a very creepy, very haunting
mystery tale. THE OPERATOR does for going to the
doctor, what JAWS did for going to the beach. Trust me,
you'll never feel the same way about disrobing and lying on
an examination table. You're warned!'
Phoef Sutton, writer of TV's Cheers, producer
of Boston Legal, crime writer

'I enjoyed this book as much as The Rotting Spot. There are
loads of twists and turns along the way, with the final one
being a complete surprise. The climax of the book is bound
to set pulses racing, as it races to the end at breakneck speed.'
Chris Longmuir, award-winning author of
the *Dundee Crime Series*

PRAISE FOR *THE ROTTING SPOT*
Bruce and Bennett Mystery 1

ALSO FROM RED SQUIRREL PRESS
(Winner of a Northern Writer's Award, a New Writing North
Read Regional Choice, shortlisted for the McKitterick Prize)

'A darkly intriguing debut'
Val McDermid.

'Valerie Laws is a fresh and talented new voice in crime-writing. The Rotting Spot takes the established form of the rural detective novel, but brings it bang up to date. Here we have practitioners of complementary medicine and a binge-drinking pregnant young Geordie; we consider the relationship between women and food and the delights of skull collecting. And all within the framework of a well-structured plot'
Ann Cleeves.

'Opens with a bang…and interweaves a suspenseful story with graphic extracts from the Skull Hunter's blog. As Erica crosses paths with DI Will Bennett, he of the blue, blue eyes, and skeletons rattle loudly in closets, Laws brings her locations vibrantly to life'
Daneet Steffens, Time Out London.

THE OPERATOR

(Bruce and Bennett Crime Thriller 2)

Valerie Laws

CRIME

First published in the UK in 2014 by
Red Squirrel Press
Briery Hill Cottage
Stannington
Morpeth
Northumberland
United Kingdom
NE61 6ES
www.redsquirrelpress.com

Red Squirrel Press is distributed by Central Books Ltd
and represented by Inpress Ltd.
www.inpressbooks.co.uk

Cover image supplied by Allan Huggins
(designstudio@aahprintersolutions.co.uk)

Cover and text design by Andrew Edwards
(www.thirdfloorcreative.co.uk)

A CIP catalogue is available from The British Library.
ISBN: 978-1-906700-782

Printed by Martins the Printers
www.martins-the-printers.co.uk

For my son Robin, who, aged 2, saw me badly injured
and bristling with steel spikes in an orthopaedic ward,
and kept me going with his daily visits; and my daughter
Lydia, for her feedback and support during the writing
of this book: and for all doctors, nurses and medical
students who treat patients with kindness, respect and
consideration. It matters more than you know.

PROLOGUE

A man and an operating table. On it a youth lay on his back, fully conscious, his whole body tense. The man standing over him felt the familiar surge of power rewarded, of anticipation which never palled however often he indulged it. He picked up the young misshapen leg, bulging and deformed where the broken bone had splintered within it. He grasped it hard with finger and thumb, pinching with the very tips as if testing an apple for the first signs of give, feeling the damaged tibia as it already laboured to heal. The youth flinched, squirmed, the conflict of trying not to in front of the man clear in his face. A gasp burst out of him, smothered but delightfully audible. The young face was white, greenish, the eyes huge and dark, and the man could read the pain in them, and it felt so good.

And even better, the boy's mother was there too. She had to sit still and keep quiet while the man hurt her son. If only he had two independent sets of eyes, to watch them both, so as not to miss a single taste, a single bite of pain from either of them. What a bonus! A two for one package. The physical pain of damage, injury, anatomy wrenched awry; and the emotional pain of the mother wincing at her son's every pang, every stab of agony, feeling it in her belly, which she couldn't help clutching behind the shield of her handbag. She would gladly, poor stupid cow, suffer it all herself if only her son was spared, but here they both were, equally helpless, in his power, where their sort belonged.

He picked up one of the delicate, gleaming metal instruments that lay neatly ranged beside him, and began to work the end of one of the thin steel spikes that he had previously screwed into the skin, flesh and damaged bone of the boy's leg, one of many, each one creating a fresh wound, each one fixed to metal rings bolted together, so that he could adjust the tension between them in three planes, twisting, shearing, pulling. The youth's face was now grey-green, and his eyelids fluttered as if he was about to pass out, strange moans burst from his mouth. But he tried to hold them back. To please the man, to impress him. And the mother sat watching, unable to help, unable to stop the torment, her eyes like her son's, wide with pain. Neither of them resisted, neither complained, they were docile, pathetic, accepting his authority. This was better than punching and kicking, the cheap thrills of easy screams and begging. Better by far the small, humiliated sounds forced out of those who strove not to express their pain out of respect for him.

The boy's skin was damp with sweat, he breathed fast and shallow, the sharp odour of fear and adrenal arousal rose from him. His mother's hands were clenched on the thin arms of the plastic chair, knuckles white as a cadaver's, as if forcing herself not to spring uselessly to the boy's aid. But the man was finished with them for now, their intimate exchange one of so many locked in his excellent memory for later recall and enjoyment over a glass of burgundy, but there was one final refinement he waited for, and it came, total submission implicit.

'Thank the doctor,' she prompted her son. As the nurse indifferently aided him to rise and handed him his crutches, pain and endorphins still zinging through his veins, he said it. 'Thank you, Mr Kingston.' He limped off back into the crowded Orthopaedic Outpatients, where so many still waited. Slowly and painfully, the next patient began to stand up as the nurse announced, 'The doctor will see you now.'

CHAPTER ONE

Erica Bruce rang the doorbell again. She was expected. Surely he'd not have gone out. She shifted her feet, jogging up and down on her toes as she looked at the expensively landscaped and tended front garden, the well-clipped constrained conifers and the ornamental pond. Too clean for frogs or newts to live in, she noted with disapproval, but with a few polished-looking koi sluggishly rotating in it. Such a retro, sixties kind of expensiveness about the house, those tacky bits of white cladding on the brickwork, those ludicrous white pillars flanking the door, too heavy and bulbous.

Was Kingston never going to let her in? Perhaps some kind of alpha male power-play? Keep her standing out here, so she'd know her place. Perhaps he had forgotten their appointment. Though she'd emailed him a confirmation just last night, belting and bracing as usual. He must be in there.

A man, on an operating table. His eyes were open, looking at the ceiling with an opaque stare. The thick thatch of black hair on the back of his head was glued to the examination table by a puddle of dark thick blood. Right between his eyes on the midline between them but

5

centred on his brow, where the third eye is said to be, a shiny metal spike protruded like a big bright new six-inch nail. It was blunt-topped with no head, strong but slender, slightly aslant from the vertical. Another such spike stuck out centrally above each strongly-marked dark eyebrow, roughly orthogonal to the skin they pierced. In the shallow bowl of each temple was another nail, at about 45 degrees to the horizontal, and another just above each ear, more or less parallel to the surface of the table. Seven spikes symmetrically placed like a crown, clean and gleaming, though there were none at the back. Small dribbles of blood had leaked out of the wounds and dried to streaks on the pale skin, trickling obedient to gravity until slowed and stopped by clotting and drying.

His mouth sagged partly open, all muscle tone gone from his face, leaving it unlined and unconcerned, but the vacant gape spoiled the otherwise handsome looks he'd had in life. His legs were together to the knee in their stone-coloured expensively casual chinos, his ankles crossed so that the left foot lay across the right. His arms were spread as far as the width of the examination table allowed, his hands palm upwards. In the centre of each palm was another nail, impaling it to the table. The fingers and thumbs, with beautifully kept very clean nails, curled inwards towards the metal spikes as if in a defensive gesture.

On the table to the left of his crossed ankles was a chunk of stained and weathered stone, about the size of an irregular, flattened honeydew melon. Small clean chips of newly exposed sandstone showed through the grubby surface of soil and green algae. Sandstone which had felt the fire of volcanoes to forge each glass-like grain, then the weathering of countless ages of ice, rain, sun, then the weight of primeval seas on its layers, eventually planted in the soil of a garden rockery or hedgerow: longer than it took for the man beside it to evolve from a single cell, millions of years just to become a crude hammer. The chippings which had been loosened from the stone were nowhere to be seen on the floor which was clean apart from a few drops of blood.

He lay on the table, alone, and indifferent. The room had been hot with fear and rage, the air embittered by the adrenaline-charged sweat of extreme emotion, of someone as full of murder as the stone was full of years, but now it was cool.

There was a smell of blood in the room. It was an unfamiliar smell, though the room had often known pain.

Still outside, Erica felt a qualm of unease, and glanced around for a moment, wondering if Stacey Reed had come along after all. Perhaps she was lurking behind a monkey puzzle tree or something. But there was no waft of Lambert and Butler smoke drifting on the wind, and no noise. She wondered for the nth time how she'd got herself lumbered with a lass she'd first seen unconscious, going into drunken labour in a filthy back lane behind a night club at chucking-out time. As usual, Erica had got involved, making sure baby Noosh made her appearance in hospital rather than onto spilled chips and vomit. Now she ran through her conversation with Stacey the day before. Had she made it clear enough that this was a solo assignment?

'Aye, he was the kind of lad who'd run his dick under the tap before a blow-job. Proper classy, like.'

The unmistakeable strident tones of Stacey Reed on her phone had entered the room just before wisps of ciggie smoke, a waft of Lynx 'Attract for Her', her almost out and fully proud breasts, followed by her muffin top, then the rest of her. Ludicrously high heels swung in one hand, and her orange spray-tanned legs ended in grubby feet at one end and a tiny tight black skirt and white top at the other.

'And they said romance was dead.' Erica hastily minimised the current window on her pc, before the ever-curious Stacey clocked anything confidential. 'He your last night's hook-up then? Bit late for the walk of shame isn't it, even for you.'

'Walk? I get fkn taxis, me.' Stacey noted Erica's defensive minimising with amusement. As if she couldn't hack into her stuff any time she liked! Honestly, Erica was a bit thick for a clever lass with degrees and shit. 'So Aa'll be comin with yer, tomorra. Yer know, for that interview with that Kingston, like.'

8

'No you won't, and stop reading my confidential stuff, and put your cig -'

'Already oot man, woman. So yer can stop naggin. Aa've gotta smoke havn'a? Keeps me weight doon.'

She dropped into a chair which shuddered at the assault. 'Aa should deffo come with. Aa mean, Aa've got rights havn'a? Aa'm yer intern, like.'

'Stacey, for the gazillionth time, you are not my intern...'

'Bollocks. Yer don't pay iz, do yer? So I'm the intern.'

'You're not any intern, let alone the definite article. And I can barely afford to pay me.' Erica began typing up an appointment report, now that Stacey was safely out of sight of the screen.

'Too right! Wodda loser! Aa spend more on a night oot than ye earn in a week! Haway, man, let iz come with.'

'Let me explain again. I have two jobs. One, I'm a homeopath. You are NOT my intern. Two, I'm an alternative health journalist, freelance. You are SOOO NOT my intern. See the diff?'

'Bet Kingston's loaded... I'd love to see inside his hoose, man!'

But mainly because it was going to be what she considered too early to get up, too late to stay up, Stacey had agreed, kind of, not to turn up. And so far, she hadn't. Erica didn't let herself think about why Stacey might be so keen to get inside a doctor's house.

CHAPTER TWO

Still on Kingston's doorstep, Erica rang yet again, stabbing at the bell, then knocked painfully with her knuckles on the front door, a white heavily moulded one with a big brass knob. Trust him to have a bloody great knob right there in your face... compensating for something? Next to the door there was a sign under the brass plate carved with his name and all the letters he'd collected in the Scrabble game of University and training. 'PATIENTS WITH APPOINTMENTS PLEASE RING AND ENTER.' Erica had not considered herself a patient. Patience had never been her strong point, and was becoming more difficult to attain as she neared thirty. Maybe she was expected to walk in. Maybe everyone he knew was classified as colleague or patient, current or potential. Maybe he was waiting to meet her in his private consulting room, the expression of his power and authority. Typical, the arrogant tosser. Now, Erica, she told herself firmly, that's not the way to get a decent interview. Get a grip. She pulled down her shoulders, shook her wrists a few times to loosen her tension, unset her mouth from its firm line and pushed hard. The door opened. She felt foolish. All that ringing for nothing.

'Hello? Mr Kingston?' Her voice seemed to bounce off the gleaming Italian tiled hall floor, the creamy, expensively distressed walls, the lofty ceilings and swooping stairwell. 'It's Erica Bruce! Hello?'

Kingston's consulting room was on the left of the hall, a brass plate on the open door. She froze. The doctor was in.

She felt a sudden giddy flush flood over her at the sight of the man on the table, and the smell she unconsciously breathed in which was interpreted instantly by the primitive parts of her brain, launching an adrenaline response. Fight was not an option, flight was, but shock, curiosity and confusion held her still. For a moment a scream tried to erupt from somewhere inside her. She fought it down and stood with her eyes shut, until the rushing in her ears became less deafening, the banging of her heart less audible. She forced herself to go over to the body. Even now, he could be alive - there might be something she could do. Though a glance at the bizarre wounds, the blank eyes, the stilled blood told her none of the little bottles she carried would be any good in this case. She had fantasised about how cool it would be if she was able to cure this man of something, anything, even piles or warts, and make him eat humble pie. It didn't look as if he would be worrying about piles again, if indeed he ever had.

'Poor guy. I hope you didn't feel too much of this. I'm so sorry...' For some reason she had to speak to him, he seemed so alone. She felt tempted to touch him, offer comfort, but she didn't.

'Just stay there, and don't touch anything,' she murmured to herself. She knew the drill. She rummaged in her large shapeless embroidered bag for her mobile and punched in the numbers for emergency services.

Murder, no doubt about it. That meant the police, and that probably meant Detective Inspector Will Bennett and his minions. Couldn't be helped. 'Well fuck him,' she said aloud. Yeah right, been there done that, very nice too while it lasted.

Waiting for the inevitable, she went back out into the garden and sat on the white-painted garden seat next to the front door with its Queen Anne fanlight, an elaborate great scallop shell moulding above it. She kept seeing him crucified on that table where so many patients had painfully lain, hoping his smooth pinkly clean hands would cure them with the magic knife of surgery, the magic bullet of pharmacy.

The gibbon call of a police siren swooped louder and nearer, a car roared up the quiet street, at first hidden by the high hedges and naff topiary, and then swirled up the broad drive, stopping abruptly just before it hit an ornamental urn of geraniums. Two officers jumped out, first to respond. Their expressions were eager but stern. Chasing youths away from bus shelters and picking up drunks at chucking-out time were more usual police activities in the seaside town of Wydsand. Though more and more, violence both domestic and random, fuelled by drugs (mostly a pick'n'mix of ket, coke, E's) complicating the proud ancient Nordic culture of binge drinking, had enlivened the job. The PC looked absurdly young in his thick cuddly sweater which seemed so unlike a uniform. Surely I can't be old enough yet to think police officers are too young, she thought. He ran into the house, while the WDC stood in front of Erica, to ask if she'd made the call and take her name.

'You know my name, Sally.' Erica squinted up at her.

'I'm DC Sally Banner, Ms er...' The young officer's elfin face, dusted with freckles, and her cropped sand-gold hair, gave her a delicate appearance but her brown eyes were hard.

'Oh for pity's sake... there's a man dead in there, let's not play silly buggers.'

'Gotta do this by the book, serious crime and all.' She wrote down 'Erica Bruce' without making Erica actually say it. Barely had she finished that when the male PC ran out again, straight past the two women to a flower bed where he vomited over a begonia. Erica felt the nausea rise in her own throat and swallowed down the bitter hot liquid, as Sally Banner hurried in in her turn, and came out again, pale and shaken, reaching for the radio with trembling hands. This really was a big one. They really would have to do everything right. And trust Erica Bruce to be right here in the thick of it. In a carefully controlled voice Sally radioed for assistance, police doctor, CSI, the works. The male PC sat down next to Erica, clearly thinking here was something official he could do while parking himself next to someone more attractive than a violently slain corpse. He opened his mouth to speak, then shut it again, as if afraid of what his voice might sound like.

'New on the job?' Erica fumbled in her bag. 'Here, I might have something you can take for the shock. '

'No thanks,' said PC Paul Lozinski, according to his name badge, in a tight voice. 'We can't take drugs on duty. I think we'll have to have a look in this bag, Ms er.'

She didn't bother to object as he twitched the bag from her hands and began pulling out tiny cylinders, reading the labels. Aconite, Arsenicum, Belladonna, Opium. His eyebrows rose at the labels. 'Poison?' he asked, eyes narrowing. There was no proper poison warning label on the bottles. What was this woman into?

'It's OK, Officer. Those are homeopathic remedies. Not only harmless, but beneficial...'

'And totally discredited. By scientists.' Sally put in.

Erica ploughed on. 'And totally legal...'

'Not for much longer, with any luck.' Sally was clearly counting the days until she could lead a raid on Erica's premises.

'...and *still* totally legal. Which is unlikely to be the case with you searching my bag. Why, do you think he might have been poisoned?'

'Oh, this stuff.' Lozinski was holding the Bach's Rescue Remedy. 'My mam has this. Swears by it.' He opened the bottle and dropped the dark liquid on his tongue from the glass dropper inside the cap.

'Thanks,' he said.

Sally Banner gave him a disgusted look. She must feel her colleague had let the side down, first by being sick in front of a witness and now this. He didn't seem a bit ashamed though. Already the pallor was washing out of his rosy fresh young face, as he introduced himself formally to Erica and began to get on the case, looking at his colleague's notes.

'Ms Erica Bruce, is it? You found the erm... him?'

'It's Kingston. Robert Kingston. It's his house.'

'I see. Why exactly do you come to be here?' It was a loaded question. Erica knew the person to find the body would automatically be a suspect.

'Maybe we should do this in the car,' said Sally. She sounded nervous. What if Erica turned out to have done it, did a runner, and made them look stupid? She could run, after all. That was how Erica and the Guv had met, running on the beach. A meet-cute over a dead puffin, according to goss. Erica suddenly swerved and stopped, and he fell over her. Erica wanted its skull. Well of course, she would. The Guv was just another scalp for her collection.

'I think I need the fresh air,' Erica said, 'I wouldn't want to upchuck in your nice clean car.' She wasn't going to miss any of the action shut in the car like a troublesome child. And she hated being cooped up.

The thought of driving a sick-strewn car was enough to give them pause. Erica watched Lozinski look at her, sizing her up, deciding she'd be no match for them in a race or a struggle. Sally looked more sceptical.

Lucky I came in disguise, Erica thought. The loose, silky jacket, spotted scarf knotted below the neck, mid-calf pleated skirt were a size too big for her, making her look even smaller than she was and hiding the musculature regular, some would say obsessive, sessions at the gym had developed. She'd borrowed the outfit from a librarian friend, thinking it would make her seem demure and a bit dowdy and unconfrontational when interviewing the great Mr Kingston, Consultant Orthopaedic Surgeon. They certainly made her seem harmless physically to the male officer, who had relaxed slightly as soon as she had seemed to share his moments of weakness by threatening their upholstery with vomit.

'You seem remarkably calm.' Lozinski still sounded dubious. Had this x-chromosome contaminated person out-toughed him? None of the other begonias seemed to have suffered.

'I took some Rescue Remedy while I waited for you guys.'

Scribbling furiously, Sally muttered something which might have been 'Sodding placebo,' before going to greet the first of the arriving hordes of CSI and related crime scene personnel.

She had learned well at the feet of her master, Will Bennett, sceptic of this parish, thought Erica.

'Placebo or not, it helps. I'm not denying it's been rather a shock. I'm guessing that's your first dead body, Paul?'

'No, it's not,' he began assertively then realised this would make his reaction more feeble, not less. 'I mean, I've seen dead alcoholics and such. Nowt like this, mind.' He tried to take control. 'So again, how do you come to be here?'

'I'm a journalist.' He looked at her warily, as if reassessing her harmlessness. 'I was due to interview Robert Kingston... the dead man.'

That's what he was now after all; all the qualifications, publications, press photos, big earnings, all came down to those two words; dead man, like the thud of the first two spadefuls of earth on a coffin.

CHAPTER THREE

'You can definitely identify the, er, deceased as Kingston? You knew him?' Sally said sharply, veering back over to them as crime scene tape began to flutter with unsuitable frivolity.

'Never met him. But I've seen photos on his online profile and in the paper's archives.' It seemed wrong, and corny, to say 'morgue'. 'It - the body - looks like him. Aren't you being a bit previous? 'Deceased' I mean?'

'How do you mean?' Lozinski frowned.

'Police doctor hasn't said he's really truly dead yet.' The officers exchanged looks and Erica realised her flippancy, a defence against her own physical symptoms overwhelming her, was both out of place and suspicious.

'Big fan of *CSI*, all those shows,' she said weakly, trying too late to undo her remark.

The truth was she was more nervous about seeing Will Bennett again, very much alive and probably kicking, than seeing the body carried out. Sally Banner had already radio'd in that they had a witness on the scene, waiting to be interviewed. Female, five foot three, late twenties, blonde, slight build, by the name of Erica Bruce.

Another car appeared. Erica's dismay was visible on her face, nearly hidden as it was by her windblown hair.

'What's the matter, Miss? Known to the police, are we?' The green tinge returned to Lozinski's face as he recalled, and regretted, taking a substance from a bottle in this lass's bag.

'You could say that.' He'd know soon enough. Sally would catch him up. 'I'm a reporter,' she said again, as if this explained it, or indeed, anything and everything. The magic of the media opened doors, and shielded its servants. In theory.

Sally snorted, looking even more sceptical than she had at Erica's homeopathy. She went over to greet and escort the new arrival, who turned out to be the police pathologist. A spare and dry-looking man, he hurried past them into the house.

'Got yourself a big story now then, haven't you?' said Lozinski. He closed in a little as if expecting Erica to race off to file her scoop with the national press. She was in at the death, on the scene of a gory story most reporters even in a big bad city would die for, and not only would the police be unable to politely but firmly shove her out of the action, but they would have to make strenuous efforts to keep her on the scene as an important witness.

Erica felt a complete fool. It had never crossed her mind until that moment that she had a big story. Must be the shock.

'I'm not that kind of journalist - I mean, I write features for newspapers and magazines. Health, alternative therapies, of general public interest. Controversial treatments, con artists exploiting desperate people, new findings, drugs and remedies.'

Editing, and writing most of, the weekly 'You and Your Health' page on the Wydsand *Evening Guardian*, or contributing regularly to 'Well Being, Body and Soul' online was hardly 'hold the front page' stuff.

Erica paused and held down the alien voluminous skirt which threatened to blow up unsuitably saucily in the brisk breeze off the nearby sea front. She wasn't going to mention the rows she had with the *Evening Guardian's* editor over her habit of introducing controversy into what was meant to be 'a cosy women's chat over the fence,' as he put it.

'However,' she added, 'of course since I'm on the spot, I will be expected to give my editor a scoop for the *Evening*.'

She reached into her bag for her digital voice recorder. Sally and Paul Lozinski were disposed to object - it was a case of 'we will ask the questions'. Who was in charge of this interview anyway?

Things were getting tricky, so it was almost welcome to hear another siren approaching, wasting its sweetness on the desert air of suburban indifference. PC and DC alike leapt up as senior officers arrived amid the CSI personnel with much crackling of radios and equipment for dealing with violent death.

Two figures were unfolding themselves from the police car. One tall, dark-haired, blue-eyed and to be avoided at all costs, none other than Detective Inspector Will Bennett, ex-lover of a certain homeopath. The other, Detective Sergeant Hassan Massum, Asian, a little older, a family man calmly and competently providing the ballast of more experience and less career ambition.

'What a pair of prats! Bring it on, boys.' Despite her brave words to herself, Erica felt the need to busy herself and her hands and find a counter-irritant to what was coming so she called the *Evening*'s editor, Ian Dunne. He was thrilled to hear the hot news as Erica gave the basic details and her role at the scene. It was beginning to resemble some nuclear disaster as an ambulance arrived and the babygro'd and booteed CSIs began to mill about like big babies.

'Great!' drawled Dunne. 'Good girl!'

Erica ground her teeth. What was she, a dog that'd just brought his slippers?

'Just stay there,' as if she had any choice, 'and I'll send one of the lads out. You'll be a bit out of your depth, I expect.' There was a pause which she knew meant another cigarette had joined its immolated mates in the blue Gitanes ashtray which was the only stylish object in his office.

Erica now became perversely convinced that she was a news hound of the toughest kind.

'Send a -? Look, I can handle it,' she snarled. 'I'm on it....'

'He'll be there in ten,' choked the voice through a fit of coughing, and he hung up. Erica felt like ringing all the national papers and giving them the story just to show him and his local bloody rag that was only fit for wrapping chips.... but that opportunity was lost. Will Bennett, she'd seen via crafty glances, had gone into the house, while Hassan exchanged words with uniformed colleagues. She saw him glance her way with a look both of recognition and confusion about the correct protocol in the circumstances, before giving a sort of nod and heading into the house as Will emerged.

Detective Inspector Will Bennett came and stood over her, his annoyingly too-blue eyes cold, his thin, dark clever face tense about the mouth. Couldn't blame him. Big murder case, something serious going down, and to top it all, herself.

'Ms Erica Bruce?'

'Oh, please. You know damn fine it is. And stop looming, I'm not impressed. Perhaps you should investigate how name-blindness is running rampant through your lot. Your henchwoman Sally Banner gave me the same treatment just before.'

He went down on his hunkers beside her, his thighs bulging, muscular as ever. Bloody gym addict... Erica couldn't resist looking, hating herself for it. 'I see you still eschew the traditional doughnuts.'

'You found the body, I believe,' he informed rather than

asked her, his voice full of cold authority. 'It must have been a severe shock.' He gave a pointed glance at the newly decorated begonias.

'That wasn't me, and I resent your assumption that it was.'

'Ah, resenting assumptions. Almost a habit, wouldn't you say?'

'We all have habits, *Inspector*. Most of mine are rather more commonplace as you may recall. And one of yours is taking control. I see you're still doing it.'

'I'm the senior officer here Eri – Ms Bruce. We'll have to take a statement from you, of course, if you can come with us now? I'll get someone to get you a cup of tea when we get to the station. And we can arrange for counselling for you too.'

Damn him, that was a deliberate insult. He knew how she'd feel about that.

Doctors make terrible patients, it is said. Similarly, this therapist hated to be offered therapy. 'Tea! Ooh, I'm *so* there! Let me guess, Rich Tea biscuits. An abomination in biscuit form and a perverse waste of calories.'

Ignoring her rant, Bennett asked for her shoes which would have to be checked for forensic evidence since she had been in the murder room. He put out a hand as if to remove them for her, then seemed to become aware that he was kneeling at her feet. Too menial, or too intimate? Erica felt a wave of heat, as if he was radioactive, and to hide it

24

she blurted out, 'While you're down there, Inspector...'

Will flushed, recoiled so that he almost fell over backwards, shot to his feet and called Sally over to harvest the shoes. He strode off to examine the scene, as Sally moved in front of Erica as if to screen her from the view of the stretcher and its contents being wheeled out. Territorial, rather than kind. Before being driven to the police station, Erica had the satisfaction of seeing her editor's ace reporter Gary Thomas arrive, to be kept firmly on the wrong side of the tape by the officers. Hassan, passing Will, saw his face flushed with anger, but just as he passed out of sight, saw his mouth twitch, as if with suppressed laughter.

CHAPTER FOUR

'Why interview Mr Kingston?' asked DS Massum. 'I mean, as opposed to all the other doctors?'

Erica was in the airless utilitarian grimness of an interview room with Will and Hassan, who had greeted her somewhat formally, unlike the laid-back warmth she remembered. With WDC Sally Banner treating her with Antarctic frostiness, clearly Erica's name was still mud at the cop shop.

'Why him? In all the hip joints in all the world? Well, Kingston had been in the papers recently. He's always been well known locally, he often goes for record breaking or headline grabbing surgery – the oldest, the youngest, the most, knee or hip replacements. In the last decade or so he's been concentrating on lower leg injuries, which can be the hardest to fix. He's been saving, or trying to save, legs which would often be amputated even nowadays. Motorcycle accidents, compound fractures, bits of leg bone missing, the works. He's on record as saying every leg deserves every effort to save it, however long it takes. A young motorcycle racer recently finished treatment with Kingston. Harry the Hawk he calls himself, he's broken just about every bone he has at some time or other. He gives Kingston credit for saving his leg and giving it back to him at full length after, I think it was nearly three years of treatment. Muscle and bone grafts, external fixators, all that. He was on TV, Harry that is, kick-starting his return to competitive riding, and brought Kingston on with him. My editor wanted me to interview Kingston, get some of what he calls 'proper doctoring instead of mumbo jumbo' into the paper, as he's a 'local hero."

Erica's quote marks were clearly audible, though she'd managed, she thought, to keep her voice reasonably neutral when talking about Kingston. All the sitting around was really getting to her now. She'd missed not only her usual mile swim but also her normal step class that morning, and was starting to get twitchy as a smoker for a fag.

Will Bennett also moved restlessly in his chair opposite her, similarly feeling caged when not in action. 'Sounds like a bit of a saint.'

'Yeah, if saints earned big bucks and massive kudos when they were still alive. Besides, I don't know if Harry can walk round the block, just that he can ride a motorbike.'

'Just the type of medical practitioner you admire, right?'

Young Paul Lozinski, sitting in, looked puzzled at this and Hassan Massum rolled his eyes to heaven. Here we go, Erica and Will, seconds out, yadda yadda, as his kids would say.

Erica swirled the dregs of her machine-made tea around and drained them in the hope of dislodging the Rich Tea sludge from her teeth. Clearly she must be suffering from shock, or she would not have let herself take in such joyless, gratuitous calories. She would have to do extra exercise to expunge them and she hadn't even enjoyed them. She wasn't going to have the alternative versus conventional medicine argument with Will again, not here, not now. But she couldn't resist making a point.

'Technology or not, he still depends- depended on the human body to heal itself when you get down to it. Some of these doctors do think they're Jesus Christ. Specially surgeons.'

An image flashed into her head, of Kingston's hands, his skilful surgeon's hands, curled around the spikes that nailed them down. 'Are you thinking of the way he ended up, crucified? Think there might be a religious connection?'

'Impossible to say at this stage, we will be making our own connections on the basis of the evidence at the scene. We are speaking to you purely as a witness,' Will intoned carefully, a spark of anger flaring in those eyes. She'd overstepped her role, but while he put her in her place, he'd do well to remember her current reporter status, humble as it was. The police needed the media's help with cases like this and local press was often more helpful than national.

'Got something personal against him?' he added.

'I never met him, alive I mean,' she stated calmly, looking him in the eye. 'I believe there's a wife somewhere, have you found her yet? Tessa, I think...I think they are divorced...'

'Leave all that to us, we will trace next of kin and so on. We know what we're doing. And,' he went onto the attack, 'I must say you don't seem very upset, finding a body – I mean, in that state.'

'Oh, you prefer women to scream and faint, I forgot. I don't happen to find dead people that upsetting, as you may recall. It's suffering that upsets me, and I assume most of Kingston's injuries took place either after death or while he was unconscious.'

'Oh really? And why would you assume that?' Hassan jumped in, glad to interrupt the tension between Will and Erica.

'Is there an alternative forensic pathology course running at your Fuzzy Logic Outreach Centre?' asked Will.

'Ivy Lodge Alternative Health Centre, as you well know. I didn't see any ropes or marks of them on his wrists. Nobody would lie there and let someone do that to them without restraint, unless they were dead or unconscious. Not even at gunpoint, unless there were two assailants of course, one with a gun, one to get close and personal with the nails. That logic fuzzy enough for you? Also there wasn't much blood from the wounds...'

'Thank you, we can manage without your *medical* expertise for now.' Will got up and walked around the room, stretching his arms above his head ostentatiously. He came back and stood over her, doing some more looming.

Hassan said, 'That's all for now. Thank you for your

30

statement. The constable will read it back to you. We'll get your shoes back to you as soon as possible. We may need to talk to you again - oh, and we'll need your fingerprints and a DNA sample.'

Will turned suddenly as he walked out. 'I'm sorry you had to find him like that.'

She wondered how much of Will's DNA was still in her bedroom. Housework wasn't one of her priorities.

Paul Lozinski wasted no time in buttonholing Sally Banner to ask about the atmosphere between Will and Erica.

'Oh gan on man, woman,' he said in his Geordie way, 'give iz the dirt!'

'They were involved in a big case together, THE big case, we all were, you can look it up, but the Guv saved that bitch's life, straight up, all she did was interfere with the investigation, and then she binned him like a used rubber. He's still cut up about it I reckon. And he should have been a DCI by now, but he's not. I reckon she's crushed his ambition.'

'That Stonehead case? Fuck me!'

'No, Paul, I won't, you'll have to use online porn as usual.'

'Can't you console the Guv, Sally? Get the feeling you'd be up for that.'

'Sod off, Paul.' Sally's gamine freckled face and Peter

Pan hairdo did nothing to disarm the anger in her light brown eyes. 'But she's bad news, and it's no coincidence she's mixed up in this. Mark my words.'

CHAPTER FIVE

Later, when Erica was home and alone in her beloved mews flat further along the coast, she found herself feeling sick. She took her constitutional remedy and lay down to meditate, but couldn't concentrate on the mantra. All that filled her head was a picture of that obscene table and its load. The spikes, the impaled hands with their pathetically curled fingers. The crude stone hammer. The sheer primitive hatred that lay behind such a sustained attack on a human being. Was it some grim mockery of religion, the crucified hands, the crown of steel thorns? Was it a parody of a medical operation, using the table he used for examining his private patients, the deliberately clumsy methods a travesty of the surgeon's delicate skill - the rock to the back of the head as anaesthetic, the bashed-in nails a crude surgical procedure?

How could anyone hate someone that much? And why?

It was no use. She had to get up and get out. She rolled off the bed, bundled up the borrowed clothes she'd shucked off and dropped on the floor, and pulled on a cropped top and lycra shorts. She tied back her hair and made for the gym on her bike, her legs going like pistons as she wove through the traffic, veins full of unused adrenaline. There was a high impact class on, and she was as late as they'd allow her to join in. She fell in through the door, took up a position near the mirror where she could study her muscle groups and check her stance and let the thumping beat of the music carry her as she began.

All thought stopped, there was no time for it, all was sensation, she reached, stretched, feeling her muscles and skin responding. She was in control, her strong heart filled her chest with its confident drum beat. That was her in the wall-sized mirror, her body small beside most of the others but strong, and not too thin at all whatever anyone said. Thin was good, thinner was better, thin enough to be safe from the danger of letting out the fat girl she'd once been, the girl who was still inside and needed to be starved into submission. Her hair lashed about, her eyes looking into their reflection. Her lips were parted, her face was flushed and her chest heaved, her breasts pressed almost flat under the tight lycra. Keep those buttocks clenched, the trainer shouted, and she did. Then she did a session on the weights and then on the stepping machine, climbing as if the devil was after her.

When the session ended, her body was shaking again, but this time like a horse that's given its best in the race. The shower was hot and stinging like needles. She turned it to cool and felt the beginning of the blissful well-earned languor that follows hard exercise. She dumped the bag of clothes in her friend's locker, glad she hadn't told her who she was interviewing.

Erica had a sudden memory of asking her for the clothes, telling her she'd arranged an interview with 'a hard man to pin down'. Somebody had managed it now. She didn't know whether to laugh or cry.

She headed home, where she pounded out and sent a full report to the paper, giving all the details she could remember, hoping that Gary Thomas had been kept at bay. She rarely switched her phone off but she'd kept it off since her police interview; it was acting like it had Tourette's as emails, tweets, facebook messages, missed calls and texts flooded in as the day progressed into evening. Not many people had known she was interviewing Kingston, but Stacey Reed made up for them with a digital bombardment like some kind of Stalky McPsycho ex-boyfriend from hell. No way was Erica going to reply, she was too wrecked. Luckily it wouldn't occur to Stacey to actually come to the flat. She would be furious to have missed being at Kingston's today. The thing she was most passionate about, even more than sex or alcohol or food, was the media, being in or on it. She'd had a taste of it at Stonehead through Erica, which was why, rather than 'work experience' to keep the Job Seekers lot happy, she was sticking close to Erica as her best chance to get more.

The *Evening Guardian* had printed Erica's name ('our very own fearless health reporter') in their write-up, so Erica had to deal with a worried call from her mother using her landline, and a few other friends who had that number, though she didn't want to talk about dead bodies any more. At least until tomorrow.

All communication with the outside world off or silent, she settled down with a glass of claret and her current Patrick O'Brian novel, where doctors used leather-covered chains to hold down their fully conscious patients while sawing off their mutilated limbs. How did a person stand that much pain? Had Kingston really been unconscious, or just badly injured enough to be helpless? It was no good, her thoughts would not stay in the Napoleonic Wars.

Surgeons thinking they were Jesus Christ. She'd used those words. Now they stuck in her mind. She had certainly met some arrogant doctors... and many patients came to her after being fobbed off and patronised by some doctor who thought any ailment not curable by a prescription must be imaginary. But she knew a lot of good doctors too, and worked in cooperation with a few. And this one was now a victim. There was something at the back of her mind, something to do with Jesus Christ. Later in the night, she had strange dreams.

'Pulsatilla!' she said aloud, waking up for the third time. This time, she had had one of her homeopathic dreams, about Pulsatilla, the Pasque Flower, which was a common homeopathic remedy. Jesus was standing in front of her, and he was holding a sprig of the purple flower in his hand. It grew and blossomed around the nail sticking out of his palm.

CHAPTER SIX

At the morning briefing Wydsand Police Station was humming with excitement sporadically suppressed every time officers remembered somebody was horribly dead. This being north east England in a seaside town, he might well be somebody their mams knew. In fact being spotted at a crucial moment by someone your mam knew had largely been the reason for the traditional shortage of serious crime in the area.

Soon they'd be getting all the latest information, and there might be some surprises. Photographs of Kingston before and after his illegal operation were on display: a headshot of the handsome, confident doctor, the thick dark brown hair, dark strongly-marked brows, the healthy colour of the keen world-wide golfer and the white teeth courtesy of an expensive dentist friend. The 'after' pictures, of his bizarrely crowned, pale, bloodstreaked, uninhabited face made a sobering contrast.

Despite the carefully custom-made coffee handed to him by Sally Banner, Will Bennett was looking grim too, but Hassan knew this was not so much about sorrow for the dead as a haunting fear that the case would be given to someone else further up the food chain. And speaking of food... Superintendent Russ 'Golden Boy' George hove into view like an oil tanker headed for scrap. Large, bedecked with stains and slow moving, he descended onto a chair like a local government planning committee on an unauthorised gazebo.

'Coffee!' he barked at Paul Lozinski, who jumped and dithered, but as no female officer rescued him he scuttled off to get some with all the courage of despair, as the Super added, 'Three sugars, milk, not that skimmed crap though, and any biscuits?'

'Er no sir.' Paul rushed over, slopping coffee over the rim, to the Super who grunted, gave him a look that promised career blight, and balanced the dripping mug on his belly adding further to the detritus already there.

Sally and Hassan exchanged looks, then dared to glance at Will whose face was carefully blank. His contempt for his 'superior' was as legendary as the Super's passion for food and his garden, in that order. It was Will who had originated the nickname of 'Golden Boy', by saying, 'George could make masterly inactivity an Olympic event and win gold medals.' It took all the will power he could round up not to show his utter disdain for the Super, to whom he had to kowtow. Erica had had no sympathy, pointing out 'If you choose to work in a hierarchy...'

Sally might blame Erica but Will himself blamed Golden Boy for his lack of promotion. He should be a DCI by now, he'd worked hard for it, he was bright, efficient, and he had a good team. He'd brought the Stonehead case to a conclusion, made arrests, what happened after was not his fault. But mud had stuck. And so had George's liking for keeping his budget down and getting Will to do a DCI's work, ably backed up by Massum, who should have been at least a DI by now but determinedly put family first, as did his equally efficient teacher wife. They had an agreement to reach a certain level of promotion and then stop there. For the present anyway, while the children still needed so much of their time and energy.

After some audible slurping, George asked Will to lead the briefing. Will darted him a gimlet look under his long black lashes. Did this mean the case was his?

Will began by giving a summing up of the crime scene from the day before.

'Surely some kind of sadist?' suggested a PC, Kev Hodges.

'Was Kingston into some kind of kinky stuff?' put in Paul. 'Anything dodgy on his computers?'

'Pretty hardcore kinky, those nails, Paul, whatever *you* like doing on your nights off,' remarked Hassan to general laughter and nudging of Paul. 'And no, nothing of significance as yet reported by the geek squad, though they've got more to do yet of course. So far, no kiddy porn, no death threats, no organised crime connections, nothing you wouldn't expect from a well to do, well-respected surgeon with a successful career. So far.'

'Dr Johnstone's doing the PM later this morning, and

of course some tests will take a while to come back after that. But he was able to come up with some provisional info from a preliminary examination of the body.' Will was all brisk business. 'Major depressed fracture to the back of the skull, causing unconsciousness, in fact probably would have been fatal if left at that.'

'Not really a lot of blood from that though Guv,' Hassan put in.

'No well I'll come to that. Looks like that stone was the culprit.'

'So Erica Bruce was right!' Paul said, deadpan. Sally gave him a furious look, and Will's face, beginning to be animated, closed again. 'She said he was unconscious or dying when it was done.'

'The nails,' Will tried to carry on regardless, looking at the initial results of Johnstone's examination, 'were driven in with the stone, almost certainly after the injury at the back, and each of the seven pierced the skull and entered the brain. Death will have occurred during this process. There were also the two in the hands which may have been driven in before the skull spikes. Hassan, you've got info about the nails.'

'Er yes. The seven spikes, or nails, or whatever you want to call them, are in fact surgical pins. They were used until relatively recently in external fixators, that is, used for fixing broken bones instead of plaster. Pins were screwed into the bones and bolted to bars which held the site still

40

while healing got under way.'

Hassan put up on the screen a picture grabbed from Google Images of a patient bristling with spikes in left lower leg and arm. 'Frequently needed for sports or road traffic injuries like tibia fractures.' He looked meaningfully at the football-mad PCs who'd been miming vomiting at the description. 'Nowadays orthopaedic surgeons tend to use Ilizarov Frames, with multiple thin wires instead of groups of two or four large pins, and a system of concentric rings as a frame. These can be used for leg lengthening as well as healing fractures.'

'So how did the killer get hold of these old-fashioned thingies?' asked PC Kev Hodges, trying to recover his credibility.

'No help to us there, I'm afraid. Kingston had some on his desk, in the murder room, loose in a dish, as well as some of the newest kind. Perhaps to show patients, perhaps a souvenir. So ironically he was killed by his own instruments.'

'Maybe a personal motive there then sir,' said Paul.

'Maybe.'

'But did the killer know they were there in advance, or just notice them at the time, Guv?'

'We don't know, Sally. But good point to consider. Any more, Hassan?'

'Well this is an example of the pins in Kingston's skull.' He held up a slim steel spike, like a six inch nail, with no head to speak of and a thin tracing of threading lower down where it would be screwed into living bone. 'It's a biggie, so most likely it was used or designed for tibia fractures. The tibia being roughly speaking the lower leg bone which forms your shin. Fractures at high speeds or with a shearing action can cause compound fractures with a lot of displacement, where the bone comes through the skin...'

'Oh yes,' Kev put in, 'a mate of a mate tripped in a hole playing footie. You could see the bones sticking out my mate said...'

'Yes well,' Hassan kept going, 'these look like tibia fracture pins, but whether they have any deep semiotic significance we don't know.'

'Semi what?' The Super seemed to wake up suddenly. 'Wossat?'

'Erm semiotic sir, it means symbolic.'

Golden Boy muttered, 'Bollix alright,' and lapsed back into what may have been deep thought.

'What about time of death Guv?' asked Paul, still trying to mend fences.

'Pathologist thinks during the night. Maybe he can narrow it down later.'

'Break-in?' wondered Sally. 'Burglary gone wrong?'

'Hit man?' Kev was getting overexcited now.

Will chose to ignore his suggestion. 'No signs of one. A break-in that is. No signs yet of any unexplained visitors, but there are reasons for that which we'll go into in a while...'

Golden Boy George reared up again with a throat-clearing growl. 'Release the kraken,' whispered Paul to Sally who dug him in the ribs to shut up.

'Right lads and lasses,' GB announced. 'No sign of break-in, objects used were at the scene, and I think we can go out on a limb and deduce,' he waved a large hand with soil-blackened fingernails at the death scene photographs, 'somebody didn't like him.'

'Er right sir.' Will was wary.

'And,' GB went on, 'we have a femme to cherchez. Viz, the wife, or ex-wife, or separated wife, wossername?'

'Tessa Kingston sir,' put in Hassan.

'Yes her. So Massum, forget for now all that semolina bollix and let's go for Occam's Razor eh?'

'Razor?' Paul was confused.

Will was startled, yet again he'd been lulled into comfortable contempt for the Super's vestigial stegosaurus brain, yet every now and then a flash of something, like a gold tooth in a tramp's mouth, suggested a glint of quality peeping through the composting manure between his ears.

'Yes laddie, Occam's Razor, ie, simplest explanation is usually the right one. I have every faith in Inspector Bennett, and I'm sure he'll get her, erm or whoever's responsible, in double quick time. And I'm sure he'll be sending some of you children off to bring her in asap. Over to you, Will!'

Further along the coast, Erica Bruce was doing her usual morning mile swim, swooping up and down the lengths and playing David Guetta tracks in her head, even occasionally singing a few lines underwater, to while away the sixty-four lengths of the seafront pool. As often in water, stroked by infinite wet fingers, and out of it too come to that, she felt horny, and it was annoyingly natural for her to think of Will Bennett, as she'd been reminded yesterday that he was fit, in both senses of the word. There'd been chemistry between them, and quite a bit of biology too, to say nothing of physics... she pictured his dark head between her pale thighs, as the delicious ache in her groin under the seam of her costume throbbed in time with a Guetta choon... shame it hadn't worked out, the sex was great and that would have been fine by her but a whole lot of relationship crap had somehow got in the way. Thought he had the right to input on her profession, her life. He was so full of himself... she wouldn't mind being full of him right now... No, stop it Erica, time to get somebody else to train up. Anyhow, Will was too tall for her. You can't get your feet over a guy's shoulders if he's a lot taller than you, flexible as you might be. And she was.

She tried thinking about the murder to get Will's rather beautiful cock out of her head (and there was another image!) Who could have done that to Kingston? Well, of course forensics would be finding out all sorts of stuff CSI-stylee. A single hair, a single grain of a rare chemical, a single fag end in an alley, that sort of thing is what you saw on TV. In real life, there'd be detritus of all kinds tracked in on shoes, blown in on the wind, dropped from coats which had picked it up on the Metro or rubbing shoulders with rush-hour crowds, over random periods of time. Murder was almost as intimate as sex, and sometimes they occurred together.

But then as she continued her fast crawl up and down, she began to picture the crime scene, and instead of all her focus being on Kingtson's poor abused dead body, she allowed herself to recall other elements in the room. Kingston's big masculine desk. What was on it? Something purple... yes, an open box of disposable nitrile surgical gloves. Surely even the stupidest murderer would have used those, so handily provided? And there was another larger dispensing box, yes, those disposable aprons they use for barrier nursing. That should complicate the forensics.

Oh well, there was no real reason she'd be involved with the case at all, apart from the accident of discovering the body, which she'd probably have to testify about at the inquest, if not the eventual murder trial, supposing Will and his gang got somebody bang to rights. The pulsating rhythms of Swedish House Mafia got her through the last few lengths before she got out and cycled home to get ready for work.

CHAPTER SEVEN

Dr Johnstone was beginning the post-mortem, dictating and recording his findings and opening up the late surgeon with instruments similar to his own. The great Y shaped incision, the rafts of ribs cut free and moved to expose heart and lungs, the organs removed one by one, weighed and set aside for consideration. The stomach contents and various samples were sent to the lab, in case some kind of sedative or poison had been used to subdue him as well as the crude anaesthetic of the large stone applied to his skull. Kingston had eaten an evening meal, a Marks and Spencer ready meal, corresponding as far as he could tell before analysis with the dirty plates in Kingston's dishwasher, presumably without realising it was his last, and its stage of digestion confirmed the rough time of death as being late at night. Somewhere between eleven and three.

The man, on the table. The killer was as aroused as Erica though for different reasons. The fresh flowering into murder felt so good, even the fear of being caught was a rush. The memory of Kingston helpless on his own examination table, as the nails were bashed in, brought a powerful surge of euphoria-creating endorphins better than heroin. A step had been taken, which could not be reversed, but at the moment there were no regrets. Except that it was over.

'So it's your case then Will.' They were grabbing a coffee before setting off, Will to see Johnstone complete the PM and Hassan to organise the team's routine investigations.

'Our case, Hassan me old marra. Or mine, in the sense that it's my chance to give CPR to my career and save Golden Boy some wonga in the process. Anyway, he's convinced it's the wife, and he may possibly be right.'

'On the old stopped clock model?'

'Exactly, though twice a day for GB's a bit optimistic. So we'll keep the uniformed lot on house to house, any unexplained visitors, suspicious characters hanging about the street, anything about Kingston that might be relevant, you know the drill.'

'Separated wife, not divorced.' Hassan had been following his own train of thought. 'She might want to inherit all his money rather than make do with a divorce settlement. I assume he was pretty well off.'

'Hell yes, those big houses backing onto the golf course are worth a mint.'

'Be handy if it is that easy, with all the forensics nightmare - hard shiny surfaces, disposable gloves and aprons, bleach sprays and other cleaning stuffs all over the place... And fancy Erica Bruce popping up again.'

'Yes fancy.' Will started pushing his hair up into spikes,

a habit he had when stressed or frustrated. He'd push it up without thinking, then realise and smooth it down again. He'd learned to control the habit when among the team after hearing they'd started calling him 'Sonic' after the hedgehog... it hadn't caught on though, some called him 'Bambi' because of the cartoon-length eyelashes fringing his too-blue eyes. Too late, he'd realised Sonic would have been a better option. Speaking of options and mistakes... he smoothed down his hair.

'Yes it's a pain. She's a pain. And it's hard to believe it's just a coincidence she discovered the body. But how can it be anything else?'

'Unless she did him in.'

'Hmm. She didn't seem too keen on him, did she?' Will sounded wistful.

Hassan was about to reply, when Golden Boy suddenly manifested between them.

'Just a word to the wise, lads. Our flesh-carving victim was a keen golfer. And so's the Chief Constable, as he's just pointed out to me. They played together sometimes. Just passing it on. No pressure!' And he rolled away.

'No pressure! Yeah, right. Well Dr Johnstone and bits of Robert Kingston await.'

'How about I get on Kingston's Will and his assets, check if he was worth murdering?'

'OK Hassan, I think Sally brought his address book back, no doubt his solicitor's in there.'

'Not really put off your game by Erica being involved are you Will?'

'Nah. She's in the past as far as I'm concerned. There's no reason she should be involved any further, thank god.'

Erica, beginning the mammoth task of drying her thick hair using a bank of three hairdryers which overheated and cut out in turn, found the local radio news was full of the story and paused to listen. Then, aware of the pile of emails and calls from patients forming, and the list of people to see today, she put on the TV local news instead and switched on the subtitles before turning the hairdryer back on. The boss of the NHS trust for whom Kingston did his national health work was all over the media telling the public how tragic it was and what a loss to orthopaedic surgery.

'Mr Kingston was an outstanding surgeon whose work has been of great benefit to the people of this area... a popular man, prominent in the community... someone I've played golf with many times.....our sympathies go out to his family.'

They didn't specify who the 'family' were. Bit awkward with the wife being almost ex. Of course, the closest family members are automatically suspect in a murder case. No doubt Will would head straight for the traditional suspect spouse, Erica thought. In some ways, so conventional a mind, if not in bed.

They'd managed to find the spokeswoman for Hip Hip

Hurrah, Kingston's local fan club and Facebook Group of people who'd had twin hip replacements under his knife. There was also Knees Up, for knee replacement veterans. Common as the op was, they all associated him with the end of chronic pain and disability, and she spoke of him in glowing terms, looking emotional.

'He was a saint, that man, a saint. He made me walk again after years in pain, it was a miracle. I don't know how anybody could do this, it must have been a madman. It's terrible these days, you're not safe in your own house....'

Hair relatively tamed, hairdryers basically buggered, Erica checked her emails, texts and voicemail, steering well clear of Facebook and Twitter, for now. Luckily she'd kept the day before free, to write up the intended interview with Kingston and do some admin, but she had appointments all day today. No cancellations. In fact several patients had rung or emailed asking for urgent appointments, unusual in alternative medicine, and Erica was pretty sure it was because of the media coverage of her finding Kingston's body. Was this proof of the power of publicity, or did they just want to get some gory details from her first-hand? Some seemed genuine, a desperate parent with a teething baby, for example, and she offered a slot for later in the day by email before cycling off to work. Parents of babies, fearful of conventional medicine, were mainstays of her homeopathy practice at Ivy Lodge, a lovely old Georgian house which was now a centre for alternative medicine. Ivy Lodge also housed an aromatherapist/masseuse, her friend Rina who was away on a long trip with her fiancé Dave. There was also a reflexologist, a chiropractor, and a hypnotherapist, Miles Fredericks. He drew up at the kerb in his Prisoner-style kit car as she walked up the steps, bumping her bike strenuously upwards to store it in the back. Extra calories used, always a good thing. The morning sun made the Georgian sandstone of the fine old terrace glow golden, and ignited the tubs of generic local authority plants dotted along the street by a council sporadically mindful of Britain in Bloom and the local elections.

Miles overtook her on the steps with his springing stride, hair flopping into his eyes as usual. He claimed it was hard to have a personal life as a hypnotherapist, because whenever he gazed into someone's eyes, they were terrified he was putting the 'fluence on them. Hence the flopping hair to curtain them, or so Erica and Rina had theorised. His partner Mel was immune to hypnosis, understandable as it meant there was still some mystery in Miles' love life.

'Morning Erica!' he chirped, disappearing into the building.

'Be seeing you!' she replied, making a circle of her thumb and forefinger to continue the Prisoner motif.

Before Erica could enter the building with time to spare for a mug of herbal tea and a read of the first patient's notes, a smell of cigarettes and a familiar voice assaulted her.

'Fuck me! Aa cannit believe ye bike to work. Ye need help, man Erica!'

'Stacey, I've told you, no swearing in the workplace!'

'We're still ootside man! Ye never answered me messages,' accused Stacey, waving the phone which seemed surgically sutured to her non-smoking hand. 'Honest man, ye need iz! Good job I'm yer intern, innit?'

'You're not my... look Stacey, I've got a lot on,' Erica struggled to hold the door open while she manoeuvered her bike inside, painfully barking her shin on a pedal in the process. 'Ff- !'

'Nee swearin, Erica!' Clearly helping with the door was not the role Stacey envisaged for herself. 'Look man it's yer lucky day!'

'Erm well it's luckier than yesterday, no corpses as yet. Ow, sod it!' The door had struck her elbow.

'That *was* the lucky bit man, eeh I dunno, yer clueless! It'll get we into the papers man, even on the telly if we tell it right!'

'Who's 'we' and no thanks.'

'Well that's alreet for ye, livin on lentils and Weetabix and that horbal tea like an anorexic rabbit, worrabout me? Single mam, struggling to get by... I've reinvented meself for the sake of me dream, haven'a? Worrabout me dreeeeem! A girl's entitled to her dreeeem! And put the kettle on when yer get inside, will yer, Aa need a coffee.'

'You needn't have bothered getting up. Must be early

53

for you.' Erica had the bike almost through the door.

'Bit late yer mean. Aa've not been home yet, man, great night up in toon, went to the after-party, shagged a DJ, well he said he was, result! I'm just on me way back. Howay, ye needn't look so stuck up, it's not long since ye were dancing every neet doon the sea front clubs, Aa remember! And hookin up with random guys...'

'Yes well something called work's got in the way a bit lately. Or maybe I'm getting old.'

'Aye Aa knaa, you're nearly pushin thorty! That's not the point, make iz a coffee and put plenty sugar in, I'll be in in a bit when I've finished me tab.'

Erica went in alone and did indeed switch her tomato red kettle on. Stacey had given herself a makeover to get the look sported by her role models on reality TV show, 'Geordie Shore'. She'd lost some weight, by smoking more and by switching to vodka and diet coke instead of beer, alcopops and cocktails, so she was thinner but with the muffin top still in place, pregnancy and bad muscle tone ensuring its survival. Her formerly blonde-streaked lank hair was now jet black beyond the dreams of any African princess, and would have drained any natural colour from her pale northern face, except that it was now glowing with orange spray-tan. Her black mass of hair was worn long, but back-combed over a pad 60s style to form a high pile on her head, with a fat wodge of fringe brushed sideways across her brow as fashion dictated. Huge black-rimmed eyes bolstered with ranks of false lashes and litres of eyeliner balanced the look, after the night's activities somewhat smudged and displaced. Her tiny tight neon pink dress was complemented by the anatomically impossible high heels dangling from her wrist, the clubbing Geordie girl's accessory of choice once a few drinks had gone down.

Hoping Stacey would stay outside or go home, Erica got ready for work, sipping a ginger tea. Suddenly her door opened, and a man walked in, waving some kind of ID at her. This was not the expected youngster worried about his acne... no it was a reporter from a city paper with aspirations to tabloid glory, Stacey hard on his heels.

A confused conversation ensued, 'your story' 'I'd rather not' 'haway man Erica!' 'our readers' 'pleeeese Erica!' 'must have been traumatic for you' 'Aa'm the intern here ye knaa' 'you are how old pet?' 'police investigation, privacy, at work, no thanks NO!' being the edited highlights before the reporter slunk off, but only after she'd added '*Guardian* has the exclusive'. Meaning the local *Evening Guardian* of course but hey.

Stacey was disgusted. 'You bliddy stupid...'

'So that's why you waited outside. I assume you'd arranged to meet him here, pretty impressive! But don't do it again.'

'You'll never get any wonga, how'll yer afford a boob job on what ye make?'

'I don't want a boob job.'

'It's aal very well not eatin and deein exercise and that, but then ye have to put the fat back in yer tits. Or plastic or worreva.'

'Attractive as that sounds, no thanks.'

'Not that Aa need any.' She looked down complacently at her own impressive frontage. 'Well it's not too late. The meedja could do a story about ye and that Will Bennett! 'A doomed romance, once they were everything to each other, their lurve flowered among the fingerprints and bloodstains, then the job came between them, until destiny brought them back together over a murdered medic's tortured corpse.' It's got everything except royalty! And it's even true!'

'It's SO not true, now go away, I've got a patient coming any minute.'

'And where's me coffee? And why haven't ye got a cappuccino machine?' Stacey picked up and threw down a handful of coffee beans from the bag next to the small grinder and caffetiere Erica kept for visitors. 'Ye have to do every bleedin thing the hard way, ye!' Stacey produced several minipacks of biscuits, and began tearing the cellophane off with her teeth and cramming the contents into her mouth. She grinned, displaying bourbon gunge round her front teeth like caries gone mad. 'That bizzie Will, he's dead fit! He was on telly last neet. Yer know what they say, 'Where there's a Will, there's a wey-hey!'

'Oh my god.'

'So what was it like? The blood, was there loads of it? D' ye miss shaggin Willy boy?'

'Not really, I don't know, and kind of. Now. Go. Away.'

'The wife did it.' Stacey had moved on to the next minipack, spraying digestive crumbs all over the desk. 'Betcha Willy'll go after hor.'

'Oh I just bet he will. Find a woman to blame. I wonder what she's like, Kingston's ex.' Erica, scooping up coffee beans, barely noticed she'd started to converse with Stacey, in the absence of her habitual pre-work sounding board and friend Rina.

'Prolly a skinny, up herself, posh RAH.'

'A woman like that might have trouble subduing a healthy man in his prime.'

'In his prime? Kingston was OLD, man! Anyhoo, Aa could subdue any man! This bloke last neet gave iz some attitude, he groped iz in the taxi queue and then, worst of aal, tried to push in front of iz, whey Aa wasn't havin that, so Aa punched him right in the face like, he went doon like a bag of hammers, blood everywhere, but he was ower drunk to really feel it like, I could see there wasn't enough pain in his eyes, so I give him a quick kick in the nads for luck.' Stacey had been energetically miming her big fight, and now subsided with a blissfully reminiscent smile and some coughing. 'See, Aa could do security for ye here! When patients get stroppy cos your dodgy pills divven't work, Aa could deck them for ye! But ye'll have to get some better biscuits in, nee chocolate on these!'

'Did you get those from Rina's office?' Erica belatedly recognised the packets. 'How did you get in there?'

'Thinking of taking over her room like, just for now. She does massage doesn't she, Aa can dee that! How much does she charge for a happy ending like?'

Erica shuddered at the thought of Rina's reaction to requests for 'happy endings' from male clients. She too could deck any man with her brawny arms.

'Keep out of there! However you got in!'

'Debit card like. Simples.' Stacey waved a card.

'Bloody hell, that's mine!' Erica snatched it back. 'You stole my...' Erica stopped, as a thin, pale youth with acne appeared outside the door, backing off when he saw Stacey. 'It's all right, come on in!' she called, while he hovered nervously outside the room.

'Borrowed it that's aal. It's hardly bent or owt. Hey, if it wasn't his ex killed him, mebbe it was some nutjob psycho, that would be mint!' Stacey allowed herself to be pushed out of the room as the youth sidled in.

'Ye look like ye could dee with a happy ending!' was her parting shot to him. 'Better for yer skin than pills!'

CHAPTER EIGHT

'Being a homeopath, you have to know a lot about people. The remedy you prescribe them has to fit the whole person - their appearance, their habits of mind, way of speaking, not just their ailment but their exact symptoms. The first time I see someone, I give them two hours just to hear them talk about themselves. Some people fit certain profiles, and their ailments tend to go along with those profiles, which are associated with a particular remedy. After long practice, I'm pretty quick to spot such people, though it isn't always so clear cut. Some remedies, such as Arnica, are good for some particular ailment or group of ailments for just about anyone, in this case, bumps and bruises. A lot of active people, and parents of young children, carry Arnica tablets with them. It was discovered when mountain goats were noticed chewing the leaves of Arnica Montana when they'd hurt themselves. The remedy stimulates the body to heal itself. Homeopathy was used as the norm in rural USA, when doctors really knew their patients and had time for them. The modern conventional drug companies rely on instant prescribing which fits modern GP's short appointment times. I offer an alternative to that.' So she'd written about her own branch of alternative medicine in an early piece in the *Evening Guardian*. Ever optimistic, she texted Stacey the link.

Having done her best for the young man with his acne and damaged self-esteem, she had a short break to give the plants fresh water, put on the kettle again for herbal tea, and check her work voicemail and emails. A couple of regular patients wanted appointments for unspecified pains and for eczema; someone wanted to know her rates; and regular patient Beccy Mitchell cancelled her appointment for the next day in a rather breathy, panicked voice.

'It's me - I mean Beccy - I can't make my appointment - I'll get back to you -'

The voice ended in a squeak as if becoming tearful. Beccy was a blonde, blue eyed young woman who behaved younger than she was. Softness personified; something of a protégé of Erica's. Will I ever learn not to get too involved, she asked herself, feeling concerned. But Beccy cried easily; in fact she was a typical Pulsatilla type. It wasn't an unusual profile. Beccy came quite often, but had no serious illness, just ongoing symptoms of stress and depression. She was determined not to go to a conventional doctor.

'They don't have time to listen to me,' she would say when Erica conscientiously reminded her of the option to see if antidepressants would help. 'You do.'

Erica often wondered if that was all she came for; to talk to someone who would listen, someone less expensive than a shrink, though more expensive than a GP. Erica had developed a protective, almost maternal, feeling for her.

And, she reminded herself, she had also treated Beccy's sinus headaches successfully. She'd have to wait for Beccy to ring again as she wouldn't take calls, and paid in cash. Apparently her husband didn't approve of homeopaths, like Will, so she explained away the expense by saying it was for beauty treatments. Some relationship that was. Erica was better off without all that crap. She thought of Louise, a wheelchair user with severe health problems, blissfully happy for the first time in her adult life after a fifty-eight year abusive marriage now that Erica and other professionals had shown her how to leave him and have her own little flat.

The first appointment of the day arrived, a young woman with a toddler whose cough announced itself from some distance away. Like someone sawing wood... Erica was already listing the exact symptoms in her head.

Later Erica did some Googling while the kettle boiled for her Earl Grey. She'd known that orthopaedic surgeons use metal plates and pins inside really bad or complex fractures, and used external fixators, but she didn't know a lot about the technology involved. Ilizarov fixators, Taylor spatial frames... the geometry of it all was fascinating. Halo... the term for a ring of spikes round the head, bolted to struts bolted in turn to wires into the chest, forming a cage and holding the head still for broken necks to mend. Even the vocabulary was religious. Had Kingston been killed that way because he was hated as a man, or as an orthopaedic surgeon? Patient with a grudge, getting nowhere with a complaint or lawsuit due to 'lost' NHS files or doctors closing ranks? A mistake by a surgeon could mean terrible consequences for someone, and their family. Plenty of possible motive there.

She viewed a youtube video of a halo being removed from a young woman who had clearly recovered enough to be freed from her mobile cage. Pins entered her head, and chest, and struts of metal formed props between them. She wore a big collar round her neck and a sort of breastplate of padding and plastic. Her children were in the room, and her husband was filming the whole thing as the surgeon started to unscrew and remove the wires and bars and plates. She was excited, but as the process continued, her smile faltered. Tears showed in her eyes. She tried to keep cheerful for the sake of her watching family, but as the actual work of removing the metal from the flesh and bone went on, unable to pretend any longer, she began to make sounds of pain like a cat yowling. Her young children watched, puzzled, clearly they'd been told this was a happy occasion, but there was Mommy in distress, while her husband kept recording. He'd probably had the same role while she'd given birth. 'You're doing well, Honey,' he kept saying as an unseen hand carefully unscrewed the stiff thin wires out of her bones where they'd been embedded for months and made themselves at home in sheaths of scar tissue, some of it attached to them and reluctant to let them go. It was strangely disturbing even though the outcome was happy. Other accounts or videos Erica found online of the removal of wires or pins mentioned pain relief of various kinds being given. Was it up to the surgeon whether to give this or not? Was cost a factor, or insensitivity, or didn't pain matter to those who weren't feeling it?

Whatever, the similarity of the halos online to Kingston's crude coronet of spikes was striking. Erica was reluctant to get involved further with the police, especially Will, after their ill-starred attempt at a fling, relationship, whatever that had been. If it has to be defined, start running, was Erica's motto. But the halo, would they realise the significance of it to Kingston's murder MO? She couldn't bring herself to call Will but she had Hassan's number from the card he'd given her at the station and he'd always seemed a nice guy. For a Detective Sergeant.

'I was just wondering...' she began, as he said, 'Will's here, I'm handing you over to him,' and Will's voice was in her ear like his tongue had once been goddamn him! His voice was brusque. Busy man, said his tone, you're lucky to get me.

'Erica. Why the call? Remembered something relevant to the investigation? Something you actually saw or heard?'

In other words, I don't want to hear any of your ideas. Erica felt her anger rise. Yeah, scared I might be right.

Controlling her irritation, she told Will about the halos.

'I just wondered if you'd considered the murder might be connected with Kingston's work as an orthopaedic surgeon - a personal grudge, a disgruntled former patient or something.'

'Disgruntled patient, yes strangely that did cross my poor pedestrian ploddish mind...'

'I meant specifically someone who had to have pins in a fracture.'

It still sounded insultingly obvious and that was fine with her.

'I mean,' she added, 'it might not be anything religious at all. The spikes could be a halo, which is the term used-'

'I think you can leave the investigation to us,' Will's voice was cold as a snowman's snowballs. 'We're looking at all the angles, and some progress is being made. We'll get in touch with you if need be.'

In other words, sod off. 'I hope you're recovering from the shock,' he said rather stiffly, and had goodbye'd and gone before she could speak again. Was there a man more annoying than Will Bennett? She was very soon to be reminded that there was.

'Why did SHE have to find the body?' Will demanded. 'Talk about contaminating a crime scene!'

'Well I don't suppose she *wanted* to find him,' Massum put in mildly.

'Bollocks! She's loving it, a chance to give me repeated

earbashings about her so-called 'ideas' and now get herself involved in police business! MY business!'

Hassan remembered Will getting very involved in sharing his ideas of Erica's business, but now wasn't the time to bring that up. And anyway she needn't have reacted so badly at the time. Will was still fuming.

'Wouldn't put it past her to have done him in just to make my life difficult... patronising little... 'oh have you poor stupid sods even considered he was killed by someone who hated him or doctors or him as a doctor or a religious nutter' of all the fucking NERVE!'

'No outstanding official complaints against him though. I've checked. But we've got plenty of avenues of enquiry Guv, so let's forget about Erica for now. Unless we find her DNA on Kingston.'

'I want him gone over with an, an, electron microscope, or a quark one of they make them. Get on the phone to CERN! If there's a single subatomic particle with a link to Erica's DNA anywhere on him, I want to know about it!'

'You certainly picked up a lot of physics crap from her,' remarked Hassan, 'it must've rubbed off. Like DNA.'

Barely had Erica ended the call than it buzzed again. It was the editor of the *Evening Guardian*, Ian Dunne.

'Erica! how's it going sweetheart?' Despite his rasping fag-sandpapered voice and the louche image it conjured up, he was slim, smart, dapper, sat alertly at his desk, had a sharp-nosed face and small hard hazel eyes and seemed to keep the nicotine off his fingers somehow.

'Fine,' she was wary. 'Obviously we won't be able to run the interview with Kingston.....do you want me to do an obituary?'

'Huh, well, yes, but first, about your eyewitness account. Sensational news for a local, so I've got young Gary to cover it, being on the spot, like.'

'What do you mean, on the spot? The police totally cock-blocked him... you mean you're not using my stuff at all?' Erica's blood was starting to boil. Gary, his blue-eyed boy, was the son of one of Dunne's golfing buddies, hoping to use the local rag as a springboard to higher, if that's the word, things.

'Course I am love. Don't get your leotard in a knot! But you're not News, you're features, and very nice they are too sweetheart!'

'You...'

'Gary's a newshound to the bone. He's got the instincts.'

'Of a plague germ.'

'Gary's done it as an interview with you, so all your stuff's in there but as you answering him, so you see I did use your piece.'

'Plundered it you mean!'

'You'll love it me dear. We've put in a lovely photo of you. It's twice, no, four times the size of the usual one!'

So much to say, so little time, so much justification for

manslaughter. 'You've put Gary's byline over MY story? How could you! Chopping up MY story and letting HIM have it as HIS fucking interview!'

'Calm down darlin, look, I know you do a good job on the page. I appreciate it, I really do. I know a lot of readers love it, bunch of hypochondriacs most of them, but it's a case of the right man for the job. That's why I'm the editor, and you're not. Don't worry, it'll do you a lot of good. The press exposure. The bigger picture! They'll be queuing up for your pills and potions now!'

'Thank you so much,' she snarled. 'That's just the advertising gimmick I need - for people to associate me with dead bodies. Every therapist's dream.'

'Wait till you see it... that Gary will go far.'

'Sooner the better.'

'Just bash out an obit for us. We'll put it on your health page instead of on our usual 'dead page'. Bye beautiful!'

He had wiped the floor with her. As per usual.

CHAPTER NINE

Will had interviewed Tessa Kingston with Sally, thinking a WDC was appropriate. There was quite a lot of oestrogen in the room as it turned out, and Will wished he'd stuck with Hassan. Tessa had turned up with a female solicitor, who protected her fiercely from any kind of attempt to suggest she'd been involved.

'If only we'd managed to have a friendly chat with her alone,' lamented Will to Hassan, after giving him a brief account of their sparring match. Sally Banner and Tessa Kingston had been little more than an audience, their heads swinging left, right, left like Wimbledon spectators while Will tried to break through the legal barbed wire entanglement thrown around Tessa by her brief.

'What did you make of her, Will? The ex-ish wife.'

'Attractive in a girly-girl way, expensively dressed, claiming to be horrified, whether by the murder of her old man or being in a stinky interview room with no soft furnishings or posh coffee, I'm not sure. Bit of a WAG type by the look of her. Oh I'm probably being unfair.'

'We've got no evidence against her have we? Only motive. That stuff I found out about his assets, he's pretty well off. The proceeds of not just one but two expensive houses, let alone other dosh.'

'Yes the sale of his old mum's house certainly fattened his bank balance. Not much progress on that motive-wise though. Because she's started divorce proceedings, her solicitor was already on the case. Wouldn't let her answer anything much just yet. Clearly trying to find out if we did have anything on her client. So we couldn't even find out why Tessa left Kingston, if indeed she did - he could have chucked her out for all we know. Hard to work out her feelings about him. She just hid her eyes in a tissue and said nothing.' Will's hair was vertical with frustration.

'So I hear. Sally mentioned when she came out to get coffee that things weren't going so well. So I had a quick skim through the neighbours' statements the house to house crew collected, in case any of them knew the grisly details of the split.'

'Great, Hassan! You're a star! And?' He started flattening his black hair again.

'Nowt.'

'Shit!'

'Sorry. Everyone who mentioned her at all said they'd seemed happy enough and then she just wasn't there, they weren't even sure when she moved out. It was only sixteen days ago as far as I can tell but that's from her and her brief. Kingston was very private about his private life. Some neighbours thought she'd had some kind of illness or breakdown and had gone off for a cure.'

'Hm, maybe rehab? Expensive addiction?'

'Surely she can't keep fending us off. Did you get fingerprints? For 'elimination purposes'?'

'Yes we did get those. Not DNA though. And the solicitor grabbed Tessa's coffee cup before we could get any off that. Smart woman. She and Tessa are obviously close, very different types but blood's even thicker than legal ethics.'

'Blood?'

'Oh yes I've kept the best till last for you mate. They're only bloody sisters! Tessa and Tara. Sounds like a burlesque act. She's staying with Tara at the mo, so there's no chance of getting her alone.'

'Wonder why this Tara's so keen to keep Tessa from saying anything about the split? I wonder if Tara's sure she's innocent, or knows she's guilty, or is worried she might have done it.'

'If we had some actual evidence stronger than tired old Golden Boy's tired old theorising... Tara was at pains to point out that Kingston changed the locks after Tessa did a runner. She doesn't have a key, allegedly. In other words she couldn't have let herself in.'

'Even if we find traces of her in the house, it's going to be hard to prove anything. She did live there after all. Traces might have survived the cleaner's efforts.'

'She admitted to going back after the split a few times, to pick up stuff. And get this, Tara and Tessa gave us this much - they both went round there the afternoon of the night Kingston was killed, to pick up some family photos and personal jewellery apparently. Tara drove her there, so they can alibi each other. They saw him, he had to be there to let them in and no doubt make sure wifey didn't nick anything of his. Besides, that woman two doors down saw Kingston alive later than they claim to have left, so it's not much use except to muddle up the forensics.'

'And Johnstone put TOD at 11-3am, most likely towards the earlier time limit. Anyway I'll check that out, see if anyone saw Tara's car and when it was there. They might have gone later. Or she might have made it up to explain any of her prints being in the house since cleaning. It's a quiet street though, and the houses are well detached from each other, neighbours not likely to see cars without looking for them.'

'Great, though I doubt we'll make much of a hole in their story. Get forensics to double check for traces of her anywhere suspicious. But if Tara's stopping her from committing herself to anything more right now, it leaves us wide open, if we do find anything she can just say it's from their visit earlier.'

It was as bad as Erica had feared. She got home to find the early edition on the mat and herself described as a 'slim, petite blonde new age therapist' next to a photo which made her look completely gormless. Worse, she'd given her supposed answers to Gary in a 'shaken voice' while her 'trembling hands clutched a mug of sweet tea, her swimming eyes huge in her pale face' as he'd 'encouraged her to face her dreadful experience'. *Sweet* tea! As if.

The police had given him some official guff about ongoing enquiries, tragic case, worst seen in a long career etc, and the neighbours said the usual belatedly complimentary things similar to those she'd heard on local TV news. 'You don't expect that kind of thing to happen here,' and 'This is a quiet, respectable neighbourhood'. Nothing from the estranged wife; presumably Gary hadn't been able to get to the new widow yet. Erica wished she could get to Gary and write *his* obituary.

CHAPTER TEN

Erica had had enough for one day. She felt tense and her shoulders were tight. She put on her running gear and set out to work it all off. The tide would be still pretty far out, plenty of damp firm sand to run on. As she jogged slowly at first, warming up, down to the sea front and then gaining speed along the beach, the moon was up already, a pale translucent jellyfish swimming in the still-light sky. The slow, slushing sound of the sea as ever had a calming effect on her spirit. She turned inland again before the track to the lighthouse at the north end of Wydsand bay and ran back alongside the cemetery.

She often took this route because it made a circuit, along the sea front, looping back past the cemetery and along a wooded track by the golf course. It just so happened that it would take her past Kingston's house, which backed onto the golf course, separated from it by a muddy worn track. She felt an urge, like a criminal, to return to the scene of the crime.

She reached the end of the asphalt path at the corner of the cemetery. The crematorium, grey stone mock-gothic, stood silent, the chimney smokeless. No risk today of inhaling somebody's mortal remains as they puffed out of the chimney straight into her lungs, as had happened disconcertingly before. She thought of them still in there, rising and falling with her breath, embedded in her lungs, living on in her body.

She turned in again to run alongside the cemetery where it ran at right angles to the asphalt track. The ground now was dirt track fringed by long grass, dock leaves, cow parsley, edged with elder, hawthorn and poplars, the golf course on her right. Where the cemetery had been on her left were now the backs of large detached houses, sixties built, their back fences having gates onto the path. Towards the end of the path, before she turned down a snicket back onto the streets that would lead her home, was Kingston's house. She was right behind it. Well how about that.

She stepped back almost into the twiggy hawthorn bushes against the golf course boundary to see what she could of the house above its high, solidly built back fence. Kingston's house itself looked just like an expensive, respectable house - there was nothing to say a murder had been committed there, apart from some sadly dangling crime scene tape across his back gate. Taking a side step, Erica felt her trainer skid on something. She looked down and found an empty quarter vodka bottle of a cheap brand keeping company with a couple of crushed beer cans and a cigarette packet, also empty. A few fag ends lay around as a garnish.

Obviously the local youths hung about here. She had seen similar caches among the newer but equally affluent clumps of houses in the area. Kids with nowhere to go. The police called their little refuges 'drinking dens', which sounded much more exciting, more reminiscent of prohibition era America with its speakeasies, bathtub gin and tommy guns than the pathetic reality of damp bus shelters or, as here, hollowed out hawthorn thickets forming scant shelter over a fence to perch their bony bums on.

There'd been a campaign backed by the local press including Dunne's papers which tried to keep in with the mayor and council, to stop outdoor drinking, and byelaws had been hastily passed. The police could show they were doing something about youth crime by stopping party-going youngsters and confiscating their bottles of Irish cider or cheap wine, pouring the contents sadistically on the ground heedless of the effort entailed in obtaining them – the careful coaching of older relatives, the threatening of older-looking friends, the labour of constructing fake ID with attention to detail of which their teachers would not believe them capable. Middle class youngsters could spice up their evenings, as not only were they now hunted and possibly beaten up by 'charvas', their natural enemies, but they had the added thrill of smuggling nicked bottles of chardonnay from their parents' stash, hiding them in shrubbery and over random garden walls at the first sign or siren from the boys and girls in blue of a Friday night.

Meanwhile, normally law-abiding adults found they

were now unable to have a glass of wine at a beach picnic or technically, even carry a bottle of immaculate vintage on public transport to a dinner party, without risking criminalisation. Erica pondered this, moving the detritus about with her toe. Sad, the driving underground of alcohol, a proud part of her Anglo-Saxon culture. After all, she could and did assert as a scientist, booze was totally devoid of calories, enabling her to get ratted while clubbing without the usual agonies of guilt caused by ingesting anything more calorific than celery. She looked up towards the house again, and tried jumping up to see over the fence, though the light was fading fast.

'Hey! What are you up to?'

A man, late middle aged, wearing light slacks, what looked like a cream polo shirt and a powder blue golf sweater was standing in the open back doorway of the next house, illuminated by his kitchen light. He had quite thin legs, but his broad shoulders testified to years of perfecting his swing.

'I saw you from the upstairs window,' he said triumphantly, as if this had required hours of surveillance and cunning. 'What do you think you're doing?'

'I was just looking,' she began, when he jumped in.

'Well clear off! It's bad enough around here with all the local riffraff hanging about at all hours, damned hoodies, say anything to them and all you get's a mouthful of abuse, the police can't seem to do anything, and now we've got passers-by rubbernecking! The street's a byword, well at least the police can be bothered to turn out for a murder, but the area's going downhill fast, young lady.'

'It was erm, me, who found Kingston,' she said, feeling that the more correct 'it was I' sounded too pompous. 'I'm a reporter for the *Evening Guardian*.'

'Fearful rag!' he spluttered. 'Had the damn nerve to call me an 'elderly neighbour!' Common little chap they sent too. You can tell them from me I want a printed apology.'

'Ah that sounds like Gary Thomas. I'll mention it to the editor.'

'You don't look like a reporter. You look like a jogger. No sign of a notebook, or anything.'

'I am a jogger. Multitasking you know. Just thought I'd check the place out while I do my run, come back tomorrow looking more like a reporter. Though I tend to use a digital voice recorder, or this.' She produced her phone. 'I can record on here. Make sure I get exact quotes and don't make any mistakes. And if you still have doubts, you can look in the *Daily Courier* today, or on the website, you'll see my picture.' Next to Gary's byline. 'Or the *Guardian* website. Health page. Hence the jogging, you see.'

'Hm. I see. But I shall be checking!' He pushed back a thin strand of grey hair which had come adrift in the breeze.

Erica was quick to take advantage of his mollified tone. 'What you said before. About the police. 'At least they can be bothered to turn out for a murder.' Implying they don't normally turn out here? I'm surprised they'd ever be needed. Such a salubrious area. Nice houses, nice class of person.' She dredged up more encouraging language she remembered from various older patients and relatives. 'What you'd call really decent types. Law abiding.' She ostentatiously put her phone on 'voice record' and held it towards him in a business-like manner.

'Oh yes, absolutely! I mean, you do expect the odd golf ball against the windows, or through the greenhouse, living here; we don't mind that too much, most of us play the game. That's why we live here, to be near the club. It's just a short stroll to the clubhouse - handy for dodging the breathalyser! But we get youths hanging about... we can't seem to get shot of the little bastards. Bloody neck-ends! We've tried all sorts. I've tried. Kingston himself was out here chasing them off numerous times. Even with his connections he couldn't seem to get anything done. Few times the police did send a bloke, they made off across the course. Back the next night! Kingston thought they put off his patients, though you can't see anything from the front of the house. But you could hear them all right. Shocking language. I told the police, that's where you should be looking for your suspect. Look, that's where the stone came from that the buggers used to kill Kingston. Right next to the den!'

He waved a long arm toward the bushes further along. A

pile of hefty sandstone chunks lay there, dumped by some gardener tired of his or her rockery. They were filmed with green, and weeds and garden escapees like honesty's pale sad satin windows had sprouted among them. One stone was plainly missing. Its place was marked by an impression in the ground, lined with bleached, flattened grass.

'Yes, that's where the murder weapon came from alright! Some scruffy young constable was round here checking to see if it fit. He didn't look much different to the yobbos, if you ask me. '

Erica wondered just how much time the old boy spent at his upstairs window. 'I'm surprised they didn't take these cans and fag ends and stuff. To test for DNA.'

'They did. These have just appeared! Tonight!'

'Bit early isn't it?'

'Police have been patrolling every so often, looking out for anyone who might have seen anything. Bloody hoodies waited til coast clear, dumped an empty bottle and fag ends and scarpered!'

'You mean sort of reclaiming their bit of territory? Quite sad really when you think about it.'

'Sad! Yes it's sad, you scrimp and save, you work hard, you make something of yourself, you buy a house by the golf course, and those little vandals…! They want stringing up. Thumbing their filthy cocaine-stuffed noses at authority. Every damned night... little buggers... they could do with some army discipline.'

'I'm not sure training them to kill would help.'

He went crimson in the face and started to swell up for another explosion so Erica hurried on, before she got hypothermia standing about in a lycra vest.

'So I expect the police asked you if you saw anything.' She rubbed her arms which were rough with goose pimples. 'Did you?'

'Not a thing. They asked me about the early morning and the late night before. Well I went to bed early, and I normally sit in my breakfast room at the front of the house in the mornings to catch the sun, when there is any. So I wouldn't have seen anything. I didn't need to! All they've got to do is put a man on watch up one of these trees, they'd soon catch the young sods.'

The thought of long-limbed Will Bennett perched in a small bushy tree all night had its attractions, though no doubt it would be one of the young officers who copped that particular bit of surveillance.

'It might be difficult to prove they had anything to do with the murder,' she pointed out, jogging on the spot to keep warm and save herself from stiffening up. She crossed her arms and rubbed her shoulders, shifting from foot to foot. 'After all, anyone could have picked up that rock and used it.'

'Hardly!' he barked. 'Most of the people who walk along here aren't the type at all. Not like those thugs...'

'Well, thanks for showing me where the murder weapon

came from, Mr er.'

'Archer. Harold Archer. Esquire.'

Erica solemnly switched off her phone, thanked him and jogged off.

It was true, anyone could have used that stone. The use of something that just happened to be lying around suggested an impulsive crime rather than premeditation. But then anyone who regularly walked that path, the hoodies, dogwalkers, golfers retrieving their balls, gardeners dumping cuttings, kids taking short cuts, might know those rocks were there, ready to hand, a safe weapon that could not be traced back to them. Even if they'd picked up the rock before putting on surgical gloves - which they surely must have unless they were stupid beyond belief - they'd have cleaned it up somehow. If fingerprints would show on rough damp sandstone in the first place.

Erica always liked getting back to her flat, in an old black and white mews which had been part of a coaching inn, historic and a bit tatty, her first proper home after the years of flat-sharing at university. She had a hot shower and made herself a quick dinner, sweet potato cooked whole in the microwave with no fat, and an omelette with minimum oil, plenty of chilli and mushrooms. She opened a bottle of St Emilion. It takes nerve to open a bottle of wine on your own without feeling like a lush. But the flowery, vanilla-scented wine was delicious. She allowed herself another glass.

CHAPTER ELEVEN

The research she'd done for the interview came in useful for Kingston's obituary. Impressive career tragically cut short at only 43; his work as an orthopaedic consultant at the Wydsand General Hospital, his private practice including spells of working in Arab countries treating rich patients who'd crashed their Mercs and Porsches... put more tactfully of course. She included his undoubted successes in surgery, his churchgoing, and being a leading light, in fact a past Captain, of Wydsand Golf Club. She didn't mention that his widow, 30 year-old Tessa, was living separately at his death, or any other controversial subjects. Not the time or place.

She wondered why his wife had left him. A guy with plenty of money, lots of status, lauded to the skies by all and sundry....maybe he shagged nurses, regarded them as his due? She wondered how he had felt about being left. Can't have made him look good to his work and golf cronies. He'd struck her as unattractively arrogant though presumably Mrs Kingston must have known him better than Erica did on the basis of their one phone conversation setting up the interview. Perhaps he was charming in private.

His manner on the phone had put up her hackles, as

did his reaction when she explained who she was. She'd told him she edited and wrote the You and Your Health page.

'What qualifies you for that?' Amused.

'I have a homeopathic practice in the town - I work on the paper freelance.'

'Oh I see. One of those 'alternative' practitioners. Alternative to real medicine, that is. All these fancy -ologies make our job harder. We have to pick up the pieces when your 'magic' fails, as it must.'

'Really?' she replied, as calmly as she could, while digging her biro into the notepad viciously. 'A lot of my clients have already been to doctors and been told there's nothing wrong with them. Or given drugs that made them ill with serious side effects. Or denied drugs on the grounds of cost.'

'Lot of hysterical women. I don't think much of those who make a living out of their delusions. Fake fortune tellers and so on, putting ideas into their heads.'

'That's an interesting diagnosis,' she managed to say without choking. 'Of course some would say that surgeons make a living out of arthritis, which might be helped more cheaply and effectively by diet and lifestyle changes. There are many points of view, aren't there? And not all my patients are women by the way. Some of them even play golf.'

He laughed, but he sounded angry. More than he had

any right to be, considering how offensive he'd been. Was he unused to people, women, who talked back?

'Surely all that homeopathic claptrap has been proved to be a load of bollocks? You should try and look at some real, hard science, if you can manage to understand it.'

Simon Singh again! And again, Erica was driven to defend her practice even though the crusade of Singh, one of her personal maths communicator heroes, sometimes tested her own faith.

'I'm a maths and theoretical physics graduate so I'm not a total stranger to science. There are many things which can't be proved by current methods. Many scientists believe in god, even though nobody's been able to isolate any evidence apart from a placebo effect there. I believe you attend St Mary's?'

'Good grief, maths eh. If that's true,' his tone made clear he doubted it, 'you should go in for accountancy and earn an honest living. Not that equations would do you any good if you sustain significant trauma.'

Horribly like Will Bennett. Recalling the conversation now, Erica kicked herself for not thinking to hit back with the mathematical geometric equations involved in the forces applied by the Ilizarov frame, Kingston's stock in trade. Still, the guy was dead so scoring points was rather point*less*.

He'd finished with, 'I'll give this interview, but I'm not debating crap like that. No-one has any right to question my work, except possibly another surgeon of equal seniority, and none of them would. I'll talk about my surgical work, and that's it. I can give you half an hour. Some of us have real jobs to do.'

She'd agreed. He seemed happier once he had, as he thought, taken control of the situation. She'd been willing to let him think so, for now. That's why she borrowed the dowdy clothes. She was hoping he would condemn himself out of his own mouth - if not, well, she was a professional journalist, even if only part time, and she didn't have to like everyone she dealt with. She'd hoped she'd never be on the receiving end of his bedside manner if it was anything like his telephone one. As it turned out, it was him who sustained the 'significant trauma.'

Good thing Will Bennett hadn't seen her biro-ravaged notepad with its blue-stained stab wounds, or he'd be giving her the third degree. However, Kingston couldn't argue for himself anymore, so she tried to leach all her dislike out of the obituary. She had to go through it several times, reading it aloud to make sure it was as bland as ricotta when she emailed it in with the regular features of her page.

She was interrupted by a phone call from Miles, the hypnotherapist at Ivy Lodge.

'Erica, can you come over, if you possibly can. Your client Beccy's here and she's in a bit of a state. I've told her you're not in this morning, but she keeps insisting. She refuses to come back this afternoon... she's going to upset the other clients.'

'OK, I'll come now. Lucky I'm not far. Take her into my room and give her four drops of Rescue Remedy, tell her I'm on my way.'

When she got to Ivy Lodge, Miles intercepted her outside her room.

'I didn't like to leave her alone, but I've got one of my smokers waiting for treatment... I've been darting in and out, reassuring her, rushing in to check on my client. I've got some of that whale music miaowing away, it's supposed to be soothing, but it's not having much effect. Maybe you have to be a whale. I'll get back to my client. He'll be dying for a fag by now as it is.'

'Thanks, Miles. Sorry you got lumbered. If she turns violent, I'll call you to come and do an emergency hypnosis.'

Beccy was sitting on the edge of the chair beside Erica's desk, hunched over, every line of her radiating tension. Her beautifully cut and streaked ash-blonde hair was all over the place, and her eyes bluer than ever under a film of tears. One hand was curled inwards, pressed against her abdomen, and the other was clenched on the upholstered arm of the chair. She had been watching the door like a child at the dentist's, and the intensity of her gaze hit Erica like a physical blow. She turned off the whalesong as she approached the sobbing girl – of course she was a woman, really, not a girl, no need to buy into her helpless habits of body language and appearance.

'What's wrong, Beccy?' This didn't seem the time to remind her about the need to make appointments in advance. She grabbed Erica's arm tightly. Erica freed herself gently. 'Let me make us both a hot drink.'

She handed Beccy a Clarice Cliff repro mug of chamomile tea. She wrapped her hands around it, and sipped, the steam adding to the moisture on her pink cheeks. She was wearing pale stonewash skinny jeans and a sugar pink short cardigan buttoned over a white tee-shirt which probably cost pennies to make in some foreign sweatshop and a fortune to buy because of the label on it, the cardigan arranged to make sure it was clearly visible. She wore high heels with the jeans. She took a hand off the mug and touched her eyes with a tissue from the box on the desk. A pile of scrumpled damp discards littered the floor under her chair. She wore no makeup, which Erica noticed from the lack of black smears on her face or the tissues. She'd never seen her without it before. She remembered Beccy saying early on that she would never go out, wouldn't even answer the door without 'putting her face on'. As if she had no face without cosmetics. Her mouth trembled and she almost spilled the drink.

'What's up?' Erica asked, sipping her own drink.

'He... It's him.'

Some people look ugly when they cry. They fight against it, their faces break up, their mouths twist, distort. But Beccy still looked pretty, her mascara-less lashes dark with tears and giving her a watery, pale mermaid look. She didn't fight against the tears, maybe for her it was OK for a girl to cry, even a girl of 30, and she let the tears run down without shame.

She blotted the tears again with a fresh tissue, careful not to rub. Some magazine had probably told her it stretches the skin and gives you wrinkles. Erica ached to see her in such distress even while feeling a stab of impatience at her helplessness.

'Your husband? Has he done something to you?' Already Erica felt a spurt of anger. Her protective feelings were reporting for duty as usual, wanted or not. She'd wondered before if Beccy's husband knocked her about, but Beccy had refused to discuss her marriage apart from to insist on confidentiality.

'He's dead,' Beccy looked down into her mug.

'Dead!' Remembering the impression she'd had of her feelings about her husband, Erica wasn't sure how to respond. But she certainly seemed upset.

'Can you tell me about it?'

She began to laugh, a barking sound like a seal, not a healthy sound.

'I don't need to,' she said. 'You know... you found him, didn't you?'

Erica put down her mug, trying to stay calm, her mind whirling.

'*Kingston*? He was your husband? But how, I mean... his

91

wife's name is Tessa.'

'That's right,' she replied with a hint of triumph, lifting her round little chin. 'I fooled him... I used a false name to come here, to go anywhere on my own if I could. He was so possessive, so controlling, he even insisted I go to a ladies' only gym. He would never have let me come here. He hated alternative medicine. To be honest, that's one reason I came in the beginning - it made me feel better, knowing I was deceiving him, rejecting his work, his world. I'm sorry I deceived you as well, but it's only a name after all. You know the real me, Erica! You've helped me such a lot. It was coming here, talking to you, seeing how you live your own life, even though you don't seem to have much money, well it gave me the courage to leave him and start doing the same. And Tara my sister and I are close again, I'm living with her just now.'

'Why are you here?' Erica tried to keep her voice neutral and quiet.

'I want you to know, because you found him, because you've helped me, you've listened to me. And because even after he's dead, I still have to be scared. It's not fair! You have to help me!'

The childlike wail came from a grown woman, but it seemed she had not grown up.

'What are you scared of?' Being alone, probably.

'I've been scared for years. Maybe it's a habit now. At first, when we got married, I was just scared I'd show myself up, not be up to the job of being his wife... he was so much cleverer, more important, older, I couldn't believe he'd picked me, just another pretty young nurse. I tried so hard to please him – but he - you mustn't tell anyone!'

'Not if you don't want me to. But he can't hurt you anymore. He did hurt you, didn't he?'

'He broke my arm once. On purpose. We hadn't been married long. When I said I wanted to go to a hypnotherapist to cure my insomnia. He just did it, like that. He hit me, he wasn't even in a temper. 'Can a hypnotherapist cure that?' he asked me. He took me to A&E himself. We walked in there and they were all over him, grovelling. Oh, I got great service! The nurses teased me. Silly me, a doctor's wife, falling down stairs. I couldn't say anything. He was their boss, the great healer; they'd never have believed me. He'd have had me put away. He told me that. Sectioned, he said, he always used the proper terms. 'Silly hysterical woman, I'd have to have you sectioned'. All women were hysterical to him.'

'I can well believe it.' Erica remembered the phone conversation.

'After that, I tried never to argue with him again. He had to be in control you see. He didn't break any more bones. Too risky. But a few times, he'd manage to give me drugs, so I passed out. It was terrifying, waking up with no idea what had happened. I'd been helpless with him... he'd done things to me, you know, sexually... He said he knew ways to kill someone. He could make it look like heart failure and one of his colleagues would back him up so nobody'd ever know. It was terrible, knowing he could do it, just waiting until one day he'd feel like going all the way. But he was so careful... and I felt I somehow deserved it. I'd always wanted children but I couldn't conceive. Robert told me he'd once got a girlfriend pregnant, but she lost the baby. Then he married me and I couldn't give him a son. My fault. I'd tricked him, trapped him into marrying me. He seemed to resent it more and more. He hurt me sometimes, ways he knew, that didn't cause injury or leave marks. And he would say terrible things – that I wasn't a real woman... I was useless, nothing... words don't leave bruises do they?'

'But you did leave him,' Erica reminded her. Inwardly she boiled with rage but tried to stay professionally detached. She'd always, though sympathetic, found it hard to imagine staying in an abusive relationship. Especially right at the start. First time he shows aggression, get out of there and report the bastard. Hurt me once, shame on you. Hurt me twice, shame on me. But she could see how hard that would be, married to someone like Kingston, not the stereotype drunken slob too handy with his fists after a night out on the lash.

'Yes, I did. For a long time, I couldn't get up the nerve. He told me I'd be useless on my own. I knew I'd never have a baby whatever happened. But then the sessions with you gave me hope; a life alone seemed better than what I had. So I just went. My sister's strong, she's not scared of him.'

'Well that was great! But why didn't you tell me about him? I'd have given you advice, addresses, contacts to turn to.'

'I couldn't tell anyone. I didn't expect anyone to believe me. But even if they did, I didn't want anyone to know; I thought it must be my fault, if he was so wonderful with everyone but me. I couldn't prove it, could I? My word against his. No. I cleared out my 'housekeeping' bank account and went. Not that there was much in it. Only what he gave me for expenses. I've been childminding for my sister would you believe! Thank god I've got Tara.'

'How did Kingston take you leaving?'

Making an effort to pull herself together, Beccy, no, Tessa took a hairbrush out of her bag which was on the floor under her chair. She began to tease it through her hair, ash-blonde where Erica's was honey. Brushing her hair she set her mouth in a firm line, the way people do against the pulling, and she looked older and more determined.

'I must look such a mess! Well, I was scared he'd come after me at first. So I went to a Well Woman Clinic, not our usual GP, who's an admirer of his of course, and said I was worried about my heart. Flutterings, pains, whatever. They tested me and said my heart was fine. I emailed him to say, you'll be pleased to know my heart's in good nick. Meaning, if I die, he'd find it hard to get away with heart failure as cause of death. I didn't expect him to smash Tara's door down or anything. He's much too careful. He has a reputation and a lot to lose. Has to keep up the godlike image in public.'

She had slipped into the present tense. Hard to believe he was dead, Erica supposed. 'That's impressive Be- Tessa. You've really made great strides.'

'I was still terrified though. I was sure he'd do - something. I don't know what. He said, 'You'll be back!' He really believed I would! That I couldn't manage on my own. Anyway, I've been doing a computer course in the daytime, spending hours at the gym getting fit in the evenings, and my sister's going to help me get a job. Couldn't use my nursing locally could I? In this region his fans and underlings are everywhere. Tara's much cleverer than me. She was the clever one, I was the pretty one, but now she looks pretty good too and she's got a good job. And children. She's a solicitor, lucky for me as it turns out.'

'So why are you still scared now he's dead?'

'The police think I did it.'

She had been calmer, thinking of how she had asserted herself and got away, but now she slumped into the chair.

'They interviewed me. Asked me all sorts of questions. It turns out there was no sign of forced entry at the house.'

'The front door was on the latch when I arrived.' Why?

'So Tara pointed out he'd changed the locks and I don't have a new key. So then it was 'Or it was someone he knew and opened the door to,' which points to me again.'

'Yes well I'm sure he knew lots of people. That's not evidence.' Perhaps someone was let in through the front door and went out the back, not bothering to check the front door.

'And the fact I'd left him... At first I thought they were just breaking the news officially, being sympathetic. Then they began asking questions about why I left. Tara was with me, thank god, it was terrifying. That Inspector Bennett, so handsome but so horrible, tall and dark, glowering over me. Tara told me not to say anything unless she gave me the nod. Why would they believe me anyway? Robert played golf with the Chief Constable up in the city club sometimes! I realised after a bit they think I must have someone else, a younger man probably. 'Quite an age difference between you wasn't there?' and so on. Tara said, well how do you know Robert didn't have women involved with him? They've checked, or so they say, don't know of any. Asked Tara and me if we do. Course we had to say no, but that means nothing does it?

'I said to them, you don't think I did it, do you? 'Oh, we're just asking routine questions. We always interview the relatives in a case like this,' they said. Tara said, Look at her, does she look like someone who could hit a man on the head with a rock? If he knew his killer, they said, easy to hit someone from behind when they trust you. It wasn't that big a rock, they said. They even looked in my bag for signs, bits of stone I suppose. Like I'd put some dirty stone in there, it's Prada! Then there were hints about all his money, would anyone want to lose half of it in a divorce when they could inherit all of it. I'm sure they're watching Tara's house. I could end up swapping one prison for another. I need to know I can trust you to keep all my stuff confidential. Tara wants to decide when and what to tell the police. But we, I, will need you to back me up at some point soon. Just confirm I told you of his abuse.'

Erica's heart sank. What could she do to help, with no official standing, except give moral support. Except that she did now have a kind of link to the case. Beccy, dammit Tessa, was her patient, her client. Suck on that, Bennett and co!

'All my patients have confidentiality, don't worry about that.'

'I was scared of Robert, but how could I have done - that, to him? I'm a nurse, I've seen enough pain and suffering. All I wanted was to be free of him for god's sake!'

'Even that last statement could be used by the police against you. They'll twist your words if you let them. Now listen, erm Tessa, the police do have to see the relatives, and they do have to suspect everybody. But having a motive is not enough, there has to be some evidence against you. Don't open your mouth unless your sister is with you. Just to be on the safe side.'

Erica was thinking, with someone of Tessa's passive

Pulsatilla character, repeated questioning and browbeating for long enough might get a false confession out of her. Kingston like many abusers had trained her to accept not only abuse, but the blame for it. Somehow she had to protect Tessa; she trusted Erica, needed her. She couldn't fail her, not like in the past, that other time at school, that other girl who needed and trusted her. She should have saved her from the bullies, but she'd failed her in the worst way, all because she was overweight. The same urge to make amends for that childhood betrayal kept her running, and starving, and swimming, and rushing in to save a series of protégées. She had the will power to give up almost anything but getting involved.

CHAPTER TWELVE

Erica sent Tessa back to Tara's in a taxi, after giving her a suitable remedy and some to take with her. As she picked up snotty tissues and washed the cups, she thought ruefully that Tessa had credited her with enabling her to leave the marriage, but she hadn't trusted Erica enough to tell her about her husband's abuse. Or even her own real name. Did I fail her in some way? The thought nagged at her.

Maybe Tessa was still not telling her everything. The police might have the wrong motive for her leaving her husband, but if she told them about his abuse, if they did believe her, it would only give her an even stronger motive in their eyes. She could understand why Tara had told her to say nothing to the police just yet. If forensic evidence was found pointing to someone else, there'd be no need for Tessa to expose her victimisation.

Could Tessa have done it? She had a passive vulnerable personality. But she was a fit young woman. She went to a gym even if it was only to make her look slimmer and more toned rather than to build up muscular strength. She might be able to hit him, knock him out, and hammer in the nails.

And his hands. The hands that broke her arm, nailed down and harmless. Soft, blonde, pretty, Tessa didn't look like a killer. But you never know. Even a worm will turn, they say. Erica had dreamed of Pulsatilla, the pasque flower, Jesus and his nailed palm, the flowers curling around the spike. She'd assumed it was the association of 'pasque' with Easter and the crucifixion, the crown of nails. Tessa was a classic Pulsatilla type. Had Erica's subconscious made the connection between Beccy and Tessa in her intuitive dreams?

Then she thought of the obituary she'd been writing for Kingston. That bucket of whitewash to be thrown over his name. She'd been so careful to bleed all her antipathy out of it. Now, knowing what she knew of him, she was left with even more of a travesty. But what could she do about it? She could just imagine the editor's face - Robert Kingston, surgeon, wife-beater... it just wasn't the right time and place for an expose. And, as he would be quick to point out, they only had Tessa's word for it anyway. Easy to malign the dead.

Her broken arm would be a matter of record, but she had gone along with the falling down stairs story at the time. Would she feel betrayed when she realised that Erica had written the positive obituary? Too late to worry about that.

Nails through his hands. Hands could do so many things, bring so much pleasure, healing, and pain. Was there blood on Tessa's hands? And did Erica even blame her if so?

Battered wives had before now been provoked into murder, and badly treated by the judicial system. It had seemed at times that a man could murder his wife, and as long as he said he loved her, but she'd laughed at him in bed or he thought she was having an affair, he'd get off with a short sentence or even probation. For a wife who'd gone through hell and finally hit back, knowing the bastard would kill her one day, it had often been life imprisonment. The fact that the judges were usually public school men, and had been basically isolated from women since infancy, was purely coincidental of course.

Usually nowadays judges and juries were more sympathetic to abused wives and partners. And of course men were sometimes victims of domestic violence. But Tessa's case was a bit different. She'd left him. To go back and kill him in that savage way, in cold blood, was harder to sympathise with. He hadn't apparently stalked or pursued her since she left. Or not in any provable way. Everyone else would say the guy was a saint. She'd probably get life, even if she pleaded provocation.

Suddenly a thought occurred to Erica. *Would* everyone say he was a saint? She hadn't spoken to anyone else who actually knew or worked with or under him. If Tessa was telling the truth, the man was a sadist, though very much in control of his sadism. A control freak. In control enough of himself to really enjoy it, long term. Was it really likely Tessa was the only one he had ever hurt? With all the power he had at the hospital, the temptation would be strong to misuse it. Maybe there were other people, colleagues, patients, out there who could tell a similar story even if broken bones were involved in a very different way. They too hadn't told anyone because they believed they were the only ones and no-one would believe them... Maybe Erica could put the record straight. Once the obituary was printed, the funeral service held and so on, she could tell the other side of the story, the dark side of Kingston.

The idea of bad-mouthing a dead man felt distasteful, but the living mattered more. If she could show what Kingston was really like, it would help Tessa if she did end up on trial and used his abuse as provocation and it would also show that there were other people who had a motive for hating and killing him. As a homeopath Erica could give Tessa remedies for her state of mind and body; as a reporter, she could perhaps help her situation. Put a whole bunch of suspects between her and the police. She emailed Ian Dunne at the *Guardian*, asking him to add a couple of lines to the obit to the effect that they were going to be doing a follow-up piece on Kingston, filling out the portrait warts and all; that they wanted anyone with personal memories of him to get in touch with Erica through her *Guardian* email address.

Her phone buzzed just as she was about to summon her first patient of the afternoon through into her room.

'What follow-up piece, Erica?' the voice of her nemesis

growled.

'I was hoping to talk to a few people about him, you know, 'the real man' sort of angle. Kingston's murder is big news here after all. It'd keep public interest simmering while the investigation goes on. Keep up the profile of the case until the trial of whoever did it.'

'All right, but try to keep the facts straight - luckily dead men can't sue.'

By the end of the afternoon, Erica was ready for some exercise. She usually swam early in the morning, but now the pool would be teeming with after-school tots, so she went to the gym and did a hard work-out with the cardiovascular machines, and then did one of her regular classes with some friends she always saw there. Then they all went out for a curry and walked home together along the seafront, the waves creaming in the darkness, the lighthouse like a ghostly beacon against the black sky. Erica drank mineral water with a slice of lime with dinner, but she felt faintly drunk, as she always did with spicy foods. Something to do with the spices stimulating the pain receptors and causing the release of endorphins, the body's own morphine. Cheap, and legal. And a good kind of pain.

In bed, she felt the spices marinading her from the inside, could smell them oozing out through her skin, and she fell asleep in an oriental haze.

CHAPTER THIRTEEN

After the obituary came out, Erica rang the hospital, explaining she was doing a further article on Kingston, and would it be possible to talk to anyone about him, a colleague or patient. At first, she got the usual primitive territory-guarding response - she must understand they were all so busy, their time was so valuable, they couldn't afford to waste it in chatting about colleagues who were no longer there, and so on. And of course talking to patients was a total no-no, confidentiality... So she sent an email to all the consultants, registrars and other staff in the orthopaedic department, saying the same thing and inviting responses.

She got one in a couple of hours. Mr Rohan would be willing to talk to her. A consultant! The only one that was on the same level, same specialism as Kingston, in that hospital, according to the local NHS trust website. He apparently dealt with fractures higher up the body, specialising in 'halos'. Erica didn't expect any huge revelations from a fellow consultant, but she should be thorough and collect the praise with the blame, if indeed there was any. And she might get talking to someone else there who might have info. She kept thinking of Tessa, who she wanted to protect and help, but who could be a killer. Though surely in a case of long term abuse, there was some mitigation? Perhaps Erica's own antipathy to the late doctor's phoneside manner was biasing her too much. She had to admit to herself that she was hoping to find some dirt on him. And her such a nice person. It didn't feel good

She managed to fit in her morning mile at the pool and with frantic hair-drying and moisturising was in time for her appointment with Mr Rohan. Not out of any special respect, but because she was chronically punctual. She'd bet herself he'd be wearing a bow tie, consultants always do, to prevent ties dangling into open wounds, blood, or private parts as they leaned in to inspect them.

Mr Rohan had a bald dome, a fuzz of grey hair round his ears and a neat little goatee beard which was still brown touched with grey. He had gentle brown eyes and a middle eastern appearance. His manners were rather formal, and he was indeed wearing a bow tie, yellow and brown plaid to match his smart brown suit.

A nurse bustled in with a tray of tea in china cups, probably this tea had never seen the inside of a machine, and some good but boring biscuits. Erica was glad she'd borrowed her respectable outfit again, the one she'd been wearing when she found Kingston's body. At this rate it would be worth investing in her own dowdy disguise.

He sipped at his tea, black. She did the same, thinking the chance of soya milk was slim to none and not wanting to trigger any prejudices about tree-hugging yoghurt-knitting veggies which might make him reluctant to speak to her.

'So, you are writing an article on my late colleague for the local paper. A dreadful business, dreadful. I believe you found him? I hope you are recovering from the shock.'

'I'm trying to take a positive attitude, Mr Rohan. It helps to do something, to tell his story and make people realise what kind of man he really was.'

That was safely ambiguous enough.

'Well, he was a fine surgeon. He'd been here for seven years, I've been here a little longer. He specialised in hip and knee joint replacements originally but lately he did more and more work on tibia fractures. Always a challenge, the blood supply being so sparse in that area, and such common bones to break in road traffic accidents or sports injuries. Comminuted, compound fractures often result....I'm more of a spinal man myself. You can contact the patients' groups, I'll get the office to give you the numbers.'

'I've already got those, but thank you. What I'd like from you is some idea of what kind of a colleague he was - the man, as well as the surgeon.'

Rohan looked a bit puzzled. 'Well, all I can tell you is he was an intelligent, able man... come in!'

The last was a response to a knock at the door. A young doctor came in, still in the white coat stage of the metamorphosis into consultant, and put a folder on the desk.

'The results you wanted,' he said to Rohan. He looked Chinese, with neat features, soft black hair like soot, his colouring set off by the extreme whiteness of the coat which looked new. A baby doc! A cute baby doc. Oh, yes. He looked back at her and smiled slightly in a reserved way. She wished she wasn't wearing the horrible shapeless dowdy clothes.

'This is Dr. Lau,' Rohan said. 'Jamie, this is Erica Bruce from the *Evening Guardian*. She's doing a follow-up piece on Mr Kingston.'

The young man's smile remained, but she thought she detected a tightening of the skin over those lovely cheekbones. Clearly Mr, or was it Dr, Lau was subordinate to Rohan and Kingston; maybe he would bear close investigation. It would be a pleasure, as well as a duty, to find out what was under that white coat.

'Perhaps I could talk to you too, if you can spare me the time, that is,' she ventured.

'Erm maybe.' His head went down, and he looked a bit awkward. Shy, or something to hide?

'Our junior doctors hardly get time to sleep,' laughed Rohan. 'They don't even have a social life, eh, Jamie?'

Jamie politely acknowledged his superior's remark and excused himself. Dammit! Well Jamie you can run but you can't hide.

'It's a tough time for him, or any young doctor,' mused Rohan, 'but he's young enough to take it. When you get to my age and experience, the pace isn't so hectic. Time for other things.'

'You mean, the better you get at this job, the less you do it?'

He looked startled. 'I suppose you could say that,' he said, still charming but with more of an effort.

Careful Erica! 'Mr Kingston had a thriving private practice, I believe.'

'Yes, he had a lot of contacts in the Arab nations and elsewhere. He went out to Saudi when he had leave from the hospital, and of course he saw local private patients, often at his home in the first instance and for follow up, then he'd operate on them at the private Hospital in town. He was a most sought-after surgeon, with a fine reputation.'

'Both here and in his private practice, you mean?'

'Absolutely.'

'So there were never any complaints or controversies about him?'

'Certainly not.' Rohan was looking less genial now. 'And now that he is dead would not be the time to discuss it if there were.'

'Of course not,' she said hurriedly. 'I only meant, it's impressive that all his patients were satisfied, considering how many he helped.'

'Yes it is.' He sounded more relaxed. 'Orthopaedic surgery is a fine branch of medicine, young lady. It may not be as, hem, 'sexy' as brain or heart surgery, but the work we do getting people mobile again after accidents is really worthwhile. And arthritis takes a terrible toll on the old, even the middle aged and the young. Not only crippling, but painful too. To see someone walk again without pain or recover from serious injury is a true privilege.'

His sincerity sounded genuine enough, she had no reason to doubt him, and felt a little ashamed of even mentioning complaints or controversies. But she would have to harden her heart a little if she was going to get anywhere with this.

She switched off her recorder and thanked Rohan for his help.

'I'll be visiting all the spheres Mr Kingston was involved in, the Golf Club, for instance. Did you play together at all?'

'No,' he said firmly, getting up to see her out. 'I know nothing about golf. We did not mix outside the hospital, and very little in it really. He had his patients, I had mine. But as far as I'm concerned, he was a valued colleague.'

In other words, Rohan knew no ill of him, and nothing at all about the man himself. Or that was all he was willing to say. The profession always closed ranks against outsiders, whatever rivalries there might be.

The waiting areas had been filling up steadily while she was in Rohan's office. Fracture clinic. She felt very conspicuous walking past them, a queue jumper, with all her limbs in working order. She tried to look like a sales rep for bandages as she walked past the suspicious eyes. There was a woman standing behind a loaded refreshments trolley. She wore a bright overall and a smile to match. An 'excellent woman', if Erica was any judge, and as a Barbara Pym devotee, she could spot the species a mile off. Clearly she was a volunteer with the Friends of the Hospital. Erica chose a mini carton of apple juice as the least harmful thing available, provided she was careful putting the straw in through the little dimple of foil. They tended to have a premature ejaculation all over you if you squeezed them too much, and everyone knows what a nuisance that can be. A fat woman sitting nearby must have read her mind, because she called over,

'Be careful, pet! Mine's just shot out all over me, like a little lad's willy!'

Everyone in earshot laughed, the trolley woman rather forcedly she thought.

'This is certainly an improvement on the departments I usually go to,' she said to the trolley lady, but loud enough for anyone else to join in. 'Horrible machine tea there and no other choice.'

The trolley woman beamed.

'We have a shop too, further in by the general entrance, with flowers, newspapers and so on. And we go round the wards. Do you know, some of the old dears never have a visitor. No-one to bring them any treats.'

'Aw, what a shame, and I expect some patients spend a long time in wards like, oh, orthopaedics,' Erica said cunningly.

'They do. There's Mrs O'Rourke. Broke her hip, but she's never been able to get up yet, complications you see, and the longer she lies there, the harder it'll be to ever get her going again, poor old soul.'

'Maybe I could visit her if you don't think she'd mind. Take her some little extras.' And get the patient's eye view of Kingston.

'I'm sure she'd be glad to have a visitor,' said the trolley woman warmly.

'Ginger marmalade,' announced the fat lady. 'Always on about it she was, when I was on Ward 5. Said it kept her regular. Missed it in here. They give yer pills instead that don't work.'

Erica felt she should have been trying to spread the word about alternative medicine while she was there, handing out samples of remedies for arthritis and so on. It would be a bit like smuggling bibles into a communist regime. But there was no need to make herself conspicuous just when she was about to do a bit of undercover work, if you could call taking a jar of ginger marmalade to an old lady that. You never read about Philip Marlowe carrying ginger marmalade. Oh, well, down these shining corridors a woman must walk.... she found out the afternoon visiting times and left.

CHAPTER FOURTEEN

Hassan and Sally were interviewing Mrs Marie Browning, cleaner to Mr Robert Kingston, deceased.

'Very good of you to come back early from your holiday, Mrs Browning.' Hassan was in full genial mode.

'No probs.' Marie blew her nose.

Paul Lozinski had spoken to her on the mobile number he found in Kingston's address book (which was boringly unhelpful, plumbers, electricians, lawn mowing service and so on but Kev was plodding his way through them all) to break the news. Marie was thin, energetic, with bright orange-dyed hair held back by blue plastic slides, wearing skinny jeans and a floral smock top. She'd been staying at her son's so hadn't been too far away. However, leaving aside fiendishly clever use of railway timetables, stolen bicycles or disguises beloved of golden age thriller writers, it seemed likely that she really had been with her son and his partner near the Scottish border, and had in fact been with them in a lock-in at the village pub on the night in question, and was therefore more likely to be informant than suspect. Paul had been told to check it all out however, just to dot all the t's and cross all the i's, as Golden Boy would say. Marie was a very hyper woman, her cleaning must have been turbocharged, and she was someone who specialised in emotional multi-tasking. She seemed upset, and angry, and pleased by the drama and attention, all at the same time. She sipped the coffee Sally had given her, and blew her nose again using the box of tissues placed at her elbow.

'You turn your back for five minutes...' She looked at the plate of biscuits with initial interest which waned when she clocked how inferior they were. 'Poor Robert!'

'So you'd been with Mr Kingston, er Robert, a long time?' Sally pushed the tissues nearer as if to make up for the biscuits.

'Seven years. I cleaned for him, and for his mum too till her house was sold. Easy enough, she lived next door! Lovely woman, lovely, but particular.'

'Ah yes we understand she died recently?'

''Bout year and a half ago pet. Oh Robert was a good son mind! D'you know he bought that house for his mum? He couldn't do enough for her!'

'So he'd have made money on the house? His mother's I mean. All those houses along by the Golf Club are worth a fair bit.'

'Oh yes. Well he was a surgeon of course, he earned a hefty wage. Deserved it too! Whoever did this should be strung up by their balls with barbed wire!'

Hassan winced reflexively at this image. Change the subject. 'So your holiday was arranged well in advance?'

She nodded.

'For the recording, please Marie.'

'Yes it was. I usually do three times a week. But with going away, I gave the whole place a good bottoming, it must've been the morning before... his last day.' She blew her nose again and finished her coffee. 'That coffee's shite. So at least he got to die in a clean house.'

'Er yes. So you cleaned his private consulting room?'

'I did. I could have been doing it all along, but well her ladyship had to do *that* room. Until she naffed off, then all of a sudden it was my job.'

'Her ladyship, would that be Tessa Kingston, Marie?' Sally could feel a galeforce bitch attack coming. 'The wife who left him?'

'S'right. Dead common she is. Did well to bag Robert. He was way out of her league. But you know what men are pet, think with their dicks if at all.' Sally daren't look at the DS.

He tried not to defend his gender but to keep on this promising tack. 'So you didn't like Tessa?'

'Never did me any harm. Just, nowt much to her. Pretty nurse who married the surgeon. Like a Mills and Boon. She was about as much use as a chocolate erm, what's the word?'

'Fireguard?'

'Teapot?'

'Condom! She just flitted about getting her hair and nails done 24/7. Speaking of chocolate, you could get some chocolate hobnobs in you know. They're bogof at Asda

117

just now. These things are false economy. Anyway, Tessa cleaned his consulting room herself, he supposedly insisted on it, not that she'd exactly have worn herself out. Had to be surgically clean. Well what do nurses know about that these days, what with MRSA and flesh eating bugs all over the hospitals? And if you want my opinion, she drinks. Broke her arm once falling downstairs, I ask you. And he was that nice to her. Well, it's the good that get taken. Poor Robert.'

'So what happened when Tessa left?'

'Oh well I had to clean that room as well didn't I? She was just, not there any more when I went along one day. He didn't want to talk about it, too upset I s'pose. But she was most likely bored, no interests but herself and her appearance, no job, no bairns, and he worked really hard operating on folk so she had too much time to herself, nice for some. Caffeteer. That's what you want in here, proper coffee. So you'd better catch the bastard that did this. Barbed wire, balls!'

'So,' Hassan summed up for Will afterwards. 'Marie doesn't like Tessa. But interestingly doesn't seem to think she did it. I mean all her comments on the killer were shall we say, gender specific to men. Though she might just make the assumption it's a male crime. Seemed to think Tessa's pretty much useless.'

'Big fan of Mr K isn't she? Blames the split on Tessa.'

'Yeah, anyway, so Tessa knew the contents of his

consulting room very well, but then so did Marie, and anyone she might have spoken to, and all the patients who consulted him privately. We can get the uniforms chasing them up. Also Marie has a key of her own. Anyone with access to her house could have copied it or borrowed it. She swears Kingston kept the front door locked, unless a patient was due. Before the split, Tessa would have been there to act as receptionist, nurse and chaperone.'

'So if the front door was unlocked when Erica turned up, perhaps the killer left that way and didn't bother to close it.'

'We can't be sure though. Kingston might have forgotten to lock it for some reason. If robbery was the motive they'd have just bashed him one and nicked stuff. It does seem a very personal murder.'

CHAPTER FIFTEEN

Erica powered up and down the pool, weightless, her lifting arms sweeping the water aside, looking through the blueness fizzing with the silver bubbles of her breath. While keeping automatic count of the lengths, instead of playing house music her thoughts roamed freely.

'42,43,...so I'm going to the hospital to visit Mrs O'Rourke. Will I be exploiting her, if I give her some time, and cheer her up, to get information on Kingston, to help Tessa?

55,56,... might be a bit awkward if I bump into Rohan... on the other hand, consultants don't hang about at visiting time, as a rule. Don't want to get buttonholed by patients' rellies. Anyway there's no reason why I shouldn't be there. I'm a fricking tax payer. When I earn enough.

63,64, a mile.'

She relaxed completely, floating on her back. Her heels drifted down to bump the bottom, her head hung heavy, her eyes shut. As she breathed, she moved up and down in the water. It was wonderful, like being unborn.

She might see that young doctor, Jamie Lau. She imagined enveloping him, as the water enveloped her, tasting him all over, biting his lower lip... it was definitely time she had a new lover. Not that his doctor status added to his attractions for her, unlike the women on the covers of those romance stories who swoon at the sight of a stethoscope and a fat salary. But she had always had a weakness for a pretty face; beautiful young men were one indulgence that was both pleasurable and slimming. Win win.

She wondered if he had any interest in traditional Chinese medicine. It would be interesting to learn more about it, and how he squared it with the western methods he had sacrificed his sleep and social life for. Quite a few Chinese medical centres and practitioners in the area these days, and not just in Newcastle's Chinatown... Her mind ran on... herbs... acupuncture...

She breathed in sharply at the wrong time, her mouth and nose underwater, and was forcibly reminded of her evolutionary status as she choked and floundered. Acupuncture? Sticking metal needles, spikes even, into the patient to tap into the energy channels that held the body in balance. Those spikes that had been driven into Kingston's head and hands. Could they be a travesty of, a reference to, acupuncture? Could Kingston have provoked so much hate in a young colleague? He was certainly in a position to misuse power, being in a superior position in the hierarchy, and Erica knew how he felt about alternative medicine. Perhaps he had mocked Jamie or his Chinese culture once too often.

There seemed no end to the interpretations of those

nails which could point to a motive and a killer.

Of course, Lau had to be a suspect like anyone who knew or worked with Kingston. She'd assumed it intellectually, had in fact hoped to increase the number of possible suspects to help Tessa, but now had to deal with the possibility of Jamie as an individual, and a fit one at that, actually being guilty. She did a few extra lengths at furious speed while she faced the fact she'd had been having erotic thoughts about someone who might have driven nails into someone's face and hands. She also faced the fact that she hoped he would not be guilty, for no other reason than that she fancied him. She was getting out of her depth - the shallows were where she belonged.

She climbed out of the pool, feeling her full weight hit her as it always did as she returned to exile on dry land, and went off to wrestle with her snake pit of wet hair.

She was hoping to visit the hospital during the afternoon visiting times when it would be quieter. The hours were 2.30 to 4.30. She had time to do some admin for the practice before lunch.

She checked her messages. One from the *Guardian,* passing on a phone number; someone responding to her request in the last 'You and Your Health' page.

What request? For a moment her still water-logged brain was puzzled. Then she remembered her addition to the obituary, asking for people to contribute to an article on Kingston.

The caller was a Mrs Hartley, a widow, who gave her address at once. It was in one of the posher streets of Wydsand, in fact a street leading from Kingston's own at right angles down towards the sea front. She had a forthright voice, pleasant and well-spoken, and said that she had been a private patient of Mr Kingston.

'Mr Kingston did a wonderful job, he gave me my life back when I got my new knees,' she assured Erica. Yes, well, knee replacements were hardly cutting edge surgery these days. He could probably do them in his sleep. And he was well paid for his work, it's not like he was doing it out of the goodness of his heart.

'What did you think of him as a man, a person?'

'Oh, charming. Attentive, polite, so concerned that I might feel pain during examinations and so on. A lovely man.'

'Did you see Mr Kingston at his house?'

'Yes, he did some consulting there. So I've seen the actual table where...you know...'

'Did you know his wife?'

'Not well, you know, but I saw her when I went to the house. Such a pretty little thing. She used to handle his appointments and so on. I don't know what happened between them - the paper said they were separated. I'd heard she had been ill. But I did know his mother a little better.'

'His mother?'

There was an angle Erica hadn't considered. Somehow she hadn't thought of Kingston as having a mother. Had he thought of *her* as 'hysterical'? She made a note to check on any relatives. Also, those elusive youths at the sad little drinking den. She must find the time to go running past there again, at a later time, and see if they had anything to add to the picture. She wrote MOTHER! YOUTHS! on the pad to remind herself.

'Oh yes old Mrs Kingston died well over a year back, as I expect you know,' Mrs Hartley went on. One possible suspect off the list. Erica did not disillusion her about the omniscience of the local press.

'She was so proud of him. It was, 'my son, the surgeon', all the time. She lived next door to Mr Kingston.'

'Next door?' A bit strange – a smothered mother's boy? Was his apparent misogyny displaced rage against a mother he couldn't leave?

'He was so good to her. Bought her the house when she became infirm, so he could be sure she was cared for.' Ah. Norman Bates off the list then. 'Another gentleman lives there now, a keen golfer.'

'I think I've met him.' Erica thought of the gent in the golf sweater, Archer, Harold Archer, she'd met out running. It would be a big house, expensive, for a man on his own. But he might think it well worth it to be so near his Golf Club.

'Well, you won't hear a word against Mr Kingston from

anyone around here,' asserted Mrs Hartley, in her double role of patient and neighbour.

Realistically, his private patients would be almost bound to sing his praises. He would hardly have showed any dark side of his character to a paying customer. Or a well-off neighbour either. Investing in another house next to his own, supposing he'd kept it in his own name, was a shrewd financial move, as a glance at the *Guardian* estate agents' ad pages for that area of the coast showed, recession or not. And besides, even if he'd given his mother the house outright, she'd died so he'd have scooped the dosh in any case. Erica felt suddenly guilty about her own stereotyped thinking when she'd heard about his being a good son. Why shouldn't Kingston be good to his mother? Why not have her living next door? It's not like he'd never left home. If it seemed a contradiction beside his abusive behaviour as a husband, well even the Kray twins were good to their old mum - and besides, a small voice in her head murmured, you only have Tessa's word for the abuse. She quashed it at once, determined to believe her protégé, but it managed another small gasp before being ruthlessly suffocated. After all, she lied to you about her identity... No, she lied to protect herself against an abusive man. She was taking a terrible risk just going to Erica at all.

'Ye's lot are fkn mentalists.' Thus Scotty, a feral youth with the skinny, round-shouldered posture and muddy, spotty complexion of a couple of generations of mums going to Iceland, but not to harpoon their own walrus. 'It's fkn prejudice that's what it is. Ye're oot to get iz. Like ye got wor Kyle.'

'Aye,' added his mother. 'Aa've lost one of me sons to ye's lot, isn't tharr enough for ye's?'

Will looked at his files as if checking, though he remembered the family well. 'Lost' as in 'sent down for nth offence'. 'Ah yes, Kyle. TWOCKING wasn't it? He certainly made a spirited attempt to outrun us if I remember rightly. His last joyride cost us a police car.'

Mother and son high-fived in celebration of Kyle's achievement, but she registered belated outrage as her hand hit Scotty's.

'Joyridin? Fkn joyridin'? Ee, of aal the nerve! My Kyle's no joyrider. He's a professional thief, man!'

'I do apologise,' Will said dryly.

'And that bizzy was a shite driver, or he'd not've hit that bollard,' Scotty was quick to contribute.

'Either way,' Hassan ploughed on, 'this is about you Scotty lad, not your brother. You are underage and have been caught in possession of alcohol before...'

'Give ower, man, worram Aa supposed to dee? There's nowt for us kids, man, we just hang oot together and we get porsecuted by ye's lot... Everybody drinks, man!'

'Be that as it may,' Will took over. 'You have previous on this, and now we find your old familiar fingerprints on a vodka bottle, dumped in a snicket...'

'Aa've nivvor been anywhere near one of them!' Scotty was as definite about this as he was unsure what a snicket was.

'Leave the bairn be!' his mother insisted. 'Aa gave the lad that voddie bottle...'

'Which is an offence,' put in Hassan, too soon.

'And it was empty when Aa give it him. Aa asked him to put it in the recycling like, burree must've forgot.' She sat back and grinned at the officers.

'Aye, she did and aal,' Scotty jumped on board. 'Aa must've dropped the bugger somewhere. Aa'm SO sorry for droppin litter, and that. Now can Aa gan hyem?'

Hassan and Will exchanged looks. This had been a very very long shot and didn't look like getting them anywhere. Families like Scotty's grew up learning to talk this kind of language. Oh well.

'The thing is,' Will tried anyway. 'The vodka bottle with YOUR fingerprints on it was dropped at the scene of a murder.'

Scotty's mum sat up. 'Now hey! Divven't ye try to pin that Kingston killing on my lad.'

'How do you know I mean that one?'

She was too smart for that. 'What, there've been other morders roond heor lately? Anyway my lad did nowt. He was home with me on the neet in question, aal neet. Yer cannit prove that bottle was dropped that neet, I'm bettin.'

'Erm naw, I think it was the neet afore Aa must've dropped it alang by his hoose.' Scotty took his cue.

'Look Scotty, I'm going to level with you. I don't think you had anything to do with the murder. But one of your mates might have.'

'Aa'm not grassin on me mates.'

'Or one of you might've seen something.'

'We - Aa nivvor.'

'Or someone.'

'Na. Them posh bastards alang there, always tellin we to piss off, when we're deeing nee harm. Just sittin, talkin, on wor phones, listnin to music, ye knaa. We've got neewhere to go man! Erm, except that neet like. When Aa wasn't there.'

'Reet, the bairn's told ye's. Now leave him alone. We're goin.'

'There've been reports of vandalism along there by the golf course. Some people have had windows broken, greenhouses, garden ornaments damaged. By golf balls at night. That wouldn't have been you would it?'

'Eee, somebody's had their garden gnome busted? Eee, that's terrible officer! Not me. Golf baals? Ower posh for us like. More likely some owld geezer playin at neet.'

'Well if you think of anything, or you saw anything, let us know. And spread the word among your mates.' Will closed the file as mother led Scotty away in triumph. 'Epic fail.'

'Yes, but you know. Let her have her win. She has a pretty crap life.'

'You're an old softie Hassan. But they did make a good double act. And I can't really believe the lads did have anything to do with the killing.'

'And it did seem that litter'd been there a night or so already. Judging by the state of the paper labels and fag packets.'

Kev put his head round the door. 'Found some drugs on that lad Scotty. Stupid git was trying to sell them to a youth waiting at the desk. Boasting he's a murder suspect! He'll dine out, or drink out, on that for months. Here you are Guv.' He handed Will an opened small brown paper packet. 'Says he's on a diet and they're sweeteners!'

Hassan conceded. 'On the other hand I suppose they might've done it. If Kingston and neighbours chased them off once too often. If they were drunk *and* high.'

Will examined the tiny white pills and the envelope. 'Yeah well I'm pretty sure they weren't high on this. I'm pretty sure I know where it came from. Crystal meth it ain't. It's a legal high, only it wouldn't work and it shouldn't be legal. I think a certain homeopath we both know is the source of these.'

'How did Scotty get that though? They'd not pay for Erica's services.'

'Well there's no label which there normally would be. I think we should get these analysed, just to cover ourselves.

130

And if they are one of Erica's useless remedies, we'll find nothing in them but sugar. I think I'll keep these in reserve, there may well be a time for tackling her to our greatest advantage.'

'I'll buy you a fluffy white cat for your next birthday Will.'

'And an underground lair. Don't forget that.'

CHAPTER SIXTEEN

Erica jogged to the hospital to visit the unvisited Mrs O'Rourke. The late autumn sun cut through the atmosphere almost horizontally, rather than down onto the trees, picking out the rose hips in the hedges so they gleamed like beads of blood, and making the leaves glow like stained glass. The yellow ones looked like translucent half-sucked lemondrops, a vivid colour which stung the eyes.

A jar of ginger marmalade bumped her back rhythmically as she went, her small rucksack bouncing with her stride.

She reached the hospital, a crouching monstrosity of fairly recent vintage, yet already with some of it marked for closure, and went in through the main entrance. Other visitors were beginning to arrive, clusters of people holding magazines, flowers and boxes of chocolates and bearing that guilty look of reverence, fear and boredom which hospitals inspire.

Uniformed staff bustled past, their gaze fixed above the suitably humbled visitors' heads to show that they were in a parallel but superior universe. By contrast, a woman who was indeed 'excellent' in a print overall smiled brightly from a small kiosk run by the same group of volunteers as the trolley in the fracture clinic. Real flowers were outlawed

133

these days, increasing the sensory deprivation of long-stay patients, so Erica bought a bunch of artificial purple daisies with built-in pot as the safest option before heading down miles of bland and featureless corridor, shedding visitors as she went. Ward Five didn't seem to get many; broken hips mostly afflicted older people whose families lived miles away and whose friends were too old to face the Byzantine complexities of the bus journey. The car park had to be paid for with a mortgage, and was still as hard to get into as Roedean.

Ward Five consisted of a row of bays with about ten beds in each. Some were all men, some all women. She tracked down the bay where Mrs O'Rourke was stowed. Two short rows of beds faced each other. Old women lay asleep or dozing, some of them with sun-starved faces as pale as the sheets but greyish. A couple of beds were empty. Their occupants sat in plastic armchairs beside the beds. Progress back into real life, Erica hoped.

Mrs O'Rourke's bed was high, with a cage of bars around the sides. The old lady who lay dwarfed by all the tubular steel didn't look capable of falling out of bed. Erica could almost see through her, she was so wasted. Her hair was white and wispy amid a rockery of massive pillows. The bed was next to the window. Through it, Erica could see the rosy sunshine lighting up the remains of broom and cotoneaster, a few ragged mophead asters and dahlias. Mrs O'Rourke just lay there, her eyes open, letting time pass.

She was unable to look out of the window herself because of the way the bed was positioned, with the casual sadism typical of institutions.

Erica put her face in the range of vision of its occupant.

'Mrs O'Rourke?' At the sound of her name, it was as if her face had been turned on by a switch. One minute she was blank, absent, the next minute she was there. Her pale blue eyes focused sharply.

'I brought you these,' Erica waved the lifeless flowers. At least they'd be a splash of colour.

'Thank ye, hinny.' She had a faded, soft voice with a hint of an Irish accent behind her Geordie one. 'Those are pretty, mind. Can you just put them on me locker, pet?'

'They're nice aren't they Tilly?' called a nearby knitting woman whose locker, that barometer of a patient's status, bristled with photos, bottles of exotic juices and piles of fruit.

'I'm Gill Webster,' she told Erica. 'My visitors are coming tonight. Tilly never seems to get one.' She spoke louder. 'Me and Tilly O'Rourke have been the longest in here. Eh, Tilly?'

'In for life, and me innocent as a newborn babby - and about as much use,' came Tilly's soft voice gamely. She was obviously mentally fit, if nothing else.

She was thrilled with the ginger marmalade.

'Eee thanks pet, there's nothing like it for keeping you regular.' The jar looked too heavy for her delicate hands.

'It's like amber.' Tilly looked into the sunlit depths of the jar. 'I had an amber brooch once. You've got bonny hair, flower,' she added. 'Lovely and long. I used to be able to sit on mine. Now I cannot even sit!'

She said this jokingly, rather than complainingly. She never asked why Erica was there, or even who she was. She had been in a long time - fracture, hip replacement which went wrong, deep seated infection in the joint, then a chest infection caused by being in bed for weeks leaving most of her lung capacity unused, and now she was almost institutionalised, her muscles atrophied, washed up on those white sheets. Erica noticed her call button had been put out of reach. As she moved it back near Tilly's hand, she glanced round and saw that every old patient's button was also out of their reach.

'Some nurses do that, accidentally on purpose like,' said Gill. 'Saves them having to come in so often.'

'But that's terrible! What if they need a bedpan?'

'Not all the nurses are like that,' she excused, 'and I can keep an eye on the old folk.'

Erica went round the bay moving all the buttons within reach, asking casually, 'What are the doctors like then?'

'Mr Rohan did my op,' said Gill. 'He's very good. Such a gentleman...'

'Yes, I've met him. Charming man. I expect you knew Mr Kingston?'

"Oh, terrible that was. Yes, some of these were his

patients, most of his have gone home by now though. They don't keep hips in long these days unless summat goes wrong like. Oh, you should have seen him doing his round, those students of his shaking in their shoes bless them. But he could do his job alright. He did Tilly's hip.'

'The one that went wrong?' Erica scented negligence. But she knew that the replacement joints did go wrong sometimes. All surgery was risky.

'Took good care of me,' said Tilly. 'He's dead now, you know. Who'd have thought he'd go before me! He was a bit hoity toity, but I just did as I was told. Doctor knows best.'

'Course he does. And there's a few others - anaesthetists, what have you - and the young Chinese doctor, the one they all call Jamie. Even the nurses use his first name. I suppose he's still in training.'

'He's a lovely lad, for all he's Chinese,' said Tilly.

'He is that,' said Gill. 'Mr Kingston used to tease him, like. When he did his rounds and Doctor Lau was with him, he'd say things like, 'I expect you'd stick a lot of needles in her, Jamie. Or give her a bit of ground up tiger bone.' And all the students would laugh though they looked dead embarrassed. I didn't think that was right, mind. Because the lad couldn't very well answer back, could he?'

That bastard Kingston. How much unexpressed resentment was the young doctor harbouring?

'I bet he felt like sticking needles in Mr Kingston,' Erica said as if jokingly, though the image was horribly like her memory of the death scene.

'Well I wouldn't go that far. He never said anything, but I saw him look daggers at Mr Kingston when he thought no one could see. They say the Chinese are inscrutable, but he wasn't then! You'll see Doctor Lau any minute, he's coming down to check on Mrs Hilton's painkillers a bit later. He's always on duty somewhere it seems.'

Erica stuck around a while, chatting and getting to know any other patients who seemed conscious. She wanted to see more of Jamie Lau. He was definitely a suspect. Not only had Kingston humiliated and baited him in front of everyone, but referring to acupuncture, he had used the actual words about sticking needles in people. Could that have led to nails, pins, like big needles, being hammered into the hated head? Young doctors worked long hours. He must be under great stress - sleep deprivation was a torture, after all. People could be made to confess to terrible crimes that way - perhaps they could be brought to commit them too.

Just then Jamie Lau came in with a nurse. He went straight over to Mrs Hilton. Erica noticed the nurse was very familiar and informal with him, and behaved as if she was indulging him when, after a quiet consultation with Mrs Hilton, he gave fresh instructions for her meds. He turned and gave a general smile and nod of greeting to the ward, pausing as his eyes rested on Erica. She did stand out rather with her lycra and bare arms, not to mention her hair. He gave a half-smile of recognition and headed out of the bay.

Erica went after him. The nurse had gone on to the nurses' station where she was talking to a colleague.

'Doctor Lau?' She had overtaken and was blocking the way. He was taller than Erica, but then just about everyone was. He looked pale and drawn. Dead tired. But he was still cute. Cute as a facebook kitten.

'Did you wish to see me about Mrs O'Rourke? Are you a relative?' His voice was soft but clear, with a trace of some kind of accent.

'Oh, no, just visiting... I really wanted to talk to you. I'm writing a feature on Mr Kingston for the local paper, kind of an extended obituary...' She watched him for any reaction to the name of his persecutor and possible victim. Was it her imagination, or did he flinch at the name? It was hard to tell, because he put his hand up over his face to push his hair back in a weary gesture.

'I saw you in Mr Rohan's room,' he said. 'I can't think why you want to talk to me; it's not that I don't want to help but I'm very busy. '

'You look exhausted, I wouldn't expect you to talk to me now when you're on duty. Why don't I take you out to dinner if you are allowed out of here for an evening? '

He looked a bit startled. She could see he was tempted, by her or the food she didn't know, but unsure, perhaps about discussing the hospital with an outsider.

'Well, thanks, that sounds great, but...' he began.

She pressed home her advantage. She had no qualms about asking a guy out.

'Come on, don't tell me that's not the best offer you've had all day! It's just a chatty piece for the local rag health page; do I look like a paparazza? I'll even feed you if you're too tired to hold a fork.'

He laughed, reassured by her small, harmless appearance and her flirtatious manner. Just another girl who wants to play doctors and nurses, he thought maybe. Well, she could live with that for now.

They agreed to meet in a couple of evenings' time at a little restaurant right on the beach which served brilliant veggie and carnivore food in terrifying quantities. The wine and decor was Mediterranean, the menu cosmopolitan. He said he had never been there. Or anywhere much, he basically lived in the hospital.

'Just think of it as care in the community,' she advised him, and let him go.

When she got back to Tilly and Gill, they were grinning significantly.

'I was just asking Doctor Lau to talk to me for the paper; you know, I write the *Guardian* health page.'

'We believe you, thousands wouldn't,' said Tilly.

'That lad could do with a break.' Gill counted her stitches. 'He was up in the night, and now he's still here; and I'm sure he was on duty yesterday. He really cares about patients you know. He spends ages checking meds, and he's so careful about lowering beds and so on to look at people in traction and so on. Some of them let the bed bounce off the floor, and that's no fun when you've got broken bones or whatever. I think that's why Mr Kingston got at him; thought he was too soft, needed to toughen up a bit.'

Cute and caring? What a killer combo. Killer? Could someone so compassionate drive nails into a living head? But then again, how sensitive could a surgeon afford to be? They did stuff like that all the time. What a mess. Hoping Tessa wasn't guilty, and now Jamie. Someone had to have done it, for god's sake.

The man on the table. You remembered the feeling of the rock hitting the pins into his head, the resistance of his skull transmitted up your arm, the give when they broke through into the softness of his brain. The way his fingers curled inwards round the nails that held them helpless. Those hands, surgeon's hands, so skilfully causing pain, carving people up like meat. That's how they operate. Doctors. Surgeons. Making incisions and decisions, and nobody questions them. Until it's too late, but even then, they all protect each other from their mistakes or misdeeds. All the clever-clever golf-playing back-slapping smug surgeons with money and status and the power of life or death. Or a life not much better than death. All in the same club. They're all in it together. Yes, he wasn't the only one. There are others. Someone should operate on them. It would be a public service. A crusade.

CHAPTER SEVENTEEN

As Erica ran up the Ivy Lodge steps, she suddenly felt light-headed and there was a buzzing sensation in her hands and feet. Hungry and dehydrated. In her room, she poured a big glass of cold water, adding the juice of a lime from the fruit bowl, and had a couple of rice cakes spread with low-fat hummus from her emergency rations before her first appointment Laura Gibson arrived. She was one of those who'd suddenly asked for an appointment 'urgently' after the report of Kingston's death, and Erica finding the body, had hit the media. But Erica assumed that was a coincidence. Laura was a smartly dressed, intelligent business woman, hardly the kind to seek shoulder-rubbing time with a corpse finder.

Today she was wearing a milky coffee-coloured tailored jacket, a cream shirt and a turquoise scarf, with black trousers which were well-cut but somewhat looser and longer than fashion dictated, to hide her deformed right leg and built up shoe. She was dark, almost Spanish or Italian looking, with black hair pulled back into a tortoiseshell clip and dark eyes. She walked with a swinging limp and a slim black walking stick and sat down with a small sigh. Erica recalled she had had the kind of tibia and fibula fractures, many years ago, which Kingston had worked on, and a fizz of anticipation ran through her. Was she about to hear something significant, or just another paean of praise to the great knifeman of Wydsand?

'Hi Laura, haven't seen you in ages, how've you been?' Casual.

'I'm fine.' Always that insistence on the positive, with a hint of defensiveness. 'Business isn't great, but hey, we're 'all in this together', allegedly.'

'Yeah, right. So is it leg problems, or lower back, or that neck trouble? All of it related to your shorter right leg of course, referring stress and pain upwards as your body strives to correct itself.'

'Yes I know, the zigzag thing.' Laura zigzagged her hand in a gesture sweeping up her own body, from short right lower leg to left lower back (sacro-iliac joint) to right neck and shoulder area to left temple migraines. 'Well all the usual aches and pains, I'm used to it. It's like my weather, I live with it.'

'I know you got good results from Ruta Grav in the past...'

'I want to be sure anything I say here is confidential.' Laura interrupted her in a sudden burst.

'Absolutely.'

'I want to speak to you partly as my homeopath, and partly as a reporter. I saw your appeal for information about Kingston.'

'Confidential on both counts, as patient and source.'

'I need to tell you. Tell somebody. Kingston was a sick son of a bitch, and he got what he deserved. Only whoever did it was too good to him, by all accounts they knocked him out with a rock first. I'd have happily helped bash in the nails.' She was trembling slightly and a sheen of sweat was on her upper lip but she looked triumphant. 'It feels horribly good to say that aloud!'

'I suppose you'd rather I didn't quote you, even anonymously?'

'Actually I'd love it... but I don't know... he may have relatives who'd be hurt by it.'

. 'So how do you know? Did he treat you at all?'

'No, and yes. The original tib and fib fractures were many years ago, as you'll know, it was treated with an external fixator of the old fashioned kind. But not by Kingston.'

The old-fashioned kind using pins like Kingston's souvenirs that ended up buried in his brain, Erica thought. She kept herself still and calm. Mustn't push it.

'Anyway, months later, pins out, plaster on, fracture clinics, all the usual. In the end, my tibia just didn't heal. Didn't unite. I hate that. I need to be independent, in charge. I used to be. That injury, somebody else's incompetent driving, took that away from me. Instead I got not just pain, permanent disability, a leg shortened by over an inch, but the feeling of helplessness, my worst fear.'

Mine too, thought Erica. Then realised what had been

145

said. Laura's leg was now considerably shorter than that. She frowned, and Laura picked it up at once.

'That's right, that's what the difference WAS. So I just got on with my life and my business, working hard, struggling a bit, walking with pain and difficulty, biting the humiliating bullet of disability, as you know I had a bad ankle fracture as well.'

'Not a good place to make new bone, the tibia, lower down.'

'Yes I know, bad blood supply. I'm an expert on this injury believe me. So fast forward fifteen years or so, about four years ago, I had a fall. Consultant checked me out, discovered the old tib fracture still hadn't united, and told me incidentally that nowadays I could have an artificial ankle joint because of the damage there. But of course, I needed a solid leg bone to fix it to. So the leg would have to be fixed first. Well all those years it was out of alignment, painful as the broken ends were able to move slightly, but I'd got used to it. But now I was being offered new treatment for that too. Previously, they'd just written me off as soon as the plaster was in the bin. I was excited. The consultant was Robert Kingston.'

She stopped, took a deep breath.

Erica put the kettle on. 'Why don't I make us some tea? Or coffee? Like that fabulous jacket.'

'Yes I look great from the waist up, don't I?' Laura laughed. Erica got busy making Laura's choice of coffee, while she continued.

'So, Kingston persuaded me to have another lot of pins and frames inserted. This time, the newer Ilizarov frame. First he explained he had to open up the fracture site, and saw the ends off the broken bones, as they were dead and he needed to get down to living bone. He said this would stimulate them to unite. While the frame was on, I had to turn the screws every day several times a day to force the bones to straighten and to stimulate the new bone to form, lengthening the leg. This was a huge decision for me to make. He was very keen to do it, a non-union that old was a challenge to his skill. I should have realised that was his priority, not my quality of life... but I take responsibility for agreeing to it. It meant at least eighteen months of limited life, worse disability, difficulty with everything, but I hoped it would be worth it in the end. So I went through with it, losing all the mobility I'd fought so hard to regain, gaining much worse pain, and now, ironically, the hospitals are dirtier and I got some foul infections, more pain, antibiotics, all that. This went on for two and a half years. My business suffered, my relationship broke down. And in the end it didn't work. And it was my fault, not Kingston's. I take responsibility for that. I have no trouble taking responsibility. It's abdicating it I find hardest. You see there was a question I should have asked him, and I didn't. So keen to believe it would work. To believe he could heal me. Him and technology. I'd lost sight of what you know to be true - that even surgery and technology rely on the body's own healing power. If it doesn't make new bone, it won't heal.'

She sipped her coffee, holding the cup with both hands.

'So what was the question you didn't ask?'

'Oh yes. 'If my tibia didn't form new bone and unite all those years ago, when I was much younger, why should it do so now?' Well there was no reason, and it didn't. But I blame myself for that. My leg, my responsibility to research fully before making a decision. So far Kingston's just a typical alpha male surgeon drunk on his own skill, caring more about his career than my life. That's not unusual, I've heard a hundred stories, we all have, doctors who didn't listen or believe until it was too late, doctors who said we, usually women, were imagining things, doctors who didn't think about the whole person. Doctors who were callous, clumsy, tactless. Gave bad news badly. And to be fair, the op might have worked, has on some patients, he did nothing I could make any complaints about. Even though I later found out a different surgeon further south was doing the procedure much less invasively or drastically... even then, perhaps he was doing the best he knew how. And if his bedside manner was - disturbing, well that's not uncommon either.'

'Medics used to have all the empathy scorned and trained out of them. Things are better now with the new students, or so I'm assured. They even do poetry workshops.'

'He was more than just tactless and callous and cold. He hurt me. His hands hurt wherever he touched me... and of course being me I had to hide it, stiff upper lip, but it wasn't easy. He'd dig his fingers hard into the injury site... it made me feel sick... and somehow, under attack.'

'There's no excuse for that, when he's in a position of power.' Erica realised the man Tessa married was pretty much the same at work as at home, but his victims there already had broken bones. And he got kudos for fixing them, the clever bastard.

'I know surgeons aren't expected to be 'kind'. Their field is the unconscious patient, the damaged area, the fixing, the skill, the success.'

'I don't think they're all like that.' Erica was thinking of Jamie Lau and his care for patients' pain and suffering.

'No, well... anyway, we're getting to the monstrous bit, and I feel really - I don't want to - so this horrible day, he gives me the bad news, my leg hasn't healed. I've gone through all that for nothing. In fact worse than nothing, my leg is now even shorter, due to him cutting the ends off the bone. From a small orthotic in my shoe and a limp, I've now got a built up shoe and a worse limp. Well he just told me right out, and I was upset. Yes, I cried. In front of him and the nurse. Know what he said? 'What are you crying for? We can just amputate your leg."

Erica felt sick herself. She impulsively put her hand on Laura's arm. Laura politely but definitely slid her arm out

149

from under. She didn't like help or pity.

'So I said no, no chance, I said you've failed to put this right, I'm not giving you another chance to mess it up. He looked furious, nobody was supposed to question him let alone criticise. 'I never offered you a guarantee' was all he'd say. So anyway, so far so ghastly. Then he took the wires out. And he hurt me as much as he could, doing it. I couldn't stop him or leave could I? The frame and wires had to come out. I asked for pain relief, he said it wasn't needed. The nurse looked upset herself but daren't say anything. So I had to lie there while he got them out, as roughly as he could, it was like a kind of violation. Because it was more than indifference, or coldness. It was more even than suppressed anger, that I'd criticised him, regardless of my natural emotional state. The worst thing - the worst thing, was that I could tell he was enjoying it. Hurting me, I mean. He was loving it. I told myself I was being paranoid, I was mistaken. But after it was done, I had a pounding headache as well as the pain in my leg, stress of course, and I was wheeled out by the nurse, but as we left the room, she caught my file in the door and opened it again, and I saw Kingston in an unguarded moment, looking at my x-ray on the screen and holding the wires he'd taken out of my bones and flesh in his hand against his - groin, and he was - aroused. His face - it was as if he was looking at porn. He switched off the look and the posture as soon as he realised the door was open, back to his haughty indifference, but

I'd seen it. He wouldn't think he'd failed, because he could claim credit for trying to save a leg others had given up on. But he was enjoying my reaction, my pain, my damage. My marred life.'

Laura was flushed red with shame. Her weakness and victimhood were as painful to her as the injury.

'I'd already been through so much, injury, years of pain, months of treatment, coping with work, my life disrupted, and yet this was somehow harder to bear. He relished my suffering. It was *obscene*. I didn't tell anyone. It was a disgusting secret I had to share with that man. A foul kind of intimacy. But what could I say? That nurse wouldn't have backed me against him. He was like god in there. They would have just said I was a fussy patient. Hysterical. One of his favourite words for female patients. 'There's no need to get hysterical.' I've felt so ashamed as if I'd been complicit. I know that's irrational but I can't help it. This is the first time I've told anyone. I mean, all of it. And I'm glad I've told you and now I think I need chocolate.'

Hm, bit like asking for condoms in a convent, but Erica went off to beg for some from Miles who fortunately had a few foil-wrapped chocolate biscuits and donated one. 'The C word? And there was more rejoicing over one that was saved...' he mocked.

'It's not for me, it's for a...'

'Friend, yes I know, I believe you.'

Erica inhaled deeply and furtively, the chocolate, rich

and sweet, dark and clinging, acting on her brain like cannabis, as Laura ate with another coffee at her side.

'Chocolate boosts seratonin levels. You need pampering a bit. I'll give you some contacts for an aromatherapy massage. Have you had reiki? It's a way of releasing old harmful emotions. There's a whole theory behind it, which the practitioner can explain, but if you don't buy that, which you probably won't, you can regard it as a ritual which can focus your mind and enable you to say goodbye to those feelings of hate and humiliation, like a kind of funeral for bad feelings. It might work for you.'

'I'll give it some thought.' Laura was closing down now she'd opened up so far. Trusting another person wasn't easy for her. She'd exposed her weakness as she saw it, and Erica wouldn't be surprised if she never saw Laura again. The way friends dump you for listening to them drone on about their lover's faults, once they're blissfully together again.

'It's entirely up to you.' Erica was speaking Laura's language. She gave her a high potency dose of Ignatia and arranged for her to come back to see if they could do something more about the leg, make it hurt less. Her resistance to pain was being lowered by her emotional state. The humiliation of the torturer's victim...forced to participate in an obscene intimacy, taking on the guilt and shame which rightly belonged to the abuser.

Before she left, she said, 'You know, Erica, I feel better having talked about it. Hearing he was dead, murdered,

I was glad, but then I felt revolted. How could I let him make me into someone like him? But all the same, I hope they don't catch whoever did it. Who knows what he did to them? Anyway, no doubt the police are hearing nothing but how wonderful he was. Nobody's going to hand them a motive on a plate. But if you have any doubts about my guilt or innocence, bear in mind I needn't have told you any of this.'

After Laura left, Erica made notes for her article, musing on what she was learning about Kingston. His murder was a hate crime, she was sure of it. The kind of impotent hate which builds up until even just killing isn't enough. She was building up a picture of a man who enjoyed power, couldn't tolerate anyone who questioned his authority. He enjoyed using his skill on the helpless victims on the table, revelling in their respect and gratitude, in the status he had in the hospital, the entourage of nurses and students following him around. But anyone who questioned his actions and attitudes saw a different side to him. A violent sadist, a clever one who could control his sadism. He could use it when he was safe from the consequences. Just the kind of person who would invite this kind of murder.

She couldn't help sympathising with all those who'd suffered at his hands, literally, but any of them might have killed him. There might be scores of them. Could Laura Gibson have killed him? She certainly hated him enough. But would she have come here and flagged herself up as a suspect? And damn it, Erica liked her!

'You can't just cross people off the suspect list because you like them. Maybe you like them *because* they're victims - because you feel you can help them, that they need you,' she berated herself aloud. So, that's Laura Gibson and other patients he hurt, Jamie the cute Chinese doctor he humiliated, and oh, the hoodies behind Kingston's house. Must go for a nighttime jog along there soon.'

She was supposed to be investigating Kingston, not the murder. Who was she, Miss Marple? No, more of a V I Warshawski, with Philip Marlowe's dialogue, given the choice. And Tessa was relying on her.

She heard Rina's door open.

'Wey that was canny intrest'n.' Stacey Reed emerged and walked into Erica's room, phone in one hand, wineglass held aloft in the other.

'Stacey, you haven't been listening in! That was a confidential consultation, Jeez! And you've no right to be in Rina's room.'

'Aa'm using it as a tempry office like. As yer intern ye knaa. And that reminds iz, ye need more biscuits in there, but better ones, with chocolate on.' She looked at Erica's rice cakes. 'Jeez, them things are beer mats, not breakfast! Anyway, if that Rina lass keeps a wineglass in er room, boozin at work, disgustin, you've only yerself to blame if it gets used agin the wall.'

'Stacey, this is serious. I could lose my job. Both my jobs!'

'Erica man, yer clueless. Aa've got ye by the Brazilian, and ye admit it! Well Aa'll not ask for dosh to keep quiet. Ye've got nowt worth mentioning.'

'Wow, thanks.'

'In fact aal I want is to work for nowt as yer intern. Can't say fairer. Safer for ye and aal. If Aa'm working for ye, Aa cannit tell anybody what Aa hear. Saw that on a Tom Cruise fillum about lawyers so it must be true. Lerriz help ye!'

'But what can you do? Apart from keep us up to date with office biscuit needs.'

'Wey ye said sommat aboot joggin and hoodies. Aa can be yer bodyguard like! Little lass like ye, ye cannit gan roond in the dark by yersel, them lads is rough ye knaa.'

'Bollocks Stacey, I've spent my entire adult life not to mention underage drinking life wandering around at all hours in the dark and in hardly any clothes, I'm not as defenceless as you seem to think.'

'Worreva. Ye've nee choice. Aa'm comin with ye when ye gan after them lads or Aa dob ye in with what I hord through the waal. Like it or lump it.'

Erica was weakening. It would be good to have company, even Stacey, and after all... as if reading her mind, Stacey played her trump guilt card.

'Ye owe iz, and ye knaa it man!'

'You mean, because I saved you from giving birth unconscious in a filthy alley?'

'Think of me bairn, little Noosh. A child of disadvantage.'

'Oh well... But don't fuck up!'

'Langwidge in the workplace, Erica! Eee mind, that Kingston was a right fkn bastard wasn'ee? Had it fkn coming, man. Aa can kinda see why that Laura wifie didn't clock him one, hor bein in hospital an aal, but that Tessa, wadda fkn wuss! Minit he laid hands on her she should've taken him to the fkn cleaners for spousal abuse, assault, the works. After operatin on his bollocks forst like. *That's* where she should've hammered the spikes in.'

'Stacey, I'm trying to prove Tessa's innocence here, get with the programme. And don't say anything like that in front of Will Bennett or he'll have you under the hot lights before you can say 'Bacardi Breezer."

'Fuck him. Oh yer did didn't yer!' Stacey was already making sure Erica's sim card had her number on it, grabbing her phone from the desk. 'Aa'll caal ye. Gotta go see aboot summat.'

She dropped the phone on the desk, and walked off, absent-mindedly putting the wineglass in her handbag. She was thinking, she'd have some calls to make elsewhere before seeing the lads with Erica in tow. There was stuff she didn't want coming out. Having a bliddy job was more bother than it was worth.

CHAPTER EIGHTEEN

Will Bennett was thinking it over again. The murderer's chosen method. He called the team together to thrash it out. The more he thought about it, the more circular the logic seemed.

'Right. This is what we've got. Stone, nails, mutilation. Let's not get bogged down in symbolic meanings just for now. What else does the murder method tell us?'

'Hatred Guv.' Sally at a nod from Will wrote it down on the whiteboard. 'Real hatred. Not just wanting him dead. Sadistic, even.'

'OK, that makes sense. But what's wrong with that scenario? What does a sadist do? What's their whole erm, driving force?'

'Making folks suffer,' suggested Paul.

'Exactly. So what about this crime doesn't fit?'

'He was knocked unconscious first, rather than tied up or something.' Hassan added a note, taking the pen from Sally.

'You see? That much hatred, that much mutilation, yet they whacked him on the head first. What does that suggest to you?'

'That he was too big, strong and fit to overpower?' Sally said.

'Yes. You see, we've been thinking could this be a woman's crime, is it possible, and in fact the very nature of it suggests it could be. A woman might be able, if she took him by surprise, to hit him with a rock. She'd have a hard job overpowering him and tying him up if he was conscious.'

'Unless it was a sex game,' put in Paul. Then blushed. 'I've er read things...'

Will ignored this. 'So that suggests the ex-wife Tessa, doesn't it? All that about going to the house in the afternoon, to explain any forensic traces... though Sally did check, and a neighbour did see Tessa in a car with a woman, possibly Tara, outside Kingston's about mid afternoon, and the car was gone by the time she walked past there on the way to pick up her kids from primary school. Nobody saw the car at night.'

'Tessa doesn't seem bright enough for that sort of clever plotting.' Sally objected.

'Maybe not, but her sister is. Maybe they're in it together. Alibi'ing each other. Soliciting for each other. Erm well you know what I mean.'

'Right Paul.' Hassan made a note. 'We better consider the neighbours too, though they don't seem murderous, but you never know.'

'He might've forgot to return somebody's lawn mower or summat.' Paul tried to lighten the moment, and failed.

Hassan kept writing. 'And add to that, that there was no

break in. She could have gone back later. OK, nobody saw the car but that doesn't rule it out.'

'Tessa claims to have no key, since Kingston changed the locks though Sarge.' Kev tried to show he was awake.

Hassan batted this aside. 'It could've been him who left the front door unlocked. Or she could've nicked a spare key when she and Tara were at the house. Or he'd have opened the door to her, surely, if she claimed to have come back begging for another chance.'

Will carried on. 'So, who would be likely to hate Kingston enough to kill him, and to kill him like that? Apart from the obvious ex.'

'Dissatisfied patients, got duff treatment or thought they had.'

'Right, Sally.' Will began to collect a list of suspects, or suspect categories.

'Guv, that might fit with the head injury as well. Someone he'd treated might be erm, disabled or physically disadvantaged in some way. Unable to take him on without knocking him down first.' Sally's elfin face was alight, she loved this stuff thought Paul, bloody teacher's pet.

'Yes that's true. Not that we've been able to find anyone who'd complained against him. Though there might be plenty who'd like to but haven't for some reason.' Frustrated rather than pleased by the multiplying list of suspects, Will raised a hand to his hair but remembered just in time.

'Somebody at work he'd cheesed off somehow?' Hassan

said. 'Not that we've been able to get any dirt on him from other docs or hospital staff. They're all singing his praises from the same hymn sheet.'

'Yes definitely a possibility,' said Will. 'But have you noticed, there's been no real warmth, no real sorrow for him as a man, as a friend. Just shock at the horror of it, and respect, and praise for him as a surgeon. The usual closing of ranks. Like if one of us got taken out, someone unpopular, you can imagine the same thing...'

Everyone but Will had the same thought - is the DI thinking wistfully of Golden Boy George speared with a pitchfork or suffocated in fertiliser?

'The lads who've been hanging around behind the houses causing a nuisance. Scotty and mates. Residents have been chasing them off for weeks. Mebbe they got sick of it and struck back,' Paul suggested.

'We have to put 'the lads' on the list.' Will did so. 'But they'd have to be high on drugs to go that far. If they were high, and drunk, and aggressive, and provoked, they might give him a kicking, even kill him, but all that careful mutilation? That doesn't sound like a chaotic mob.'

'They're just kids,' said Hassan. His wife worked with lads like these. 'Even though they are a right pain and commit crimes like theft and possession and so on, and yes OK, if they suddenly got a mob mentality taking them over they might go off on one. But let's not forget the crime scene. The use of those nitrile gloves, plastic aprons, such care not to leave traces. Not exactly what you'd expect of a drug-crazed mob.'

'No you're right. However, they're not all that daft. You never know, one of them might be a clever sadist in the making.'

'Guv, some crims torture folks to get their PIN numbers from them,' suggested Paul.

'Actually that's a good point,' mused Will. 'He'd be unconscious, brain damaged, but perhaps he came to, briefly? Brain injuries can be hard to predict. They might've thought it worth a try, not realising how bad his injuries were.'

Paul looked triumphantly at Sally. 'I read about this bloke, he shot himself in the head with a shotgun and then walked away, left most of his brains all over the inside of a bus shelter, didn't collapse until he was back home.'

'A clever sadist among the lads might be worth following up. Also this case is getting nationwide publicity, somebody might be enjoying their fifteen minutes of fame.'

Both Will and Hassan were thinking of their interview with Scotty and his mum, uneducated, ignorant even, but not stupid.

'Guv,' Sally had been thinking. 'There may be a family member after Kingston's dosh. Or a girlfriend. He might've been boffing the nurses.'

'Be a waste not to,' muttered Paul, dodging Sally's kick.

'Anyway we've got this list and we'll just have to keep

asking questions, at the hospital, in the street, and hope people will talk to us about Kingston.'

Hassan sounded madly optimistic even to himself.

At home, Erica poured herself a glass of Chateau Neuf du Pape and listed her suspects in a new Word document.

Tessa/Beccy, abused wife. Laura G's story backs up Tessa's about K's abuse. Independent testimony that K got his jollies dishing out pain & getting away with it/ being rewarded for it. Gives Tessa v strong motive, but OTOH too scared to take him on?

Jamie Lau, humiliated trainee doc + all other students K probs treated the same.

Laura Gibson? + others with similar stories, not come forward. Wd she tell abt her motive if guilty? Risky. Disabled so poss probs handling him dead or alive. Accomplice?

Hoodies in drinking den. Robbery gone wrong? Drug fuelled attack after he caught them vandalising?

And who else? Could she really find anything out when the police had all the expertise and personnel? On the other hand, who would confide in the police if it made them a murder suspect? No-one with any sense. Picturing herself running along the edge of the golf course, Erica remembered she hadn't yet followed up the Wydsand Golf Club, or the church, in delving into Kingston's life. But would Kingston have ill-treated the kind of influential people he liked to impress, who brought business his way or cemented his status?

All in all, with suspects and sources multiplying madly on every side, she was running out of time and avenues she could legitimately explore before she had to submit her article on Kingston.

She didn't know it, but the situation was soon to become even more complex.

CHAPTER NINETEEN

Stacey had insisted on a pizza before they set off.

Erica objected. 'It's a strain on the heart to run straight after eating.'

'It's a strain on the fkn belly not to eat man. Aa'm not dragging meself doon a damp muddy track heaving with morderers and rapists, and even dog crap, without some decent scran inside iz. A nice big four cheese pizza will set iz up nicely. And Aa'm entitled to me expenses. Yer gettin off light man.'

Stacey now dripped molten cheese into her scarlet mouth from a height with something like ecstasy. 'And Aa'm not runnin.'

'Maybe you have a point. Captain Jack always insists the men have their dinner before going into action. In O'Brian's novels. Napoleonic wars. Salt pork and plum duff. Maggoty biscuits.' Erica nibbled some of her extra thin pizza crust, and picked off the roasted veg and goat's cheese from the top.

'Eewww! Bet they'd have fought better on four cheese pizzas.'

It was properly dark by the time they set off for the affluent street along the golf course, joining Erica's regular jogging route just at the start of the path past the crematorium where the graveyard ran alongside the golf course. It seemed odd to be using a taxi to go jogging, and Stacey's help was proving expensive, but they were both very merry, considering Erica had had nothing stronger than sparkling water and Stacey only a treble vodka and Red Bull. 'Fitness drink, innit?'

Erica had her mobile, some emergency remedies, an attack alarm, and a perfume spray. Someone had given it to her for Christmas, someone who didn't know her very well. She'd never found a perfume yet which didn't smell like artificial chemicals and alcohol, and not in a good way. The smells which make life pleasurable are the sea, creosote fences, gorse flowers, hot bread, fresh ground coffee, new paper, books, vanilla, cloves, and of course the way people smell, all different and all interesting, if not always pleasant. But sprayed in an assailant's eyes the scent might be of some use. They both had torches too, in an attempt to avoid standing on anything left by the neighbourhood dogs.

There was a thin yellow smile of moon and a haze of smoky mist in the air. The few stars that showed were turned down to minimum, with the muted glitter of lead.

They set off along the golf course boundary track with the high fences of Kingston's neighbours on their left, the dark hedges fringing the green sweeps of the course on their right. They were 'jogging' very slowly, Stacey complaining all the way, and Erica fizzing with impatience.

Enough light spilled out of the houses' upstairs windows to help them see their way though they couldn't see their feet. As they got nearer to the drinking den and Kingston's house, they could see a ghostly glow ahead. The track finished there and turned sharply down the snicket alongside his house and onto the street. The source of the glow was an old lamp-post with a battered, archaic look. A bit like Narnia.

They were almost in its pool of light, Erica jogging ahead, Stacey walking behind as the trodden part of the track there was rather narrow, and brambles and hawthorns kept catching at them, trying to trip them up. Their torch beams swayed in front, illuminating strolling slugs, damp fallen leaves, unidentifiable dark patches. Erica, unable to resist looking at wildlife, spotted something moving on the ground, to the side of the track, and bent to have a look. Just as she registered the bright pin-small eyes and questing nose of a small hedgehog, there was a loud thock! and something smacked into her left arm. She staggered, then stood, disorientated. For a few seconds, she was only aware of the impact, then a deep burning pain seemed to drill into her bicep.

'Fuck, fuck it, what the fuck.'

'Erica?' Stacey caught up. 'What the buggery was that?'

She shone her torch around and it picked out something fluorescent yellow. A golf ball. She picked it up.

'Look at this! Some posh bastard on the fkn golf

course...at this time of neet! It could've hit yer head! Hey, it could've hit *me*!'

Stacey shouted into the grassy blackness over the fence, where the serene greens and fairways lay quiet. 'Wanker! Aa'll fkn morder ye, ye bastard, come on, man, bring it! Haway, if ye've got the balls!'

Nobody was willing to 'bring it'. 'Here's yer fkn ball back then, ye twat!' Stacey hurled the golf ball as far as she could into the dark.

'Oh shit, Stacey. That was evidence. We'll never find it now. There'll be golf balls all over the place. Can you shine the torch on my backpack, while I get the Arnica out?'

Erica put two tablets of Arnica under her tongue to dissolve, after shaking out two tiny tablets into the lid to avoid touching them with her hands. Not just hygiene, but remedies aren't supposed to be touched by fingers. A few doses would reduce the bruising a lot, but there wouldn't be any miraculous cure from a blow like that. Just helping the body to help itself.

'I need to get some witch hazel on this...' she rubbed the place where the muscle burned. 'At least it wasn't my head.'

'Coulda been. If ye hadn't bent doon just then... Aa've a good mind to go up to that Golf Club and play war....'

The mental picture of Stacey invading those hallowed portals did a lot to get Erica over her initial shock. 'I don't suppose they'd let you in... you're not wearing a tie, or a penis.' Erica was flashing her torch about at roughly shoulder and head height.

'What ye looking for? Aa need a drink.' Stacey lit a Lambert, bored. Her fag end glowed like a firefly.

'This hurts like hell, but it could have been a lot worse. I'm wondering if the ball ricocheted off something before it hit me. If it came directly from the course, it would have hit me on the right arm....and it wouldn't have made that loud noise. It could've hit the fence and then my left arm... unless it came from further over this side, like one of the back gardens or the bushes behind them...'

'Who cares, neebody's dead.' Ever the philosopher.

Erica found a dent in one of the planks in the garden fence which looked fresh, a few gleams of newly exposed wood showing in the torch beam. She tried to photograph it with her phone, doubting it would come out.

'Anyway, golf baals'll be hitting the fence aal day lang,' Stacey pointed out. 'Nee way yer can prove that was the one what got ye.'

'Very good point, intern mine, it might've been easier if you'd not got rid of our evidence.'

'Soz.' For once Stacey was contrite. 'Aa could've been on TV if Aa'd kept it. Even *Crimewatch* is better than nowt.'

They moved on into the light pool. Erica showed Stacey the pile of stones where the murderer had got the weapon to bash Kingston. It seemed like a long time ago, and already the depression looked less marked, growth had started as nature erased the rock's absence. Blades of grass were starting to stand up and turn green.

They shone their torches along a bit, where the drinking den had been. Now the trodden area was decorated again by the traditional loitering youths detritus – empty fag packet, crushed beer cans, and a couple of miniatures of voddie.

Looking at these, Stacey was moved to a sigh of nostalgia. 'Eee, worrit's like to be young!'

Erica bent and stirred the little heap of refuse, her left arm hanging useless. It felt numb, but fizzy electric shocks were running up and down it.

'This crap's been dumped here recently. What's this?' A glint under the debris.

She moved the miniature bottles and uncovered a syringe. 'Looks like vodka's not exciting enough for someone.'

'Eeewww! Don't touch it man Erica! It'll be heavin with Hep C and shit.'

'Do you think it could have come from Kingston's house? Nicked while he was being offed?'

'Fk knows. Aa think we should tell the bizzies about it. And yer arm and all.' The police often leaked stuff to the tabloids...

'I might take the syringe in, just in case, but I doubt it's important. What happened to me was an accident, I hope. If not, it's hard to prove otherwise. '

She could just see Will's sardonic features when she told him she'd been whacked by a golf ball. Yeah, right. Like she was going to act the helpless female. He'd like that way too much.

'Wanna go to A and E?' They had to raise their profiles somehow or they'd get sidelined out of it. Sod Erica and her weird hang-ups about Willy Bennett!

'No thanks. I'll treat it myself. I don't think anything's broken. I just hope the bruising and stiffness won't be too bad. What if I can't swim, or do my gym class?' A feeling of panic rose at the thought.

They turned back, Erica sucking Arnica tablets.

A door in the high wooden fence opened suddenly and a woman looked out at them. She was wearing a thick fleece, more sensibly dowdy than sporty, over a flowered dress and slippers. The house was about two or so away from Kingston's; as far as Erica could tell, next door to where the man in the golf jumper had spoken to her last time.

'Is everything all right?' The neighbour came further out, seeing that they were women. She held a black and white cat in her arms. 'I came out to the garden to call Siggy, and heard a bang, like something hitting the fence. I listened for a bit, and all I could hear was women's voices, so I thought it might be safe to look out.'

'My arm got hit by a golf ball. Some idiot forgot to shout 'fore', and couldn't even keep the ball on the course. What kind of person practices his shots in the dark?'

'Nobody plays golf at night, dear. It would be those young thugs,' said the woman positively. 'We've had plants broken, greenhouses damaged, streetlamps vandalised at night.'

'Mr Kingston as well?'

'Oh yes, specially him, and Mr Archer. Because we're at the end of the track where they hang out. In fact it's a lot worse now than it's ever been. It used to be more day times, the odd golfer off their game, but those damned hoodies! They do it on purpose. They find the balls golfers have lost on the course and let fly. Bloody vandals, pardon my French.'

'Surely they won't still hang about here straight after the murder, with the police about.' Erica's arm was throbbing but she wanted to continue the contact. Stacey had sloped off into the darkness to smoke. No point talking to some posh wifey.

'Well it's a more exciting place now, isn't it? Way cool, as they'd call it! And as for the police! It took a murder to get them here, all the times we've called about the vandalism, did they take a blind bit of notice? And anyway the police aren't patrolling here any more. We believe they're on drugs.'

Presumably she meant the youths rather than the police.

'Horrible squalid litter they leave behind. Underage drinking! Smoking. Something should be done about it.'

They left the neighbour to her indignation and Siggy's supper and got a taxi back to Erica's. Stacey watched as

172

Erica put cotton wool soaked in witch hazel on the big red mark made by the golf ball.

'I'll keep topping this up.'

'Ice, man woman, ice!'

'Yeah yeah. You go home, I'll be alright.'

Erica had trouble sleeping that night. Her arm throbbed, and her mind raced. She was reluctant to believe that someone would deliberately aim a golf ball at her. Surely it must have been a random throw or hit which just happened to be in the wrong place at the wrong time. She couldn't help thinking, though, if she had not stooped to look at the hedgehog, it might have been her head that took the full force. The loud 'thok' as the ball hit some part of a fence or tree trunk could have been the sound of her skull splintering.

But would a few youths do such a thing? They were more likely to go in for some low-level intimidation, threatening remarks and body language, or just keep out of sight and enjoy their contraband booze. Was it likely they'd had anything to do with Kingston's murder? But he was a doctor. And doctors with private practices might have drugs at their houses. If it was a burglary gone wrong, Kingston having a go in true alpha male style, a hoodie or hoodies high on ket and e's might respond with such bizarre savagery. But would they return to the scene of the crime, and leave more evidence behind, if so? Surely the police would test the previous lot of rubbish for DNA

CHAPTER TWENTY

The next day, her arm was stiff and painful, and there was a dense dark bruise despite her efforts with arnica, ice and witch hazel. She had a long hot shower before Weetabix, soya milk and hot grape juice. What to do about the syringe? She'd picked it up in a plastic bag she found under the hedge and it still lay, wrapped up, in her bag. Tonight was her dinner date with Jamie, the cute young doctor. Maybe she should show him her bruise.

She decided to take the syringe into the police station at lunch time. It might be evidence of a kind. She tried not to admit to herself she felt a strong urge to keep poking the bear, a certain blue-eyed bear, with a stick. Before work, she needed to swim, all the more so as she was desperate to know if she still could, and how much her injury would cramp her style. And as for her style tonight...

Swimming was painful. Each time her arm left the water it burned, but she pressed on. She kept thinking, I'll just do half a mile, then I'll stop. Then, I might as well press on to forty lengths. That's two thirds. Ish. Then fifty. Then, it might as well be a mile now. Doing her hair was difficult too. But she felt better 'in herself' as the local saying was. The idea of not being able to exercise was scary. Especially today. She wanted to enjoy dining out, and it was hard to do that if she hadn't earned the calories up front.

As it turned out, she more than earned any future calories during a very packed day. She arrived at the police station and asked for Inspector Bennett. She was asked to wait.

If there's anything that Erica hated, it was being forced to hang about at someone else's pleasure, wasting precious time in a state of inaction. She went over to a bench seat and sat down on the edge of it, fidgeting, unable to keep still. She hated hierarchies and everything they imply. This place with its uniforms and badges brought back unwanted memories.

Then Tessa and a woman, presumably Tara, walked through. They'd been called in for another interview with Will and Hassan, and Tara had suggested she and Tessa, who was becoming distressed, have a break to get some coffee and consult. Tessa fell upon Erica with glad cries, and introduced them. Tara was like Tessa pared down and hardened. She wore a dark blue suit and high heeled court shoes, and her blonde hair was severely cut and bobbed into sleek head-hugging place. She had an attractive face with good cheekbones, and small pearl earrings in her lobes. She smelled of Pears Soap. It was a pleasant note in the mix of disinfectant, tobacco smoke drifting in from outside, and cheap coffee that filled the air.

She invited Erica to join them in the most charming manner. She was clearly keen to get Erica onside, and was pleased to find out that Erica had brought the syringe. As she said, anything which kept the field of suspects as wide as possible could only be good for her client/sister, if only to create reasonable doubt, should things get as far as a trial.

'I know Tessa feels she owes you a lot.' Tara took a precise sip from her police canteen coffee, and made a face of disgust. 'We could do with any help you can give us.'

'Absolutely. I'll back Tessa, and what's more, I've no intention of stopping my own investigations. Despite what happened last night.'

She showed Tara her golf ball injury, feeling rather foolish, but Tara took photographs, and made copious notes. 'This may have been a deliberate assault on you, rather than random mischief. It could suggest the real killer is out there, watching the scene, and feels threatened by you. I'd only anticipated your backing up Tessa's account of Kingston's physical and psychological abuse, however. It's not normally the thing for unlicensed people to undertake their own investigations.'

'The thing is Tara, people talk to me. I'm used to it, as a homeopath, our whole job is talking to people to find out what they're like. Or more to the point, we listen to them talk. About all sorts of aspects of their lives. Plus, I'm a journalist, or sort of. I've got reasons to ask questions. I know people don't much trust journalists with all the phone hacking scandals and such, but they don't feel that way about the local paper. Well maybe not so much. I can find out whether Kingston made enemies elsewhere. I can suggest other avenues of enquiry to the police. I want to help!'

'That's great, Erica. The police are getting more focused on Tessa...'

Tessa had been holding her machine hot chocolate in both hands, gazing into the sweet depths as if looking for her reflection, but she looked up at this.

'I'm so stressed, Erica, I don't know what to do! Thank god for Tara, and you.' She looked terrified, gazing at each of her champions in turn with truly touching faith.

'I've been getting Tessa to hold back on Kingston's abuse of her, as it makes her motive stronger. But now I think we need to introduce it. Just in case.' Her cool light blue eyes bored into Erica's and she read the message in them without difficulty. If Tessa was charged, being an abused wife would be her defence, and mitigation if the worst came to the worst.

'At the moment it's just her word that it ever happened.'

'Nobody'll believe me!' Tessa sobbed a little as she spoke but kept herself under more control than usual. Tara seemed to be a good role model. 'They'll say I should have done something, said something, sooner. I could kick myself now, I went along with his falling downstairs story. But at the time I was so shocked.'

'Don't beat yourself up, you've had enough of that

treatment from him.' Erica patted her arm.

'You had no proof, and they'd not have believed you Tessy. So let's deal with the situation we're in now shall we?' Tara's tone was both fond and a tad exasperated, as if this was her habitual feeling in dealing with her younger sister.

Tara resembled Tessa, there must have only been a couple of years between them, but she looked like a mature adult, fit, strong and decisive. She was more attractive than Tessa to Erica's eyes, though dressed in a smart professional way instead of going for kittenish cute like Tessa did. She continued speaking to Erica. 'So if you could confirm what Tessa told you about the abuse that would be very helpful. You can also confirm that she suffered from symptoms related to stress and trauma perhaps.'

'If Tessa agrees I can break confidentiality, sure. And I've got some information for you.'

She gave Tara and Tessa a brief round-up of what she'd gleaned at the hospital, and from Laura, not mentioning that Laura had come to her practice let alone naming her, but making it clear that there were other areas of his life where Kingston could have made himself hated even if none of those people ever talked about it before. None of them would expect to be believed, given Kingston's status and social standing.

Tessa gave Erica an impulsive hug and went off to the Ladies' to prepare her 'face' for the next phase of the interview.

'I'm so glad Tessa has you,' Erica told Tara. 'She's a Pulsatilla - I mean, she's easily influenced and I'd be worried she might be browbeaten into a false confession.'

'Over my dead body! Or somebody else's!' Tara was fierce. 'I let Tessy down badly, leaving her to that monster's abuse. Letting him separate us. I'm not letting her down again. Whatever it takes to get her out of this, I'll do.'

'You seem like a good influence on her.' Erica rather enjoyed the thought of Tara and Will going head to head.

'Yes well I'm trying to set her up to take control of her own life after all this is over. Getting her to take courses, think about a career. She's already so much better for Kingston being - well, out of her life. She's really helping me with the kids, I'm getting out more in the evenings, we can do so much for each other. I even sleep better, knowing she's in the house. It's tough being a single parent. She's really very sweet you know. She actually looked at his medical records and the pathologist's report, which I know cost her, she gasped, she went white and nearly fainted, but she read it all right through, and do you know what she said? 'I just wanted to be sure he didn't suffer too much.' Huh! Didn't suffer enough more like. The police are still sniffing about for a possible lover who might have assisted her with the crime. I'm certain there is none. She'd have told me.' She looked at Erica as if seeking confirmation, perhaps not being so certain as she claimed.

'I don't know of any. And that's just typical! Not only

do the police assume it's a woman, they don't even give her the credit of being able to do it herself!'

Tara gave Erica the low-down on the forensic situation, and why it looked potentially bad for Tessa.

'No evidence of a break in. No evidence of anyone being in the house, no clear outsider's DNA except Tessa's, oh and a fingerprint or two of mine. From our visit that afternoon of course. The mutilations were carried out in the consulting room, apparently, but the first attack, which caused catastrophic head injuries, happened elsewhere.'

'Hence the lack of blood in the room.' Erica remembered the small rusty trails from Kingston's wounds, the sticky mass under his head glueing it to the table.

'Kingston insisted on a high level of hygiene, appropriately enough. There was a lot of bleach and cleaning materials for his consulting room. Sometimes he saw private patients with wires and frames and inspected their wound sites. His nitrile gloves and disposable aprons could have protected the killer from blood spatter.'

'They could have dragged him through to the room unconscious, on a sort of raft of surgical aprons to keep blood from the head wound off the floor. And the stone used to bash his head in was from outside the back of the house. So he may have been attacked outside on the footpath.'

'Not sure what he'd be doing out there at night. But it's all they've got. No signs of break in, remember. I wouldn't be surprised if the police have been watching my house to see if Tessa's imaginary boyfriend-stroke-accomplice makes contact with her.'

Just then Will Bennett appeared. His face looked thinner, and a suspicion of dark stubble showed on his usually well shaved chin. Erica felt a pang of concern, instantly dispelled by his look of displeasure to see Erica and Tessa's legal eagle sister in close conclave. It had not occurred to Will that Erica would be able to get any further information on the case from anyone but the police, and that would be carefully controlled information to suit them, not Ms Bruce. He ushered the two interviewees through to resume their ordeal. Just as Erica was realising she'd not be able to speak to him now as he'd be interviewing Tessa, he came over.

'Inspector.'

'Hello Erica, I hear you have some 'information' for me.'

'Aren't you questioning Tessa Kingston? Again.'

'The Super and Hassan are taking it from here. Anyway, I thought you were bringing information, not seeking it.' Will switched to official-speak, knowing it would wind her up. 'We have no statement to make at this time, my Superintendent is now following up a promising lead and the press will be informed if anything definite transpires."

'Yeah, right, like I don't know Golden Boy only follows promising leads to hot dinners or cake. I'm not just 'the press', Will. I'm Tessa's therapist. That makes it my business.'

'Not in my book. She's entitled to a solicitor and a doctor. A real one, not a so-called 'homeopath'.

'Oh yes, she was married to a *real* doctor. That turned out well!' Better say nothing more on that for now.

'And I hear you've been asking questions at the hospital. I hope you aren't thinking of interfering in our investigation.'

'Just doing my job as a reporter, *Inspector.*' She glared up at him. 'You can't control the hospitals and you can't control me.'

'Come on then let's have this information. Then get out of my hair.'

He motioned her into a small room of depressing aspect. DC Sally Banner was there already. The look she gave Erica made Will's look like true lurve.

'You looked different when we last met.' She looked pointedly at Erica's lycra leggings, short skirt and black zip-up stretch top, state of the art trainers, and loose hair.

'I don't think dressing with intent to disarm is an offence, is it? I brought you this. To help Tessa Kingston. I know you don't want any help from me.'

She placed the syringe in its tatty bag on the table. The two officers looked at it.

'What's this? A new hobby you've taken up? Skull collecting not exciting enough for you?'

Sally couldn't resist a dig. She looked at Will for his approval, but Will just looked uncomfortable, remembering how he and Erica got together over a dead bird on the beach as she stooped to harvest its skull. And how her skulls watched them having sex at her flat with their huge hollow eye sockets.

'I found it in the lane behind Kingston's house. At the hoodies' drinking den. It might have come from Kingston's medical supplies, stolen when he was murdered perhaps.'

'I see. Well, thank you for bringing this in, Ms Bruce.' Sally was as frosted as a Magnolia Bakery cupcake. 'Of course, it's pretty much useless as evidence because we haven't had a chance to examine it in situ.'

'Exactly.' Will's blue eyes, bright in his dark, thin face, fixed Erica's. 'A break in the continuity of evidence... it's been removed from the scene, put in a contaminated bag, handled by god knows who... And how did you come to have this in your possession? When did you find it?'

'I was jogging along the path last night. I thought I'd bring it in case it suggested other suspects. The hoodies who hang about there for example.'

Will sighed. 'We have considered all eventualities, believe it or not. Mr Kingston either opened the door to his assailant, unlikely in the case of a bunch of youths, or they used a key, again unlikely. The final attack took place in the examination room. It's unlikely Kingston let strangers into his house, especially at night, don't you agree? It seems likely he knew his killer, perhaps *very* well.'

Sally went in for the kill. 'We only have your word for it that the syringe was there at all.'

Erica's eyes narrowed with fury at this slur. 'It's not just my word, someone else saw it there.'

'And who was that?'

'Stacey Reed.'

Will laughed. 'Oh we know Stacey.'

'You, and Stacey Reed, were jogging? Stacey, charva queen, jogging!' Sally couldn't stop laughing. 'Hahaha, good one! You're keeping some strange company these days Erica!'

'That's nothing but class prejudice, and you both know it! Stacey happens to be my intern.' Wild horses wouldn't get Erica to disown Stacey as an intern now she'd been mocked by these two smug bastards. Stacey was now her official intern as of, well ages ago.

'Intern!' Will snorted in derision.

'Yes intern. She needs work experience.'

'You can say that again! She's spent her whole life avoiding it.'

'Yes well she's changed. People do change you know. I want to help her. A young single mother trapped on benefits... I owe it to her.'

Will and Erica locked eyes.

Will finished her off. 'Believe it or not, we are quite capable of processing evidence WE took from the site for things like, ooh, I dunno, fingerprints, or even DNA, yes we have heard of that, and with a leap of genius, comparing it with any records on the system. And, taking the massive risk of not consulting a homeopath, we have nevertheless stumbled on the idea of checking those against any evidence found in Mr Kingston's house, so you can sleep easy in your bed.'

Erica and Will were still holding eye contact, until the word 'bed' fell between them onto the table, at which they broke away and looked down as if it lay there like an embarrassing memory.

Sally horned back in to the conversation. 'You could have got the syringe while you were at the murder scene, before we arrived. You admit you want to help Tessa, who you say is your client. It's not like you're not involved.'

'No,' said Will. 'You seem to be a lot more involved than we thought.'

Erica bit her lip. She wasn't going to tell them, not now anyway, that she'd not even known Tessa was her client until after she'd found Kingston's body.

'And you are taking a risk running about behind there at night, even with Stacey Reed as bodyguard, sorry, *intern*. You could come to harm, so please don't do it again.'

Erica's arm was hurting but she wasn't going to admit she'd already come to harm, not until she was sure it would help Tessa. 'Right, well I'm very sorry to take up your valuable time. I realise now I should have left the syringe there to give hepatitis to any passing child, and waited for it to be found by your assiduous officers. I'll let you get back to the more congenial task of browbeating a young widow. I'm sure you need all the manpower you can muster for that. Anyway, I must go now. Work to do, and I've a hot date tonight.'

Erica left, fuming. She'd been unable to resist telling him she had a date even though it was childish point scoring. Why did he have this effect on her? Clearly Will Bennett was determined to keep her out of things. Shame he was so fit, even now she couldn't help clocking his muscles, but they were wasted on a git of a man who spent his life saluting and grovelling to so-called superiors like that oxygen thief Golden Boy George. Wolfman, she used to call Will, after his homeopathic remedy type, Lycopodium, aka Wolfsbane. Ambitious and driven, but where did it get him? Again she thanked her stars that she lived her own life. Though the editor was a pain, at least Erica was freelance and didn't have him breathing down her neck all the time, and her homeopathy practice was all her own. As was her overdraft.

As she worked through the afternoon, she was thinking on and off about her dinner date with Jamie Lau who was gorgeous and not a bit like Will. Luckily the restaurant added cheapness to its many other virtues, as she did not have an expense account from the *Evening Guardian*. What would Jamie be like to spend time with? What would happen between them? And would he be any help in her quest to find out about Kingston? Though she felt almost guilty to be planning an evening out, when Tessa was being put through the third degree by Will and Sally and those other muppets. But Tessa did at least have proper support from her sister, and her being squarely in the frame for the murder made it all the more important that Erica find out all she could. It was an obligation to go on this date. No question.

She hoped that being a reporter, useful as it was as an excuse for asking nosy questions, would not put Jamie off confiding in her. As a practitioner, or a person in the bus queue, Erica was always being told the story of people's lives, but they might be more wary with a journalist, especially in Jamie's situation. The hospital was just as soulless a hierarchy as the police force.

She hoped Jamie didn't smoke. She certainly hadn't smelled it on him at their last encounter. She liked the smell of a man's clean skin. Will didn't smoke. Not that she cared, any more, about that.

It was too much to hope Jamie might be a vegetarian. But please let him not be an out and out carnivore, into blue steaks and lobsters and suchlike. She didn't fancy kissing a mouth which had just had bits of barely dead flesh stuffed into it. 'Lips that touch liver shall never touch mine.' Sometimes she wished she wasn't so fussy, but she couldn't help it. And didn't want to help it either, most of the time.

CHAPTER TWENTY-ONE

Erica had time for a good session at the gym to earn her dinner calories in advance. She went to her usual high impact aerobics class, working off her rage at Bennett and his arrogance, to say nothing of that jealous bitch Sally who was plainly panting for Will's truncheon. As the instructor exhorted the class to kick or hit out, Erica kept his face in mind, determinedly preventing her thoughts from venturing anywhere further south. She was barely aware of the others, a blur of moving shapes around her, a thick atmosphere of body heat. Take that, you bastard, and that.... it felt good dishing out some punishment if only in her imagination.

She left the shower cubicle naked. Friends, other women from the class, milled about, showering and changing. Most of them were superb specimens of health and fitness, and she took pleasure in the sight of their athletic bodies, and the knowledge that she belonged there among them. Nothing would ever erase this pleasure, this setting right an old wrong, this achievement, after the early years of skulking about, fat and useless at games, at best ignored, at worst scorned by the effortlessly athletic girls who were already wearing bras and makeup... last girl in her year to wear a vest... and what happened because of her unfitness.

'Coming for a curry?' one of her gym mates asked.

'No thanks, I've got a date.' The thick white towel felt good on her skin with its mixture of softness and harshness. She pulled out a rolled up bundle from her bag and shook it out. One of her favourite dresses. All her dresses were 'body con' cotton and lycra, short, tight and clinging but moving freely with her. She liked to wear clothes instead of letting them wear her. She'd chosen this H&M dress for its nearly elbow length tight sleeves, to hide the bruise on her arm. It had a scoop neck and was a plain dark red crushed velvet. She stuffed her sweaty bra top, leggings and skirt into her bag, put the black zip top on as a jacket, and pushed her feet into wedge heel strappy sandals. Her trainers she tied on to the outside of the bag with their laces.

She fished out a silver pendant and matching earrings and put them on, touched up her mascara and brushed out her crackling, rebellious hair.

A volley of remarks of the 'don't do anything I wouldn't do' variety accompanied her, to which she made the time-honoured replies.

'Where'd you get that socking great bruise?' asked the girl next to her, raising her arms one at at time to apply roll-on deodorant which to Erica smelt almost as bad as sweat. At least she didn't spray chemicals around like some of them did.

'Got hit by a golf ball.'

'I didn't know you played! You don't strike me as the type.'

'I'm not. I was jogging along by the course.'

'Golf is sooo dangerous! My dad's in Wydsand Golf Club, mad keen he is. He was telling me, some old geezer got hit on the head there a bit ago, he's still in hospital with head injuries. Mostly they keel over with coronaries though. That Kingston, that doctor bloke you found, he was a pillar of the club. They thought a lot of him there, according to my dad. He was Captain one year, or something lame like that. '

'Really?'

Erica looked at her open expression, her swinging pony tail of auburn hair, pretty triangular face. Younger than her. She didn't know her name. They'd never been actually introduced.

'I was thinking of going up there myself, to the club I mean,' Erica said. Well she was thinking of it now.

'To join?' she laughed. 'After someone whacked you with a ball? They're a load of dinosaurs in that place, I can't see you getting in! They only take women on sufferance as far as I can tell. You should hear my dad and his mates going on about women 'cluttering up the course.'

'Not many ethnic minorities either I suppose.' Erica was getting the smudge of an idea about a new possible motivation.

'Not many of any minorities. Not that they're missing

much if you ask me. You know what they say, golf is a game played by men with little white balls! '

She laughed delightedly at her own wit.

Erica was thinking aloud. 'But it might be important to join, from a work as well as social point of view. If anyone felt they were excluded , it could have an impact on their careers or businesses. That might make Kingston unpopular in some quarters.'

Erica was thinking of Rohan, Kingston's surgeon colleague, and his remark about not being in the Golf Club. Suppose Kingston was keeping someone he knew out for racist or sexist reasons.... maybe even Erica's dinner date....

'Yeah, right! I think they all kid themselves about that side of it. It just stops them feeling guilty for spending so much time hacking about in sand pits if they can call it 'work'. Anyway, Kingston had nothing to do with membership. There's a bloke to do all that, I'm sure. Membership secretary or something. I think he was the one got whacked on the head. Dad was complaining he has his own special parking place, I mean, sad, or what!'

This could be checked, but it sounded as if it would be a cold trail. After all, Rohan was just as successful as Kingston, without the privilege of playing golf. Or seemed to be, to an outsider. But did Rohan miss out on lucrative private medicine opportunities because he was excluded from the camaraderie of the nineteenth hole?

'Oh, well, better get going.'

She was a bit dressed up for the restaurant really, but she hadn't worn a dress in what seemed like ages and she felt like it.

She walked down through streets of shops closed for the night, except for fast food places. The sandals broke her stride annoyingly, so she changed back into trainers for the walk. They went well with a short skirt or dress and she felt a lot better swinging confidently along. Amazing what a difference shoes make to a woman's walk. She was used to high heels for clubbing, her feet were often more covered than the rest of her even in winter, but she often ended up going home barefoot with her shoes in her hand like so many drunken Geordie lasses.

She got down to the sea front, where clusters of lads in short sleeved shirts, mostly Newcastle United black and white stripes, and girls wearing a great deal less, were going in to the various winebars past dinner-jacketed bouncers, though it was early yet for the masses of drinkers. Tonight she went through a gap in the railings and down a concrete slope to a dark little row of buildings tucked under the promenade, a couple of metres above the sand. It was dark, and the sea was glossy like tar, edged with white froth like toothpaste spit. Tiny lights glinted far out where fishing boats hunted shoals of elusive silver fish in the bitter cold of the unforgiving North Sea.

She was ten minutes early. Being there first might make

her look too eager, but sod it. She was chronically early like all control freaks, allowing for a list of 'what ifs' that didn't happen. But they might! She leaned on the railing and changed her shoes again.

Light spilled out of the restaurant and she went in to the warmth, taking a blast of cold sea air with her. Jamie waved from a small round table at the back. He had out-punctualled her. She felt a flicker of annoyance at this, despite being already prepared to be more annoyed if he turned out to be late.

He was wearing a striped blue and white shirt and black jeans from Urban Outfitters.

'You're early.' She sat down, unable to keep an accusing note out of her voice. 'It shakes my faith in human nature.'

'I've never been here before, so I wanted to leave plenty of time in case I got lost or...'

'...or got mugged or fainted or was kidnapped by aliens... that's just what I do.'

'What would you like to eat? What do they do well here?'

'Everything. Shall we have some wine, or are you driving?'

'Wine would be great. I don't have a car at the moment. I live in at the hospital, and I don't get much of a life outside it at the moment.'

They studied the chalked list of specials.

'I'm wondering about the veggie burritos. They're

wonderful, but it might be fun to try the aubergine and apricot tagine....'

'You're a vegetarian?' he said. 'Then I'll eat veggie too. You won't want to sit and watch me eating meat.'

Although this was a point to him, she immediately felt guilty.

'Don't deprive yourself on my account.'

'I don't each much meat anyway, and I like veggie food. Would you eat meat if you were really hungry?'

His dark eyes challenged her. She looked right back.

'If I were really hungry, and I am, I would eat you.'

When they were facing a barrage of food, and trying to find space for the wine glasses and bottle by putting salt and pepper on the floor, she remarked, 'You haven't been here before then? Where do you usually go?'

'Anywhere near the hospital. I'm very much concentrating on work right now. I had a great time as a student, and I'm going to have a great time when I'm established as a doctor, but now, I hardly get any sleep, let alone time to go out. Still, I should go out more. I've sort of got into the habit of erm, not.'

'I've heard you're very conscientious.'

'Heard? Who have you been talking to?'

'Patients. I was visiting Mrs O'Rourke and she and the other lady were singing your praises. They think you're a wonderful doctor.'

'I try to be,' he sighed. 'It's not easy, what with...'

His words trailed away.

'It must be difficult working in a strict hierarchy like the hospital. I imagine Kingston gave you all a hard time - rather an autocratic man, he seemed to me.'

Jamie ran his finger round and round his wine glass rim, looking down into the ruby depths.

'That's what you want to talk to me about, isn't it. Kingston, for the newspaper.'

'Well, sort of. It's as much an excuse as anything. I've talked to a lot of people, but you're the only one I've taken out to dinner. All work and no play... You don't need to worry, Jamie. Though I know you've no reason to trust me.'

'My family come from Hong Kong, my mother is English but she lived there too. Both my parents are doctors. It's all I want to do, and I want to do it well. But being good at the job isn't enough. I have to fit in, get good references, good reports, refrain from rocking any boats or blowing any whistles. Sometimes it burns me, but it's the system, and I'm stuck with it for now. I'll do things my own way when I've finished training. That's what I tell myself anyway. Even though Kingston's dead, the hospital wouldn't like me to criticise him in any way. It's all about closing ranks.'

He sounded bitter. She decided to change the subject for now.

'Do you have any interest in traditional Chinese medicine?' Too late she realised it sounded crass, even verging on racist. She was thinking of the nails, and the possible reference to acupuncture needles, but that would sound even worse if she explained. He bristled a bit.

'Not really. There's no reason why I should, any more than I should assume you morris dance.'

'OK, sorry, I only asked. I do work in alternative medicine. And you should see me leaping about with my bells on, waving a daffodil.'

He laughed. 'I'd like to see that. '

'I asked you because I would like to do an article on Chinese medicine for the paper some time.'

She told him more about her homeopathic practice.

'Well I have doubts about most alternative therapies,' he said. 'I'd rather see some scientific proof. Hasn't Simon Singh pretty well destroyed homeopathy? They can't find anything detectable in the massively diluted remedies...'

'Well I don't want Simon destroying my evening as well. But do you believe in gravity?'

'Erm yes.'

'Well we know it exists because we see and measure its effects. And we can predict the effect it will have. Einstein's general relativity... well suffice to say, mass seems to warp space-time. But we still don't know what gravity is or exactly how it works. You can analyse space between two masses, earth and sun, and you won't find anything which might be gravity. How can it act over huge distances, instantly, when there's nothing detectable there?'

'Physics isn't my thing. But I'm willing to believe in gravity.'

'It's my thing. Part of my degree. So homeopathy has been 'proved', in the old sense of tested, on people over years. We see its effects.'

'Placebo effect...'

'The effects match particular remedies. Those are very diluted, so maybe we just can't yet measure what's there or it's some other mechanism working. It works on babies and animals too, so it's not all placebo. Not that there's anything wrong with placebos. Fool the body into healing itself, hell yes, I'll take that any day of the week. Look, people pay for alternative treatment because conventional medicine, which is free, has let them down. Left them with side effects worse than the illness. Refused them drugs on the grounds of cost, when the drug companies seem to be allowed to set the prices. Refused to believe they are ill in the first place. Aspirin's made from willow. Digitalis from foxgloves for heart failure. We're all on the same side or should be. Sorry to be lecturing, I went through a lot of this with an ex-lover. He's been getting in my hair lately so it's all coming back.'

Jamie topped up her glass. 'Well I've had my revenge for you mentioning Chinese medicine! You look great when you're defending something. Now I've made you suffer, let me state for the record, I'm not into Chinese medicine any more than herbalism or homeopathy. If someone of whatever ethnic background or belief system smashes their leg they need an orthopaedic surgeon, don't they?'

'Absolutely. But when you put someone's bones back in position, it's their own body that heals them, and how well it does that is down to the vital energy that body has. That's where alternative therapies can help however they work.'

'Maybe so.' He was careful.

She wasn't. 'Surgeons like Kingston act like mechanics, applying procedures and techniques, forgetting there's a person involved,' she ploughed on, seeing his face tighten as the hospital line to be toed unreeled before his well trained, or washed, brain. 'I know you are different, I've heard how you care about the patients, and their pain relief, and how you treat them with respect.' His face relaxed a bit but he looked conflicted. She'd just praised him for something his superior had been trying to humiliate out of him. The new ways of empathy hadn't reached everybody.

'Well that's nice of them, and you, to say, but a doctor has to remain detached to some extent...'

'But the caring, the empathy, that's all part of the healing process, surely. Recent studies have confirmed that old detached scientist, doctors without feelings, model is flawed as well as undesirable. People have to heal themselves, whatever treatment they get, and that is inhibited when they feel scared or threatened or insecure.' She thought of Laura Gibson and her non-united tibia fracture.

'I've always thought so,' he said, suddenly choosing

which side to jump to. Probably glad to speak his heresy in a safe environment. If a journalist, even one on her level, could be called safe. 'Not that it's an approach which gets me respect in the system.'

Erica remembered the way the nurses had used his first name rather than title and surname. The way their obvious liking for him was tempered by a sort of fond contempt.

Seeing him suddenly opening up, Erica took a risk. 'So why would Kingston give you all that racist abuse about acupuncture and tiger bones if you have nothing to do with traditional Chinese medicine?'

'How do you know all that?' He was suddenly alarmed. 'Seems like you've been checking up on me.'

'Relax. It's nothing sinister. Patients and visitors observe staff as much as staff observe them. The staff seem to forget the bodies in the beds are actually conscious human beings as well as pulses and blood counts. We have eyes and ears just like you, and Rohan, and Kingston, and the nursing staff. So you see, I could write about you if I wanted to without having the pleasure of dining with you first. I won't though. I've no wish to spoil things for you in your chosen profession, and your chance to rise through the ranks of golf-playing consultants, for the sake of a piece about a dead man. Who seems to have been a bit of a racist among other things.'

'I don't think he was racist. I think he looked down equally on everyone and he used any ammunition to get at someone when they'd displeased him, to put them in their place. He made it clear he didn't like me. We had different attitudes to patients and to medicine. I once – once - questioned his judgement on the grounds of patient well-being. Very tentatively, just a question, but it was enough. He had it in for me from then on. He could have done a lot of damage to my career.'

Erica didn't like the sound of this. Did he realise he was giving himself a motive for murder? She looked at his hand lying on the table, fingers curled round the stem of his glass. Slender fingers which could feel a bone was broken, and feel the pain it was causing too. Slender but strong. He was a man devoted to healing, but doctors had killed before, inevitably being christened Dr Death by the press. Look at Harold Shipman.

'Kingston couldn't take having his authority questioned, could he?' she said softly. 'Perhaps he was afraid of it.'

'I think so, yes,' said Jamie thoughtfully. 'I might as well tell you. But it's not for printing. It was just a matter of opinion... he might well have been right.

'There was a patient, an old woman who had bilaterial tibia fractures and he fitted Ilizarov frames on both legs - she was ninety nine years old. I questioned the wisdom of doing the operation at all.'

'But surely it had to be done?'

'Not necessarily. She could have just had the fractures reduced, superficially healed and made painless. She wouldn't have been able to walk, but then she couldn't much anyway before the accident. An operation is traumatic for an old person. The anaesthetic is risky, and sometimes it makes them seem senile afterwards for a few days. The shock does that. Then there was the recovery from the op. Physiotherapy, and rehab. They tried to get her walking again. She went through a lot. She found it agony trying to walk or even stand with those wires in with all the swelling and bruising, and the injuries. She'd also had head injuries by the way. The body's reluctant to heal at her age. She dreaded the physio coming round. Kingson got her family to encourage her to stand up, told her she'd have to walk to be allowed home. She was desperate to be home, and safe, among her own surroundings. But she just couldn't walk, or stand the pain. Nobody understood what it was like for her. The family accepted whatever they were told. They wanted to believe she could get better. She said to me, 'That physio, doctor, it's the cruellest thing.'

'The other patients couldn't sleep for a few nights after her operation. She was talking to herself all night, reciting poems she'd learned at junior school. Bits of Shakespeare, Wordsworth... She got MRSA in the sites where the wires went in. And the bones didn't heal anyway. They kept adjusting the frame, but it was no good. When she eventually left hospital, she went to a care home, and she never walked again anyway. By then she was pretty much institutionalised, she'd been in so long. All that pain she went through at the end of a long life. All that blackmail about going home if she just walked. I can tell you all this because she's dead now.'

'Kingston said at the time that the very old deserved the same care as anyone else.'

'And it's true. But in each individual case, the treatment doesn't have to be the same, just equally good. Sometimes that might mean doing nothing, just making someone comfortable and helping them adjust. Anyway I just wasn't sure. It would be a difficult decision. I'd hate to have had to make it. And I know I will have to make those kinds of decisions. But the temptation is to do what you can because you can, regardless if it's the best thing for that person.'

'To get headlines, and status.' What she'd learned of Kingston didn't fit with a commitment to grey power.

'Maybe, or maybe just because you want to use your skill. But she was never given a real choice, it was never explained to her; her mind was sharp enough. At least at the beginning. But I still don't know if he was wrong or right. I just asked whether it was the right thing to do, and that was it. I was condemned from then on.'

He took a mouthful of wine and she watched it go down his throat.

'Will things be easier for you now he's dead?' she asked bluntly.

'Maybe, maybe not. I wasn't the only one he got at.

There was a bloke, a mate of mine - anyway it depends who comes in Kingston's place - they might be worse! It's caused a lot of talk among the staff, the murder that is. Sent a shock wave through them. People don't kill doctors! They usually seem to be complaining a doctor killed their loved one. There's been some publicity recently about a heart surgeon up in the city.'

Clearly Jamie was wary of giving away any of his mates' stories and who could blame him.

'Oh yes I think I saw something about that, all this Kingston stuff sent it out of my head.'

'Bereaved family accusing him of killing their child. Not just putting in a complaint but making sure they get publicity. They're angry, grieving. It's natural they want someone to blame... makes me glad I'm not in that field, where people die more often than they do of broken legs. From what I've read he did all he could, and more. Surgeons seem to have the power of life and death but we're not miracle workers. But Kingston's murder... the nails... the stuff of nightmares. We're so used to thinking of ourselves operating on people, it's a nasty feeling to think one of them wants to operate on one of us. Just hope it doesn't catch on.'

'I can't help hoping I'll turn up some useful information while I'm digging around for this article.'

'You should be careful. You might dig up something very unpleasant, and dangerous.'

Was that a warning? Erica shivered slightly. Someone had just come in with a blast of cold air. She had some more wine.

When they took away the remains of the main course, which was still enough to feed a family, she suggested they go outside and look at the sea before deciding whether to have dessert. There was no-one else out there, although above them the road teemed with winebar crawlers, taxis cruising among them like sharks.

They leaned on the cold metal rail, its paint blistered by salt, and looked at the dark sea, always beautiful, always deadly, creaming in under them.

He put his arm around her. She couldn't help flinching, and he moved his arm away instantly.

'Sorry, moving too fast?'

'No, it's just, I hurt my arm.'

'Do you want me to look at it?'

'Oh it's nothing much, I got hit by a golf ball while out jogging, and besides, this is supposed to be your night off. Anyway, this sleeve is tight, I'd have to take this dress right off.'

There was a silence. They were facing each other now. His face was a glimmer in the dark and his eyes and hair were black as the sea.

'I'm treating it myself. I like to do things for myself. Well, most things, anyway.'

He cupped her face in his hands and kissed her on the

mouth. He tasted of wine and spices, and the salt that stuck to their skins from the sea spray. Erica wound both arms around his neck and kissed him back. She felt a shock go through him as her tongue slid into his mouth. They went on kissing and his hands moved over her and she put her cold hands up under his shirt and felt his warm skin.

They decided to skip dessert. They almost skipped paying the bill but remembered just in time to escape criminal records.

They took a taxi back to his place and had brandy there. Her hair was sticky with salt. She brushed it in his bathroom. His utilitarian rooms reminded her of student days, being in live-in accommodation, coming back after some party with a hook-up. She went back into the bedroom.

'All this wonderful hair,' he murmured. 'You know you said you would eat me if you were hungry enough...'

'Why d'you think I had no dessert?' She pulled off her dress in a single movement, her hair fizzing with static as it emerged. 'So, you're a trained expert on human anatomy?'

CHAPTER TWENTY-TWO

Erica was stroking the long hard bone of his skeleton's thigh when her mobile buzzed. Jamie had gone off to work much earlier.

'Ms Bruce?' Will at his most pompous.

'Inspector Bennett! What an unexpected pleasure!'

'I'd like you to come to the station to assist us in our enquiries,' he said stiffly. 'Are you at home?'

'No, actually I'm at the hospital.' She gave him the finger over the phone.

'Nothing serious, I hope?' An audible quickening of interest. Like he'd care.

'Erm, I don't know yet - I've been sort of kept in overnight for observation. Are you going to give me a lift, or will you pay my taxi bill?'

'I'll send someone to pick you up.'

'I'll be at the main entrance, if I can find it.'

While she was waiting she rang Tara. She felt sure this new move by the police was something to do with Tessa. Tara answered, sounding rather breathless. In the background were sounds of family chaos.

'They want me at the police station. Do you know anything about it, and do I need you to find me a solicitor?'

'Tessa has told them about Kingston's abuse of her

during their marriage. She has used you as confirmation of her story. All we need is for you to back her up, that she displayed behaviour or symptoms consistent with those of an abused spouse, that she told you he broke her arm and subjected her to prolonged intermittent physical, verbal and psychological abuse, constantly ran her down and criticised her and terrified her. We haven't told them everything he said or did. Tessa can't bear the humiliation of going over it all and she's suffered enough. Oddly enough some of the words and phrases he used to her are harder for her to admit to than the broken arm. They can't hold you unless they arrest you and tell you your rights, but just in case, here's a name.'

Erica rang off, and scrabbled among the bits and pieces on Jamie's desk to find a scrap of paper to note the details. She wasn't going in to Will's lair without some protection. There was a packet of what looked like thick wires. Steel, shiny, but with no heads. She went cold, then shook herself. What more natural than to find pins used in orthopaedic surgery on the desk of a trainee doctor on an orthopaedic ward, after all. She looked at them, imagining having them drilled into bone and then slowly unscrewed, as her patient and Kingston's victim Laura Gibson had described.

When Paul Lozinski swung the police car up to the hospital entrance, she climbed in, still wearing the red dress with her top over it but with her trainers on, her heels back in her bag. Her bare legs were cold, and the fug of the car was almost welcome. The officer wasn't as friendly as he'd been when they met over Kingston's corpse. Rather distant, in fact. Obviously the officers were taking their cue from Will.

Soon she was in what they called an interview room, which had no view at all, and was greatly in need of some proper interior design. As she waited she wondered how the timid Tessa had coped with these surroundings. So good she had strong clever Tara there to bat for her. She tried not to breathe too deeply, it smelled like people had been smoking in the room, or maybe just heavy smokers jonesing for a drag and sweating tobacco, and there was a smell of disinfectant under the strong scent of plastic upholstery. Not a room to follow a night of pleasure.

Will Bennett entered. A heavy scruffy man with woolly bear caterpillar brows and a pursed mouth followed, Superintendent 'Golden Boy' George himself. He looked as if he lived on the kind of meat pies they sell at football matches. Had he come in with Will to protect his underling from the wicked woman he'd dated? Or was it Will he didn't entirely trust not to go easy on her? As if!

'Carry on, Will,' he said, after acknowledging her existence with a preoccupied nod.

Will tried not to look at her legs. Erica didn't much look like someone who'd spent the night in hospital, and she could see he wanted to ask, but was trying not to do that either. Shame he was so repressed.

'I haven't got long. I've got patients to see. At my homeopathy practice,' she added for the Super's benefit. 'You haven't arrested me, so I can go at any time, am I right? '

'Absolutely,' said Will. 'We only want to clarify a few matters. As you may know, we have been questioning Tessa Kingston, purely routine. Mrs Kingston has informed us that her late husband was violent towards her. She says that you know of this and that you can confirm it.'

'I can confirm that she told me of it, and also that her behaviour while I've known her was consistent with that of someone afraid of her husband,' Erica said carefully. Don't mess with a mathematician, Will.

'Tell us more.'

'She told me of specific instances, like, he broke her arm, and psychologically abused her and that he gave her drugs and made her pass out for his own sick power games. She made it clear to me that she was scared of him and didn't want him to know she was seeing me.'

'I see. And you have records to back this up?'

'I have detailed notes yes. Confidential. '

'I think we can insist on seeing them.'

She sighed. She'd had no breakfast, and a long night. How best to help Tessa? Or Beccy, as her records were labelled. Will was probably right. She'd better make a virtue of necessity.

'OK. Look, my records will show she was afraid of him. But I should tell you she saw me under a false name. Also that she is not a violent type of personality. She's a Pulsatilla. It's a homeopathic remedy type.'

For once united, Will and the Super exchanged superior smirks at this. 'False name? Didn't she feel she could trust your discretion?'

Erica glowered at Will.

'Look, it was her husband she didn't trust. He would have taken it as a gross affront for her, wife of a surgeon, to see an alternative practitioner; the ultimate rejection of all he stood for. She was terrified he'd find out.'

GB joined in. 'Then why would she take such a risk at all? If he was that much of an ogre.' Faint emphasis on the 'if'.

The Super's little fat mouth was pulling itself in and out like a sea anemone. She wrenched her attention from it with an effort.

'She didn't trust doctors, because of him, and because he knew most of the doctors in the area, and she probably thought they might tell him over a friendly game of golf. And maybe it was her rebellion, a secret of her own to show that there was a part of her he didn't own and control. It might be worth a risk to have that knowledge. Look at the risks taken by civilians in occupied countries, French Resistance helping Allied airmen for example...'

'You seem very protective of Mrs Kingston, Ms Bruce,'

remarked the Super. 'Her innocence would mean a lot to you - if you're emotionally involved.'

There was something significant in his tone. Almost as if he was implying something between Erica and Tessa, more than a therapist and patient relationship, more than friends? A definite creepy vibe. She noticed Will shift in his chair, uncomfortable at his Super's tactic.

'Emotion - the number one crime for any medical practitioner, and the one every woman is born guilty of!' she snapped. 'Her innocence does mean a lot to me, she had just begun to get her life back when all this happened. I like to think I was able to help her. And still can.'

'We will have to see those records to confirm not only that she told you about the abuse, but that she did indeed see you under a false name. I hope for your sake she did.'

'Why?' Erica felt sticky with sex and kept feeling little trills of aftershock that made her shift in her seat. It was hard to concentrate.

Will made as if to speak but Golden Boy stopped him with a look. Things were getting more like an interrogation and less like confirmation of Tessa's story, and he knew Will and Erica had been an item.

'Because,' GB barked, 'if you knew your 'patient' was Tessa Kingston all along, whatever name you put on her file, we'd be wondering very much why you didn't mention it when you found her *allegedly* abusive husband dead. When we assumed you had no personal connection with

Kingston at all. And suddenly you turn out to be the not so grieving widow's avenging angel, and start showing up here with dodgy bits of evidence.'

'That syringe, there was nothing in it, by the way,' Will put in. 'And no fingerprints apart from yours. Anyone would think someone was trying to incriminate the hoodies.'

'Of course, we only have your word for it that it was outside his house at all. As a matter of fact, there were a few odds and ends missing from the murder room.' Gloves, aprons, pins, she was thinking. 'But we can't be sure that was one of them. Does anyone where you work use syringes?'

'Not to my knowledge, and it occurs to me, from this threatening line you're following, that her *guilt* means rather a lot to *you*. Perhaps you are equally emotionally involved, Superintendent, Inspector. I'm not trying to fix blame on some probably blameless teenagers, just trying to show that the obvious line isn't the only one. You know, 'reasonable doubt.''

'As you know, Ms Bruce, Mr Kingston let in his killer, which points to someone he knew.'

Will sighed. GB was astray. Erica wouldn't buy that as their only conclusion. They'd already discussed it. She knew fine well the rock used to club him was from the back of the house. Sure enough she pounced.

'Someone visiting at night, carrying a rock? I can think

of an alternative scenario. Kingston hears a disturbance behind his house, maybe a window broken, runs out the back door in a temper to catch the young louts, leaving his door open, the killer nips in, and when he goes back in they're already lying in wait to attack him. I'm surprised you didn't think of it yourself.'

Will's dark face darkened some more. His Superintendent was breathing hard, trying not to defend his man and make him look worse. Of course she knew Will would have thought of it, he wasn't stupid, but they'd tried to wrong-foot her and hoped she wouldn't have thought of it herself. He must think I'm stupid, she thought. Like every blonde in a short dress.

'We aren't sure the rock attack took place outside. Just that the rock came from there. The room was well cleaned up as you saw. Surgical equipment was used.' Will's voice was brutal as he tried to cover himself.

'Could Tessa get a man up onto a table?'

'There are ways a woman can get a man to lie on a table, without having to do any heavy lifting.'

'What a mind you have Inspector!'

She was near to losing her temper; beneath the anger was fear. Any left-over arousal had evaporated. She was trying to hold back the claustrophobic feeling of being buried in this grey bunker, away from daylight, with rooms and corridors patrolled by hostile powers and a series of doors between her and the free fresh air. She clung to the memory of her conversation with Tara as a life belt in an icy sea; at least someone knew where she was, someone who knew her rights and needed her support.

Erica controlled her breathing, using her meditation techniques to repeat a mantra in her head. She must not show weakness in front of Will Bennett. Him and his bloody boss.

'We're talking about someone who cold-bloodedly bashed nails into a helpless human being, Erica. They don't deserve any protection from anyone.'

He'd used her first name at last. Like it mattered. Pompous git. 'That's why I don't want them to go free while an innocent person pays. I don't think an estranged wife was the only enemy Kingston had made.'

'No.' The Super was back on the offensive. 'You didn't like him yourself, did you? Your editor says you had quite an acrimonious phone conversation with Kingston; apparently Kingston was not impressed by your form of 'medicine'. More or less accused you of being a fraud and a charlatan.'

Will's sneer made it clear he still felt the same way about homeopathy strongly enough to agree with his nemesis the Super. Just another chasm between him and Erica. Will had claimed to care about rationality and logic, when really, as Erica well knew, his scepticism of all alternative medicine was purely based on emotion – protective anger on behalf of his sister, who had been conned out of much needed money by a fake therapist who claimed to be able to cure Will's adored nephew's learning disability by 'destroying' her 'bad, possessed' money.

'When we found you with Kingston's body, it seemed that you had nothing to do with the case. Now we find that you didn't like him, and that you had been treating his wife without his knowledge, and sympathising with her supposed ill treatment by him. Encouraging her to leave him.'

'I did nothing of the sort. I didn't know she'd left her husband. I didn't know he, Kingston, was her husband then.'

'We only have your word for that. Even if your records show a false name, that doesn't mean you didn't know who she really was. You're trying to save her from suspicion now. Perhaps you were trying to save her from him then. Perhaps violence seemed the only way. And a parody of conventional medicine, such as an alternative therapist might think up.'

'What? You're insane! Look, I didn't know the details of his abuse until after the murder. Just that she was scared of her husband to the point of using a false name.'

'If that's true,' Will began.

'What do you mean 'if'?'

'You lied to us!'

'I didn't. I just... didn't mention when I knew.'

'So IF it's true, then your evidence that he was abusive

is worthless. It makes her look more suspicious, not less! She fed it to you after his death! You must be very naive to believe her.'

'I wasn't surprised... it matched her previous behaviour and her symptoms too. Look are you arresting me?' She touched the slip of paper with the solicitor's name on it like a lucky charm in her pocket.

'Not yet. But perhaps you should think about the risks of playing detective just for the sake of a story in the local paper.'

'I'm not 'playing' at anything, believe me.'

She was no Philippa Marlowe. She wanted to defend Tessa, yes, but in the last analysis, she just had to *know*. Couldn't bear not to. She'd not told the officers about her golf ball injury. On the one hand she could claim it might be a deliberate assault, and point to another suspect. But that would mean more or less admitting she'd been poking about behind the house on very shaky 'journalistic' grounds, and Will would pounce on what could have been an attempt on her life to triumphantly point out that she should keep out of things.

'Good to know,' he said, patronisingly. 'Luckily for you, Kingston had been dead since the previous night, or being found with his body would look suspicious for you. Course, we're checking and double checking your movements the night before as best we can.'

'That's me, lucky. Now I must be going. I have work to

do, and I don't want to take up any more of your valuable time.' She hated Will for making her hungry, this was a dangerous situation when she might easily lose control and eat too much, left with a bellyful of calories like an unwanted pregnancy.

As she left, her knees were shaking and her arm was aching where the bruise of the golf ball still throbbed. Ravenous, dehydrated, and filled with unused adrenaline, she didn't have time to go home before her first appointment at Ivy Lodge so she stopped at a small coffee shop and had 'breakfast' tea and toast. It was sliced white bread and the jam was the kind you classify by colour rather than fruit, but she was so desperate, the whole thing combined to make a sensual experience almost as blissful as her night with Jamie. As the hot strong tea warmed her belly, she remembered that night and began to feel good again.

She still had her life, after all, a life mostly on her own terms, and Tessa was in good hands with her sister even if they charged her. Erica was convinced Will would only charge Tessa if he was on safe ground. He was the type who'd rather die than be shown up as wrong if he jumped the gun. Typical Lycopodium. And if Tessa was charged and tried, Kingston's violence would be a powerful argument in mitigation.... she could easily convince a jury she was a victim, a moist-eyed kitten in human form, even if it was harder to convince Will and his master GB. How could Erica herself fancy a man who came to heel every time that giant charity bag of rags and stains gave him a look?

Erica's amateur research had shown that there were others who had hated Kingston. Where did that leave her? She didn't want to defend Tessa by putting other individuals in the frame. How could she throw suspicion on Laura Gibson, who had confided in her, who had suffered? On Jamie, whom she'd slept with? And each of them could represent a host of similar colleagues and patients who felt the same way about Kingston. She could keep trying those areas, but more and more suspects might emerge. Without actual evidence, the motive alone would not be enough to get her any further.

Will was wondering about Erica. She'd been in the hospital overnight? Or was she just yanking his chain? He'd not liked to ask why. And yet sitting there, she had that look, the one he remembered so well, kind of soft-eyed and dishevelled and not quite all there, the look she usually had after a night of hot sex. He remembered what she'd said about having a date.

'Wassup Will, you look narked.' Hassan came in with some printouts. Will jumped.

'Oh, just frustration - with the case. Any news?'

'Well I was thinking we'd better follow up Kingston's cousin. His mother's sister's son, a - erm' he looked at his notes, 'Stephen Blair. He's Kingston's executor and he inherits half the proceeds of Kingston's mother's house sale. It gives Blair a motive, especially considering he's in credit card debt up to his eyebrows.'

'Is he indeed. Maybe you and Paul could have a word with Mr Blair. He might turn up at the inquest tomorrow.'

'Bound to be a verdict of murder isn't it? We've got samples and so on from Kingston, and they'll be releasing the body for cremation.'

'Speaking of samples, no drugs found in him. Whoever clocked him one, he was very much alive and capable of kicking when they did it.'

'Your point being?'

'Pretty risky, for a lass like Tessa, taking on a healthy alert man she was scared of.'

'IF she was scared.'

'No defensive wounds, so there was no struggle. Not easy to creep up on someone you're terrified of, it happens all the time in films and on TV but the chances are they'd look round and then you'd be in trouble.'

'Maybe she wasn't that scared. We only have her word for it. Tara and Erica are backing her up but they don't have any real evidence. And knowing he'd change his Will after a divorce makes her motive even stronger.'

'Actually I'm surprised he didn't change it when she left him. The thought of her nabbing all his dosh...'

'He seems to have been an arrogant bloke though. And doctors don't expect to be patients, or corpses. Maybe he just didn't think he'd die in his prime. Or at all!'

'Perhaps he thought she'd be back.'

CHAPTER TWENTY-THREE

At Ivy Lodge, Stacey was being very conscientious about her internship all of a sudden. For a start she was physically there, at an hour when she'd normally either be going home to sleep or sleeping. Occasionally she gave a surface or two a once-over with antiseptic wipes, when someone was looking, and spasmodically manned the entrance like some sort of meeter and greeter in place of the receptionist they couldn't afford. Her instincts were telling her to be around, in case something went down that might give her something to sell - anything which might bring the notoriety of her dreams. Erica might find something that would make both their names known.

'So how was yer hot date with the baby doc? Yer gonna give him another ride round the block, like?'

Erica gave her a brief summing up of her night of passion followed by questioning at the copshop. 'I suppose the police variety of porridge is at least calorie-free. And as for Jamie, he had to rush off to start work, and then I was in chains at the station... He's a great kisser, and adorable with it. And for a first time he was very promising. I can train him up. But his work is so all-absorbing of his time and attention. And I doubt if I can compete with all those pretty nurses.'

'Hadaway man, Erica, nurses are aal ower shit n' vomit, sooo not a good look yer knaa. And most of them are fat lasses.'

Erica forbore to point out that Stacey herself was often in a similar condition of a night time.

'He's sent me some sexy texts.'

Stacey made a mental note to read them as soon as Erica left her phone unattended. 'And Wild Willy Bennett as well. Two fit blokes after ye!'

'Please don't call him Willy...'

Just then Miles Fredericks, her hypnotist colleague, dashed by her open door and paused to stick his head in.

'Bit late!' he panted. 'Some sodding kids made a disturbance outside my house late last night. Kept waking me up. Have you got any of that night-nurses' remedy available? I could do with some to take home.'

'You mean Cocculus? Just a minute.'

Erica fetched him some tiny white tablets in a brown paper envelope.

'Usual procedure, as with all my remedies. No coffee, no mint, no food or drink, no touching the tablets. Tip them into your mouth. And I think your next victim is waiting.'

A man was sitting on a chair outside Miles' room, twitching with impatience. Something about the wrinkles round the eyes and mouth, and the body language, said 'repentant smoker.'

It was a very long shot, but she wondered if the hoodies who used to hang about behind Kingston's house had moved their drinking den of vice near Miles' house instead.

Miles lived on a modern estate of what are called 'executive homes'. They always have very pastoral sounding names, which are all that's left of the land they've covered up and destroyed. True to form, Miles' estate had been built on the fields of a vanished farm, and it was bounded by an overgrown disused railway track beloved of walkers and cyclists during the day, which formed the boundary of the far side of the golf course. So it was not so unlikely that the youths had merely crossed the course to a new hangout.

She managed to buttonhole Miles later on.

'Those youths who woke you. Could you text me next time they turn up? I'd like to talk to them. I'm erm, researching a feature on youth drug and alcohol abuse.'

'Well I had been thinking of ringing the police. But if you really want me to I'll ring you instead.'

'Last time they annoyed you, did you go outside to chase them off?'

'Yes, I did. Bloody cold it was too.'

'Did you shut the door behind you when you ran out?'

'Come to think of it I don't think I did, I just ran out and when they'd gone, having given me a tour of the Anglo-Saxon history of the English language, I went back in.'

'And you ran out of sight of the door?'

'Yeah, round the corner of the house.'

'I bet you've got alarms all over your house, but then you go running out leaving the door open. Someone could have got in while you were chasing the others away.'

Miles was inclined to scoff at the idea. Besides, his partner was inside to fight off any invaders. But his actions in leaving the door open had illustrated how easy it would be for the killer to have got into Kingston's house without breaking in, or being someone he knew. Or, slipped into his back garden, waited for him to come back through and bashed him over the head as he passed by, before dragging him through the house for the rest of his punishment. Bit handy for the killer, them being there, but then they had been making trouble for some time, it was common knowledge.

Erica was feeling the lack of sleep and the lack of time to shower properly. Once home, she would collapse in a heap. She changed back into her sports top and bundled her now icky dress into her bag with the strappy sandals. She got a suitably erotic text from Jamie. Maybe it was going to be more than a one-night stand. She rather hoped so; but not tonight, please not tonight.

Staggering in to her flat, she stripped, piled everything but her shoes into the washer and set it going. Desperate times, desperate measures, she thought recklessly as she microwaved some frozen mature (lo-fat) cheddar before slapping it on wholemeal toast and bunging it under the grill. She collapsed on her bed and ate the golden molten cheese, salty and oily, gulping a mug of hot juice. Must organise some salads.... she made do with a handful of red seedless grapes. Damn things have more calories than blueberries but the ones in the fridge had gone squishy and white-ended and disgusting. As usual, she tried to burst the grapes one by one against her palate with her strenuous tongue, but they were too firm. Grapes must have changed since Keats' time. Still it was good exercise for her oral technique which might be getting a lot of use in the near future. The washer rumbled and swished, carrying her away on a wave of soapy sound. She crawled under the duvet.

She woke next day, still filthy, and had a hot bath. It was almost better than sex. The bruise on her arm was a pale mauve already, fading outwards to yellow.

Golf balls, Jamie, texts... her thoughts swirled like water down the plug. She belatedly texted him back.

Must friend him on facebook. But she'd asked him out. Next move should be his. As she towelled herself, the black cotton against her pale skin reminded her of his dark silky hair against her belly. A woman cannot live by work and exercise alone. Or even cheese on toast.

The inquest came and went with no surprises or revelations. Your basic 'murder by persons unknown'. Robert Kingston's cousin and executor Stephen Blair, a skinnier, younger version of Robert but with a rather down-at-heel look, had been questioned by the police but not held. Erica presumed he had some sort of alibi.

CHAPTER TWENTY-FOUR

The health page all done and delivered ahead of deadline, Erica was reading the latest Ann Cleeves on her kindle, curtains drawn, glass of claret at hand, perfect Cox's Pippin chill against her leg as she curled on the sofa, limbs relaxed and mind at ease after a good gym session. A delightful work-out with Jamie had enlivened the previous night, and they had woken together to renew their efforts. Then he'd bogged off to work and she was now blissfully alone in her home, realising that she needed both parts of the equation with him or any man, the being with and the bogging off which had to be in balance. More equations, it was all about the Maths. Her mobile vibrated against her thigh. It was Miles.

'Erica? Those lads are round the side of the house again. I don't know if you want to come round now. Personally I think you're barking.'

'Oh god. I don't feel like it... bugger the lads.'

'No thanks!'

'I've just got cosied in for the night,' she grumbled unfairly. Do I still need to follow up this lead? With the police still suspecting Tessa...

'Mel thinks we should just ignore them. So if you want to forget the whole thing... '

'No, I'll be there. Give me a while. I'll be on my bike. I didn't realise Mel was back. Sorry to disturb.'

'Don't be silly. Come in and have a drink when you've finished being beaten up.'

He rang off. Miles' lover Mel did something fairly well paid and financial and was often away in Europe and the US. Another keen golfer, which was probably why they lived by a golf course. Duh.

Erica's tyre needed pumping up, of course, and she couldn't find her bike lights at first. She put on warm clothes, feeling insecure and tired. Needn't worry she might inflame adolescent passions, to them she'd probably seem ancient. She texted Stacey to say where she was going and why, on the very slim chance she wanted to come along. It was unlikely she'd be available at such short notice and she certainly wouldn't have transport to hand but in fact her presence could be useful with the hoodies. She probably knew some of their older brothers and sisters from the Wydsand coastal clubbing scene. Also some native caution made Erica feel somebody should know where she was going and why.

It was cold when she set off, with a brisk wind blowing the stars about and playfully gusting against her as she pedalled. Why don't I do something well paid and financial and get sent abroad all the time? A question which occasionally popped up.

She pedalled up the winding paths set between grass

verges which the designers of the 'executive estate' had laid out so that happy pram-pushing yummy mummies could stroll about traffic-free between culs de sacs. As it turned out, those who moved into these little ghettos tended to have several cars per family, so the drives and streets were littered with glowering 4x4s and the separate footpaths became sad and leaf-strewn.

Miles' house was on the end of a row, its side parallel with the footpath. It was easy to pick out because of his kit car parked outside, looking very eccentric in this setting. She wondered how the neighbours felt about having a hypnotist in their midst. She also wondered why all the cars were parked outside when nearly all the houses had huge double garages. How much of a modern house was redundant? The requisite separate dining room, never used due to the equally requisite 'dining country kitchen, the heart of the house'. The garage that held no cars. The study where nobody studied.

A light went on at the side of Miles's house. She glimpsed movement. Then it went off again. A security light fixed high on the wall. The wind brought a snatch of noise, garbled by the weather and unrecognisable. But someone was definitely there. She went back the way she'd come until she reached the previous street, turned down it and cycled along Miles' street as far as his house. She parked her bike between his car and Mel's, which was something shiny and curved like a crouching beast. She didn't think she'd gain cool points being seen arriving on a bike. Only losers use buses, went the youthful creed thereabouts, god knows what they thought of two wheels propelled by your own legs once you were past eleven years old.

She walked round the side of the house where a few dark figures lurked close against the wall where a whimsical wrought-iron arch heavily decked with clematis montana and the like formed a kind of shelter. The wind still buffeted them, belting straight down the path. They were more or less out of range of the security light, occasionally making it go on out of defiance or carelessness as they jostled each other. She stood under it and it went on, illuminating her in all her unthreatening smallness and spilling enough light on them for her to see what sort of nest of iniquity she was dealing with.

A small bunch of lads in the inevitable low-hanging jeans with crotch stretched between knees, waistband and more of their keks showing, knitted beanie hats and baggy t-shirts, thin and inadequate for the weather and season. Little points of orange light glowed from their cigarettes, and glanced off the straight sides of beer cans and a bottle of something clear, vodka or tequila probably. Wary, arrogant, defensive, and ball-shrivellingly cold. As true Geordie males, torture would not have made them admit this last however.

'Want something, pet?' Asked with the obligatory adolescent sneer.

'Aa wouldn't mind giving her somethin!' another said in a voice heavy with innuendo.

They laughed. Men, the lords of creation, reminding Erica of her place in the world. Infuriatingly, they could indeed be a threat to her physically. She hoped she wouldn't have to use the pepper spray she'd bought online and now had in her pocket.

'Want a fag, darlin?' The sneerer was holding out a packet, the light cruelly illuminating his acne like the craters of the moon.

'Not right now thanks. I just want to talk to you. OK?'

'We've got a right to be here,' said the innuendo chief. 'Neebody can tell we to piss off.'

'Or we'll fkn tell them to piss off.' Another was keen to show off his bantering skills.

'I'm a journalist, I write for the *Evening Guardian*.'

She passed round the card which repeated the fact in print. It was too dark to read it but they didn't bother trying very hard.

'Oh yeah?'

She showed them a page of the paper with her name and photo on, glad she'd had the nous to bring it. They were probably not regular readers of the local paper. Doomed to remain ignorant about the WI's latest speaker on 'Dutch Tulip Fields' and that hardy perennial topic, public ire re dog mess.

'Ye should get yer tits oot, that'd get folks readin,'

opined one.

'Thanks for the suggestion. I'll mention it to my editor. My page promotes healthy living.'

Laughter.

'Fuck that,' the first one said. 'Live fast, die young, leave a good-looking corpse, man pet, that's us.'

'Well, you might manage two out of three.' Before they could work that one out, 'I'm doing an article about young people and attitudes to drinking, drugs, smoking and so on. What do you think? Anonymous of course.'

'How much do we get paid?' demanded one.

'It's the local fkn rag, not a proper tabloid, man!' scoffed the apparent leader.

They clustered round, treating her to a barrage of boasting about their alcohol consumption, cigarette smoking and drug taking, all of it sensational and much of it probably wishful thinking.

'E's, Ket, weed... owt we can get... hey, why aren't you taking notes, or recording iz?' one of them asked suspiciously.

'I've a good memory.' But she took out her small digital recorder and began to record their pathetic boasts. She felt sorry for these lads. To have nothing better to do than hang about outside in the damp windy cold, drinking, smoking and self-medicating, seemed a terrible waste of youth. It seemed a long time since Erica's own earlier days of foolish excess. Now even her excesses were carefully planned, earned, and atoned for. God help the girls for whom these boys were the available boyfriend pool.

'I'd heard you lot hung about in the lane over the other side of the golf course, behind Robert Kingston's house. '

They knew his name alright, it had had enough publicity.

'Aye, well, the fkn bizzies've been aal ower the place since,' said the would-be Jimmy Dean.

'Somebody was saying a lot of windows got broken,' she kept her tone neutral. 'Fences damaged, greenhouses vandalised.'

'Fkn crap! Well, one or two mebbe. It wasn't us, like. Erm it was some *other* lads. We used to find golf baals lying aboot and try and get rabbits and that with them. A couple of windows did kind of get broke... hey, ye cannit prove it was us!'

Would it be worth mentioning her own painful encounter with a golfball? They would just laugh, deny it. And if it was them, they'd be pleased to know they'd hit her. Why give them that satisfaction?

'Did you ever get any rabbits?' She was sceptical. You'd need a lot of force and accuracy to hit the most obese, arthritic rabbit with a golf ball, except by accident.

'Aye,' one of them began, 'buttloads of rabbits, man,' but their leader punched him in the arm and shouted him down.

'Shurrup! Did we fuck! We'd find dead ones and tell other lads we'd killed them. That's aal.'

Erica was surprised they weren't boasting of bringing down rhino and elephant, let alone rabbit. Perhaps they weren't sure if it was legal?

'You know, I was the one who found Kingston after he'd been murdered.'

An excited outcry. The security light blinked on and off as they milled about. The stars were extinguished and revealed, tiny celestial fag-ends.

'Mint!'

'Was there loads of blood?'

'Serve him right, stuck-up bastard!'

'Was there really nails in his heed?'

'Really. Don't you have any sympathy for the poor man?'

'Nee way! He was always oot threatening us with the police. Called us rubbish! Human jet something.'

'Jetsam?'

'We hated the bastard. Stupid fucker...'

'That other owld gadgie was worse...aalways on wor case, I fuckin hate him and that cat...'

His leader kicked his leg so that he hopped around comically. 'It was the owld wifie with the cat, man, always coming oot moaning at we.'

'Sad losers. Kingston should've got a fkn life!'

'Bit late now, like!' They all fell about laughing.

They wanted all the grisly details. None of them gave away any intimate details of the crime.

'Did it occur to you that you might be in danger, if there was a killer hanging about that area? A psycho, who might have thought you'd seen too much?'

They looked warily at one another. Was that why they'd moved their meeting place, rather than a heavier police presence?

'We didn't see nowt! Wish we had. We could have got money from the tabloids. Or off youtube. That bastard Kingston come out all radgey, yelling at we; we went, we were going anyway. 'Fuck off n drop deed!' Aa shouted – pretty good eh?'

'The night of the murder?'

'Erm no, mebbe the neet before... Mind we'll not tell any of this to the bizzies. They'll try to pin it on we. Then we saw on facebook, Gibba's mam n'dad were away, so we all went roond there.'

Her heart went out to Gibba's parents, imagining their homecoming.

'So will ye give we owt at aal for wor stories since it's for the meedja?'

'You've just said you saw nothing, you know nothing. If you want me to use your stories of underage drinking and buying booze from off licences, I could maybe give you a few quid when I've got your names and addresses. Which I won't print.'

'Me mam'd kill iz!' one muttered.

'Anyway, why've you picked here to set up home?' she

asked. 'Not exactly luxury, is it?'

'Well doon that path and along a bit is an offie that's not too fussy about checking ID. And this light, it's handy for seeing to open the drinks and fag packets.'

'Gadgie in that crib there, he come out and tried to chase we off. But he's got nee right. It's a public path, innit?'

Poor Miles. How to get these lads to leave him in peace... Just as a bit of frivolity, she remarked, 'That guy is a hypnotist. Good one too. He can make people do really stupid things. He can hypnotise them before they know it. Just catch his eye, if he's pissed off at you, he'll make you impotent.'

'Fuck off!'

But they exchanged uneasy glances. She fished out a tenner to give them, groping in her bag in the uncertain light, and spilling a couple of remedy pill bottles on the ground. She was just trying to retrieve them when she heard feet pounding towards them. Surely Stacey hadn't come, and surely she wasn't running? But it was someone a lot bigger than Stacey, at least height-wise. Will Bennett was suddenly there doing his best looming act, dressed in jogging gear. Erica shot upright.

'Scotty!' he greeted the pimply leader of men. 'Fancy seeing you here! Are you harassing this woman?'

'Are we fuck!'

'For pity's sake Will!'

'It's ye doing the harassment! Me mam tellt yer I'd done nowt.' His cohorts were backing away and making sure their faces were out of the light. To no avail.

'And hello, Gaz, Robbo, Big Steve, Little Steve... the gang's all here. Isn't that nice! Drinks and smokes as well!'

The objects in question had been hastily jettisoned as soon as Will appeared at a signal from Scotty, but they were still visible, glinting amid the greenery and twigs.

'They're hers man! She brought them for we. She's grooming we for sex!'

Will and Erica both burst out laughing at this piece of brilliant improv.

'Is this true?' Will asked her, unable to resist.

'You know me, Inspector.'

'Yes I do. Hm, also I think a certain off license will be getting a little visit from my colleagues. Now what's this?'

Erica had relaxed and he suddenly swiped a bottle from her hands. He shook it and it rattled merrily. 'Little white pills! Exactly like the ones Scotty was trying to sell at the station! What a coincidence.'

'Did ye get them from her?' Scotty asked Erica, at the same time as Will asked him, 'Did you get them from her?' indicating Erica.

'Who's her?' Erica answered Scotty first, then Will. 'And of course I've not given any to these lads, they're not clients of mine.'

Scotty switched attention to Will. 'Aa tellt ye them were sweetners man, and Aa divn't knaa what this lass has got! She's a dealer man, take her in!'

The lads had been receding further and further, behind

Scotty, and at this point having thrown Erica to the wolf, Scotty shouted 'Leg it, lads!' and the whole crew ran for it across the golf course.

Erica and Will were left alone.

'What are you doing here?' they both said.

'Being a journalist.'

'Patrolling.'

'Yeah right, you just so happen to patrol here, randomly, when I happen to be talking to these lads.'

'Yeah right, you just so happen to be interfering in our investigation when I specifically asked you not to. Come on Erica, let's go.' He took hold of her arm and she yelled, 'Ow!'

'Oh for god's sake surely you're not claiming police brutality.'

Then he realised she was hurt. He tugged her gently into the lamplight and looked at her bruise.

'Golfing injury. OK, I got whacked by a golf ball when I found that syringe I brought in, if you must know. No doubt you suspect Tessa of hanging about the golf course lethally wielding a nine iron or whatever.'

'So you thought it a good idea to give whoever it was another chance?'

'Don't change the subject Will. I'm still waiting to hear how come you turned up here and now.'

'Got an anonymous tip-off that a woman was being harassed by youths here. Call came from a phone box, not a mobile. Very strange. Though it was probably made before you even got here, thinking about the timing.'

'Oh really.' Stacey was the only one who knew where Erica was going, apart from Miles and he'd not be using phone boxes when he was in the house next to them. What was Stacey up to? Would she even know how to use a phone box? 'Well I was fine.'

'Oh, I know. It's the lads who are the victims. Harassed, groomed, offered drugs. You're never that nice to *me* these days.'

It was strange how being alone in the night together had made them start to behave more naturally despite the occasional spat. She'd put a stop to that. 'Well I'm not a victim so you don't need to ride in on your white horse and rescue me. Ever.'

He was stung. 'Right, how about I arrest you instead? So help me, I will.'

'You're not seriously going to act on those ludicrous accusations! God you must be desperate for some arrest-action.'

'It's not their accusations, it's our forensic evidence.'

'Forensic bollocks!'

'I'm writing that down. Anything you say may be given in evidence.'

'OK, then, Inspector Bennett, you have a beautiful cock.'

Will flushed, she could tell even in the intermittent security light.

'Well aren't you going to write that down? Take me in, and I'll repeat it at the station and sign a statement to that effect if you like.'

'Thanks for the reference.' He was recovering. 'But I was serious about the forensics. Young Scotty there had some pills which he was trying to sell as Es, and on analysis they turned out to be sugar. They look exactly like the ones you dispense, and true to form, there was nothing else in them.'

'Nothing detectable by you and your minions.'

'It's like gravity, yes I know.'

'There are other homeopaths. And the fact that Scotty was trying to earn some money selling them isn't my fault.'

'Those lads wouldn't buy anything from you for their health and you know it.'

'I wouldn't sell them to anybody for any other reason, and YOU know THAT.'

'So they've been stealing them, is that what you're saying?'

'Not necessarily. Someone I prescribed them to might have a lodger or a son or daughter who's nicking them to sell.'

'Well take this as a friendly warning. Stop interfering in the investigation or I may do something officially about your possible involvement.'

'I've told you before, people tell me things. Things they wouldn't tell a police officer. I can help if you'd let me. And since when was it illegal to peddle sugar? You going to raid Cadbury's?'

'You know fine well they were selling those pills as illegal drugs.'

'Well you claim they are harmless and have nothing in them. I bet you can't get any of the lads' customers to complain they weren't real drugs. Interesting point. Is it fraud to sell illegal drugs that are legal and harmless? And it must have been obvious even to you that those lads didn't know me before tonight. I had a feeling I was getting somewhere... something they might have been about to say, perhaps... when you came along and ruined it.'

'Keep out of it, will you Erica! There are those who still wonder if you had any part in the murder, knowing your tendency to go overboard for one of your protégés... even as an accessory after the fact. You're not in any position to investigate anything. If need be I can hold you in a cell...'

'Ooh, Inspector!'

'On suspicion of selling - erm, well while we further investigate the pills Scotty had.'

'You know me, I treat sugar like you treat cocaine. I'm not going to dish that deadly stuff out to youngsters for a few quid for anything but therapeutic purposes. Now thanks for the threats, it's been lovely, I shall get back to my boyfriend now.'

Why was she saying such a tragically immature thing? She just couldn't stop.

'Oh really, and who is this boyfriend?'

'Mind your own.'

'It wouldn't be someone involved in the case would it?'

'Mind yours.'

'So that's how you get people to 'tell you stuff'! Well I certainly can't compete with that.'

'Oh you undersell yourself Will. I'm sure you could. Being held in handcuffs and shown your well-lubricated truncheon could loosen a lot of tongues.'

'Go home Erica. Take care of yourself with that arm. Look, I'll give you a lift home.'

Erica refused and cycled home, thinking over what had been said. Setting aside her indignation at Will's suspicions, the feeling that she might have got something important out of the lads was buried under more immediate and obvious clues. 'Did ye get them from her?' Scotty had asked her, about the pills. Clearly he didn't know they'd originally come from Erica herself. Put together with the mysterious phonebox call from 'a woman' not using her mobile number, there was only one solution. Stacey had been stealing and selling Erica's remedies, sweet stuff more profitable than Rina's biscuits. Well the Tory government *had* been banging on about encouraging young entrepreneurs. It was work experience of a kind. She only hoped Stacey wasn't going to be claiming expenses. She texted Stacey. 'Have spoken to police. We need to talk.' That was Hollyoaks enough for Stacey to understand she was in bother. There was no reply.

To distract his mind from thinking about Erica in bed with another guy, lucky sod, Will checked in with Kev who was gloomily parked in front of Tara's house 'surveilling his arse off' as he described it.

'Nothing guv.' He sounded terminally bored. 'They know I'm here so Mrs Kingston's not going to do owt.'

'I know, I told you to let them see you, it's just to rattle them. Make sure you do follow though if she goes anywhere.'

'The sister went out, so Mrs K is probably looking after the sprogs.'

'You're doing a grand job there Kev lad. Keep it up!'

'Aw Guv. When she goes to the gym, are you sure Sally's not available to do the surveillance there?'

'Only occasionally. What's the problem, you don't like watching the lycra-clad gym bunnies come and go?'

'Yes but I don't see them in action. It's a women only gym Guv remember! They won't let me in without a warrant. It's like bein' stranded outside a brewery on free sample day.'

'Tough. We can't make her join another gym just to feed your filthy fantasies.'

CHAPTER TWENTY-FIVE

A man, on an operating table. The man standing over him had taped his penis vertically to his belly, to give uninterrupted access to his scrotum. He was now kneading the right testicle with sterile-gloved forefingers and thumbs, as it slithered about in its loose bag of stretchy, stippled skin as if desperately trying to evade his invasive fingertips. He seemed to find what he was looking for, diving into the skin which gave and gave beneath his probing, to isolate and clamp the vas deferens, the flexible whitish looping tube which carried sperm to the base of the penis, or had done until now. Now part of it was a pale tight bulge like the head of a boil protruding from the clamp. The man on the table offered no resistance as his most private, protected and tender area was punctured by needle-fine forceps which were then prised apart to make a bigger hole in the forgiving skin. Deeper, deeper, the layers of fascia were split and parted, the white pearl of the clamped portion of vas showing through clearer and clearer until it popped out and stood exposed, lifted clear, a short sinewy loop of it now free of the scrotum's protective sac, held tightly stretched between two clamps. The man now cut through the vas, burning his way through with electrically-produced heat, and the two cut halves writhed like a tortured earthworm, until the longest section was sliced again, leaving two short truncated open-ended tubes poking up like sea-lily stems, as the burned-off section was removed, a sad downward curve of severed tissue, to be discarded. The open ends, yearning to join back together, were prevented by further diathermic application, sealing them before they were tucked back inside their shielding layers, now breached. The clamps all removed, leaking blood and fluids mopped, the man operating looked at the face of the man on the table below him, noting his responses were satisfactory, checking that he was fully aware, before turning his attention to the left testicle and repeating the process. Once the punctures had retreated into the folds of coarse loose skin, they wouldn't even need stitches.

'You'll be fine to drive home, and back to normal in a week. Keep using condoms, and don't forget to provide test samples over the next few months, it's all in the pamphlet I gave you. Some of the little blighters will still be swimming around in your system for a while. Any persistent pain or hard lumps, get in touch right away.'

The man on the table was sweating but relieved, looking forward to some worry- and latex- free sex. Consultant Urologist Paul Chambers continued to talk cheerfully to his vasectomy patient, trying not to think about the man who was stalking him online, pursuing him for doing his job as well as he knew how.

When Erica got home, windblown and feeling the cold leaving her cheeks as she stood in the warmth, her browning apple and glass of wine were still waiting faithfully. She binned the apple and slurped the wine as she rang Miles. 'Sorry I went straight home without popping in.' She updated him on the night's adventure.

'Ah, so you're not under the hot lights? I saw the police car on the front street and your sexy ex dismounting from his white steed. Then a bunch of lads making off across the greens. That golf course hasn't seen so much excitement in years.'

'Yes, a lot of things seem to take place round the golf course.' Erica recalled her conversation with the girl at her gym about the Wydsand Club. 'It might be worth investigating there. I'll bet Will and co are too grovelly to the well-heeled and respectable to go bothering the men with little white balls. And they'd not let me in without checking my uterus at the door.' She paused. Miles could feel a favour request forming through the phone. 'Hey, isn't Mel in that club? Could he get me in?'

'They've got one of their tragic 'dinner dance' do's coming up soon. Christmas Chicken Dinner or Captain's Coronary or something. You could go with Mel as his 'plus one'. It's not my sort of thing. Be an interesting study for you. Human nature at its most basic.'

'Ooh, I've never been a beard before! I might, thanks. As you say, something interesting might turn up.'

'It's very quiet outside now. What did you do to those lads? '

'Told them you'd put the 'fluence on them and make them all impotent. Seems to have got rid of them.'

'Until they come back and put a brick through the window.'

'There's no pleasing some people.'

Time was passing. Kingston was already history. But while their conversation shifted to an Ivy Lodge night out, and how they needed to book for Christmas really early this time, someone else was mercifully unaware that they had already seen their last Christmas nearly a year ago.

As Erica reviewed her night so far, she envied writers of classic detective novels their small isolated group of suspects; the lover, the spouse, the business partner, the butler. As each suspect is investigated, they can be crossed off the list and the list gets shorter.

Not here. As she spoke to people who might have motives, even when she felt like crossing them off, the list lengthened rather than shortened. One embittered patient might stand for legions of them she couldn't discover. One humiliated colleague might be one of many, scattered wherever Kingston had worked. One abused ex-wife might stand for several abused ex-girlfriends. Kingston had been getting on a bit for a first marriage. He must have had relationships before Tessa. Hadn't Tessa mentioned a previous girlfriend who'd got pregnant and lost the baby? An image of Kingston's fist slamming into a rounded belly flashed into her mind. Was that how she'd lost the child? Had Will Bennett looked into that?

Scotty's posse might have done nothing worse than minor vandalism, but any one of them, or of other similar disenfranchised, dystopian feral groups might have done the killing, maybe for shits and giggles, maybe out of their heads on pills as a change from, and in fact easier than, killing rabbits on the golf course.

Speaking of which, was her own golf ball injury an accident? Or a random attack by youths? Or someone trying to get her out of the way, knowing her to be the reporter who had discovered Kingston and was now jogging past his house and showing too much interest? Even if there was a connection, it didn't narrow down the field at all.

Of course there was more than motive to be considered. How many of those few she had identified had alibis for the night Kingston was killed? How many innocent people ever did, in real life? Lack of an alibi need not be significant, but the existence of one would help to narrow the field a little. Anyway, alibis were Will's department. She could hardly interrogate people directly about where they'd been.

Jamie texted. 'The Pleasure Dome tomorrow, my treat, 8pm? xxxx' Kisses instead of emoticons. He was raising the stakes.

An invitation to the pleasure dome. It was a Mongolian restaurant in the city where you chose from buffets of fresh raw ingredients, designed and built a sauce to cook them in, then they cooked it for you in minutes. The food was basically Chinese with Indian bits and they had lots of vegetarian choices. A fun place to go. She replied 'Love to dine on honeydew and drink milk of paradise, 8pm, see you there.'

She went to bed wondering whether he had that afternoon free as well. Late night loving is all very well, but she preferred to do it when her senses were unaffected by alcohol or fatigue, when she was at the peak of her powers, or as Will had called it, 'match fit'.

It turned out that Jamie was free in the afternoon, something she found out by cornering him at the hospital and shamelessly propositioning him. He seemed to like the idea. They didn't get much conversation, since he was working, but the sight of him confirmed that, whatever their relationship was or was to be, the chemistry was definitely there. Her reason for being in the anaphrodisiac surroundings of the hospital rather than just texting him was to visit the old lady, Tilly O'Rourke and her feisty fellow-patient Gill Webster in the orthopaedic ward. She took them some remedies for building up the immune system, badly undermined by antibiotics and undignified treatment, dire food and disturbed sleep; also nets of clementines and some magazines not forgetting Tilly's ginger marmalade.

It was Saturday, so it was also a busy day for the Toon Army, as Newcastle United were playing at home in a local derby match that afternoon against Sunderland. Feelings would run high and alcohol would run low, and as she waited for Jamie to arrive at hers that afternoon, she spared a thought for Will Bennett's city colleagues, who would be under a lot of pressure keeping the peace. Chances were, extra officers would need to be be called in from outside the city. Stress and bad backs were rife and long-lasting. She enjoyed a childishly spiteful fantasy of Will standing on the touch line to keep order, having to keep his back turned to the game and watch the Toon Army's antics instead.

For those not going to the actual match, the wine bars and pubs would be showing it on TV live and later at night, and the streets would be eerily quiet until after the match, when lads and lasses would erupt onto the streets to take out their frustrations or celebrate by making a lot of noise and possibly damaging property and each other. Apart from being careful to avoid being on any dubious streets at the wrong time, she saw no reason why this sporting fixture would have any effect on her at all. She was wrong.

Jamie arrived at the flat, which she had even cleaned, well, tidied for the occasion. Could it be love? He was wearing denim jeans and a close fitting white t-shirt. She followed him in, to enjoy looking at his cute ass from behind. The three most beautiful sights in the world are supposed to be a ship in full sail, a field of crops ready for harvest, and a new mother and baby. Somewhere not too far down the list is the sight of a firm male bottom in a tight pair of jeans. Sheer poetry.

He paused to look at her skull collection, small but choice, which might have spooked a new lover who was not an orthopaedic surgeon. His strong slim fingers caressed the bones and articulated the lower jaws of the array of birds, mostly seabirds, a deer, sheep, badger, rabbit, dolphin, and her horse skull.

'Where do you get these from?'

'Most of them are from when I lived in more rural surroundings. You cut off the head, put it in the garden for ants and so on to clean; then when it's rotted, you boil it in bleach. A lot of them turn up as roadkill or on shingle beaches after storms, the birds and dolphins for example.'

'You're not after a human specimen are you, Erica?'

'Don't worry, you're quite safe, from decapitation anyhow. The chiropractor at Ivy Lodge has promised me his old one when he gets a new specimen. Surely you've got one already? Apart from the one you're wearing right now.'

'Passed him on to a relative who followed me into medicine.'

She lifted the heavy horse's skull from his hands, its small pod of brain space and great flat planes of bony cheeks, the worn teeth, giving it a patient and hopeful look, and put it back on the shelf where memories belong. She hadn't been actively collecting since events at Stonehead. More interested in the immediate future, she sat astride Jamie's legs as he sat on the couch.

'I'm more likely to be worried about you. You might have my leg off in an absent minded moment....'

She ran her hands down the outsides of his bare arms. The muscle was hard under his smooth skin.

'You're very strong for a slim guy. I suppose you have to be to wield a saw.'

'It's not all sawing off legs you know,' he placed his hands on her thighs. She could feel the heat of them.

'That's what Stephen says. He gets fed up when people assume that.'

'Stephen? Is he a doctor?'

She'd done it again. Of course, Stephen Maturin was fictional to Jamie, if not to her. Damn that Patrick O'Brian. She began to explain about the novels, but she was experiencing sensations which even reading a novel cannot give, and her speech was becoming confused.

Before he gave her something else to do, he stopped to ask, 'Should we be thinking where this is going, Erica?'

Uh-oh. 'Here's fine, or the bed, or both.'

'I mean, thinking about what's happening between us?'

Best put a stop to this nonsense toot sweet. 'It's up to you.' She went on rubbing herself over the warm hard dome poking up through the crotch of his jeans in a silent lapdance. 'You can think, or you can be fucked senseless. Which is it to be?'

Her silver-tongued eloquence did the trick, and they had a wonderful afternoon. Better than football. So it was in a warm and happy mood that they sat in the Pleasure Dome that evening eating and talking between trips to the buffet which Erica enjoyed guilt-free, another benefit of spending the afternoon in vigorous and prolonged exercise. She watched Jamie, in that haze of sexual gratitude people have often mistaken for love, watching his mouth close around his food and thinking about what he had been doing with it earlier on, feeling twinges of ongoing pleasure.

'What is it men of women most desire? The lineaments of satisfied desire,' he quoted. 'Don't look so surprised at me quoting Blake, doctors don't only read Grey's Anatomy you know.'

'I adore Blake, and Grey's Anatomy too for that matter. All those people shamelessly showing their internal organs.'

Jamie and Erica went clubbing in the city which was just starting to fill up after the match. The streets rang with tribal chants and ran with vomit. Not with blood, though. The local team had won. Strangers embraced, thugs took a night off beating their wives, thieves smiled at passing cops. Everyone was happy, except for the other team's fans, who had been hustled out of town by the police before the locals could add injury to insult. And except for one other person who was past happiness or any other emotion by the night was over.

CHAPTER TWENTY-SIX

A man on an operating table. Another room, still and silent like Kingston's. Another room of shiny clean surfaces, sharp instruments and nitrile gloves like hand-shaped condoms. Another long narrow table. Another man. He too lay quiet and passive, the back of his skull soft and pulpy, a puddle of dark blood for a pillow. A heavy ashtray, clean of ash but bloodied at one end, lay on the table between head and left shoulder. The man's grey hair lay in a soft fringe on his brow. His face was untouched, his clouded eyes catching a stray photon of light as he gazed at the ceiling, seeing nothing. The same patch of ceiling so many men had gazed at from this table, feeling cold, scared, suddenly small, shamed and vulnerable. This man wasn't feeling anything. Not now, not ever again. Which was just as well. Protruding from the palms of his hands two scalpels appeared to pin them to the table, gleaming softly in the diminished light. His comfortably casual checked shirt was untucked and turned back, his trousers unzipped and pulled down to mid thigh. Beneath the short, sad, collapsed tube of penis, his scrotum had been sliced open and his lap was full of blood.

Next morning, Erica woke first and lay looking at Jamie's sleeping face. So pretty. It was good having him there in the morning in her bed, warm and waiting, just as it was good between their trysts to have her bed luxuriously to herself. He seemed to feel her scrutiny and opened his dark eyes, a slow smile beginning to widen his mouth. His skin smelled fabulous. She breathed him in as he reached for her and she kissed him, her hand swooping down to scoop up his balls and lift, squeeze carefully, feeling him harden and gasp under her as she fell upon him like a female praying mantis in a hungry mood.

After Jamie went back to the hospital, she went for her usual swim, then with her wet hair tied up under a beanie, straight out of the sea front building for a run along the beach, wintry and deserted except for a few hardcore dog emptiers. She was in such a good mood that she took off her trainers and ran through the edge of the waves. It hurt, it was so icy, belying the silvery beauty of the pewter grey sea. She had trouble getting the trainers back onto her damp, numb feet when she left the sand, and ran home as the feeling seeped back painfully into her toes. She had a hot shower, the sand swirling chaotically down the drain. Life was a bower of bliss, she thought prematurely as she reached for a crusty white towel.

Her phone buzzed. A chirpy male voice assaulted her ear.

'Erica! It's Gary!'

Pause as if for round of applause.

Why was Ian Dunne's young protégé, ace reporter in the making, ringing her up on a Sunday morning?

'What do you want?'

'Come on, don't go all snooty on me. I'm calling you up to tell you some hot hot news. If a feature writer knows what that is... don't hang up! Only kidding...' He sounded excited, and more than usually pleased with himself. 'There's been another one!'

'Another what? You've had a second wet dream? Congratulations.'

'Another murder! And it's a wet dream alright! Hope you've got an alibi for last night - got the impression the Inspector fancied you for the last one – or just fancied you!'

He chortled at his own wit.

She wondered if this was his idea of a joke. Probably somebody got killed in a fight outside a pub - murder was uncommon in the area, but manslaughter could follow beer like a whisky chaser when a brawl got out of hand.

'Go on then Gary, unburden yourself.'

'Ooh, is that an invitation?'

'Groogh... hang on while I fetch a bucket.'

'I can't fill a whole bucket, but thanks for the compliment! Anyhoo, I was out and about last night, watching out for trouble, and causing some and all, what am I like...'

'Let's not go there until we've got a world-class psychiatrist handy...'

'...and I heard a call-out on the police frequency... it was about half two, the clubs were just coming out, I had a feeling there might be more trouble, then, call it an instinct, reporter's instinct...'

Erica sighed, towelling her hair while Gary's voice chirped out of the phone like a deranged sparrow. He'd rung up to boast, no doubt all hyped up at being on the scene of some poor bloke getting glassed or having his ear bitten off by his erstwhile 'bessie mate'.

'Very impressive, Gary, now if you don't mind...'

'Listen, Erica! Didn't you hear me, I said there's been another murder! Like Kingston!'

Now he had her attention. 'Go on, tell.'

'Oh, now you're getting your knickers in a twist! Well, since I owe that great Kingston story partly to you, OK...'

'Entirely to me.' Now desperate to hear she was still unable to help contradicting.

'Another doctor's hung up his stethoscope, gone to that waiting room in the sky, put on heavenly scrubs. God I'm on fire! Might use those... I'm surprised you haven't heard it on the news. The media are flocking and I was on the spot! First kid on the block, again! Yes!' She could see him punching the air like a triumphant Toon striker.

'Get the focus off yourself, Gary, and onto the story.'

'Guy called Paul Chambers. Lives up in Jezzie.'

Jesmond, one of the more salubrious suburbs of Newcastle, a middle-class ghetto heaving with university lecturers and doctors as well as students with rich parents and bohemian trustafarians. More recently its main street had become a clubbers' paradise of purple lighting, patio heaters and herds of prowling taxis as the hotels became bars and filled up with noisy drinkers who fancied a change from city centre or seafront, while any residents who objected were marooned there by massive mortgages and the housing slump.

'He's a cutter too, like old Robert K, but not an orthopaedic surgeon! Though thinking of bones... And he works, worked, at the Royal Elizabeth Infirmary. Quite a bit older than Kingston, in his fifties, not far off retirement actually. Poor sad git lived alone. Wife died some years back. Cancer. Never got over it. With all them pretty nurses just gagging... well anyway, there he is, in his own home, in his own private consulting room, on his own examining table, another one doing a spot of private work as well as NHS, nailed like a charva lass in a nightclub toilet.'

'Nailed how exactly?'

'Same as Kingston, according to the police.'

'The police gave you info instead of chucking you out?'

'Well the city bizzies were there, local DCI quite a media fan I think, then your pal Willy-Boy and DCS Massum showed up, called in because of the similar MO. They must have burned rubber up the coast road and changed out of their jimjams on the move. The two lots of cops were circling each other like territorial bisons on heat... 'it's my case, no it's mine you bastard', type of thing. I kind of did a tap dance amongst them to get max info.'

'So, the info you so skilfully gleaned from these gladiatorial buffalo?'

'Eh? Right. Well. Whacked over the back of the head with a heavy object, a marble ashtray this time, hands nailed to the table, pinned with some sort of blades. Isn't it fantastic! A serial killer, right here in the north east, oh thank you god!'

'You really are vile Gary, cut out the gloating will you. For one thing, this Paul Chambers was a person, not just a story, and for another, you're going over the top. The Archers is a serial. This is two similar murders.'

'Oh, yes, a serial killer, and he's got a name already. And wait for it, I, Gary, invented it! I got it tweeted straight off, hashtagged it asap, shared it everywhere, and the media are running with it!'

'Disgusting image...'

'Aren't you going to ask me his name? Well it's 'The Operator'. How cool is that?'

'About as cool as you're sexy.'

'I knew you'd not resist me for long! And you haven't heard the best bit yet. Erm, I mean, the worst. I said Chambers wasn't an orthopaedic surgeon. Aren't you interested to know what he was?'

'Go on, tell me.'

'He was a urologist! Specialised in vasectomies. Did

them privately in his own consulting room as well as on the NHS. So what did the bastard do to him? A very messy vasectomy, kind of, with one of his own blades. That is one smooooth Operator...Hmm, wasn't there a song? Maybe they'll play it when I'm on the TV news... Anyway, if Chambers had lived, he'd be singing soprano. Gross, eh!'

Erica visualised the scene. Blood. A hideous wound. Thank god she didn't walk in on this one. But some poor soul must have.

'Gary, you're the one that's gross.'

'Can't help it Erica, I'm high as a kite, had no sleep all night, I've got more coffee in me than Costa, and anyway, Chambers was probably dead or deeply unconscious and dying before the cold steel did its work. Probably never knew what hit him. Reunited with his dead wife, eh? Quite heartwarming, that angle. Hmm...'

'You'll have people queuing up to be murdered, you silver-tongued bastard. Do the police think it's the same killer?'

'Looks like it! I've been able to get some background on the victim from Dunne - our esteemed editor's come up trumps. Chambers belonged to his Golf Club, the city one.'

Her mind was racing. Why did golf of all things keep cropping up? Or was it just that consultants and golf go together? And what would this mean for Tessa? She must get information from Gary while he was high on adrenaline and ego.

'So how come the murder was discovered in the early hours, if this guy lived alone?'

'Young clubber, lives with his posh parents over the road from Chambers, came home after a night out, saw lights on, unusual apparently, then noticed the door was open, went in, saw the body, raised the place, lost all his designer lager in the hall. Not a pretty sight. Must have happened last night when everybody was watching the match on TV. Anyway, I thought I'd ring you, old colleagues blah blah, and I did owe you one. And I'll give you one any time you like! Boom boom! Can't hang around, I've got the nationals to talk to, but maybe we could get together for a drink soonest -'

Gary thought a glass of wine bought him full sexual favours. Not for a whole vineyard, with him.

Erica finished drying her hair and made tea. While she had been in bed with Jamie, some poor lonely bloke was being murdered. Sex and death, twin pillars of existence, not to mention the media. And a murdered vasectomy surgeon was a dream combo.

At least this time Erica had an alibi; Inspector Bennett and his gang couldn't try to frighten her off with their suspicions. Jamie had been with her all evening and all night, bless his little cotton socks. And she had been with him all evening and all night... Yes! Gary-like, she punched the air, sploshing Lapsang Souchong over herself as the significance sank in, more slowly than the tea.

If Jamie was her alibi, she was his. Although she had not seriously suspected him, she had been unable to forget that he did have a motive, or at least hated Kingston. The demands of her rampant libido had drowned out the small voice of caution. But it was a relief to know that he was innocent. At least of this second killing, her mathematician's mind tried to butt in, this one might be a copy cat, but she suppressed it firmly. Maybe it was too soon to speak of a serial killer. But it looked as if the killer of both of them was someone who was down on doctors, to paraphrase the Ripper, rather than someone who had a personal motive against Robert Kingston.

All the research she'd done into Kingston's life and relationships, all the muck that had floated to the top of his whitewashed existence. Tessa, his abused wife. Jamie Lau and many others, bullied at work. Laura Gibson, embittered patient who had endured his sadism helplessly. Again, many others, each believing themselves alone. Relatives of patients put through unnecessary suffering to boost his career. Plenty of room for resentment there. The hoodies. All that, and then it might turn out to be some random nutter who hated doctors.

Kingston was news again. Without him, no serial killer, no Operator.

Another result, Tessa would be free of suspicion now. What motive would she have for killing Chambers? She could move on, find a new life, perhaps rewarding work, or maybe just another husband who wasn't a sadist. Surely after the police had released Tessa, being unable to hold her any longer without charge, they would have been watching her. Will had believed she had a boyfriend somewhere. If they'd been watching her that night, the police would be her alibi. A nice thought. Though it was ironic that Tessa had been cleared not by Erica's well meant efforts, but by those of a deranged killer.

Erica could get back to her homeopathy practice, and her writing, and keeping fit. If only her intern would take a break from her arduous duties, Erica could relax and enjoy her flourishing sex life.

She knew the police would be up to their helmets with this second murder, and its apparent significance after Kingston's. But she couldn't forget Will's treatment of her and his infuriating way of hinting that she was a possible suspect or even a dealer in fake drugs. It was pretty low, to use his position to strongarm her, just because their relationship hadn't worked out. He couldn't pretend to suspect her now, and she was determined to let him know she knew it.

She rang him, and explained that it was about an alibi for the murder.

'A what? Alibi?' His voice sounded weary; a stark contrast with the hyped-up euphoria of Gary Thomas. The reporter thrilled with the story, able to pile pressure on the police. The police officer, up all night, expected to come up with the goods, sickened by the horror of the crime.

He sounded sceptical as well damn him.

'For the murder, yes.' She was beginning to feel angry again, remembering him questioning her in that horrible interview room, trying to pin the crime on Tessa, angry with her for interfering, for being there, for backing Tessa up. 'I got the impression you thought I might be involved. So I want you to know I have an alibi.'

'May I ask why you haven't told me this before?' he asked, testily.

'It's only just happened! For God's sake, I've only just heard about it myself!'

'Sorry, I don't understand. How could you have just found out about your own alibi?'

'Two men are dead. Let's not play silly buggers. I've rung you up voluntarily, to tell you that I have an alibi for the murder of Paul Chambers, last night.'

He sighed. 'I see. I assumed you were referring to the murder of Robert Kingston. I couldn't understand why you hadn't told us before.'

'I have no alibi for Kingston's murder, and I shouldn't have to provide one. But you took it upon yourself to suspect me, and this time I have got an alibi, and I want you to know about it!'

Really the man was infuriating. Perhaps he was stupid. Perhaps his supreme physical fitness and intense blue gaze had blinded her to his lack of brain.

'Is there any reason why anyone *should* suspect you of the murder of Mr Chambers?' he asked. 'We really are very busy here, you know. We don't need frivolous calls from the public clogging up the system.'

Gah!

'Assuming the same person killed both doctors, obviously you've got a nutcase with a medical fixation on your hands. Surely this new development must clear several suspects from the first case, for example Tessa Kingston?'

'And why should we assume the same person committed both crimes? Do you have information about them? Been doing some more nocturnal jogging?'

This sounded like some kind of obscene double entendre. She resisted the temptation to say 'Ooh, Matron!' 'The two killings have features in common, haven't they? The bash on the head, the pierced hands, the mutilation relating to the victim's medical specialism...'

'That's rather more information than has been given out so far,' he retorted sharply. 'May I ask where you obtained this information?'

'You may, or you may ask who told me.' She was sick of his pompous police-speak. Any minute now he'd say 'whilst', or 'commence'. Well backatcha! 'Ay was hinformed of the crayme by a journalistic colleague, whose name Ay ham not at liberty to reveal. We journalists must protect our sources.'

'I see. I should have known.' That little scrote from the *Evening Guardian*! Mouthy git. 'All I can say is that the police are keeping an open mind.'

'Really? Is this a new policy? I'm sure Tessa will be pleased to hear it.'

'All I can say at this time is that we are investigating a possible link between the two killings.' He spoke as if through gritted teeth. 'If you can give a checkable alibi for the evening and night, fine. In the event we want you to come in and sign a statement we'll contact you.'

Don't hold your breath, he implied, as if she was foisting herself on the police for her own entertainment. It was as if he had never hinted she might be a suspect.

'Alright then, I spent the afternoon, the evening, and in fact the whole night, with a doctor from the hospital - you know, Kingston's old stamping ground. Jamie Lau. He will be able to confirm that. And of course, I stand alibi for him.'

A brief silence. When he spoke it was in a more hostile tone.

'I see. I must say, you 'journalists' go to great lengths to chase up information.'

His tone implied she was some amoral hackette willing to sleep with anybody who would give her a few lines for the paper.

'It was no hardship, believe me, and yes, it was a case of 'great lengths," she said sweetly, hoping Will hadn't been

267

laid in months and serve him right.

'Anyway,' he went on, 'there is no reason to suppose Dr Lau was ever a suspect in the Kingston case. Unless you have information to that effect, of course?'

'If you want information about Jamie, you can get it yourself, I'm sure you have your own methods. Not the same as mine, I hope, I don't want him exhausted. I assumed anyone who knew Kingston was a suspect, that's all.'

CHAPTER TWENTY-SEVEN

'We'll be in touch, if we need any more assistance,' Will barked, and slammed the phone down. Like he didn't have enough to contend with, she had to go rubbing his nose in her filthy slutty goings on... Will muttered and threw innocent papers about until his long suffering colleagues had gathered for a briefing on this new development. The station was buzzing with the news of Chambers' murder, and the phrase 'serial killer' was being passed round like a fat joint, getting the younger officers high as kites.

'Right.' Will put up photographs of Paul Chambers, alive and dead, next to those of Robert Kingston, and Hassan gave a brief summing up of the crime and how things stood. The close-up of Chambers' scrotal wound caused a group wince among the male officers and the excitement about serial killers took a rest while they took in the reality of what had happened to a man like themselves.

'Due to the obvious similarity between the crimes, we have to consider they might have been committed by the same person, or persons. There are some confusing factors however. Sometimes it's hard to tell if a feature is a difference or a similarity.' Hassan pointed to the two photographs of Kingston's head and Chambers' groin. 'Different wounds, yet both seem to be references to the victims' specialisms, orthopaedics and urology.' He pointed to the two pictures of the hands with their metal piercings. 'Both had their hands pinned down with sharp implements. Different implements were used however.'

'Sarge, the implements also refer to their specialisms.' Paul got in first before Sally could start her arse-kissing routine.

'Quite right lad.' Hassan was all approval.

Paul wanted more. 'So that suggests the Operator did both of them...'

Will blew up at this. 'The *who*? *What* did you say?'

'Erm, the Operator, the serial killer Guv...'

'I only hope you'll be as quick to catch this serial killer as you've been to adopt the sensationalist name invented by that excuse for a reporter who was getting under our feet last night, and whom I suspect of using police radio frequencies.'

Paul subsided.

'I'm afraid the media are already riding on that bandwagon,' Hassan said philosophically. 'It's going to be hard to avoid the term.'

'Yeah I know.' Will pushed up his hair into spikes. It already looked rumpled due to lack of sleep. 'But I don't want you all assuming this 'Operator' actually exists. As DS Massum has been pointing out, the evidence is ambiguous. Yes, the killer used implements on the hands in a similar way, and used the surgeons' own tools, which seems like the same MO. BUT the killer or killers used implements already at the scene. Is that another link? Or is it a sign that one of these killings was dressed up to look like the other? If pins taken from Kingston's room had been used on Chambers we'd have a definite sign of a single killer. We've got nothing from forensics yet except it looks like Chambers' killer used one of the scalpels on his um, privates before pinning his right hand with it.'

'Is Chambers right or left handed?' Paul was back in the game.

'What, you think he might have done it himself?' mocked Sally.

'Hardly. But maybe it's significant you know. Symbolic like. The hand that did the operations, being spiked with the scalpel that he did them with after it had done his operation...' Paul was getting lost in a chain of connections.

'Fair enough, Paul. You could follow that up. Hassan?'

'Right well as I was saying, at the moment it could be the same killer. But we are not dismissing the possibility of two separate crimes. There are such things as copycat killings. Also, murder for personal gain or other reasons can be disguised as a motiveless killing, and how better than to give the impression of a crazed serial killer on the loose? Even Agatha Christie thought of that one.'

'Maybe we should bring her in on suspicion,' muttered Kev to Paul.

'So, we need to follow up all the possibilities. Are there

any suspects in the Kingston case we can eliminate, if it does turn out to be the Op- the same killer?'

'We don't have many named and identified so far. But there's Tessa Kingston. Kev, you were watching her last night I think?'

'Yes Guv. She was at the gym, till late. For nearly three hours, as per usual.'

Sally added, 'She does a long session each time, longer since Kingston died. Working off her grief perhaps? Or guilt. She does classes, machines, has a swim, sauna, steam room, you name it she does it there. I checked all that with the desk a while back.'

'Kev. Could she have slipped out the back, assuming you were alert enough to spot her leaving by the front doors?'

'I suppose it's technically possible, but she'd have to get back in, in order to come out the front doors at the end of her session, and the back doors, fire doors, only open from inside. And yes Guv, I was watching. I'm sure she didn't slip by me.'

'Why would she murder Chambers anyway? Doesn't mean she didn't kill Kingston,' asked Sally. 'And if Kev was following Tessa, nobody was watching Tara.'

'Oh come on,' Paul scoffed. 'Why would she go after Chambers?'

'To get Tessa off the hook, of course. She's emotionally involved, wracked with guilt for letting Tessa stay in an

abusive marriage for so long... I mean if that story's true...'
She tailed off.

Hassan resumed. 'Connections between the victims. Both surgeons. They both played golf, at different clubs, though Kingston was once a member of the city club too so presumably knew him. They trained at the same university, though Chambers is older - he'd done some travelling before he signed up to be a medical student. But they only trained together until they began to follow different specialisms. So far we've not found that they were close friends or saw a lot of each other. Lots of doctors in this region know each other.'

'Could be some nut who hates all doctors. Could be some wannabe doctor who didn't make the grades!'

'Good point Sally. Maybe you could check out that angle?'

'Is it still our case though Guv? Chambers lived in town. Won't the city lads and lasses take over?'

'No, we've agreed on an approach. Bearing in mind they might be two separate killings, the second disguised to look like the first, City are looking into Chambers' case and we are still looking into Kingston's. Any connections either of us find, we share.' Will flattened his hair down. It had been standing up for record time. 'But just to say all we've found out so far about Paul Chambers is he was a quiet, hardworking, rather sad lonely man, at least since his wife died. Not at all like Kingston. And you don't tend to get so many failures with vasectomies. Serious complications are rare.'

'You'd not get me under the knife,' said Paul.

'Not after seeing those crime scene pix.' Kev shuddered dramatically.

Sally snorted. 'Huh. Try childbirth!'

Erica was sure this new murder, tragic though it was, would at least let Tessa off the hook, though Will had been evasive. Not to mention downright nasty when he heard about her and Jamie. Like he had any right to an opinion of her morals! A couple of days later she was just thinking she hadn't heard from the blonde sisters lately, when she had a call from Tara to say Tessa had moved back into Kingston's house.

'Not the most pleasant associations, but she's determined to stay there. She says it's her home now and she wants to start standing on her own two feet. I think the new murder has made her feel less under suspicion though personally I think they still have her in mind. I know she would love to see you. You've been such a help and support to both of us.'

Erica decided to call round. She hadn't been back to Kingston's house since the night she'd jogged past it and the golf ball had hit her arm, narrowly missing her head. The first time she went there, she'd found Kingston's body. Not her favourite venue. As her therapist, Erica wondered how Tessa was coping. She decided not to ring first but to 'drop in' when 'passing', to get more idea of Tessa's state of mind.

She rang the doorbell, feeling a new chill as she relived standing there waiting to interview Kingston, bracing herself to put up with his patronising manner, his aggressive arrogance, unaware that he had been rendered harmless for good by someone who had objected to him much more drastically than she had.

Tessa answered the door and broke into a warm smile. Her loose blonde waves were styled into natural-looking order, and she wore black cropped leggings, gold gladiator sandals, and a furry white sweater with little pearl beads sewn on in swirls.

'Erica! Come in!'

Erica followed her through the hall, noticing that the murder room door was shut. Tessa led the way into a big living room with an arrangement of seating put together like gigantic pricey Lego with occasional square glass tables. The floor was polished hardwood with carefully scattered rugs to trip over. A wall hung gas 'fire' flickered quietly.

'I hope you don't mind me calling, but I was out on a run, and I was passing.' If her relationship with Tessa was still therapist/patient, she was technically out of line turning up unasked at her house. She was hoping that they'd progressed beyond that after all the trials of the past few weeks. Tessa hadn't rung Erica herself. Was that progress to independence, guilt at getting Erica involved, or was she embarrassed at having told Erica about Kingston's abuse? Tessa might want to back off from her after confiding in her so freely. It was a common enough reaction.

'You look wet. And a bit muddy...' Tessa glanced at the floor.

'Sorry.' Erica kicked off her trainers and took them back into the hall, leaving them by the front door.

Back in the living room she perched on the edge of a seat, aware of her mud-splashed legs and the pale cream of the suite. Luckily it was the inevitable leather. The coffee table was scattered with leaflets and brochures. Colour charts from decorating firms. Swatches of fabric. And details of houses for sale from estate agents in the town.

'Thinking of moving?' Erica asked, Peter Wimsey to the life.

'I might. Or I might just have it completely redone. When probate's granted, I'll have enough money to live on for a good while, so I can take my time deciding. This place needs a makeover anyway even to sell. And so many bad memories here.'

She gazed into the ersatz fire. A house where she'd been a terrified wife, and where her husband had been murdered by some intruder. Was moving back in, planning the future, a step towards independent adulthood? Or was Tessa just waiting to live on her husband's money? Erica had launched herself into investigating Kingston in the hope of proving her innocent, or at least not the only suspect. As usual, she had felt too protective of her patient, too involved, hoped to save her, set her free, while it seemed that Tessa preferred to have Farrow and Ball repaint the bars of the cage. But was she just trying to control Tessa, mould her in her own image? But then denial, and surfaces, were what had sustained Tessa for many years, maybe always. No big surprise she'd cling to a strategy so familiar when so much else had changed.

'You're so fit, Erica. And thin. I've been spending more time at the gym myself since all this happened. Gotta keep in shape, haven't we, us girls? Got to be a bit careful to pick the right exercise though. Men don't like a girl to have too many muscles.'

And there it was. Forming yourself according to what men liked. Had this woman learned nothing? Erica stopped herself pointing out that a few more muscles could have helped her fight off Kingston at the beginning and avoid living in terror for years. Her period of self-analysis was over, it seemed. Back to the airhead. Well why shouldn't she be an airhead, Erica you control freak, she was berating herself, when Tessa topping up her cup paused to pick up a strand of Erica's hair, feeling it with her fingers like fabric in a dress shop.

'How do you get yours that colour?'

'Choosing the right parents, I suppose. Being outside in

the summer. Ow!'

'Oops sorry. My ring...' Tessa disentangled her ring, which flashed through Erica's hair. Erica felt trapped and impatient, wanting to pull away but unable to.

'It's gone all curly and big now with the damp. I hate that.'

'I use these new straighteners, they're just as good for curling. You can only get them from Harrods. Or Bendel's in New York City.' She released herself from the hair. 'This ring came from Tiffany's on 5th Avenue! Robert bought it for me to celebrate something, being made Captain of the Golf Club or some big payout from private work or something. It cost a mint. He was good to me sometimes.'

To Erica, the hoop of diamonds and sapphires crisscrossed with platinum looked like barbed wire. Symbol of ownership and wealth. A sign of his success.

'Erm yes very nice. Tessa, have the police been in touch with you, since the second murder?'

'They've asked me to stay in the area. Tara told me all the details. That must have been some grievance the killer had. She thought it would confirm my innocence but that snide Inspector Bennett as good as hinted that *I* might have done it, the second one I mean, to cover up my tracks, make it look as if a psycho serial killer did both killings! Tara says it's just police desperation. She told them, the risk of doing a second murder, when they've no hard evidence against me for the first one, well, it would be insane.'

'I did think the police would be watching you after releasing you without charge. They should be able to provide you with an alibi themselves.'

'That's what Tara said. Most of the officers were called up to the city for the big match. They admitted, when she pressed them, there was one man watching me at the relevant time. He must have been very fed up sitting outside a women's gym instead of watching the football.'

Will must be spitting nails; his own man gives Tessa an alibi.

'Did you know Paul Chambers?'

'Really, Erica, you sound like the police sometimes. No, well I've probably met him, I don't remember though. He might have been at some big do or other when we were. It seems Robert knew him when they were younger and through the city Golf Club. But he never talked about him that I can remember.'

'I was only thinking the police would have a job linking you with him if they can't prove you knew him at all.'

'Well I'm trying to stay positive, like you've always said. They're bound to catch the Operator soon. I'm not sure yet whether a murder happening here will be good or bad for selling this place, if I do. Usually, these houses go for a bomb, you know.'

'Even with the occasional golf ball crashing through the conservatory?'

'Absolutely, Erica. When Robert's mother died, he had

no trouble selling her house at an inflated price. That sad old guy Harry Archer jumped at it. Literally, about an hour after the FOR SALE sign went up, he was round here! Golf's like a religion, you should hear them all at the club droning on about their scores or whatever they are. Robert used to make me go to the social do's of course. Thank god, never again!'

Was there any point in going to the Golf Club do with Mel? It didn't sound like much fun. Still, they couldn't *all* be that bad. Tessa was bound to be biased, associating the sport with Robert Kingston and all his cruelty. Speaking of which...

'Tessa, you know I write for the *Evening Guardian*. I've been researching a piece about your late husband. I've turned up a lot of things, like your experiences of him, which are at odds with his public image. Legally, I can write what I like. And there don't seem to be any close relatives to be upset, apart from you.'

'Oh no, Stephen Blair and Robert weren't close. Robert didn't feel he was worth spending time with. Bit of a loser. He's left him some money, which I was quite surprised about, but I suppose blood's thicker than water.'

'Good because I'd like to write the piece warts and all.'

'Ooh yes. I'd love all his stuck-up cronies to know what he was really like. I'm sure they all despise me for leaving him, not that any of them have bothered to contact me. It's time they knew why I left. Well that he was violent and abusive. I don't want you to quote anything he used to say to me. I couldn't bear people here to know that intimate stuff. But go on, give the rotten bastard hell!'

'By the way, Tessa, what about a funeral? I can see how difficult it might be for you.' As the almost-ex, do you turn up in veil and hankie, sobbing? Or dance on the grave? Or not turn up at all? Hallmark should do a card for this tricky social situation.

'Those old bores at his church are going to arrange a memorial service and the Golf Club have offered to do the drinks and nibbles afterwards. They pushed a note through the door here to let me know. As his executor, Stephen will be sorting out the funeral. Some people would expect me to be there, but I don't want people pointing and staring. And gossiping about whether I killed him! I couldn't bear it.'

After a pause, she went on thoughtfully, 'I expect Stephen's been hoping I did. He'd have got all the money then. And I hear he's hard up. I don't want him staring at me, giving me the evil eye.'

Erica jogged home along the sea front, the sea darkening to violet, the sand to brown, the wind colder though the fine drizzle had stopped. As she ran, just as when she was swimming lengths, her mind ran on tracks of its own. Two murders. Two doctors, surgeons, consultants, but in different spheres of medicine. What were the possibilities?

She listed them mentally, as her breath chilled her throat and her feet pounded the damp ground.

1. A serial killer was on the loose, aka 'The Operator', a nutjob who had it in for doctors in general. It was unlikely that a patient had personal grudges against an orthopaedic surgeon *and* a vasectomy specialist. This being the case, there could be others to come. The speculation about Kingston's death had alarmed the medical profession. Now normally complacent consultants would be going around in pairs, feeling the fear that women so often felt, though this time there'd be no helpful police messages for surgeons to 'stay indoors' as there were when women were attacked. Would the Operator stick with male surgeons, or include female ones? An interesting thought... anyway, if this was the case, Erica didn't have the resources and computer software to collate all the factors in common between the two victims. Both were men, and not young. But then most consultants were. Both were involved in private practice as well as the NHS. But then again, so were many hospital doctors. Both played golf; so did lots of doctors and white collar workers, and they weren't even in the same club. They lived in the same area, but not the same place.

Even if the police had DNA, unless they had the profile on record already, how would they find the killer - they could hardly test everyone in the area.

2. Kingston had been murdered by someone with a personal motive, hatred and resentment, a desire for

revenge. Someone Erica might have spoken to already, or not. A patient, a colleague, the possibilities were potentially endless for all practical purposes. Then, after that, someone else had done a copycat crime, killing Chambers for some reason of their own, either personal or professional grudge, hoping to pass it off as the work of the first killer and disguise it as a serial killing. Would she be able to find out about Paul Chambers as she had about Robert Kingston? Maybe the editor would let her do an article on Chambers as well. Good excuse for making enquiries. Erica's thoughts leaped over the little obstacle of Dunne reading her exposé of Kingston as her trainers did over puddles.

3. Kingston had been murdered by someone with a personal motive, someone so concerned about being caught that they killed Chambers to make it look as if a serial killer was on the loose. Very risky. But possible, given someone so twisted by hatred that they could hammer nails into a human head with a rock.

The two killings were similar, but not the same. The killer had echoed the first killing by pinning Chambers' hands down after bashing him over the head. Had the second killing been done by someone else or the same person varying the mutilations to match the speciality of the victim? It seemed to be open to question, perhaps deliberately so. Where to go now, apart from the shower, and to work.

CHAPTER TWENTY-EIGHT

Erica's pregnant patient was preparing to give birth by taking Caullophyllum, and was now asking for Staphysagria to take with her for pain after childbirth. She'd had a rough time in a Dickensian hospital with her first baby, a combination of modern technology and medieval morality having ruined the experience for her. This time she wanted to get it right. She had of course already been drinking raspberry leaf tea, an ancient herbal strategy for an easy labour. Erica had converted her to homeopathy by curing her horrendous morning sickness.

As they came to the end of the consultation, her patient remarked, 'You know, I'm really grateful to have you to talk to, and to have the remedies. It makes me feel more in control. I'm glad you're willing to prescribe these remedies, but you don't lay down the law. Some alternative practitioners are very extreme. A friend of mine was having bad morning sickness, and when I told her how you helped me, she went to a homeopath up in the city, where she lives.

'He refused to help her unless she turned over all her health care to him, and insisted she didn't see her GP any more or even go to antenatal appointments at the hospital. So she left him and bought herself some tablets like mine, and it didn't work. So now she's sceptical about alternative medicine.'

Erica sighed. She wasn't surprised they hadn't worked, since they hadn't been prescribed specifically for her. Some other remedy might have been perfect.

'Who was this guy?'

'He's called Craig Anderson. He hasn't been in the area long. He makes a religion out of alternative medicine, it seems. But he does get clients, especially those who have had bad experiences of GPs and hospitals.'

It might be worth contacting Craig Anderson for the health page. Extreme views were good for stirring up readers' interest. It would have been good to have done the interview with Kingston with his disdain for alternative medicine, and then one with Anderson with the opposite views. Clearly Anderson was going to end up in the newspapers one day anyhow. Probably being sued by some patient's family. He was playing with fire keeping people away from all medicine apart from his own. How can people like Kingston and Anderson be so sure they're right? Erica, devil's full time advocate, almost envied that certainty.

The certainty and extreme viewpoint of the Operator. How powerful the killer or killers must have felt standing over a man with his hands nailed down, rendered unresisting by a skull fracture. If this is a serial killer who hates doctors in general, there's no way he'd give up a buzz like that. The ultimate thrill. The kind of thrill Kingston, ironically, might have enjoyed if his tendencies had been allowed to get out of control.

Now there were two murders, #theOperator was well and truly trending on Twitter. Erica watched with fascination and sometimes disgust. On Twitter, or in comments on online newspaper columns, on facebook or messageboard discussions, surprisingly large numbers of people had their own tales of woe at the hands of doctors and surgeons. Sometimes incompetence or negligence, but most often lack of empathy, a callous uncaring attitude which left scars. Sadly unsurprising was how many others were making a sick joke of it ('Paul Chambers is asking, can he have his ball back?'). Others were outraged on behalf of such eminent victims and were blaming the government for NHS cuts, the police for incompetence, and a list of other regular blame-ees for assorted sins. There were troll-like provocative statements ('smug middle-class bastards had it coming!') and speculation about The Operator's psychology, blaming his/her mother, father, ('he must have suffered appalling childhood abuse!') the government ('NHS cuts inspiring hate crimes'), even the victims ('they must have done something to provoke such violence').

Another more local effect of creating the monster that was The Operator was that Stacey came in from the cold. She rang to face whatever music would greet her unmasking as the homeopathic drug dealer of Wydsand nightlife, unable to resist the possibility of being near the epicentre of a publicity earthquake. Erica's investigations were her only way of getting in on it. Erica greeted her with anticipation. How would Stacey handle this?

'Hi Erica. Just thought Aa'd call to say, you're welcome!'

'I'm sorry?' Why am I apologising, Erica asked herself.

'You're welcome. Ye knaa. Me ringin the bizzies to tell them ye were in danger.'

'Oh I see. What made you think I was in danger Stacey?'

'Whey, them lads is bad news man. That Scotty... Aa knaa his bro. Hard bastard, and not in a good way.'

'So you thought I'd need rescuing by Will Bennett? Gosh thanks.'

As ever, sarcasm was wasted on Stacey. Not that she wasn't bright but she couldn't be arsed to listen carefully enough to pick up a tone of voice.

'Nee probs, pet.'

'I thought you'd resigned from your 'internship'. Not hearing from you.'

'Yeah well. Bored out me tree at home. Me mam expects iz to help look after our Noosh. Aa mean, Aa love the bairn to bits ye knaa, but kids are so bliddy full-on! And Aa didn't want to upset her routine like. Aa mean, it gives me mam sommat to dee, looking after our Noosh. Gives meaning to her life poor owld soul. Aa wouldn't want to come between them. So, can Aa, ye knaa, come back like? Aa've felt bad about letting yer doon.'

'Oh, you mean by stealing my remedies and selling them as E's?'

Silence. Stacey's mind raced as she tried to work out whether denial or confession would be least effort and most effective at getting her back into Ivy Lodge.

'Aa nevvor. Whee sez? Aa'll sue!' she tried.

'Will Bennett says. He found the tabs and analysed them. They are homeopathic pills. And one of the lads asked me if I got them from 'her' presumably meaning you.'

'Fuck. Busted.' Erica heard her mutter. Aloud, 'Whey ye cannit prove it was me, nor your tablets. There's loads of homeos aboot. And neebody'd die of them tablets would they? It's not like there's owt in them but sugar.'

'Remind me to remind you what I do here Stacey.' She launched into a lecture on stealing, trust issues, illegality, risking her business and reputation, feeling it had to be said. 'And I can't have you nicking my stuff!'

'Aa won't! Aa promise. Not that Aa did, mind. Please man Erica, lerriz come back. Aa rang the polis to help ye. Honest.'

'So why the phonebox?'

'Me mobile was chargin...'

'The anonymous tip-off? Let me guess, it was in the hope the police would show up and chase the lads off before there was any chance of me finding out about the tablets they had. Sadly, the police already knew about it and so do I. Not impressed, Stacey.'

'Aw haway, man Erica, Aa'll get we a takeaway the neet. Me Jobseeker's just come in. My treat. Look, Aa'm sorry, OK? I didn't think them pills were worth owt. Aa mean, *ye* sell them way dearer than Aa did! Haway, we're a team, ye and me.'

Omigod. Really? Erica's turn to switch off her ears as Stacey launched into a tirade of denial, promises, rash claims, and guilt tripping.

But if she took Stacey back, she'd be saving little Noosh from her ministrations, just as she'd saved Stacey from giving birth to her in a filthy alley. And Stacey had shown admirable self-control, not mentioning Chambers' murder and her own relentless quest to be where the media might suddenly be at any moment. Erica had no illusions about why her company was so attractive to Stacey but she felt a responsibility to Noosh, the beautiful baby who'd fought her way out of Stacey's belly.

'So, chips or rice? Indian or Chinese? Aa bet ye've had enough Chinese lately ye dirty bugger.'

Erica recognised this as an endearment. She was already calculating whether she'd done enough exercise to 'earn' a takeaway, even a carefully calorie-conscious vegetable-heavy option. God it was wearing to have this inner voice, like carrying a school bully in your head. But the alternative – no, let's not go there. Nothing tastes as good as skinny feels, in the immortal words of Kate Moss. Stacey's voice cut into her thoughts.

'Ye bring the booze. Aa'll get we some chips, fried rice, giant battered onion rings and curry sauce.'

In the Indian takeaway, the TV news was all about the killing, and Erica saw Paul Chambers for the first time, smiling soberly in the photo taken before someone bashed his head in and slashed his genitals like a bag of boil in the bag rice. Thick grey hair, grey eyes creased narrow as if he spent a lot of time concentrating; pale skin, firm mouth. He had a fleshy nose with a suggestion of a cleft in the tip, echoed in the dimple in his chin. An indoor face of central heating and windowless corridors; he looked as if he'd spent more time in hospitals or seeing patients at home than on the golf course.

The men waiting for meals looked away from the screen, shuffling uncomfortably on their plastic benches as if to shift their beloved balls away from any stray scalpels.

Erica and Stacey lugged their fragrant bag of food back to Erica's, nibbling poppadoms. So they were a team now. Oh well. Erica told Stacey what Gary Thomas had told her about the murder.

'It's aal ower the meedja. Everybody's talking about it.' Stacey was wistful. 'Ah mean, just think what the Operator might do to a gynaecologist, or a brain surgeon... or an eye surgeon...' She ladled bright crimson chunks of chicken tikka masala onto the alp of colourful rice and rather flaccid chips on her plate. Erica had shelled out for the non-fat and non-carbs food groups.

Erica forked the more interesting bits from her sag paneer onto a spoonful of rice. 'I'm going to see Craig Anderson. A fundamentalist homeopath.'

'He been pinching your patients? Aa'll get him for ye.' She tore a naan bread asunder as if it were Anderson's liver.

'No thanks, but he might be putting off a few prospective ones. He's asking for trouble.'

'Aye. Aa can see your Gary and the like crucifying him in the meedja. He'll kill somebody and their family'll take him to the cleaner's.'

'*My* Gary? Eeewww. He's ecstatic about this new murder, no doubt already heading to London for a career in one of the national tabloids.'

'Yeah? What's Gary look like? He shaggable?' The magic word 'tabloids' had its usual effect on Stacey.

'Only if you hate yourself.' Erica wondered if she could get any more information from him about Paul Chambers before he went. 'Anyway. This Anderson is just as arrogant as Kingston.'

Stacey licked the serving spoon clean. 'Hey, mebbe he doesn't just go for proper real doctors and that. Mebbe he goes for weirdy types like this Craig thingy and aal. Or ye! Eeh, ye'd better be careful.'

'No way. He'd be more likely to go for a high profile therapist.'

'Yeah, like a health writer with her picture in the paper every week?'

'That's ridiculous. I'm so - harmless.'

'Makes you all the easier to kill. Hey, Aa could be your bodyguard. That'd look great on me CV. Aa could get a job as a club bouncer. Get in free. Get all the lads after iz. And if the Operator tried to take ye out, Aa'd kick his ass for him.' Stacey went into a happy dream of headlines and TV appearances, invites to be on 'I'm a celebrity, get me out of here' and the like. 'Only Aa'm not eating worms.'

'What?' Erica was mystified by this reference to ordeal by invertebrates on reality TV. 'They might never catch the Operator. I can take reasonable precautions, but they can hardly ask all the health professionals in the land to stay behind bolted doors for ever.'

'Precautions like not jogging along creepy golf courses past murder scenes at night?'

'This nutter attacks people in their homes.'

'Erm, who got hit by a golf ball?'

'Hardly the same as being nailed to a table and having your pride and joy pruned. Are you going to say the golf ball was hurled by the Operator, aiming to fire it down my throat as a deadly mockery of a homeopathic tablet?'

'Omigod! Hells yeah! Erica, ye nearly got Operated!' Stacey punched the air in excitement. 'What's Gary's number?' She made a grab at Erica's phone.

'I wasn't serious... give me that back! You don't think?

Nah. Get a grip Stacey. Where were we? Oh yes, Craig Anderson. I must admit I hadn't thought that someone like him could also be a target. I was thinking, could the Operator *be* someone *like* Anderson - an alternative therapist who is violently anti-doctor? I was already thinking of interviewing him for the health page. I bet he'll jump at the chance to publicise his views. And it'll give me a chance to find out if there's any chance he might be the Operator.'

'Aye, even better! Investigate now, headlines later. Bigger ones.'

'Besides, the Operator will feel I'm on his side when he reads my piece on Kingston.'

'Yeah, brilliant. Aa'll open another bottle eh. We can drink to bein celebs! Aa'll have a Lulu Guiness handbag... Noosh'll have designer clothes... mebbe Victoria Beckham...'

CHAPTER TWENTY-NINE

The next day, Erica googled Craig Anderson and called him. A quiet, confident but restrained voice answered.

She introduced herself. 'I've heard you have some interesting views on conventional as opposed to alternative medicine... I wondered if you'd be willing to talk to me about your practice and your opinions on the future of homeopathy?'

'That sounds interesting. I welcome every chance to spread the word about the work I do.' He sounded wary though.

'Might get you some new patients too.' She was poking him with a stick.

'That would not be my primary purpose.' She could feel the drop in temperature over the phone. 'It's about truth. I would insist on approving everything you write in advance of publication, of course. Would there be a proper contract and an honorarium?'

A what? Who did he think he was? If she wasn't on a fishing expedition, she'd have told him to get lost. Here she was, offering him a free advert, and he was making conditions. Swallowing her irritation she explained that no, there wouldn't be either of those, it was a local paper and she had no budget for that. He still went for the bait of a public platform though and she agreed to meet him at his practice later in the week.

Will Bennett and Paul Lozinski sat in a scruffy flat carpeted by pizza boxes and filmed with dust. Will felt his usual mix of pity, exasperation, and revulsion at the total human defeat which was writ large on every surface of the place where Pete Barnes existed, nursing his groin and his grudge. Paul was less concerned about the interior design, the place didn't look that different to his own bedroom when he wasn't forced by some lass to tidy it up. Still, he was relieved when the Guv refused mugs of tea for both of them; there's muck and there's other folks' muck and you don't want it in your mouth.

They'd driven up the coast to Blyth to interview Barnes, as his name had been on Chambers' records as a patient and he lived in their area rather than that of the City force. They'd been systematically checking patients of both dead doctors to find grudges or motives, cross-checking any relevant details with complaints to the Hospital Trusts. Sally had the bright idea of looking up complications of vasectomies and orthopaedic operations to see if they came up on any blogs or forums. Barnes' name had come up after exhaustive searching of key words from the medical records. Bright lass, mused Will. She'd be a Sergeant soon at this rate. And always keen to take advice or learn from him...

'Here you go.' Pete Barnes came in with three cans of Pepsi and handed them round. He popped his own can and started drinking as Will put his down unopened. All that sugar! Paul wiped the top unselfconsciously and started glugging too. The two younger men belched simultaneously and grinned at each other briefly. Barnes, late thirties, looked years younger for a moment then relapsed into what seemed to be his customary strained look. He was very tense. They could smell it in his sweat. His belly flopped out over the belt of his jeans under a baggy old tee shirt. Will kicked off.

'Mr Barnes, we're investigating patients of two surgeons recently found dead. You may have...'

'The Operator. Yes I know.'

'I believe you were a patient of Mr Chambers?'

Barnes nodded. His hand clenched a little round the can. Will noticed the paper-thin metal dimpling.

'You went to him for a vasectomy about three and a half years ago?'

'You know I did. Or you wouldn't be here.' He'd become sullen. Well, nobody likes being suspected of serial killing. Don't read too much into his body language.

Will glanced at Paul, who took over. 'Made a bit of a mess of it didn't he? Horrible thing to happen, mate. You have my sympathy.'

'The hospital trust don't seem to think I have any right to complain. And most other people seem to think it's funny.'

'Some of these surgeons, god complex you know, they don't like admitting they slipped up...'

'Chambers told me it sometimes happens. He couldn't do anything, he said. Couldn't, or wouldn't.'

'So Mr Barnes how do you feel now he's dead?' Will cut in from the other side. Formal cop, friendly cop.

'I...well I don't know. The news, they said he'd probably felt nothing. That makes him better off than me.'

'You're still alive.' Will was cold.

'I know I'm alive because it still hurts. Otherwise, what kind of life have I got? Marriage gone, sex life gone...'

'You've still got the internet. We found this on the forum you've been frequenting.'

Paul read the extract aloud. 'Be warned guys, don't get the snip without checking all the things that can go wrong. I had mine more than three years ago. Everything went fine, until five months after the op. Left testicle swelled up, hurt like buggery. Hospital said I'd got epididimytis. It's a complication of vasectomy they don't tell you about, well nobody told me. They gave me painkillers and antibiotics and sent me home. It still aches a lot of the time, and often it flares up into a stabbing pain, like a knife in the balls. My wife ended up leaving me with all the stress on our marriage. We wanted a carefree life without worrying, we thought kids would be a pain, now I can't have any and I've got no marriage. No relationships neither. Oh and my ex-wife? She's got a kid now and another on the way with her new bloke. Changed her mind. But I don't blame her. It was me wanted the snip. Didn't want the bother of condoms. If anybody knows anything that would help, PLEASE PLEASE PLEASE TELL ME.'

As Paul read, Will watched Barnes tensing up still more, his face set. Poor bastard he thought, unconsciously crossing his long legs.

'Well people should know!' Barnes burst out. 'Chambers took my money and I lay down on the table and let him carve up my balls and I can't do nothing about it!'

'Mr Barnes, where were you on the night of...'

'You can't think I did it!'

'Well let's see, 'stabbing pain like a knife in the balls.' You wrote that. And 'I lay down on the table and let him carve up my balls and I can't do anything about it.' You just said that! Somebody did that very thing to Chambers!'

'God mate, I wouldn't blame you, wanting some payback for that.' Paul Lozinski did the sympathy bit. And in fact he meant it. Well almost.

'So I ask you again, where were you...'

'I was here, watching TV, drinking beer, like every night.'

'So you have no alibi.'

'No. But I didn't do it! And you'll not prove I did. You can look at CCTV for days and you'll not find me anywhere near him. And all his troubles are over, mine aren't. It's a rare complication, they said. He didn't do anything wrong,

299

they said. No negligence. He warned me there could be pain for a time in some cases. He didn't say permanent pain!'

'Thank you Mr Barnes, for your help. And we're sorry to have troubled you. We'll be in touch if there's anything further.'

On the way back into Wydsand, the two officers were silent for most of the way, thinking dark masculine thoughts. Just as they drove past Sainsbury's, Paul said, 'They've got a bogof on Mates condoms this week. I'm stocking up. Poor bugger. Gives a whole new meaning to 'a bag for life'.'

Meanwhile back at the station, Masum and Sally were discussing their visit to a fairly well-to-do couple, the Milligans, who lived in Wydsand. She was younger than him. The second wife. They'd talked to them separately, Sally following her into the kitchen while Hassan did the blokey bit with husband.

'He seems OK with it all. Shocked about the murder. His then wife insisted on him having a vasectomy after their second child. She had a bad time with them both and didn't trust contraception. Chambers counselled them to wait until they were older, more sure, but they went ahead. No problems, until the marriage broke up and he marries wife number two. So he goes for a reversal. But it doesn't work. Rotten luck but he's an educated guy. He

knew it was a long shot. Doesn't seem to blame Chambers
for that. Says him and his wife were together that night at
home. I can't help wondering if it's worth chasing up all the
reversals that didn't work from Chambers' records, unless
the blokes made a fuss or threatened him. Most people
know the score.'

'Hm. Alright for *him* to be rational and fair. He's got
two kids. He sees them weekends and holidays. She's got
no kids of her own and never will. She's got to share him
with his kids. She's got to watch him with his kids playing
footie and what not. She said more or less what he said, but
I could tell she minded. D'you know Sarge, when they got
married they asked for money instead of presents, to fund
his reversal? So their friends and family could help create
their new baby. Like, I don't know, like it was some kind
of magic, the more people involved wishing and praying
and hoping, the more likely the miracle would happen.
But it didn't. And she says they were together at home that
night as well. But they both have motive, irrational yes but
wanting kids isn't rational is it, and they are alibis for each
other.'

'Poor buggers. But yes, their alibis aren't much use.'

Will and Hassan compared notes. 'So', Hassan closed
another file on the computer, 'that's most of the known
disgruntled patients of either Chambers or Kingston who
live on our patch. I'll email this lot off to the city lads and

lasses and then we'll see if they've got anybody in their neck of the woods who fits either crime.'

'Right. Too much to hope we'd find somebody who'd had the snip from Chambers and a leg or arm pinned by Kingston and wasn't happy with either... Most of them don't seem to bear any grudge. They accept things go wrong sometimes. Like that patient of Kingston's, Lozinski and I called on her last thing. Seems philosophical about the result of her treatment. Didn't express any ill feeling it didn't work. Have you got her file there, it's a Laura Gibson.'

Over the next few days, in between seeing patients, Erica worked on her article on Kingston, typing and rewriting between appointments and late at night after the gym, trying hard to achieve some sort of distance, trying to be fair to both sides of his character. She described his undoubted skill as a surgeon, cited the positive opinions of some patients, how he'd changed their lives for the better, freeing them from crippling pain and stiffness with successful, if nowadays routine, joint replacements. How he enjoyed the status of consultant; how he tried to push forward the boundaries of his specialism, sometimes perhaps beyond what was of benefit to the individual patient, without mentioning names of course. She mentioned his position in the hospital, how exacting he was of students and staff under him, and how sometimes this could be overbearing, especially towards those who questioned him. Any information which had come from Jamie Lau, Laura Gibson, Gill Webster and Tilly O'Rourke she described as 'anonymous sources.'

Then, she told of how he had a somewhat cavalier attitude to pain relief. Even writing about it, she felt tainted by the obscene pleasure of the sadist. She wrote of him as a keen golfer, popular among professional men. Lastly, she described him as a devoted son who had bought his mother a large detached house next to his own. With Tessa's permission, backed up by Tara, she wrote about the apparently devoted husband, who had abused his wife if she crossed him to the point of violence and injury. Asking, why should we assume someone in a caring profession is perfect in every aspect of their lives? And that he did not deserve the horrible death which had found him at the hands of the killer now known as the Operator. He should have lived to face up to his treatment of his wife, as she had found the courage to assert herself and leave him.

At last it was finished. She emailed it feeling good about writing a balanced account. She stretched luxuriously, and went off for a hot shower. She emerged to find a mass of missed calls on her mobile and furious messages on her landline from Dunne to 'ring me back pronto!' She made a hot drink before ringing him, to have a gale force bollocking roaring into her ear.

'What the fuck are you playing at Erica? No way will

I print such scurrilous, libellous rubbish about a pillar of the community. You've lost your mind! How could I face the manager of the hospital trust? I play golf with him for Christ's sake! Way to give the *Evening* a bad name, throwing dirt on a local hero who can't speak up for himself. You should stick to your quack remedies and stop bothering the big boys.'

He ended the call.

She was raging. Bloody local golf clubs, hospitals, police hierarchies, male dominated, class oriented, money and status driven bunch of bastards. Probably all Freemasons as well. She'd heard Dunne was. He'd join anything if it would get him well in with the local movers and shakers, the bloated fish jammed into the regional puddle. He'd be drummed out if he allowed anyone to slag off a fellow trouser-leg roller-upper. He'd probably had to give some secret oath to uphold the honour of fellow members. She imagined him bedecked with arcane regalia, which in her mind was some kind of apron like her gran used to wear to wash up in, but with a Masonic design on it. A set square, wasn't it, their sign, and a pair of dividers, and wasn't there a hammer somewhere? Masons used hammers surely. Or was that the Soviet flag?

Dividers; metal spikes. And a hammer. Oh god. What if there was a Masonic connection here? What if the nails and rocks, after all even the ashtray used on Chambers was marble, used to hammer them into the victims' hands, and in Kingston's case, head, were meant to refer to the Masons? And wasn't it generally believed that top cops and judges were Masons? Was Will...? No, more likely the Superintendent. He'd rather die than wear an apron at home of course, but in a secret society of men, oh he'd be strapping on his pinny with the rest... She rang Will and left a message.

She had to get out and run off her fury, so she headed along the sea front. Increasingly she'd been running in the opposite direction to the lighthouse, crem, Kingston's house and the track behind it. She'd been running, or cycling the first part, south along the seafront, towards the great river mouth with its castle standing guard on the cliffs, and out along the pier to the smaller lighthouse on the end of it, which together with its twin on the south side of the river guided ships into their outstretched protective arms. It was a longer, stormier run, more open to sea wind and fret and huge waves washing over the pier if the sea was in a violent mood. She'd told Will where she was going so he could meet her if free, or ring back and arrange to talk.

Eventually having followed the curves of the succession of bays and the long stretch of pale gold beach between them she reached the lee of the castle, standing behind her high on the cliff as it had for centuries. She carried on along the pier on the north bank, waves boiling white crashing against it on her left, smoother but still heavy grey swell on her right, to the lighthouse on its end almost surrounded by sea. She watched the waves for a while, thinking about death, and murder, and bodies. She wanted to be here, when she died, in the North Sea's cold and boundless heart... the squat lighthouse straddled the end of the pier, hollowed underneath to form a rough stonework chamber open to the land side, and she was standing in there breathing hard, out of the worst of the wind, when a shadow filled the doorway and she turned to find Will Bennett there. He'd been running too, and was in his shorts and top, long and lean and dark, Wolfman to the life only a lot less hairy.

Will looked at Erica, so small and determined with her wild hair, her chest heaving with effort.

'It should be you that's called Will,' he surprised himself and her by saying.

'I did call you,' she said, confused.

'I mean you always look so determined. So much will power. Are you OK?'

'Of course I'm OK!' He'd put his foot in it already. 'Why wouldn't I...'

She made an effort to start again. 'I had an idea about Kingston.'

'Oh.' His chest was moving too, deeply but not as much as hers. Not that he was fitter, oh no, he must've run a lesser distance. Probably drove to the car park and then along the pier. She'd left the message saying where she was running. Maybe she'd hoped to meet like they had the first time, two runners by the sea, united in their driven self-punishment.

As she poured out her Masonic theory his eyes narrowed to chips of blue glass like the fragments of Victorian medicine bottles on the beach, now 'boody' polished by the sea. Her residual anger at Ian Dunne spilled over into her telling which didn't help.

'So are you saying the Superintendent is the Operator?' He indulged in a nanosecond of fantasy of himself with a knee in a prone GB's hated back with handcuffs poised...

'You know I'm not. I'm saying there might be a Masonic connection you could look into.'

'Well thank you very much Erica. It's alright for you, Ms Warshawski...'

'I'm more of a Ms Harriet Vane at the moment, I'm rereading the Wimsey books.'

'Ah yes, more amateur sleuths. It's alright for you to cherry-pick which aspects of the case you are going to interfere in, and which you are delegating to me and my team. I don't have that luxury. I came out for a run because I was going mad indoors, chasing up leads and scores and scores of possible suspects of one, both or either murder.' He gave her a quick run-down of some areas they'd explored. 'To say nothing of chasing the usual knife fights, alcoholic punch-ups, vandalism, car theft, and drug dealers.'

Erica opened her mouth to reply but he went on. 'Speaking of which, I assume it was definitely your Stacey who's been nicking your sugar pills and selling them on?'

'She's not my Stacey but I'm saying nothing. Not even if you dangle me over the railings.'

'Don't think I'm not tempted.' He took a step towards her and she stood firm, looking up at him like a furious little cat at a big dog.

'That's where I'm going when I'm dead, but not yet.' She gestured towards the restless waves heaving themselves endlessly against the stone, wearing it away with all the patience in the world.

'Check the wind direction first. You'll end up like ground black pepper in somebody's fish and chips.'

They both laughed, and as a particularly ambitious wave splatted across the wall and landed behind them on the pier path, they turned as one and began to jog loosely back along the pier, scurrying past the damp patches where waves had scaled the wall and might again.

'Hard luck about your article.'

'Thanks. Yeah, well it's my own fault. I've chosen the wrong paper, editor, time and place to be a hard-hitting writer of exposés. Maybe Dunne's right, I should give up trying to be a proper journo and just do the recipes.'

'That's not going to happen Erica.'

'You think so?'

'Yeah. The readers would starve trying to live on what you eat.'

'Cheeky bugger!' She clouted him on the arm.

'Actually I wish he would print it. It might stir something

up... provoke some sort of reaction in the case. Though I think you might be at risk yourself if you're not careful.'

'You and Stacey, two minds with but a single thought.' She told him about their conversation about the golf ball. 'But I'm going to write a feature about a fanatical homeopath instead. The kind you hate even more than me. The kind you'd like to lock up.'

'I look forward to reading it. Seriously though Erica be careful.'

'I am. If anyone really wanted to kill me they'd not have left it at one near miss with a golf ball. They'd have plenty of chances while I'm out running, or at Ivy Lodge, or at home. It must have been a one-off, an accident probably. Anyway I've got Stacey as intern and now bodyguard as well.'

'Thanks for the warning. I suppose there's no point in telling you to stop interfering?'

'I suppose there's no point in asking you to say Tessa's totally in the clear?'

They stopped at the point of separation, looking at each other, hot inside and cold outside, feeling very aware of how near they were to each other. And how well they knew each other's skin, body, scent, feel, heft.

'You've got a boyfriend,' Will said. And Erica had a flash of annoyance, not wanting it to be true right then, and after all she'd made no commitment to Jamie and wasn't going to, but Will was old-school like that, she'd be handing him too much ammunition if she said let's kiss anyway and pulled his head down to hers and fastened her lips on his and opened her mouth to him... Abruptly he spun round and set off, raising a hand in farewell without looking back.

A good work out at the gym helped get her remaining editor-rage out of her system, and a good night out on the lash put things in proportion. While there was house music with heavenly synthesiser tunes and infuriating beats, while she had a body to move with it, in motion with all the other ecstatic bodies, while she could move her hips against the body of a beautiful young man and feel how much he wanted her, that was all that mattered. At least, at the time.

She never knew when she'd see Jamie much in advance, his hours were horrendous, and when he was free she might not be. Much as she longed to spend time and energy with, on, under and around him, she didn't want to be hanging around waiting to rearrange her schedule for him. Not a good pattern to get into.

However, until such time as Erica took over writing about how to use left-over cauliflower and banana yogurt to make an amusing supper dish for two, she was still editing the health page, despite that dickhead Dunne. So although she had got over the first flush of fury, she was not in the mood to indulge overbearing men. Pity, really, that she'd arranged to see Craig Anderson, the purist homeopath. As with Kingston, she'd have to control her own feelings to get an interview and maybe some information out of him.

CHAPTER THIRTY

Anderson's terraced house was quite a walk from the metro station. It had leaded windows, a square porch, and a grey front door. Below the doorbell was a plaque: 'Craig Anderson, BA, MNCHM, R.S. Hom, Homeopath'. She rang the doorbell. This time she'd made no concessions to conventional fashion which might lull the suspicions of an establishment figure. Anderson was right-on alternative by all accounts, and he would probably know she was a homeopath herself. She wore black skinny jeans and a cerise sweater, with pink Converse high-tops.

Craig Anderson opened the door. She was pleased to see no one had nailed him to a table. Always a good start to an interview.

It was obvious the guy worked out and with serious weights. He was stocky, muscular, his arms bowing out from his sides slightly as they do in body builders. His neck was thick. His smile was thin. His eyes were very pale grey; a shaved head with a dusting of fair stubble; a conspicuous crucifix on a thin gold chain round his neck. He wore a black, blue and white striped Adidas polo shirt, tucked into grey jeans which barely contained his bulging thighs. A bit like Will, if a heavy weight had fallen on him from above. His bottom though was almost flat, she noticed when he turned to show her in. Too much exercise had distorted his body instead of perfecting it.

Several things were immediately clear. One, that he would have no trouble bashing someone's head in with a stone, would barely work up a sweat in fact. Two, that he would be a hard victim to kill unless they brought a machine gun. Three, that no one would ever question his bill.

She followed him down a long, narrow hall. The house, though small from outside, went back a long way. It was the kind of place that has a back yard with a high wall around it, so not much light gets in except through the front windows.

She could only hope that this being a formal interview for a newspaper would keep her safe if Stacey had been right in her speculations that Erica might be a target; Anderson could theoretically be the killer. Just in case, she claimed that her editor had sent her. He showed her into a room looking onto the back yard and switched on the light; the shade was a large white paper lantern like a swollen moon. The room was painted all in white, with the original stripped and polished floorboards. She was not surprised to see woodchip on the walls under many layers of paint. He himself was too young to be that out of date. He must be aiming at some kind of retro chic. A bit of Seventies spirituality, perhaps. Or just indifferent, leaving the previous decor as it was.

There was a black ash desk, another retro box ticked, and lots of books bending built in shelves. A wicker chair painted white faced the desk. She perched on it at his invitation. He sat down on the black swivel chair behind the desk. Obviously he was keeping his distance. Maybe he was scared of her. Yeah right.

On the stark white walls were framed texts in big swirly calligraphy of the 'Desiderata' type. Texts like 'PHYSICIAN, HEAL THYSELF'. 'A GOOD TREE BRINGS FORTH GOOD FRUIT'. 'IF THINE EYE OFFEND THEE, PUT IT OUT. IF THY HAND OFFEND THEE, CUT IT OFF'. 'IF YE WILL NOT HEARKEN UNTO ME, I WILL BRING MORE PLAGUES UPON YOU'. She sighed inwardly. A fundamentalist, with the fun taken out, and the mental left in. He was religious, and not just about homeopathy. Great. She switched on her digital recorder and placed it on the desk between them. He made no objection.

'Well, Mr Anderson, thank you for agreeing to talk to me. We've covered the subject of homeopathy and most of the alternative therapies in our health pages. Perhaps you've seen them.'

He went on calmly looking at her, not yet responding. His desk was arranged so the light went onto his face, lighting up those pale eyes. His stillness was disturbing, except that she suspected it was conscious and contrived.

'My editor and I felt you might offer our readers a

different slant on homeopathic practice. Perhaps you could tell me why you became a homeopath?'

'Because I believe it is the natural way to good health, the *right* way. I'm against drugs that alter the mind and work against the body's own immune system. Alternative medicine is a way of life, not just correcting malfunctions, but a whole philosophy.'

He'd learned the knack of speaking quietly in such a way as to make people listen hard. A good teacher's, or preacher's, trick.

'Like these texts on the wall? Some of them sound a bit drastic....'

'People need to realise they are responsible for their own health, their own God-given bodies. It's a sacred trust, Ms Bruce.'

'I see. And how did you begin - how did you come to be a homeopath? Most of us start out as something else....'

She held his eyes. He wanted to seem in control; the desk between them, the steady stare, the unnaturally still body language, but she could sense a tension in him and something, maybe an emptiness at the heart of him.

'I started out as a cost and management accountant for a big firm down south. Kent, actually. '

The bathos of this unlikely start almost made her laugh. She choked it down. Maybe she could spur him on a bit.

'Really! That's most unusual. Most people would think that alternative therapists are too impractical for such careers. Did you find you couldn't handle it?'

'No!'

His stillness held but his hands whitened, tensed on the desk top.

'I was good at my job. It was a good job, with prospects, we - I was doing very well. But I decided that this would be a more socially useful line of work. So I retrained.'

'I see. And had you always used homeopathic medicine?'

'A little. '

He'd clammed up again. She tried to shake him loose another way.

'Rather like me. I took a course in homeopathy just for treating myself and family and friends, ended up being more interested in that than in following up my degree. I don't like too structured a life. Was that how it was for you?'

'You can't really compare us. 'Therapists' like you just play at it. Handing out pills, just like doctors.' He almost spat out the last word. 'It's pointless, giving remedies to people who swallow paracetamol and ibuprofen like sweets, go running to their GP between appointments, smoke, drink, eat bad food, take no exercise, ruin their health. It's a kind of sacrilege. They've got to be made to see. Health is life. They've got to live healthy lives, and then they won't need doctors.'

Erica controlled her anger at his jibes. No way was she going to get into a row with this guy. There was something fuelling his agenda though, she could feel it. Both of them had given up conventional careers to become alternative therapists, but he'd also moved to the other end of the country. There was also that hastily corrected 'we' which made her wonder. Time to push him further, see what popped out.

'The health page I write deals with issues of prevention, good health and natural remedies of all kinds. But we can't tell people not to see doctors. We'd have deaths of cancer patients on our hands, and the law on our backs. Surely you're not telling me you can cure cancers, or put back amputated limbs?'

'Most cancers are caused by bad lifestyle choices. So are accidents, come to that. Drinking and driving.... drugs... and doctors are just sales reps for the drug companies. If they knew that arthritis could be cured by a change of diet, or by, say, chewing an oak twig, do you think we'd ever get to hear about it? No way, it wouldn't bring any money to the drug companies' shareholders and directors. No, they'd go on developing anti-inflammatory drugs which have side effects and don't cure the condition, so long as the money goes on pouring in. There's no profit in prevention.'

Much of what he'd just said could have been, in fact had often been, said by Erica herself at times. Yet this whole black and white, people must/must not, was totally alien to her. Go further, get him to say it so there's no room for doubt.

'Is it true then, Mr Anderson, that you only take patients who agree to leave their GPs' lists?'

'Absolutely. And change their lifestyles. Live as God intended. Don't abuse their bodies. Then any small imbalances in the vital force can be corrected by homeopathic remedies.'

'What if someone's in an accident, caused by someone who hasn't adjusted their lifestyle choices? Broken bones, damaged joints. Surely they need a hospital?'

'In a properly regulated society, surgeons would be regarded as simply mechanics. They would put the body back into anatomical order and then homeopathic remedies would help the body heal itself.'

As usual, her devil's advocate tendencies were coming out. When talking to Jamie, she had made many of the same points as Craig Anderson, but now hearing them in a more extreme form, she felt like arguing for the other side.

'What about pain, Mr Anderson? Surely some conditions are helped by pain relief. Surely you agree that a parent cannot see their child suffer pain without wanting to relieve it? That doctors can sometimes...'

'Doctors! I'd like to see them forced to suffer the treatment they dish out!'

He was on his feet, bulky and threatening. His face was white. She forced herself to stay calm. This man needed help of some kind. Or maybe she did. Somehow she'd found the button to press. Not so sure now she wanted to know any more, just get out of there with her own temple of a body intact.

'Well, thank you for your frank expression of views,' she was trying to sound breezy while getting up and scrabbling her recorder back into her bag. 'I'll put a piece in the paper, but I'll have to be careful about some of the more extreme opinions...'

'Of course,' he muttered but dully, without the usual scorn.

She still wanted out, but his hostility seemed to have gone back into hiding. It wasn't directed at her, amateur therapist as she was in his eyes, but at doctors. She risked another question, really wanting to know.

'So do you treat yourself? Do you find you can diagnose any imbalances in your own physical or mental health? Most of us find that difficult, and if you are so erm, purist, it must be hard to find another practitioner with similar views.'

'I haven't needed any help so far, Ms Bruce. I eat only healthy, unpolluted unprocessed organic food, exercise hard, don't drink or smoke, and therefore I'm in perfect balance.'

Physically, possibly. Mentally, she wasn't so sure. He followed her back towards the front of the house, it was like tunnelling to freedom, the light from the street through the front door panes increasing like a view of heaven. Erica was trying not to scurry, run for the light, intensely aware of his bulk behind her, though he moved quietly. Captain Jack Aubrey could always feel the 'loom of the land' when out at sea. Well Craig Anderson was looming like a cliff. He could out-loom Will Bennett any day. She reached for the door like an alcoholic for a gin bottle.

At last she stood on the garden path, in daylight and in public. This was her last chance to ask about the killings. 'By the way, what do you think about the two murders of surgeons? Do you think the killer, the Operator as they call him now, might start on alternative therapists?'

'I'm not wasting any sympathy on those two. It's usually doctors that do the killing. Look at all the doctors who've killed in history. All those 'doctors' who killed thousands of women in childbirth by spreading their filthy germs in the lying-in hospitals. Doctors in Nazi death camps. How did Shipman get away with it for so long? Playing on peoples' misplaced trust. It's probably another doctor who's the killer. They're all jealous of each other you know.'

'Know a lot of doctors, do you?'

'Know thine enemy.'

'I thought you were supposed to love the enemy.' She remembered the framed biblical texts on Anderson's walls.

'He that is not with us, is against us,' he replied.

And closed the door.

She jogged back to the metro station. The wind was cold on her cheeks, seemed even colder as she stood waiting, the approaching train preceded by gusts of suddenly animated junk food wrappers.

Had she just been alone with a murderer? The way he had behaved showed him to be anything but in perfect balance, whatever his claims. His feelings about doctors could only be described as murderous. But would he ever put those feelings into action? Should she tell the police about him? She had no actual evidence. Will had suggested himself that an alternative therapist could be the killer, but only, she was sure, to scare her off getting involved with the case, and hence with his life. She wondered if the police had in fact looked at that avenue of enquiry.

But would Anderson have sounded off so freely if he was guilty? Surely he would have dissembled, smiled and smiled and been a villain, to avoid drawing attention to himself. Maybe not, if he was really unbalanced to the point of madness, really believed he was right, a lone avenger doing the world a favour by ridding it of doctors.... a sort of folie à un.

Kingston had had quite a high media profile, clearly putting his own glory and status before the patients' wellbeing, certainly as Anderson might have seen it. But why would Anderson target Chambers? Perhaps he disapproved of vasectomies? Surgical birth control as some sort of heresy, a denial of the god-given life force?

CHAPTER THIRTY-ONE

As the Metro neared her usual home stop, she felt the familiar urge to be close to the sea. Though standing on the platform with its chilly desolation had made her fleetingly wonder why everyone didn't desert the north east coast and move en masse to the Côte d'Azur, she never felt like leaving the north sea and didn't care how bleak or icy the wind while she was in sight of it. They say you can never step in the same river twice. You can never see the same wave twice either. The rising wind would be driving the waves hard against the piers at the mouth of the river Tyne with all its spectacular drama, and she felt a need to be there amid all that raw energy where thought and belief were alien and redundant.

So she stayed on the Metro for a couple more stops and jogged down the short street to the river mouth. The two piers with their small lighthouses on the ends curved out their welcoming arms to make a relatively safe harbour after centuries of lives lost mere yards from dry land, as ships foundered on the Black Middens rocks.

She jogged slowly, not having proper trainers on, to the end of the north pier. She liked it best when the water was stormy. It was a brighter day than when she'd met Will here but the sea had built up to a fine display of power. To her left, the waves flung themselves against the pier wall with a loud 'Ger-DUNSH!' sending plumes of glittering white spray sprinkled with rainbows shooting up like geysers. The wind tried to blow her sideways as she ran.

A great splat of water fell right next to her as a particularly mighty wave managed to storm the battlements of the pier. Sometimes, quite often in winter, whole waves washed right over the pier, and even leapt the lighthouse on the end. People would gather to watch the spectacle from the land end of the pier on a viewing platform after the harbourmaster had emerged from his little hut and walked to the end and back, shepherding all the walkers and anglers off the pier before locking the big wrought iron gates to keep them off. It wasn't far from those conditions now.

She leaned on the green-weed-coated salty wall, watching the waves, thinking as her hair whipped her face. Weren't journalists supposed to protect their sources? But she was not a journalist, Ian Dunne had made that very clear when he rejected her article. And what if she told the police that Craig Anderson might have a motive, albeit an irrational one, and he found out? Even if he was innocent of the murders, any hint of persecution might push him over the edge, and she didn't fancy facing his rage. Not with those muscles. Could she trust Will not to dob her in? Throw her to the batshit crazy wolf in wolf's clothing?

But then, Anderson had given her an interview freely.

He'd let her leave with her recording intact. All she had to do was write up the interview, add some researched relevant info and it would be published on the health page. No chance Ian Dunne would be so defensive about a mere nutcase homeopath as he'd been about Kingston. Then it would be in the public domain, and it was up to the police to do something about it if they wanted to. There must be loads of others who hated doctors, with or without reason. A bungled vasectomy leading to a disastrous pregnancy; or a regret at having it done being turned against the doctor who did it; these could be motives for Paul Chambers' murder if it was a copycat killing.

She headed back along the pier. More and more waves were managing to throw their crests over the wall, and several times she was soaked with icy spray. She knew from soggy experience that what looked like a graceful lacy arc of droplets felt like a ton of bricks if you were right under it when it landed. Luckily she avoided a direct hit which could have knocked her down. Home, she changed into dry clothes, made a much needed mug of Earl Grey, and sat down then and there to write up the interview. Fearless Erica Bruce, exposing all that was weird and wacky in the world of health. Writing it was a breeze compared with getting a brush through her salt-sticky windblown hair.

Now it was a question of waiting until it was published in a few days time, together with another article about what to do if your child bumped its head and a few letters with replies.

Re-reading her Kingston article now, she felt a shudder at the thought of the swung stone crashing against the back of the head, the bone caving, shards of skull piercing the brain. She wondered how it felt. Did you hear it, that huge sound of your death? Did you feel the shock, or just enter a state of unconsciousness or semi-consciousness? How much time was there to realise what was happening before blackness descended? Had Kingston and Chambers realised they were doomed from the moment the weight made contact with their skulls? Or was puzzlement their last conscious feeling? She ran a hand over her horse's skull. Bone seemed so solid, rounded, a safe box for the brain, yet a fall backwards could breach it.

Covering herself and of course Dunne and the paper, she added a rider to the article on Craig Anderson. 'Erica Bruce advises that the opinions voiced above are the subject's own, and the *Evening Guardian* would recommend seeking the advice of your GP as well as that of an alternative therapist.'

She felt a twinge of shame. Didn't she have the courage of her convictions? Didn't she believe in her own branch of medicine? She was still reeling under Simon Singh's attacks on homeopathy, yet had so much personal experience of how it worked so often and so well. And so much knowledge of how little scientists knew about quantum theory, and the Big Bang, and before the Big Bang, and yet felt able to make definitive statements about the universe with what seemed like no more proof than homeopathy. They even said that asking the sensible question 'What was there before the Big Bang?' couldn't be answered as it was meaningless. Lots of scientists were religious, with no scientific proof required.

She reflected how all the really scary people in history had been as sure as Anderson, and felt better. She knew going to the GP wouldn't stop people seeking the help of homeopaths and chiropractors, hypnotherapists and other more dubious 'ologists'. Most of the patients they saw had already been shown the door by GPs and consultants who said it was all in their minds. Got to keep Jamie in work, she thought fondly even though it meant she wouldn't see much of him.

The next evening Erica was working a late session at Ivy Lodge. She'd been there all day, and was coming to the end of a solid batch of patients. True to form for this time of year, colds, coughs, earache, and various related symptoms predominated. This was one area where homeopathic medicine could really come into its own. All conventional medicine could offer was paracetamol in assorted disguises, often mixed with caffeine for a quick lift, some lemon flavouring for comfort, anything that would temporarily mask the symptoms. 'It's something going round,' as GPs said of most common illnesses. 'Drink plenty of fluids, rest, and it'll go away by itself.'

She'd seen her last patient and was bringing her computer records up to date when darkness filled her doorway like an extra wall. It was Craig Anderson.

Stacey had been around, but had vanished into Rina's room mumbling about 'mint neet oot' preparations involving a nap, then later hair re-building and root blackening, and front loading with cheap voddie. If she had her earphones in, Erica was as good as alone in the building.

'Evening, Ms Bruce.'

He moved forward, light on his feet in spite of his bulk, and sat down. Something heavy in his jacket pocket clunked against the chair frame when he did so. Erica put her hand on her mobile in her pocket.

It was her turn to keep her distance behind a desk.

'What can I do for you?' She tried to keep her voice light. Her turn also to attempt the still, in-control body language. He was doing it too. They must have looked like a couple of dummies, she thought, but she wasn't ready to see the funny side just yet.

She could sense that tension in him again. His eyes were narrowed as if against the light, as if it hurt.

'I want to be your patient. Please put my details on file.'

He said it like an order. Her patient? With such a low opinion of her as a practitioner?

'Do you have a health problem at the moment?'

'I - have headaches. Bad headaches.'

328

'I see.'

She didn't see at all. Hadn't he claimed to be in perfect balance and therefore in perfect health? Hadn't he spoken with scorn of her as just playing at homeopathy? And he had turned up here, at a time when there would be no-one much around. Perhaps he wanted her to pull the article.

He seemed to bulge out of the chair, packed with muscle, tight all over with repressed energy. She didn't like this situation at all. But she mustn't show it. And she mustn't confront him with the apparent contradiction of his earlier statements. No point in antagonising him until she knew more of what was going on.

Besides, she was a health practitioner, and maybe he did need help. She could well believe he had headaches with all that tension.

An acrid scent was coming from him. The room seemed very small yet the door seemed very far away. As her fingers moved slowly over the keyboard, making mistakes and trying not to shake, trying to spend as long as possible in contact with her pc, opening a Word file, typing his basic details at his prompting, name, address, DOB, phone, email, her mind was racing.

What if Craig Anderson was the Operator? What if he attacked her, gave her a permanent headache with whatever was in his pocket? If he killed her, it would be easy for him to erase his details from the computer. Before or after bashing some nails through her hands? And what other mutilations would he consider she deserved? Now she realised that all her questions during the interview, challenging his anti-doctor stance, might have sounded like support for what he clearly saw as the enemy. His parting words rang in her ears. 'Those who are not with us are against us.'

If he attacked her, she wouldn't stand a chance. All her exercise would be useless; she might as well have spent her life lying on a sofa eating chocolate and chip butties.

She was tempted to secretly speed-dial a number on her mobile to let someone hear what went on. Will, preferably. But Anderson might be a bona fide patient, entitled to absolute confidentiality. Why oh why had she insisted that Stacey stopped eavesdropping on her sessions with patients. Right next door she was probably asleep on the massage table.

Erica made three decisions. 1. If it came to it, she'd go down fighting and try to hurt him for the sake of her honour which suddenly seemed a very real thing, as solid as the desk. The thought of being murdered or violently attacked, and not having done anything about it and never being avenged in any way seemed unbearable. 2. She resolved to mark or scratch his face, get his skin cells under her fingernails or get some kind of forensic evidence so at least he'd go down for her murder even if she wasn't around to see it.

3. Make sure he couldn't erase his visit from evidence. While busy at the pc, she contrived to move her phone

onto her lap and start the voice record. She could only hope it would pick up what he said and to some extent, did. She then hastily called up her minimised facebook window, clicked on messages and brought up the thread of messages exchanged with Stacey, copied and pasted Anderson's details, after 'listen in! Might need u' and hit return, all while asking Anderson more questions about how to spell his address and so on. At least there'd be some record of him being here at this time, private but on the pc in Rina's room even if Stacey didn't hear the 'ping' sound of a message alert. She knew Stacey kept facebook open at all times.

While doing this, fidgeting with her hair and generally gesticulating to create a diversion, she managed to keep talking. She asked finicky questions from the Homeopath's Materia Medica. Usually she'd be getting a new patient talking about everything to do with their lives as she assessed their physical and emotional type, their body language, their characteristics to get the full remedy picture. This was different. She just had to spin this part out before she had to face whatever he really had in mind. He'd come for something, and she doubted it was for his headaches.

The message was sent, her window hastily closed before any reply from Stacey would start her pc pinging. So that was all right. There would only be the tiny formality of being murdered to cope with.

'OK Mr Anderson. Now about these headaches.' Her

331

voice sounded almost normal.

'I get headaches.' His voice was dull. His eyes fell. His hands lay on his massive thighs, rubbing the material of his jeans up and down. 'Bad headaches.'

'Could you describe them? Is it like a tight band round your head, or is it in one temple, does it feel like a nail being driven into your he-?'

Appalled to hear herself asking this standard question in these circumstances, she stopped short, feeling a flush of heat whoosh up her body as if she was doing high impact aerobics. Sweat broke out all over her and nausea made her weak.

He was looking directly at her. She forced herself to look back at him without making actual eye contact, a valuable bit of body language when dealing with confrontational or aggressive people. She looked at his third eye, between and just above his eyes. Not so confrontational and challenging as direct eye contact, but not submissive as looking away might be.

'Do you know what it feels like? Do you want to know what it feels like?'

Was this a threat? 'Why don't you tell me what it feels like?' She hoped her voice wasn't as strangled as she might soon be.

'It's like being in hell.' He leaned forward, putting his huge hands on the edge of her desk, his knuckles white. 'Do you know why I came?'

Oh god. He didn't give her a chance to answer, but took a deep breath, his great chest expanding. She was wondering how to cope with the onslaught when a rush of words poured out of him.

'I hate doctors. And you seemed to be defending them, even though you're supposed to be one of us. I want you to know how much I hate them, and why. I had a wife and son. Now I have neither. All because of the saintly medical profession. Pretty good reason for hatred, don't you think?'

As the sweat cooled on her skin she shivered slightly. She kept quiet and let him talk. She couldn't tear her eyes away from his, but she had a feeling something was moving on the periphery of her vision, behind Anderson and to the side, by the door. She didn't dare take her focus away from him as he spoke.

'We both had good but demanding careers in finance. We had a son, Matthew. He was our world. We decided to stop at one child. One child seemed to be all we could deal with and both work as well. Everything was perfect.

'Then he became ill. Feverish, very feverish, it was terrifying. We were worried that it might be meningitis - it was far, far worse than any of the usual viruses that little children get. He couldn't bear the light... he screamed... I can still hear it. We took him into A & E.

'Just a virus, they said. They sent us home. They sneered at us. They made it clear we were just neurotic parents, as if we didn't know our own child enough to know he was seriously ill.

'It was meningitis of course. He died three days later. He was four years old.'

No tears in his pale eyes now, just cold anger and hate.

'Do you know what they said when he was rushed in again? It was too late - treatment should have started right away. As if it wasn't their fault!

'My wife couldn't cope with it. Not just the grief but the guilt. She felt she should have somehow forced them to treat him that first time. We couldn't help each other through it. We were sealed off each in our own private grief. A year later she took an overdose. I found her dead when I got home from work.

'So yes, I do feel as if someone has hammered a nail into my head, and I don't think you or anyone else can do anything about it. My guilt keeps me alive to suffer their loss. I didn't come here for treatment; I meant it when I said I treat myself. Your practice is corrupt. You've lost your true faith, if you ever had it.

'If I'd known about homeopathy then, I could have prevented Matthew's illness from developing. I'm sure of it. I don't expect a cure for any suffering of mine. I don't even want one. I came here as a patient because I wanted to tell you about Matthew confidentially. I couldn't trust you as a journalist, but I thought I could trust you as a therapist. Even if you had no ethics, you'd soon go out of business if people felt they couldn't trust you. You're the first person

I've told about it since I moved up here. So now you know.'

What do you say to someone who has lost a wife and child like that? She didn't have to say anything; he got up, turned and walked out, the heavy object in his jacket clunking against the door frame as he went. Erica vaguely noticed the door had come partly open. Presumably that was what had moved, he mustn't have shut it properly.

Bang! The door crashed open again, making her jump as she poured herself a glass of water, spilling it all over her desk.

'Oh, ye're OK.' Stacey sounded almost disappointed. 'Worra fk'n nutjob! Jeez! Aa thowt he was gonna morder ye.'

'So did I!' She sipped water while with the other hand dabbing at the spills and shaking her keyboard upside down. 'So you got the facebook message!'

'Aye. Divven't worry, Aa was on the case.' She waved her phone triumphantly. 'Aa was ready to act in a split second man.'

'Thanks Stacey. Though by the time you called the police, I'd have been dead meat.'

'Kind of ironic for a veggie. Oh, aye, spose Aa could've called the bizzies.'

'Well what were you going to do? Rush to my rescue?' She was really quite moved.

'Nah! Share this on Youtube of course! Aa'd have had a thoosand hits by the time he got oot the building! Aa got it aal on here!' She waved the phone again. 'Take him on? Aye, right, the guy's got arms like legs! He's fkn massive, man! Thick as mince, though. He never saw iz open the door and start filmin. Aa'm a fkn genius man!'

Erica stopped in mid-fumble for the Rescue Remedy. 'You haven't, please tell me you haven't, put that on Youtube? Oh fuck... it's supposed to be confidential! I only sent the facebook message so there'd be proof he'd been here, if he did go apeshit.'

'Calm doon, pet, Aa didn't. Aa was waiting for the morder. But it didn't happen.'

'Sorry about that.'

'Never mind, Erica. Aa've got this aal safe if he torns oot to be the Operator.'

'Will you send that to me now, and then delete it?'

'Course Aa will.' Stacey shared it to Erica's email address. Would she fuck delete it. He might yet turn out to be the serial killer. She'd made contact with Gary Thomas who'd suggested she keep him in the loop if Erica found out anything.

'I tried to record him on my phone but...' Erica tried it out and could barely hear anything. 'It's pretty rubbish. I had to keep the phone out of sight so's not to provoke him.'

'He doesn't think much of ye, does he?'

'No. Poor guy. I wish I could do something for him. Perhaps it helped him in some way just to talk about it.'

'Aye. He's had a crap time of it. If my Noosh had that meningitis Aa'd take a fkn gun into A and E if they'd not help iz.'

'He didn't give away anything about the murders though.'

'He could deffo be the Operator. He'll more likely go to your house. He was waiting for ye for ages and folks saw him here today.'

'Comforting! He had something in his pocket, something hard and heavy.'

'Just pleased to see you mebbe!'

'It might've been a stone. Or just a jar of jam he'd bought.'

All in all, it was a relief to arrive at her warm flat and curl up with Lord Peter Wimsey, a glass of wine and a quorn steak.

When her article on Anderson was printed, Will rang.

'Great, always nice to hear from a reader.' This time, Erica, try not to let him antagonise you...

'I wouldn't normally read it,' he went on, with his usual charm. 'But he seems to have an obsessive hatred for the medical profession. Do you know any more about him? Did he tell you anything else that might be of value to us?'

'Well he's now my patient, so technically anything else he told me is confidential.'

She heard Will's angry intake of breath.

'For f- god's sake, Erica, that sounds very much like obstruction to me. I thought you wanted to help! I thought you wanted Tessa Kingston off the hook!'

'Yes, and YOU told me to keep out! Make up your mind! This is just typical, one minute you want rid of me, the next you're asking for information! I have my ethics you know. Professional ethics.'

'Really, from where I'm standing you don't have either a profession or ethics. Or morals, come to that.'

'Well sit down then, take the weight off your prejudices. Look Will, OK it's a matter of public record that he hates doctors. And has extreme views on medicine. And I can tell you he has his reasons. You'll be able to find those out yourself as they will all be on records you can access if you look him up. There, that's helpful of me isn't it? But I can also tell you something negative. I don't know of any link to either of the dead surgeons. If he hates doctors, he could have gone for specific ones elsewhere, and you will be able to check on that more easily than I could. I hope that's enough to satisfy you for now? I know how hard you are... to satisfy I mean.'

The police computers would have all the info about his medical and employment history, the death of his son and his wife's suicide. Even someone with no imagination could deduce what his feelings were likely to be.

'Well I hope you're not withholding anything vital. Think how you'd feel, with your bleeding heart always ready to take on lame dogs and lost causes, if somebody died because of your 'ethics.' And I think it would be wise if you keep away from him from now on.'

'Not your call. He's a patient so I'm not going to avoid him.' She wasn't going to tell Will that Anderson shared his low opinion of her work.

'Surprise surprise! Look, we may contact Mr Anderson in connection with our enquiries. Please do not warn him. Such a move could be regarded as obstruction.' A pause. 'Or dangerous to you. Be careful!'

He rang off.

Anderson and Will, despite their diametrically opposed views on alternative therapies, had a lot in common. Both uptight alpha males. Too much muscle-building exercise, not enough relaxation. Not that she seemed to be getting much of that herself. Still, she had managed to keep her temper this time despite his jibes.

CHAPTER THIRTY-TWO

Christmas was thundering closer like a herd of rabid reindeer. Before that was the Wydsand Golf Club Christmas do, which Erica had promised to attend with Mel, if it was still worth following up Kingston's murder. Still, that obstinate oaf DI Bennett hung on grimly to the idea of Tessa as a possible suspect, as The Operator might be imaginary - one murder, one copycat murder, for different reasons personal to two killers. So since Mel was giving her a chance to dip her oestrogen-contaminated toe into another of Kingston's worlds, she might as well follow it up.

'What do people wear at these shindigs?' She nabbed Miles at the water cooler.

'Suits. Dinner suits.'

'OK, I'll wear a suit.'

'I dare you... oh, but women aren't supposed to wear trousers. They don't wear long dresses any more, either.'

'Jeez, why does Mel bother with all this bollocks?'

'He likes the game. He and I don't socialise with that lot but he usually goes to the Christmas bash. I think he enjoys going in disguise.'

It seemed that Miles and Mel were happy in their comfortable golf closet, though they were very relaxed about their relationship when hanging out with normal folk. Miles and Mel, Tessa and Tara, alliterative pairings everywhere thought Erica. How cosy.

In the end Erica wore a dinner suit. She had to adapt it though in case of being refused admittance altogether. And she wanted to look hot. She found a man's vintage dinner jacket with satin lapels in a charity shop with a silky printed waistcoat which she wore with nothing underneath, having had it taken in to be body-hugging and making sure the buttons were firmly stitched on. She wore a red silk bow tie round her neck, and a short red skirt and high heeled black sandals.

Jamie loved the outfit, which was great except she had to sew all the buttons on again afterwards.

Mel picked her up in a taxi in which they had the obligatory conversation about football with the driver. There was some hanging about at the Golf Club bar drinking gin and tonic first, at least they had some Slimline thank god, during which her outfit was stared at expressively by both male and female guests. Well it wasn't like she'd ever come again. The joining fees were astronomical to say nothing of the waiting list. Dinner was the usual dreck inevitable when feeding a lot of people at exactly the same time: lukewarm, bland, greyish slices of some kind of meat with a puddle of gravy on top and little dishes of veg swimming in butter. Her goat's cheese tartlet 'veggie option' managed to be flaccid and pretty tasteless too. What a waste of calories! Her starter mushrooms had turned up armoured in deep-fried breadcrumb shells which she had to chip off in order to eat the teeny fungi hidden within. Then there was chocolate pudding or 'xmas pudding' or 'fruit salad' which wasn't worthy of the name. So far she wasn't sure if this had been worth it. Luckily she'd brought iron rations, a quorn steak which she shamelessly ate with knife and fork and nobody seemed to notice. People at dinner kept asking what she 'ran' to which she'd say 'about five miles usually' and they'd look puzzled. Later on it turned out this was Golf Club speak for 'what kind of car do you drive.'

At the coffee and mints ritual, a man got up rather unsteadily and gave a speech. The Captain, Mel whispered. He did the usual overview of the year, mentioning various golf events and awards which meant nothing to Erica, giving out some silver trophies to delighted winners. Then he went on to say it had been a bad year in some ways what with their invaluable membership secretary sustaining head injuries, from which he was thankfully making a slow but good recovery, and the death of valued member and friend to them all, Robert Kingston. While he listed Kingston's virtues, Erica looked carefully around for insane hatred or evil glee but could see nothing but agreement and decent expressions of restrained sorrow on the listening faces. Nobody looked heart-broken though.

There was some chatting and mingling afterwards. The nearest she got to a familiar face or name was hearing a snatch of conversation from a couple of fruity-voiced geezers chatting at the bar.

'Good thing nobody's brought old Archer, always banging on about the rules and so on. What a king-sized bloody bore!'

'God yes, and of course he's not quite...PLU.'

PLU? Wasn't that 'People Like Us'? Snobby gits! Archer was surely Harry Archer, who had bought Kingston's mother's house. Old! These two guys looked older than him. And a bore!

'Pot, paging kettle,' she said aloud. Mel grimaced, clearly not a fan either.

Her eavesdropping was interrupted as a man landed heavily in a temporarily empty chair next to Mel who introduced Howard, his regular golf partner. Large, plumpish, but with small hands and feet, and hair that stood up, he grinned eagerly, his gaze flicking over her fishnets.

'I was hoping Mel would introduce me,' he chuckled genially, 'bit of a dark horse, is Mel, keeping quiet about you for a start.'

He had clearly found the wine to his liking to say nothing of the gin.

'Some precious secrets are worth keeping.' Mel mischievously put his hand on hers in a show of faux possessiveness.

'We call them the odd couple, Erica. Mel here, and

344

Miles. Living together - I keep telling him, people will talk! Still, it makes sense, two divorced guys sharing a house, specially since old Mel here is always jetting off to foreign parts, eh?'

'Erm absolutely. Did you know Robert Kingston?'

'Oh yes. Well, not *know*, if you take my meaning, but, well...bloody shame. Decent bloke all round, by all accounts. Never heard a word against him at the club. Have you, Mel?'

'No. Not that I ever actually spoke to him, just knew him by sight.'

'Really?' Howard was puzzled. 'I thought you knew him better than that - what about that time on the fourteenth green...'

'Don't remember,' Mel drawled. He seemed bored.

Mel had an even voice, curiously unexpressive. She looked at his eyes, remembering that Miles had said he could not be hypnotised. She got the feeling that he enjoyed living a double life, keeping secrets; that he didn't do it out of fear of homophobia, but as a game he enjoyed as much as golf.

She danced with various men, some of them were quite fit, and when possible, introduced Kingston into the conversations about holes, greens, woods, irons, and cars and their vagaries. She heard no opinions that differed from Howard's. Howard himself claimed a dance, as his wife was dancing with the Captain and pretending to be fascinated by his golfing anecdotes.

'What was that you were saying about the fourteenth?' She sipped mineral water with lots of ice to keep dehydration at bay.

'Oh, just one day Mel and I were playing a round.' She suppressed a grin at his unintentional double entendre. 'I'd gone off to get my ball out of the rough, and I saw Mel and old Robert talking on the green, very close and serious. Probably about an awkward lie or something...'

He saw her startled look. 'Awkward lie of the ball! Golfing term.' He chortled and stood on her foot rather painfully, gazing soulfully down her cleavage.

In the taxi home, she was quiet beside Mel. Just how important was it to him to keep his private life secret? What would he be prepared to do to keep it that way? For all his seemingly relaxed attitude, it would not be comfortable to be ostracised and possibly hounded out of the club, all the more so because he seemed to feel superior to them. She could imagine how much Kingston would have taken delight in exposing him, or even more, in making him live in fear of exposure, if he had found out about Miles and their true relationship. After all Mel had lied about being divorced; that was a step further than just not telling anyone he was gay. He was a strange guy, so contained, so unknowable. An awkward lie..... she was starting to see conspiracies everywhere.

As Christmas approached, the media kept alive the interest in the two bizarre murders. Though they explored every angle it was clear they believed in a serial killer. The Operator was good copy.

Erica almost felt sorry for Will, Hassan and co, though not that snarky bitch Sally. It was a major investigation now, and they would be checking and cross-checking lists; who was known to both victims; who had operations in the two fields represented by Kingston and Chambers; anyone who had threatened staff in hospitals, or threatened or carried out legal action about real or imagined negligence. Not much of a Christmas for the officers involved but then it never was. As usual, every single weekend and often during the week, A&E was awash with drunks who often took aggressive exception to being treated for their ailments free of charge by exhausted and expert staff.

The media were, she felt, waiting for the Operator to strike again, in fact hoping he would. Two was, it seemed, a puny effort for a serial killer, even though he used interesting and unusual methods. There was a sense of dread and anticipation among the medical profession. Security was stepped up in hospital wards just in case the Operator branched out.

Memos had been circulated, warning staff to be careful who they let into their homes, and, incredibly and yet inevitably, warning female medical staff to go about in pairs and avoid being out late at night.

Typical! Erica fumed, considering that the two victims, both male, had been attacked in their own homes, possibly by someone they knew. Any excuse to keep women locked up.

CHAPTER THIRTY-THREE

Erica went 'home' as it persists on being called throughout adulthood to spend the Christmas weekend with her mother, arriving on Christmas Eve to a warm hug. Her mother looked her up and down.

'I hope you're eating properly.'

Coming back to the village Erica grew up in always brought back disturbing memories, mingled with the usual blend of comfort and boredom induced by being at home in what was no longer her house.

'I've got you a Linda McCartney pie in the freezer,' her mother said with an air of going the extra mile. Oh, god, pastry. Might as well stick my head in a bucket of lard, Erica was thinking. 'The rest of us will be having turkey of course. Christmas isn't Christmas without a turkey.'

'I don't remember that in the bible.' Erica was already returning in spirit to the rebellious teenage daughter.

'I'm not happy about you living alone with that Operator about.' She stopped herself there but her silence spoke volumes. Erica had made coming home for Christmas conditional on 'no freaking out, no fussing' about finding Kingston's body. They had already had words enough about it.

Erica went on peeling sprouts waiting for the next

question.

'Are you seeing anyone at the moment?' Always keen to get her married off despite her own divorce. Erica knew her Mum wanted her happiness. Perhaps she also wanted some kind of closure, to feel Erica was off her hands, so she could stop worrying.

'I'm 'seeing' a Chinese doctor, an orthopaedic surgeon if you really want to know.'

'Oh? Why didn't you bring him?'

'I'm just shagging him Mother, we're not engaged.' She cut increasingly savage cross-shaped notches on the sprout stems.

'Perhaps they don't have Christmas.' Erica's home village was about the most undiverse place on the planet.

Erica sighed. 'Of course doctors have Christmas. He's with his parents. He's only half Chinese, so you only need to be half worried.'

'I'm not worried. Which half of him is Chinese?'

'Erm, what?'

'Mother or father?'

'Oh - mother is English, as if it matters.'

She cheered up. It was easier to imagine discussing wedding plans with an English mother. Erica threw a sprout at her.

'Which half!' They got the giggles, and got out the gin.

So Christmas trundled along its well-worn tracks, her sister Livy's three children filling the house with noise and dead batteries, the smell of roasting flesh and satsumas; pine needles dropped, tempers frayed, muddy walks were trudged through in bitter gales and icy rain and Erica's jogging was preceded by pleas to 'wear something warmer than that pet.'

Erica avoided the pub and shops where she might meet anyone from her old school; though the family most concerned in that childhood disaster had moved away years ago. Being here reminded her of the fat child she'd been, so hopeless at sports; so excluded from the skimpy fashion clothes when she became a fat teenager. When Paula arrived at the school, poor, skinny, wispy, short-sighted, cringeing Paula, Erica made a discovery. While she'd flinched away from taunts in the past when they were aimed at herself, she found she could be a fearless champion in defence of someone else who made better bully-fodder. Her weight, used effectively, made her formidable, her tongue learned to lash. She protected Paula, who by her weakness enabled Erica to assert herself. What a team.

Until the day the non-stop barrage of nasty jibes and sly kicks were replaced by a new entertainment; they discovered Paula was scared of moths. Erica could still see the ring of happy faces and cupped hands surrounding her, this was something they could do which would not really hurt, just a joke, but the pleasure in their eyes was obscene. A cloud of fluttering moths swirled around Paula. Erica saw her face for a split second, white and stretched, and then she ran, chased by cheering kids, and Erica, puffing after them, left behind as always, her heavy body refusing to keep up, hot and sweaty, her breath labouring, unable to do anything to help, as they all disappeared from sight.

The pursuers were already falling back, bored, but Paula, like a fragile, fluttering moth herself, blinded by terror, ran onto the main road through the village and was killed by a van. Erica arrived on the scene just in time to see her in the road, no longer scared of anything.

After that, the adults took over. Police officers, doctors, teachers, counsellors, kind and powerful and reassuring with their uniforms, instruments, words. But where had they been all those days and weeks and months of her friend's torment, her own? And where had Erica been when she ran and when she died? Miles behind, useless.

She'd learned some hard lessons. That she needed to take control of her body, so that she could look after herself; those in authority always came too late. And so that she could look after anyone else who needed it too. As she dieted, exercised and willed the hated fat away, her mother feared anorexia; but that would be another loss of control, a weakness. Ironically, as she grew fitter and thinner, she became pretty, accepted, desired, but she didn't enjoy that until she'd moved on from the village school. Paula's white little face, seen again in Tessa's scared helplessness, haunted her dreams for a long time, but she knew that if anyone else needed her, she was ready; she would never again be left behind. Each time her homeopathic remedies helped someone, it was a brick building a wall between her and guilt.

Now she looked forward to getting back to her flat; but then, on the day after Boxing Day, the day before she was due to go home, the Operator was back in business.

A man, but no operating table. He lay on the cold ground but he did not shiver or curl up against the cold. The brittle stalks of winter-dead plants caused him no discomfort as they dug into his back. The night's damp soaked into his clothes and hair and froze, so that he was misted with frost. Beneath it his face was dark, and beneath the darkness of his skin his flesh was pale and greyish. He wore a woollen scarf, a flicker of true red in the greyscale winter garden, where he lay behind the shelter of a high garden wall. Dark brownish blood had seeped into the earth of the border under his head. His arms were stretched out to form a crucifix. Two nails stood up drunkenly from his hands. His shirt was wide open as was his warm winter coat. On the left side of his chest was a great gash, the edges of the flesh standing proud and white rib bones showing. The ribs had been cut and levered apart in an apparent attempt to reach the heart, but the ribs had guarded it too well or time and equipment had been inadequate. The heart was exposed as much as blood and rib would allow. It was still, hard and frozen like the White Queen's. Up the sweep of drive with its herringbone block paving, the house stood waiting, chill and silent. A holly wreath hung on the door, a gold ribbon catching the sluggish filtered streetlight. The house was not his. His own house too waited for him to come home. And the woman in the street waited, increasingly irritated in the bitter cold, for her little dog to return from the garden and continue their walk. She waited until she had overcome her well-bred reluctance to trespass on someone else's property and then she went in, to see her pooch snuffling at a frozen bloody corpse.

CHAPTER THIRTY-FOUR

It was like a repeat of the Kingston crime scene. Cars, vans, crime scene tape, same officers and CSIs, busy in a quiet leafy street at a quiet, affluent house. This time however the murdered man was outside and it was night, so powerful lights were being set up and a crime scene tent was to be put up over the body so that after a while it would seem as if he was encased in a glowing lantern. It was very cold but Will, Hassan, Sally Banner and Paul Lozinski weren't feeling it. Revulsion, pity, and a guilty excitement kept them warm. Sally, needless to say, had been despatched to talk to the sobbing woman whose dog had been first on the scene, together with the DS. Important witness, hence DS Masum; woman in distress, hence herself, Sally couldn't help thinking resentfully.

'He was *licking* it! He was *licking* it!' the witness Mrs Hodges kept saying, trying to reconcile her little fuzzy friend of the big brown eyes and baby-substitute position in the household with this unwholesome and unhygienic behaviour. Anybody would think there was an animal, a carnivorous animal with no sensitivity at all, which had poked its snout out of her sweet little Cupcake like an alien parasite.

'Er yes.' Hassan exchanged looks with Sally at the 'it.'

But that was unfair, he realised, you can hardly judge a person by an impersonal pronoun in these unexpected circumstances. It was Hassan who cleaned the blood off Cupcake's muzzle so that his owner wouldn't have to, and also in case of any DNA issues.

'Do you know the deceased?' Sally asked.

'No, no we don't, do we Cupcake? We don't know the poor man... well I say don't know...'

'Well do you or don't you?' Sally was snappy, watching Will and Paul put their heads together over the corpse.

Hassan frowned at her before turning to Mrs Hodges with a reassuring look of sympathy. 'Can you tell us anything about the deceased?'

'I don't know his name and we've never talked but I've seen him walking along this street before. Cupcake and I go for our last little walk every night at this time and sometimes I've seen him walking along in this direction,' she pointed along the street, 'and we've kind of nodded you know or said 'good evening' but that's all.'

'You mean he used to pass this house routinely?'

'I suppose so. Can we go home now please?'

'Yes of course. Though please come in tomorrow as soon as you feel able to give us a statement. Sally, could you check round the back of the house and I'll make sure our star witness,' he patted Cupcake's furry head, 'gets home OK.'

Shepherding them off the premises into the tearfully

summoned husband's waiting 4x4, Hassan thought of his own daughter. He hoped that by the time she grew up she could afford to be compassionate without losing cred and wouldn't have to keep proving herself like Sally.

Dr Johnstone had certified death and was examining the body. Will was going through the dead man's effects. His wallet, debit and credit cards, phone, change, keys, business cards, all the usual impedimenta were there in various pockets. No chance of a robbery gone weirdly wrong.

'Nobody's answering the doorbell. House looks all quiet. His key doesn't fit the front door.' Paul had tried to show some initiative.

'He doesn't live here.' Will was collecting info. 'Come and get this lot listed. It's all here. Name, address, phone numbers.'

Paul eagerly returned to Will's side and began to take notes.

'His name is Raj Gupta. Paul, take a look at him, and tell me what you think he did for a living.'

Paul looked at the body, now spotlit in the dark garden, arms outstretched as if acknowledging applause. He looked at the chest wound.

'I'd guess he's a doctor. Surgeon I mean. Heart surgeon, Guv?'

'Correct. Cardiologist to be more technical about it.'

'The Operator!'

'Oh god not him again. Annoying little scrote.'

Paul was startled at this, then he turned and saw Gary Thomas approaching. You could almost see him drool.

'Get shot of him!' Will strode off to talk to Hassan, leaving Paul to deal with the reporter. Will showed the DS the wallet, open to reveal a smiling photograph of a woman and children. The two men looked at each other, feeling sick with dread. As Sally came back round the side of the house, they turned and looked at her, and she stopped in her tracks, her face white in the darkness. She knew what that look meant.

Will held a briefing the following afternoon when they'd been able to gather enough information to make it worthwhile. In the meantime they had uniformed officers out doing house to house in the streets round about. When it transpired that Gupta worked at the local hospital, and liked to walk home from the Metro station, leaving his shiny Merc at home, they also covered the streets from the station, as well as riding the Metro to talk to passengers. Though Gupta had been regular in his geographical habits, his timetable varied according to his workload which often involved emergency surgery at all hours. Will gave instructions that any information picked up was to be passed on to him immediately, so he could include it in the briefing.

'Raj Gupta. Consultant Cardiologist.' Hassan added

a crime scene photo and a living photo of Gupta to the display. Three of them now. Kingston, Chambers, Gupta.

The Superintendent waded in, shedding fruitcake crumbs as he moved, and sat down on a couple of chairs. 'Our patch.'

'Erm yes sir, this one's on our patch.'

They all gazed for a moment of silence at the picture of Gupta alive, a serious, fine-boned man.

Heart surgeon. They all felt a difference this time, rightly or wrongly. This was a man who saved lives, who fought with death on a daily basis. A man whose work was vital. And it had been fatal to him.

'I might need a bypass one of these days,' Golden Boy rumbled, his mind running on similar lines. 'We need all the heart blokes we can get.'

'His heart got bypassed years ago,' whispered Paul to Kev.

Will shot them a look. 'He had been on duty at the hospital, yes Kev, Kingston's hospital. He liked to walk home from the Metro to relax his tension and exhaustion after long hours of surgery. He always used the same route from the station, though at random times of day or night. It looks like someone attacked him from behind with a stone, inflicting lethal head injuries, in fact they hit him twice, dragged him into the garden of that house and there tried to cut out his heart. It's a quiet area, especially at night. Few of its inhabitants walk anywhere except to walk their dogs; we haven't found anyone who saw what happened. He was cold when found, but then the night was freezing. Dr Johnstone reckons he must have been there for a couple of hours, which fits with his movements as far as we can check with the hospital. He was probably attacked about nine o'clock, as a working hypothesis.'

Sally chimed in. 'The house owners are away for Christmas. They are in New York City, which checks out, and seem to be in the clear. The Operator may have noticed the house was dark and empty and even waited for Gupta in ambush behind the wall with its high hedge, though how they'd know when he'd come past is anyone's guess.'

'Maybe the Operator was willing to wait, even several nights in a row, to get him. For some reason he was targeted.' Hassan resumed. 'Now what are the similarities and differences between this and our previous cases?'

'He was attacked outside,' said Sally. 'And not in his own home.'

'That's one major difference.' Hassan wrote it down under 'diffs'. 'In fact two.'

'His family were at home though,' Will put in, 'which would suggest that perhaps he personally, as opposed to any old cardiologist, was targeted, and the Op- killer had to change MO. The other victims lived alone.'

'Or even that it wasn't the Operator but a copy-cat,' Paul suggested. 'Or if it is the Operator, I mean if he exists, maybe that's the only reason Kingston and Chambers were targeted. They both lived alone. There can't be many surgeons that don't have wives or girlfriends.'

'Or husbands, or boyfriends,' Sally put in.

'Yeah, if they're gay,' conceded Paul.

'Or even women, you git!' Sally snorted with derision.

Will sighed. Round and round we go... 'Well we've not found any girlfriends for Kingston or Chambers, or any exes with any evidence against them. Any other ideas?'

'The nails in the hands, Guv.'

'That's a similarity, Kev, right,' Hassan added it to the 'same' list. 'The killer seems to have got the nails from the garden shed which wasn't locked. At least, the door was open and some identical nails found in there.'

'That's good enough for us.' Golden Boy stirred like a primeval swamp with a gas upsurge. 'Let's not make things complicated.'

'Like Chambers, Gupta was a quiet sort of bloke according to his wife and the colleagues we've had time to speak to. Worked very hard. Committed. Conscientious. More than competent.' Will spoke up.

'Any enemies?' GB rumbled. 'I'm thinking a lot of his patients probably died on the table with his mitts groping around in their chest cavities.'

Will winced. Hassan shot him a warning look.

'But sir, heart patients are often at death's door. Even patients' families would understand that.' Paul too felt the Super was kicking a man when he was more than down.

361

Will looked at Sally. The task of informing the family, Mrs Gupta and their son and daughter-in-law who'd been waiting at home for him, had fallen to Will. It had been a given that Sally would be one of the tellers. Lucky her. Will felt sick remembering Mrs Gupta's hands fighting the air as if to fend off the impossible, the unthinkable news, before her face seemed to dissolve like sugar in rain.

Sally took the cue. 'Not everybody appreciates that surgeons aren't magicians. His wife told us. Gupta had enemies.'

Much of this detail emerged publicly over the next few days. Gupta's family were too upset to comment and it was left to the hospital trust to parade a spokesman to trot out the usual platitudes. Whether he'd ever actually knowingly met Raj Gupta was doubtful.

The media were not shy about giving their opinions. The Operator had clearly struck again, and this time, outside. He was 'devolving' or 'escalating' or whatever vocabulary they'd picked up from TV crime series about serial killers. The police came in for criticism for not making the streets safe; they in turn were appealing for witnesses. The only sighting that had emerged was by another dogwalker, in a nearby street, who had seen a couple of separate joggers relatively near the time Gupta would have been approaching; a broad-shouldered man, wearing jogging clothes and a knitted hat, and a dark-clothed youth in a hoodie, hood up. He had not seen a face clearly, nor any obvious blood on either of their clothes.

Police wanted to talk to the joggers to eliminate them from their enquiries, or as witnesses. The police further infuriated the media by refusing to confirm that Gupta was a victim of the serial killer known as the Operator. They were keeping open minds; members of his immediate family were not under suspicion, having been at home together with some dinner guests; Mr Gupta had been heading home to join them. When he had not arrived, they assumed some emergency had come up, and that he had not had a chance to contact them, which was unusual, and had stayed the night at the hospital, which was not. But officially police were considering a racial motive for the attack as another possibility. No-one else was.

Wasn't he a doctor? A surgeon? Hadn't he been killed in a way which referred to his specialism, coronary surgery? Weren't there nails in his hands? Wasn't his wallet still in his pocket? What more did anybody need to know?

As any pleasure at being in her own place was spoiled by this new murder, Erica thought she might as well make herself thoroughly annoyed, so she rang Gary Thomas.

'Come to your senses, Erica? Realised only I can give you what you need under the duvet?'

'In your dreams. I just wondered if you had any inside info about this new killing.'

'Ah, the Operator strikes again! I hope... Well, I might

have, but I'm much in demand right now, pretty busy, and let's face it, Erica, what's in it for me?'

'I thought you might like to show off your inside knowledge now you swim with the sharks from the big nationals, that's all. You never know, I might be in a position to give you an exclusive one day, if my researches into these killings pay off. And if not, it won't cost you anything to drop a few words in my ear.'

'Well, I did pick up one or two things. But that's enough about my evening, ha ha! The police need to be seen to be looking at a possible racial motive here, but no-one I've spoken to thinks that likely in this case. The Operator's an equal opportunity psycho. Gupta had an excellent record, considering them with dodgy tickers are likely to kick it at any moment. Some evidence is contradictory or confusing. The nails in the hands weren't properly driven in, just a token really - but then he was on the ground, not a table. The killer would be in a hurry, afraid someone would go by and notice something.' He gave her a brief run-down of the killer's MO and the figures seen in the area at what might have been the relevant time. 'Doctors' organisations are screaming for protection, hospitals are issuing them all with attack alarms and they're going about in pairs when possible. Even the men! But you'll know all about lonely doctors needing protection at night, won't you?'

'I'm not rising, Gary.'

'Well as long as he is, eh?! Fnarr, fnarr. Of course, some

are saying the Operator is a doctor or health professional himself. Be easier for him to find out where doctors lived and if they lived alone. Could have a grudge against the medical establishment. Or a failed medical student. There's some argument about how much medical knowledge is involved in the mutilations.'

'Yeah, right, like Youtube hasn't got films of every operation you can name in glorious close up.'

After she'd got rid of Gary, she thought about Jack the Ripper. Old Jack had operated in dark alleys, near places where people were going by. He had been in a hurry. In one case he had killed twice in a night, the first time doing little damage to the body, apparently interrupted. So, his perverted needs still driving him, he had killed again and done his ripping. But the worst mutilations had been reserved for the only victim to be attacked inside a room. The added time and privacy had enabled him to go to town on his victim. Intestines draped over picture rails and so on. But the Operator had done it in reverse, going from indoor attacks to outdoor. Maybe it was getting harder to get surgeons to let him in as they were getting very wary.

Gary's point about whether the Operator could be a doctor himself was another parallel with Jack the Ripper. Some had believed that the mutilations were proof that a medical man, or one trained in medicine to some extent, had been guilty of the killings. But surely the crude nature of the present killings belied that. The murder of Gupta had been rather a botched job. The killer had made a mess of getting at the heart, being unable to prise the ribs apart. She knew from descriptions of roadside emergency operations that the ribs had to be cranked apart with retractors before the heart could be reached for massage by hand, or in this case, presumably, removal.

On the other hand, the ancient Aztecs were adept at removing living hearts from sacrificial victims armed with only an obsidian knife. But then, they got plenty of practice.

Such gruesome speculations were cut short when emails and texts started piling up. Jamie wanted to see her. It turned out he hadn't been away after all, but had had to stay on duty over Christmas to cover for sick staff. Funny he hadn't let her know but then she'd been away herself and they'd been sexting over Christmas rather than exchanging news. Her patients, suffering from holiday excesses, expected her to put them right with a pill. Some wanted hangover cures in advance for the New Year parties where they intended getting paralytic. Sometimes she could see Anderson's viewpoint.

She organised some appointments, texted Jamie to arrange a meeting, and decided to get outside before cabin fever set in. A run along the beach would put things in perspective as always.

It was a bleak afternoon, with tiny dry wisps of gritty snow whirling suddenly out of a sullen sky, like a heavy lead lid over the earth, with the sun sending some dull yellow rays under it. A large golden retriever bounded up, its coat matted with sand and water.

'Go away, pooch,' she said, but the thing shook itself all over her. As she was brushing wet sand from her clothes, the dog's owner also bounded up.

'Hi,' he said enthusiastically, with the same simple expectation of welcome as his dog. 'Lovely to see you! Alone, are you?'

She was about to repeat herself when she recognised him. Mel's golfing partner, whom she had met at the Golf Club dance, and had danced with. Howard, that was it. With the networking wife. There was no sign of her today, which probably explained the enthusiastic welcome.

'Had a good Christmas Erica?'

'Very quiet.' She gave the conventional answer everyone gave, even if they'd spent the festive season in a haunted castle with a rock star lover of each sex and a few minor royals.

'Saw old Mel the other day,' he remarked. 'Boxing Day, in fact. In the street, near his house. Thought he was going skiing - oh, god have I spoken out of turn? I assumed he'd be skiing with you. You haven't broken up have you?'

'Mel and I have nothing serious going, Howard. He was going skiing with Miles. They enjoy going on the hunt together, you know - each other's wingmen - some very attractive women there, all that apres ski social scene...' She was burbling, awkwardly trying to keep up the pretence of the Odd Couple which Miles and Mel seemed to maintain at the Golf Club.

'Ah, right.' Howard brightened. Omigod, he was pleased she was fancy free again. 'Maybe he came back early. Only saw him from the back, maybe it wasn't him. '

The conversation was brought to an end by a boxer dog which was taking an unhealthy interest in Howard's retriever. Erica ran off while he was attempting to disentangle them and avoid a black eye from the boxer's bulky and aggressive owner.

The further she ran from the car park the emptier the beach was. She revelled in the open space and the boiling wintry sea. She thought about Jamie. She felt about Jamie. Her few days away had intensified her desire for him; as she ran, the little shocks of her feet hitting sand seemed to climb up her legs and collect as an ache, a pool of heat in her groin. She was awash with lust, and couldn't wait to see him, touch him and taste him. She remembered their pre-Christmas dates and how he always seemed so quiet and nice, in the old fashioned sense, and how it contrasted with his total lack of inhibitions when they were alone. Sod Mel, Howard, dogs and all murderers. Except that Jamie had been around for the third murder… and possibly Mel too, from what Howard just said.

Had Craig Anderson also been around over the Christmas holiday? He could be described as broad-shouldered like the figure spotted near the scene, in fact it would be an understatement. He did hate doctors after all.

She dismissed the thought from her mind, until the papers reported more on the Gupta killing. Confirming Gary's words, he seemed to have been a respected surgeon with an excellent record. However, being a cardiac surgeon, he often operated on people who were near death, and unavoidably, some of them died in spite of his efforts. Almost a year ago, a complaint had been made against him. A young girl had died on the operating table, and her parents had accused him of negligence. He had come out of the investigation well and been cleared, but they had been bitter and unhappy with the verdict. The girl's father had threatened Gupta: 'It's not over yet!' That was said in front of other staff.

The media tried to chase up this couple for a quote but they had gone quiet. Presumably they would be questioned by the police. Erica hoped they had an alibi.

The similarity of the situation with that of Craig Anderson, whose son had died of meningitis which had not been spotted by hospital staff, and who certainly felt bitter about it, made Erica wonder. Could he have heard about the case and taken action like some muscular avenging angel on behalf of the parents? In which case, was this killing inspired by the other two murders, or was he involved in all three of them? She couldn't see why he would kill Kingston; most of the hatred Kingston inspired would not have been known to Anderson. As far as you know, Erica reminded herself.

Similarly, Craig Anderson had nothing she knew about against Paul Chambers. Though there was something in the bible, something ludicrous, which she'd used in arguments whenever someone quoted Leviticus to support persecution of gays. 'He that is wounded in the stones, or has his privy member cut off' is an abomination or ought to be killed. Or something like that, among a whole lot of bizarre rules about mixing fabrics and suchlike, all with OTT punishments, texts conveniently ignored by those who cherry-pick holy writ to back up their own prejudices. But maybe to a zealot like Anderson, a vasectomy specialist like Chambers could be seen as performing an operation which effectively excommunicated his patients, cutting them off from heaven and perhaps making them unfit to live. That would give him a motive, if his religious mania was extreme enough and combined with his hatred of doctors.

Perhaps Anderson had such a fund of hatred building up inside him he had turned to murder to assuage it, bypassing his residual conscience by seeing himself as an avenger for the weak. Finding each time it didn't heal the pain of the loss of his wife and son. And it was significant that those killed by the Operator had been powerful figures, high status men. Maybe he regarded them as fair game, and in some twisted way felt he was protecting the helpless from them.

Anderson worked out seriously and would have no trouble overpowering and killing another man, especially white collar workers like surgeons, especially as they had all been taken by surprise - the first wound in each case was on the back of the head.

She remembered how Anderson had come to Ivy Lodge and how scared she'd been. His tension, his suppressed violence. But perhaps some kind of chivalrous impulse made him leave women alone, especially small ones like Erica; it might not fit with his macho image to attack a woman. On the other hand, if he seemed in danger of getting caught for the other murders, self-preservation might kick in and chivalry would be kicked out double quick. For the sake of his personal Crusade. Fundamentalists could always find justification for their actions.

It would be dangerous to antagonise a loose cannon like Anderson. Erica pictured him like Patrick O'Brian's character Awkward Davies, rushing into battle waving a butcher's cleaver and foaming at the mouth; or perhaps he would be more like Stephen Maturin, surgeon and secret agent, who could kill when need be, coldly and efficiently with a steel blade. Either way, she had to know more. Poke the bear.

'Mr Anderson? Erica Bruce here. I was wondering if you still wanted to be considered as my patient. You did give me your personal details. I have them on file. I'm just sorting through my records for the new year, and in view of the opinions you expressed when I interviewed you...' She let him pick up the cue.

'Oh - right. Well I think I made it clear that I don't need any professional help except my own. I just signed on as your patient to secure confidentiality. So by all means delete the file. I won't be making any other appointments with you. You just put bandaids on bloated bodies which are already damaged beyond your skill to repair.'

What a charmer.

'Erm, OK. Just as you like, Mr Anderson. Did you have a busy Christmas period? Do some of your patients, like so many of mine, expect miracle cures for their own excesses? Or do you have them trained yet?'

'My patients know better than to ask me for magic bullets, Ms Bruce. I deal with more serious imbalances of the vital forces within the body.'

As always, talking to Anderson made her want to rush out and get legless and overdose on Belgian chocolate. One last try. A long shot.

'I expect they still want you on hand over Christmas though. Did you see there's been a third murder?'

'Yes, but it's of no concern to me. I was away visiting relatives down south, and I'm busy right now, catching up on my work, so please delete my file, on the assumption that what I told you remains confidential.'

If he thought that only she in this area knew his exact

motive, that gave him a motive for getting rid of her, if suspicion was gathering round him. Had Will Bennett taken her hint and looked into Anderson's past records? 'Down south:' what of the medics there he blamed for his son's death, surely he'd have gone after them if anyone?

Was there any way of checking on whether he really was away at the relevant time? Short of asking his neighbours on some crazy pretext... Besides, even if he had really gone south, he could have travelled back to do the murder and whizzed back all in a day. Maybe hired a car under an assumed name. Taken a train and bought a ticket for cash. That was all Will's department, checking facts and CCTV cameras.

CHAPTER THIRTY-FIVE

'Ye must be hornier than a Viking helmet, man.' During a break at Ivy Lodge, Stacey was slurping a caramel macchiato to go, Erica drinking smoky Lapsang Souchong from her own stash. Stacey was scoffing chocolate hobnobs ('vital office supplies') while Erica watched her. 'That lad of yours works too bliddy hard. Crap job if ye ask me.'

'He's got an insanely busy time over the next couple of weeks.' Erica swam, jogged, and did gym classes, but apart from giving her the usual exercise high and filling her with energy, they did not act as any kind of anaphrodisiac, rather the reverse. 'Good job I'm self-sufficient and able to care for my own needs as a woman should.'

'Aa'll bet ye get yer AA batteries delivered by truck.' Stacey nudged Erica painfully in the ribs and sloshed coffee over her sleeve. 'Jeez, yer ribs hurt me fkn elbow!'

Miles breezed past. 'Hi girls!'

'Miles! How did the skiing go? Howard said he thought he saw Mel over Christmas. I thought maybe something had gone wrong.'

'Oh it was great, but Mel had to cut and run, some crisis at work, as per usual.'

So Mel *had* been around over Christmas. Erica remembered Howard's conversation at the Christmas dinner dance, how he'd mentioned Mel and Kingston being deep in consultation on the golf course, though Mel claimed to hardly know Kingston. An awkward lie, he'd said. Was it? Also Erica had a nagging feeling that somebody else had lied at the Golf Club. Not a big lie, or she'd have noticed it consciously. An awkward lie where there was no need for one, or so it seemed. Any lie might be significant, if she could only remember it.

One way of recovering a lost memory was through hypnotherapy. But she could hardly ask Miles to hypnotise her, only to hear her casting suspicion on Mel. She could go to another therapist, but how could she know they were trustworthy or reliable? And Miles would think it so odd...

Jamie too had cancelled his trip to stay with relatives to be on duty in the hospital in case any amateur Santas fell off the roof. Of all the many suspects she'd collected for Kingston's murder, only those who had been away and could be shown to have been away at the time of Gupta's killing could be eliminated from suspicion. Unless of course there was more than one killer... Was she really considering Jamie as a suspect, she thought with shame?

Combining genuine convictions with cunningly setting up further investigations, for her next health page she dealt with remedies of all kinds for SAD, Seasonal Affective Disorder, which makes sufferers gloomy and torpid, some to the point of disability. Remedies like daylight simulation light bulbs, for example, and where to get them. Herbal remedies like St John's Wort for depressive symptoms. Getting as much daylight as possible. So many people must go to work in winter in the dark, come home in the dark, and spend all day in artificial light.

She suggested getting out for walks outside when possible, even in cold or wet weather, and told how when she was feeling down, or had thinking to do, she made for the sea, and how she would often run south along the seafront and along the north pier to the end under the huge empty sky and watch the waves smashing against the stones. She had been going there daily recently. She went on to recommend exercise, as even when exhausting, it is paradoxically energising.

So, it would now be natural to follow up with a series of features on sports and outdoor hobbies which would look into the health benefits but also into the social benefits of, say, golf. Her research would enable her to penetrate the Golf Club and ask questions. Although Chambers was in a different club, and Gupta - did he play? He hadn't been at the dinner dance. Nobody of any skin tone darker than 'Antibes Tan' or 'Coronary Crimson' had been there... still, somehow the Wydsand Golf Club kept cropping up.

What about Mel, and Howard's description of him being in close conversation with Kingston. Mel's bland unhypnotiseable gaze came into her mind, his air of concealing some private joke. Did Mel have a motive to kill Kingston, maybe something to do with being outed, or some business deal perhaps? The other two murders could have been copycat killings, or done to hide the real motive - although again, to think someone she knew could have inflicted those mutilations was horrible.

'Selwyn Blackett here,' said a jovial voice when she rang Wydsand Golf Club.

She explained her mission. He was suddenly less jovial.

'Well, I don't know, Miss Bruce. We don't, that is to say, the members come here expecting, I mean to say, it is a private club you know. There are rules about non-members and *ladies* coming into the bar... and a *journalist*, well...'

Hm, lady journalist, two strikes against her.

'I'm doing a health article, Mr Blackett, not an exposé - not that you've anything to expose, I'm sure. Just one visit and a chat will do, and a few facts I can get from your website. It will help to give golf a boost in the area, encourage people to join.'

He laughed. 'We've a long waiting list for this club, Miss Bruce, we've no need to sell ourselves. We make a point of being extremely particular about what sort of people we allow to join. The members like to think they'll meet here their own sort of people, people they feel at ease with. People who know how to behave.'

Ah PLU, like Kingston? He knew how to behave all right. She bit back enquiring exactly what he meant by 'own sort'. The first job was to get in there, any questions about ethnic minorities and women could wait.

'Oh, dear. I was hoping you or someone there could spare me a few minutes. You were all so friendly at your Christmas dinner dance - such an enjoyable evening.' She hoped some personal connection with a member would help.

'You came to the dance? Yes, it was a good do. With whom did you come?'

'With Mel.'

'Oh, I see.' The joviality was back in place. 'I think I remember you. Red and black outfit, rather striking? Yes, Mel is a sound chap. I should have thought you could just talk to him.'

'You know how it is, Mr Blackett, it's better to get information from an official source, it looks better in the paper. What exactly is your role at the club?'

'I'm Membership Secretary. Well, I'm standing in for our Membership Secretary, whom you may know was injured by a golf ball. Damned disgrace! Bloody people get onto the course you know, whacking away like maniacs. He's recovering, I'm glad to say, but we'll be having our first committee meeting of the new year soon and a new Mem. Sec. might well be elected. Why don't you come along at lunchtime and I'll show you round, and you can take a look at the course.'

The Golf Club bar looked rather dissipated in daylight,

as bars do. A pale sun shone through the big picture windows, glinting on the bottles and trophies. Outside, the green landscape flowed in gentle undulations, decorated with fawn sand bunkers and clusters of trees and bushes. Colourful figures strolled in pairs, towing trolleys bristling with clubs. Erica managed a glance into the distinctly inferior 'ladies' clubroom', but was allowed to perch on a stool in the main bar where a few men looked at her with alarm. Maybe they were afraid she'd menstruate on their furniture.

She met Selwyn Blackett, a powerfully built man with a small paunch. He had bushy eyebrows that met in the middle and thinning hair on top. He was smartly dressed in golf gear. She'd noticed that golf clothes were in bright, even ice cream, colours. Baby blue, primrose yellow, fancy patterns, even pink... all the colours and designs the sort of solid businessmen who joined Golf Clubs could never wear in any other part of their lives. Maybe that was one of the main appeals of the game, the chance to let loose with colour and feel it was conventional, even de rigueur. A kind of respectable version of cross-dressing? She mentioned the colours, not her speculations.

'Safety. Make you stand out on the greens. Helps to avoid accidents. Golf balls are very hard, you know, and they travel at a hell of a speed. Still get the odd whack, when a ball goes astray, or some idiot doesn't look out where he's going.'

'Yes, I know how dangerous they are. Someone hit me on the arm with a golf ball while I was running down the track along the side of the course.'

He bristled and opened his mouth to defend the honour of his members.

'I'm sure it wasn't any of your lot. It happened at night.'

'Oh, I see. Those damned yobs find golf balls and break windows with them, the little vandals. Envy I suppose. Can't be arsed to work for money themselves, but resent others having it. A pity the police can't seem to do anything. They could do with some healthy exercise.'

'Like golf?' Erica said with faux innocence.

Blackett chose to ignore her comment. 'D'you know, a full eighteen holes of golf is a good four miles' walk. Most of our members drive everywhere and have desk jobs so it does them the world of good. Shall we go outside?'

She gladly abandoned her drink and followed him out. They'd probably fumigate the bar when she'd gone.

Even though it was winter, the course was green and soothing to look at. They strolled along, Blackett hailing various players who looked at her suspiciously. She should have brought a leper's bell to ring.

'That's Robert Kingston's house over there isn't it?' She could see only the upper storey windows of the houses from here. It seemed a good chance to bring the conversation round to the murder.

'Yes. A bad business, that. Respected member and a

good golfer too. Very keen, when work allowed. They still haven't caught anyone, you know. It's a disgrace. Those neck-end lads were hanging around... haven't heard the police have arrested any of them. Though there've been those other murders. The Operator. Some lunatic.'

'Of course Mel knew Mr Kingston.'

'Possibly. A little. I don't think they knew each other well. Old Mel's away so often. I did hear Robert once mention that Mel'd put him onto some shares. But they weren't what you'd call friends.'

This didn't sound like a row or anything, unless the shares had plummeted. But who would be able to tell her that?

'I wonder if Kingston's widow will sell the house,' she fished.

'It'll be snapped up, you can bet on it. Plenty of members would give their eye teeth for that. Well, not much point in giving their right arms, hey?' He laughed.

'Yes, so Mr Archer was telling me. Mr Kingston's neighbour. He's thrilled to bits to be living so near the club.
'

'I'm sure. Actually his mother used to be a cleaner at the clubhouse, and his old dad was a groundsman here. Grew up with golf... Ah, times change, eh?'

He sounded a bit regretful, as if them as cleaned the club should stay on the right side of the j-cloth. As they strolled back towards the clubhouse, Erica glanced back at the houses and caught a glimpse of movement at Archer's window. He was gazing out over the course. Blackett raised a hand in a kind of ironic salute to him, and he returned the gesture.

'I'm surprised he isn't out playing this morning.'

'Maybe he'll drive up later.'

Drive? So much for all the healthy walking and open air. She said as much.

'Oh, he's not a member of *this* club yet, goodness me no. He belongs to the city club. He's on our waiting list. Very keen. Always wanted to be a member here, and live right there in those houses. Lifetime ambition. Bit of an upstart, you know. But getting that house was a long-term investment for him, and well worth it.'

Erica was surprised. Surely Archer'd given the impression he was a member already. Was that the awkward lie that tugged at her memory? Then she remembered the Christmas dinner dance. Someone said, 'Nobody's brought old Archer'. That should have told her; if he was a member, he wouldn't need to be brought as somebody's guest. She looked up at his window, but he was gone.

'He loves that view,' Blackett said. 'There's none better, in my book. He often sits by the upstairs window, even in winter, watching the players.'

Erica cycled back home, wrote up the piece on golf and emailed it in. Ian Dunne should be pleased she was featuring his own favourite sport. Not that he was any advertisement for healthy activity, with his perennial fags.

Researching among old and new books of homeopathic

remedies for various patients, she was amused to find one for 'exhaustion due to partner's excessive sexual demands'; she must tell Jamie about it, especially as it was 'China'. Though China was not an oriental remedy, but made of Cinchona bark, like quinine. Jamie was often worn out from the demands of his job, the problems of bureaucracy and politics that plague any hierarchy, funding problems, and so on, but being young, he was always up for pleasure. Hers, in particular. And his demands were every bit as excessive as her own.

Her erotic musings were interrupted by news headlines on the radio, tuned to the local house music station. A man had been found with severe injuries and loss of blood. A man who worked in the medical sphere, the newsreader yelped breathlessly and ambiguously. Police were not able to comment on whether there was any connection to the Operator killings. The man was alive, but his condition was critical.

Another one, and so soon? It seemed incredible. She tried contacting Gary Thomas but he wasn't answering. Out covering the story no doubt. It had just broken, after all.

Between late afternoon and early evening appointments at Ivy Lodge, Erica managed to keep googling and following Twitter until she could glean a little more. The injured man was said to be 'an alternative therapist'. He was still critical, having lost a lot of blood. The man's name was being withheld until next of kin had been informed;

they must be still trying to contact them.

Did this mean the Operator was branching out? Should Erica, Miles and their colleagues start looking over their shoulders? There was as yet no clue as to whether the Operator had been involved. The news media made the connection cunningly, mentioning that 'three murders involving members of the medical profession have been committed lately by a killer dubbed 'the Operator', but police are so far refusing to link them to this attack.'

The tone implied that the police were a bunch of party poopers and of course any fool would see there was a connection.

Erica thought about the injuries inflicted on the other victims. Nails in the head, castration, the heart exposed. And now the Operator – or whoever - had botched the killing, maybe left the victim with injuries as horrible as those, but still alive. Was that better, or worse?

Her next patient came in to talk about his piles. Harriet Vane and Peter Wimsey never had this trouble.

By the time she was at home, making a mushroom stroganoff with fat-free bio yogurt, the news was more detailed. Surgeons were trying to re-attach the man's right hand which was almost severed, but there had been major blood loss. There was also an injury to the back of the head.

The man had been identified as Craig Anderson.

CHAPTER THIRTY-SIX

Erica mechanically stirred some French mustard into the sauce, but it was hard to eat any of it. She picked at her green salad, the news going round in her head. She couldn't believe the Operator had attacked Anderson. With his pumped-up muscular body, tense awareness, he'd be a hard man to take on. Even a blow to the back of the head would be risky. Craig was a loner, isolated by his hatred and bitterness, so who could get close enough to him to hit him without him noticing?

Also, why would the Operator attack someone so totally opposed to the medical establishment? Someone who hated doctors, who practised alternative medicine almost as an act of war. It didn't make sense.

The doorbell rang, making her jump. It was Jamie. As soon as she opened the door, he put his arms around her and they kissed for a few blessed and absorbed moments before she pulled back to look at him. He looked shattered, his face almost grey, his eyes narrowed with fatigue.

'This is unexpected. Aren't you on duty?'

'Have been, for more hours than I can make sense of. But I wanted to see you. I heard the news about Craig Anderson. I remembered you talking about him. I know he wasn't exactly what you'd call a friend, but what with finding Kingston's body, and now this man you know being injured, I was concerned about you. If that's alright.'

'It's alright. I've been trying to eat, without much success. '

'We can eat together. We've got to keep our strength up, as our mothers would no doubt say. Though sometimes I wonder what for.'

'Jamie, how did you know it was Anderson? The news just gave his name when I was cooking, and a few minutes later you arrived.' A frisson of doubt.

'I heard it over the medics' grapevine. He's up in the city hospital, but the word reached our dump pretty fast. We've all been jumpy with these Operator killings. Any news gets passed around like gonorrhoea.'

'I thought he *was* the Operator when he came to Ivy Lodge all hyped up, and I thought he was going to kill me. Well, the thought crossed my mind. But I couldn't help feeling sorry for him. He was so bitter and screwed up. And now this has happened. His right hand. How is he, have you any details?'

'Sure you want to hear about it?'

She poured wine for them both. 'Hell yes.'

Jamie sank back on the couch, his eyes almost closed. His voice was soft and slow, he'd only had one glass of wine so far but he was all in.

'They think he'll live. The head injury wasn't drastic, though there was a skull fracture. He was unconscious when he was brought in. The hand might be saved, it's not quite as bad as the media makes out, but it may not function the same way as before. Nerve damage. Recovery will be long and slow. He could be effectively disabled. '

'As if the poor guy hadn't suffered enough.' She was thinking of his dead son, his dead wife, and now this. He wouldn't be pumping iron for a long time, if ever, with that hand.

Her thoughts were interrupted by the doorbell. Now what? Will Bennett stood on the doorstep like bad news personified.

'It's about Anderson – I know you visited him recently, I thought that, you know, finding Kingston and now this… I thought I'd check you were, you know, all right.' He looked rough, his eyes two dark hollows. Ah, the pressure to get a result was starting to tell.

'Yeah, right. You mean, check up on someone who keeps meeting Operator victims, suspiciously often? Anyway, Inspector, it's very kind of you but I have a guest…'

'Oh, I see.'

'Who is it Erica?' Jamie's clearly non-female voice drifted down the hall.

'Ah – well, a good thing you're not alone. I hope… well, good night,' Will almost barked, as he strode off and she returned to Jamie.

'I think the Inspector is losing it. Thought he could scent weakness and homed in, huh! Suspecting me because

I met Anderson probably, or trying to. Anyway, what were you saying about Anderson before?'

'He has two black eyes.'

'I can't see anyone taking him on in a frontal assault.'

'The word is,' Jamie said in a voice that was almost a sigh, 'it's a contre coup injury. The black eyes... contre coup... what was I saying?' He pulled himself up and forced his eyes open. 'I'd better not finish that wine.'

'Oh, yes... I've heard of that. Bouncing brain in its little pond of fluid.'

'Yeah. Certain types of head injury cause the brain to bounce up and hit the facial bones from behind, causing black eyes; usually it means that the moving head hit something, rather than that something moving hit the head.'

She put her glass down. 'You mean, he fell over backwards and hit his head on something? Instead of being hit? Maybe someone found him unconscious and carried out the hand injury; a copy-cat Operator type assault, do you think? Or could someone have knocked him down with a punch to the face, hence a black eye which wouldn't show after the contre coup.'

'No, now look Erica, this is very much inside information, the police haven't released details yet obviously.... but it looks very much as if he might have done it himself. Cut off, or tried to cut off, his hand, passed out, fell over backwards, and hit his head on something hard - a tiled hearth, I think it was. There was some kind of banner or poster lying across him.'

'Oh, my god.' She grabbed her glass again, and swigged back the wine. 'I knew he was in a state, but this..... I can't believe it.'

'Well, it's not official yet, and there may be more to come out, if the police decide to make it public.' He rubbed his eyes.

'You really are exhausted aren't you? They work you too hard at that place - I hope it'll all be worth it when you're on the golf course as a highly paid consultant.'

'Been a shit day. Accident; child hit by car, driver didn't stop, horrible injuries, distraught parents, and I can't do enough. Pain relief isn't powerful enough, our skills, my skills, aren't good enough to do more than a patch-up job. Even nature won't be able to put everything right, with all the healing power children have. Keen footballer, this kid. Was.' He sat up and took her hand.

'Sorry Erica. One day I'll learn not to care so much, I suppose. '

'I hope not. There aren't enough doctors who have the empathy you have. Come on, you need rest.' She hauled him to his feet and supported him into the bedroom. He had thought of her in the middle of his own troubles. He needed some TLC too.

'I don't usually get much rest here,' he murmured, as Erica peeled off his jeans.

'You will tonight. Though I'm not promising anything about tomorrow morning... One unselfish act deserves another. I'll give you a massage to help you relax.' She trailed her hair down his body. 'With my tongue, if you like.'

She woke up in the night to find her cheeks wet with tears. Craig Anderson. She was crying for him. What was happening for heaven's sake? Beside her, Jamie was so deeply asleep he seemed to be scarcely breathing. The light picked out the fine bones of his face and the smooth skin of his shoulder. Somehow, while she was sleeping, the shock had worn off, and she could feel something of the despair Anderson must have felt to do that to himself, if he had. To have the willpower to try and cut off your own right hand with your left; such a horrible, fundamental mutilation, such a way to die, as he would have expected to if he hadn't been found in time.

Erica felt she had let him down. He had come to her, in denial perhaps, but he had come. She should have realised he felt this way. She should have been able to do something about it. What remedy could she have given him for this? All his anger had seemed turned outwards. What could have happened to make it turn inwards against himself? He was religious, in a fanatical way. She remembered the biblical texts on his wall, his way of speaking. Surely suicide would go against his creed. But then, thoughts of revenge and hatred had not seemed to go against his beliefs. Suicides usually took pills or hanged themselves or slashed their wrists. To try to cut off his hand - a picture jumped into her mind. One of the biblical texts on the wall, written in big black curly letters on a white banner similar to the other texts on Anderson's walls. IF THY HAND OFFEND THEE, CUT IT OFF.

How had Anderson's hand offended him? He had seemed so sure he was right about everything. Two possibilities came to mind. Either he had made some drastic mistake over the treatment of a patient, in which case she could well imagine he would turn his anger on himself at having been proved wrong, fallen short of his own faith. Or he had used his hand to do something else unspeakable. Like slit open a scrotum or a chest? Like hammer nails into a person's hands or head? Anderson could be the Operator after all. Surely the police would think so.

But then why would he suddenly get a bad conscience about it, if he did it in the first place, and more than once? Traditionally it's said that killers get a taste for the work, they escalate, as the rush killing brings fails to last and they need higher and higher levels of stimulation. Though some killers behaved as if they wanted to be stopped. Her brain whirled. She got up stealthily for a drink of water. She couldn't put the light on, or read, or anything else she might have done if she'd been alone. It was wonderful to have Jamie next to her, but there was a downside to sharing a bed.

She opened a new bottle of sparkling mineral water and it fizzed out all over her. She swore, getting back into bed wiping droplets of water from her belly and thighs. Jamie's dark eyes were open, two faint glints in the dark.

'Sorry, woke up thinking about that stupid git Craig Anderson. Stupid, stupid thing to do!' Her voice rose.

'Erica, you couldn't have done anything to help him if he didn't choose to be helped. You know that. Don't beat yourself up over it.'

'Listen who's talking!'

'Yeah, well, I'm as daft as you are. Come on, lie down. Mm, you're all wet. My favourite kind of woman. Trust me, I'm a doctor.' He disappeared under the duvet.

Next day the police, anxious to quell the excitement about another possible Operator attack, issued a statement that the injuries were not thought to be the result of an attempted murder such as those carried out by the person known as the Operator. Craig Anderson was stable, surgeons were optimistic about re-attaching his right hand which had been practically severed. His skull injury meant he was still very ill and police were waiting to interview him about the circumstances in which he was injured. They could have a long wait. Erica was desperate to know what was behind Anderson's self-mutilation or suicide attempt.

There was only one way to find out. She would have to ring Will. She could try the city force, but they would probably refuse to speak to her at all. Awkward, after their last brief meeting on her doorstep when he'd done a runner at the sound of Jamie's voice.

He was unavailable. Damn. She rang the city hospital. She would have to be careful here. They would probably regard homeopaths as witch doctors. She asked after Craig Anderson. No, she was not a relative, she responded to the inevitable question. Nor a journalist. (Well she wasn't wearing her journalist's visor at that moment.) She was a private therapist and counsellor Mr Anderson had been consulting. This was technically true. She still had his details on file. He had consulted her. She was a trained counsellor. Hospitals used counselling staff these days, so they shouldn't be too suspicious.

She piled it on a bit, saying she'd been concerned about him, and he had confided in her about certain anxieties which had been preying on his mind. She was concerned that his injuries could be self-inflicted. She knew that detail had not been made public so far. The voice on the other end hesitated, while Erica waited. They could ask the local police about her to check if she was genuine. They might then find out she was a feature writer and assume she was after a news story. They might well check with the police officer who no doubt was hanging around Anderson's bed waiting to be able to talk to him.

The decision was made, presumably without checking. She would not be able to see him, he was too ill, immediate family only, but she could talk to one of the staff looking after him.

She was put through to a Dr Mackson. Erica told her that Anderson had been in a tense and distressed state, very bitter about past bereavements. Mackson seemed to know about his wife and son, though she didn't say so directly. They were dancing around each other, both trying to keep confidentiality. Presumably his relatives had told the hospital. Since his opinions about doctors had been in the newspaper interview he gave, Erica didn't feel the need to keep that secret, so she mentioned his attitude to the medical profession. She said she was worried about how he'd react to find himself in a hospital, a hostile environment as far as he was concerned. Mackson said their own counsellors would look into it.

They were getting quite cosy now, and the doctor went so far as to confirm that it did look as if the injuries were self-inflicted, and that there was something clearly on his mind. He had been unable to make any statement, only muttering about 'blood on his hands', presumably, she said, referring to the bleeding caused by the injury. Erica could ring again in the near future and maybe see him when his condition had improved.

Erica thanked her and rang off. Blood on his hands? Cutting off his right hand? The police would not be slow to make a connection, especially given Anderson's opinion of doctors. She could see the hunt for the Operator being scaled down. She could only hope Anderson's family had a good solicitor organised.

At work in Ivy Lodge that afternoon, she got a call from Ian Dunne.

'It's my elbow.'

'Excuse me?'

'My elbow, woman. You know, pointy thing halfway up my arm. It's giving me merry hell. Ruining my game and, what's worse, I can hardly raise a glass. Lucky I'm an ambidextrous drinker, eh! The doc's tablets are doing bugger all. Thought you could slip me some of your eye of newt or rat's arse or whatever.' His elbow must be in agony, his mind had been deranged. 'Your article on golf. I like it. I didn't realise you could treat real illnesses, like golfer's elbow. Thought it was all stuff that people imagined they had. So I'll give it a whirl.'

Oh great. She arranged an appointment, giving him some advice to follow in the interval. Why oh why had she written about golf? Dunne would swallow the remedies with a mouthful of Scotch and fag-smoke instead of letting them dissolve in a clean mouth. His mouth hadn't been clean since he was weaned. Then he'd sack her if they didn't work.

She suddenly realised how much writing features meant to her. It was something different, it was interesting, challenging, socially useful, and although the constant deadline hung over her like a cloud of blood-starved mosquitoes, she would miss that buzz if it went.

CHAPTER THIRTY-SEVEN

The media seemed to be holding its breath. From being claimed as the Operator's newest victim, it was now being hinted that Anderson actually was the Operator. Someone had leaked or sold to the media some of the phrases from his office walls, which seemed to clinch it. Public discussion on social media and online comments made it clear they'd made up their minds. According to Jamie, the mood of paranoia among medics, consultants in particular, was lifting even as the days lightened with the promise of eventual if reluctant spring. Evidence, proof and trial were just formalities. Erica was beginning to feel, perversely, protective of Anderson. A mixed-up mess, yes. The Operator? Not so sure. What if Will and cronies stopped looking and the real one was still out there?

The weather was unsettled too. Sudden freezing winds would blow up, whipping the sea to a cold fury. She would run down to the pier to watch the mighty waves and think, and was frequently shepherded back by the harbour master as huge waves began to hurdle the wall, first as spray, then as great bodies of water that could wash a person off into the lethally icy, boiling sea. The unruly water matched her mood and even the wind brought a bitter pleasure of its own.

Ian Dunne arrived at Ivy Lodge with his golfer's elbow. It did not bode well when Erica politely asked him to put his cigarette out. He was not pleased. Her attempts to talk to him about his background, to learn about him so she could use her intuition and the Materia Medica to choose a remedy were stymied amid gruff demands to 'just give me the bloody pills, woman!' He made it clear that he had no intention of giving up golf to rest the joint, even for a couple of weeks. She explained how to take the pills, by tipping them into the cap, tipping them into his mouth and letting them dissolve slowly, at least half an hour before and after eating, drinking and smoking. She showed him a helpful exercise and where to apply ice and heat and for how long and how often. She prescribed Rhus Tox.

'These look more like contraceptive pills. Are you sure there's enough in here to do any good?'

'It's your own body that will heal you. The remedy just kick-starts that process.'

He stowed the little envelope away in his pocket. 'Take a hell of a kick-start for that Anderson to heal himself! Poor guy's obviously a raving nutcase. Bad conscience, if you ask me. They'll never send him to prison. It'll be the funny farm, you can bet on it. Hey, we can run a follow-up feature on him when the trial's over. 'My lone meeting with the Operator, by Erica Bruce. How our health correspondent met a multiple killer and lived."

'I'm glad you read my stuff so attentively.'

'I read every word of the paper like it was my daddy's Will! I read your golf piece, didn't I? I was glad to see you listed all the local clubs, including mine. Wouldn't want all the publicity to go to that lot at Wydsand Club. They've got a waiting list as long as an orang utan's arm. Still, they've had a bad year in some ways. We've been joking about it in our club bar. Harry Archer's been getting some stick I can tell you! Wanting to join a club where you get murdered! A waiting list to be whacked!'

'That's a bit extreme, isn't it? It was only Kingston. Gupta wasn't in a Golf Club from what I gather, and as far as I know, Paul Chambers was a member of your club. '

'Yes, but Chambers was going to join Wydsand Club as well. He was on the waiting list, same as Archer. Meant to retire to the coast. Anyway, I'll give these pills a try. Thanks, pet. Glad to see you've packed in trying to be a proper reporter. It just isn't your area.'

He left just in time to save his life, cradling his elbow and taking with him the stench of stale Marlboros. She opened the window, regardless of the wintry blast which charged in without so much as an appointment and chased paper all over the room.

Somehow she had to calm down and get her brain into gear. She re-established order, ran home, had a hot shower and sat down with some Thai Quorn casserole she'd made and frozen in portions, and a glass of wine.

401

What had Dunne said? Wydsand Golf Club had had a bad year. Kingston, a prominent member, was murdered. Paul Chambers, who was waiting to join, had been murdered. People were dying to get into that club. Even their membership secretary had been put out of action for a long time. He could have been killed...

There might be a connection. Suppose Gupta's murder was a one-off copycat crime, a big assumption admittedly, the whole thing could centre on Wydsand Golf Club. Harold Archer was also on the waiting list to join, but had not been attacked. Though he wasn't a doctor. But Kingston was already in the club. Why him and Chambers? A lie, an awkward lie. Archer had lied to her. He had given her the distinct impression that he was a member of Wydsand Club, said how good it was to stroll down to the club, when actually he was still having to drive up to the city. And after he'd bought Kingston's mother's house for a premium price. But surely he'd have known about the waiting list at Wydsand before he bought the house? Dunne did.

Surely it wasn't about the waiting list? No, that was ludicrous! People might be dying to get into the club but surely they weren't willing to kill to get in. It was just a game after all. A respectable hobby. If the waiting list was that long, you could hardly murder your way down it until your name was at the top. Could you? Unless it was all about resentment, revenge for injustice. Someone getting their name above yours, or something similar.

She called the club and found out when Selwyn Blackett, who'd shown her round on her previous visit, would be in. She possessed her soul in patience until then. They refused to give his home or work numbers. The next day she trekked back to the club and once more upped the coronary rate by invading the testosterone-ridden bar at lunchtime, after parking her bike among all the shiny cars. Its handlebars seemed to droop dispiritedly but Erica charged in all guns blazing.

'Has it occurred to you that this club could be the centre of these so-called Operator murders?'

Blackett choked on his single malt, spraying whisky all over his cuff. 'Good God! you journos do get carried away. That's rather far-fetched, you know. That Gupta bloke didn't even play, and Chambers is in the City club.'

'Yes but Chambers is on your waiting list. Think about it.' She outlined the basic connections for him. 'Maybe the membership secretary's golf ball to the head wasn't an accident. I took one on the arm that was meant for my head. OK, it could have been random vandalism, but put together with Kingston's and Chambers' deaths, it makes this club look like an unhealthy place to be. Harold Archer, Kingston's neighbour, is on your waiting list, isn't he? And pretty desperate to get in, after buying that house he's saved for all his life, watching you lot playing outside his window.'

'What, and he could be next? You ladies and your idea

of logic! The Operator kills doctors, dear! Hence the name, Operator!'

'Well *sweetie*, possibly somebody on your list, like Archer, could be - well, shortening the list.' She was sticking her neck out.

'Now look,' he spluttered. 'Archer is a respectable chap, or we wouldn't have him on the list at all. He understands how it is. My predecessor, the Membership Secretary you claim was knocked for six on purpose... he explained to Archer, that whatever he'd been told, living by the course did not put him top of the list, and he had no choice but to accept that. He's getting on, and it's a long list, but the rule was, anyone belonging to another club was put further down the list unless they resigned from the previous club. Bit strange really, you never know, perhaps the next Mem. Sec. will see if we can bump him up the list.' He winked, clearly expecting his position to be made permanent. 'Naturally he doesn't want to resign from his old club until he's safely in here. Otherwise he could be left with nowhere to play for an unspecified time.

'The rule was originally to stop people joining several clubs and not giving allegiance to any of them, clogging up the membership lists and stopping other men joining. Fair enough, though in his case it could be argued that the rule was a bit unfair. But, you have to have rules, and they have to be seen to be enforced.'

She listened impatiently to all this. 'You enforce an

arbitrary rule, which you admit is unfair, then merrily scrap it if the Membership Secretary changes? Seems a funny way to run things. Was Paul Chambers ahead of Archer on the waiting list?'

'Yes he was. So were other chaps. You're not suggesting... our club has to take *murderers*? Some must advertise, but we don't. All our applicants must be proposed and vouched for by members to get in. And wait their turn on the list. There's no-one here with any dark secrets, I assure you.'

Like Mel and his male lover? Kingston and his violent sadism?

He spoke again before she could reply. 'You're laying yourself open to slander accusations talking like that. It isn't right. You'll have to leave. '

Their attempts to keep their voices down were getting more and more forced.

'Look.' Erica was practically hissing now. 'You've just told me Archer expected to be a special case because he'd bought a house here. Where would he get that idea from if not from Kingston who sold him the house at an inflated price? I agree, it sounds weird to think anyone could kill their way to the top of the list. There's a lot I haven't worked out yet. And there's Gupta. But what are you leaving your club open to, if it turns out Archer's guilty and you've bent the rules to let him in? What will that do to your reputation? If I were you, I wouldn't let any one through your own front door at night until this is all sorted. And I'd be watching out for flying golf balls.'

'Well I've certainly heard a lot of balls today. You really must go, Ms Bruce. Or I'll have to consider calling the police. I must say, I wish I hadn't agreed to let you in here in the first place. Some of the members didn't like it at the time.'

She got riled then. 'Nice to know you're willing to admit murderers, as long as they aren't female or Asian of course!' She stormed out of the club, but the thought of having to unlock her bike and pedal off in a rage watched by Blackett was cringe-making. She sat down on the boundary fence, in sight of Kingston's house, to cool off. She was uncomfortably aware that she had her own prejudices against organisations like the Golf Club and its rules. She mustn't let that cloud her thinking.

Did she have to tell Will? It did sound daft, and the police were well satisfied that the medical connection was the valid one. She might be maligning a harmless man looking forward to playing golf in his retirement. On the other hand, if she did nothing and someone else died horribly, the blood would be on her hands, at least in a sense. Her thoughts lurched aside for a moment. It was possible to feel that one had blood on one's hands through doing nothing, as well as something. Might that apply to Craig Anderson? Punishing a sin of omission, instead of commission? Could he have been guilty of the Gupta murder, if her theory was correct? Gupta was accused of a similar act of negligence, albeit wrongly, to that of the medics Anderson blamed for the death of his wife and child.

She phoned Will as the wind chilled her rage-hot cheeks and numbed her phone hand unheeded.

'Erica!' his all too familiar sardonic tones stung her ear like lemon juice in a cut finger. 'What can we do for you?'

'I've a theory about the Operator murders. Seriously, I think I might know who it is.'

There was a silence. 'Some of my colleagues think the same, actually. We're getting close to making an arrest.'

'If you mean Craig Anderson, I don't think he committed the murders. At least not two of them. Gupta perhaps. I think the medical connection is just a blind.' She explained about Harold Archer. 'Surely it's worth looking into.'

'Do you expect me to take this seriously? Or are you wasting police time? One minute you're hounding me in defence of Tessa Kingston, now it's Craig Anderson. It's a very ingenious idea but it defies common sense.'

'I was right about Tessa.'

'Erm... I have no statement to make at this time.'

'Oh come on Will! Have you established any connection between Tessa and the other victims? No, I thought not. OK my theory sounds a bit out there, but since when did murderers use common sense? A loss of proportion is typical. Plenty of killings are for motives that seem senseless to sane people. I'm sure there's something in this,

Will. Think how you'll feel if someone else dies while Craig Anderson is still in hospital. Think how I'll feel. Do you honestly think I'd ring you up for fun, after the way you've been treating me just because of - the past? Do you think I enjoy being patronised and my ideas rubbished? I can get that from my editor!'

'For heaven's sake, Erica, why can't you learn to keep out of police business! Apart from anything else, you could be putting yourself in danger.'

'Ah, so you admit the Operator might not be Anderson! Or how could I be in danger, since he's bedbound? Did you research his background?'

'Of course. We know about his son, and his wife.'

'Yes, and he hates doctors because of all that, so surely if he's the Operator he'd go south and kill the doctor who made the decision to send his son home from A&E?'

'This may astonish you Erica, but I checked up on that. He wouldn't have killed that doctor, because he's already dead. Died earlier this year. He was killed in a car accident, he'd taken to drink sadly. Possibly conscience over Anderson's child, possibly stress over Anderson's accusations.'

'Oh.'

'And there's no evidence it wasn't an accident, but I'm going to get them to reopen the case to double check it wasn't murder. Anderson may have started with him, and carried on, or he might have killed the other doctors after he'd been thwarted of his revenge on the one he blamed.'

'Well fine, but look, since Anderson's on ice for now, it can't hurt to keep investigating other avenues.'

Will gritted his teeth. 'Of course we're still following up leads, jeez I'm the one being patronised here. Nothing is certain. There are inconsistencies.... the Gupta murder doesn't fit the pattern in some ways. And yes, we've checked up on the Morrisons, the couple who blamed him for their daughter's death. They had alibis, though admittedly only other family members, but we've got nothing on them anyway.'

'Isn't there any forensic evidence?'

'Nothing conclusive. It's not that straightforward. Believe it or not, we have checked for connections between everyone we know to be involved.'

'Did you know Chambers was on the waiting list for Kingston's Golf Club?'

'Well no. So thank you for that vital piece of information Erica.'

God he'd find out who'd missed that and throttle them even though it was a beyond insane idea. He'd said 'find ANY connection' and the team should have caught it. 'I'll add it to our database... yes we've even created one of those. Sally Banner's brilliant with computers.'

'Yeah, she'd like to defrag your hard drive for a start.'

'Everybody doesn't have a sex-crazed mind like yours you know.'

'Poor you! Good luck finding another like me. Anything in there on Archer and forensics?'

A pause while Will raked through Sally's database. 'Erm... yes, Harold Archer, known to both the first two victims. He'd been to see Kingston about some aches and pains, and to drinks at his house, and of course he'd bought his mother's house, though that was all done through solicitors and estate agents. He'd been to Chambers' house too, through their mutual Golf Club connections in the city. So even if we did find the odd hair or fingerprint it wouldn't necessarily solve anything. Please, leave it to us!'

'Peter Wimsey would've listened to me. He's got imagination.'

'No, he's imaginary. Get a grip Erica. You really think Harold Archer is so eaten up with envy and rage over not getting into a Golf Club...'

'Yes! Can't you just imagine Kingston, selling him the house at an inflated price, enjoying the fact that it took a lifetime of effort for Archer to afford it, letting him think his dream is about to come true, lying to him about getting into the club, then making sure he has to languish on a list? Do you think guys often leave that club, apart from feet first? Can you imagine how that feels? Kingston next door, gloating! Sneering at him every day. Conning a man out of his hard-earned savings, just for the sadistic pleasure of it.'

'OK. So I can see how Archer might feel like bashing Kingston on the head, maybe when they're both outside trying to chase those lads away from the path... but Chambers, just because he's on the list?'

'Not just because, partly to hide the true motivation, keep you thinking it's all about doctors. Gupta may have been a copycat, maybe that was Anderson, or maybe it was Archer, *because* there's no link! The media had run with 'the Operator', what better way to draw suspicion away from himself, confirm it's a medical motive and a serial killer!'

'Erica this is an oldish kind of geezer, he's in his mid fifties, a serial killer with slippers and a pocketful of Werther's Originals...'

'Will! That's the most egregious ageism! I can't believe I'm hearing this... what appalling stereotyping! My god...'

'OK, OK, I was being flippant, your theory is so insane! There was something I was trying to say... god you do my head in. Ah yes, so he might have crept up on the three surgeons with a rock, stretching credibility to breaking point, so how about the membership secretary, and you? How many serial killers have two distinct MOs?'

'I don't know. That's your job.'

'He'd have to be unfeasibly accurate with a golf ball to aim straight at somebody's head! I know he missed yours, but he got pretty near. Remember what the hoodies said, they have to lie to the lasses about hitting rabbits. What? Hang on Erica... What is it Hassan?'

Will's end of the conversation went mute leaving Erica on hold. Hanging on to memories and words... what had those lads said? It wasn't quite the way Will remembered it. She was used to listening to people and remembering, noticing what they said and how they said it. Something about a cat... It wasn't Archer with the cat, it was the woman next door, Ziggy or Siggy. And something they'd said about the rabbits had surprised her. In fact, she'd been recording them at the time. She'd not bothered listening to it, as all sorts of events, Stacey's call, Will's arrival, Stacey selling remedies to the lads, had intervened and anyway she'd only been doing it to impress them.

She dug it out of her bag and found the file for that night. She played it, fast forwarding.

Here it was. '*...used to find golf baals lying aboot and try and get rabbits and that with them. A couple of windows did kind of get broke...*'

'*Did you ever get any rabbits?*' Her voice, sceptical.

'*Aye, buttloads of rabbits, man,*' then a tussle sound and an oof! of pain from the speaker before their leader Scotty's voice came on.

'*Shurrup! Did we fuck! We'd find dead ones and tell other lads we'd killed them. That's aal.*'

That's what had surprised her. That Scotty would deny hitting the rabbits instead of lying that he had. She searched a bit further on, glad that Will was keeping her on hold.

'*We hated the bastard. Stupid fucker...*' meaning Kingston.

'*That other owld gadgie was worse...aalways on wor case, I fuckin hate him, and that cat -* 'Another sound of violence

412

and the voice was cut off. Again, Scotty took over.

'It was the owld wifie with the cat, man, always coming oot moaning at we.'

Twice Scotty had stopped a lad from speaking and glossed over what he'd been trying to say. What did it matter who had the cat, and whether they'd killed rabbits with golf balls?

Thinking hard, she didn't notice Harold Archer watching her from his upstairs window. She was watching Blackett through the Golf Club bar window, speaking on the phone and glowering at her. Snobby git. His words came back to her, 'our club, take murderers? some must advertise, but we don't...'

'Murder Must Advertise!' she said aloud. Dorothy L Sayers' novel in which Lord Peter Wimsey solves a crime involving a pebble, no, a scarab, propelled by a catapult. A cat - ! What if those lads had made or bought online a catapult which could fire golf balls, and they'd used it to break windows, damage plants, and take pot-shots at rabbits? Oldest naughty boy meme in the world. 'Just William' and Scotty, twins across the decades. Quite clever too. Golf balls lying about the course, ammunition that couldn't be traced back to them. Golf ball injuries could be blamed on someone practicing on the course at night. Scotty hadn't wanted her to know about it. Did this mean it was the lads who'd fired at the Membership Secretary, taking him out of action with head injuries, and at herself?

With murderous intent, or poor impulse control?

'I hate him, and that cat' the lad began, speaking of Archer. Had he been about to say, 'that catapult was ours'? 'that catapult took ages to make', 'cost a packet on ebay'? Had Archer copied, or taken, or found, their catapult, and used it against the Membership Secretary, and herself? Did that make it more or less likely he'd killed Kingston? Her mind was whirling. She had to think it out. If only Will would listen to her. She ended the on-hold call with Will, then called him straight back. It went to voice mail.

'Will, it's Erica. It was a catapult. Archer's got one, or the lads have, anyway that's what was used against the membership guy, and me, and possibly something to do with Kingston's murder... listen.' As she relayed the recorded dialogue she was retrieving her bike and beginning to push it. 'I'm going for a run to think things out and work off my adrenaline. Meet me on the pier if you're free or call back.'

She finished the call, got on her bike and pedalled off as if she'd been fired from a catapult herself. She barely noticed the biting cold even though she'd been still for some time.

Bloody Will Bennett! To think, that arrogant bastard had once held her in his arms when all her defences were down, given her orgasms, all the while holding what she did in contempt. All the time, smugly convinced he'd saved her life back at Stonehead, and that she needed his protection. She just couldn't forgive him for that.

CHAPTER THIRTY-EIGHT

'Bloody Erica Bruce!' Will stormed to Hassan, sitting next to him in the car. 'S'alright, she's on hold. She can't hear. She doesn't bloody listen, more to the point!'

Hassan had taken a call from the station to say a Mr Selwyn Blackett, of Wydsand Golf Club, had rung to complain about a Miss Erica Bruce who had been making allegations about members or would-be members which could damage the club, especially as she might publish some of this 'dangerous twaddle' in the local paper... and Blackett had ranted on in this manner when Hassan rang him back to find out what was going on, interested at first simply by the proximity of the club to Kingston's house. He'd put Will on the phone, cue a re-run of the same rant, before he could break in and try to pour oil on troubled vinegar.

'She suggested that Mr Archer might be murdering his way up the waiting list?' Hassan was hearing this for the first time without any of Erica's reasons and couldn't help grinning. Will grinned back at him as he tried to soothe Blackett.

'Do I hear amusement, Officer? It's not funny I assure you. This club has spent decades building up a certain reputation...'

Will tuned out briefly, looking at his own mobile which was silently ringing, Erica's name showing. He let it go to voicemail while he offered Hassan's mobile back to him, and Hassan made a great show of refusing to take it, Blackett's voice quacking out of it as it hung in the air between them. Will put it back to his ear, to hear Blackett winding up, 'I hope you're going to follow this up, young man. She ought to be arrested, or at least silenced, threatened with legal action... members of this club have had a bad enough time, press hanging round, members attacked or murdered... Mr Archer is desperate to get in, I've just been telling him, this kind of allegation won't do his bid for membership any good...'

'You've spoken to him?' Oh shit, Erica was in trouble now. Archer could sue her, the daft bint. 'Was that wise, sir? If you're not happy with that sort of erm, rumour, surely spreading it yourself is counter-productive?'

'Yes well I thought Archer ought to know what was being said, and to be frank with you Inspector, he is well, fanatical about joining this club, it's a lifetime ambition for him, and I just thought... well I told him, I hope you've got an alibi for some of these attacks Mr Archer, because we don't want this sort of mud sticking to the club!'

A feeling of unease began to form in Will. 'How did he respond?'

He pressed mute and hissed at Hassan, 'Drive! Archer's house, next to Kingston's!' Better safe than sorry.

Hassan started the car and set off, while Will kept listening to Blackett on Hassan's phone.

'Archer was furious! Said he'd seen her outside the club, and was going to sort her out. She'd just bicycled off by then but he said he'd catch her up, and then he hung up on me. Rather rudely too. Then I saw his car go haring off. Though how he'd know where to look for her...'

Will cut Blackett off, 'rather rudely' too, and grabbed his own mobile to ring Erica. No reply but he saw the missed call from her. As he listened to her message he snapped, 'Archer's after Erica, he's in a car and she's on a bike and he's out of his mind with rage... she'll be heading to the pier. To 'think it all out'. She's got a new theory and new evidence and she won't know what to do with it.' Since I've shown no interest in her ideas.

'Hang on.' Hassan slewed the car round. 'Maybe Archer will lose her? She could cycle anywhere, alleys, footpaths.'

'She said in the paper that's where she goes to think and to run. He might know where she's heading. Best head straight there, though we'll keep an eye out for her.' He asked the station to put a call out on Archer's car, and for any officer to look out for Erica on her bike. Hassan was making all the speed he could on the residential streets, towards the sea front and heading for the river mouth.

'Long shot though,' Hassan said. 'We don't know which way they went, there are loads of streets you can cut along. We'll try the obvious, the sea front road.'

'She had more to say about her theory in the phone message... you'll never believe this, she thinks he's the Operator.'

'Archer!'

'She thinks he killed at least the first two, yes I know it's far-fetched, but actually he may have attacked the Membership Secretary which could be attempted murder. And Erica herself was attacked. Possibly. And she is so very attackable.'

Will brought Hassan up to speed on the catapult theory. 'It sounds fairly harmless... but that Golf Club bloke nearly died of his head injuries. As it is, he may have long-term brain damage. Foot down, mate, Erica's in deep bother and this is when she decides to go running.' *Because I wouldn't listen to her.*

Running. What else could Erica do now? Go to Archer's house and accuse him? Fat lot of good that'd do. He might murder her, or more likely, just laugh in her face. She had no proof at all. She had no way of contacting the lads at a moment's notice. And they'd just deny everything. Will wouldn't be interested, even if he ever listened to her message. The theory did sound crazy, even to her. She could just imagine his sardonic expression, his blue eyes narrowing. Battling against the wind along the seafront was an outlet for her pent-up rage, as she headed for the river mouth and the northern of the twin piers. Along the promenade, past the grotty bit with the boarded-up souvenir shops and amusement arcades full of young kids wasting their money and their lives, along curving rows of hotels and B&Bs, most proclaiming vacancies or full of weekend stag parties; past the church and the long sands, where as usual some brave souls were belly-boarding or trying to surf.

The ruined castle on the headland of the river mouth got nearer, as her breath came harder, the wind kept rising, and the thoughts in her brain kept coming but getting nowhere. The sky was darkening to a slaty wet mussel-shell colour, and the matching sea moaned in sympathy with the wind keening in the overhead wires. Waves were beginning to lash the sea walls below to her left. She could hear the familiar 'wump!' as tons of water met solid rock and concrete, flinging up curtains of spray.

There must be something I can do, she repeated like a mantra. Suppose Anderson never recovers fully, or is brain-damaged? He'll never go to trial, but they'll assume he did all three killings. She wasn't convinced he'd killed Gupta either. No, Erica. Keep to the point... A bus swung past, its slipstream all but sucking her and her bike into the traffic. It was a relief to get off the road and down the hill to the beginning of the pier.

Waves were appearing over the top already in puffs of smoky spray. The big wrought iron gates at the entrance to the pier were still open. Hardly anyone was on the pier itself in the bitter cold wind and rising sea. There was a clutch of people on the concrete platform on the open sea side of the start of the pier, watching the waves from safety as the wind built them up higher, stronger, whiter. At this rate the harbourmaster would be emerging from his little hut soon to close the pier. She felt a strong urge to get to the end, even if she'd only have to turn round and run back again. Standing out there, as if on an island, just her and the sea, she'd find calm in the heart of the storm, and answers.

She ditched the bike against the salt-corroded railing, and ran through the gates. As she pounded along the pier, waves flew higher on her left, trying to climb over the pier wall. On her right, inside the harbour, it was calmer, but the contained swell was still impressive. The moored fishing boats and the green and red buoys marking the safe channel for big ships bucked frantically like rocking horses on crystal meth.

A father and his two children and a middle-aged couple passed her heading back to land, already wary of the increasingly dangerous waves. Dark irregular patches on the path showed where water was landing, and the two children were sopping wet. Kids could never resist daring the waves. Soon, larger and larger volumes of water would leap the wall, swill across the path, and gush from the pier through the railings on the right into the harbour. She kept going, heading for the stubby little lighthouse on the end.

She focused on getting that far, determined to go round its hollow body, stand if only for a minute on the very end of the pier.

She'd always shaken her head sadly and wisely when newspapers reported that someone had been washed off a pier or some rocks, or fallen from a cliff, or capsized a boat while not wearing a lifejacket. Now the risk didn't matter. Getting to the end was something she could set her sights on and achieve, and that seemed more important than anything at that moment. Something she had control over.

Her hair whipped about her right ear, the icy wind knifed her left with a horrible earache. The sound of the waves hitting the huge stone barricade beneath was accompanied by plumes of spray stinging like hailstones. She kept running. As she got to the last third of the pier, a huge mass of water leapt up, threw its multicoloured tentacles above her, and fell. From the land, it would look like a fine spray. It felt like buckets of icewater thrown over her, including the buckets. She ducked under the weight, checked by the freezing cold shock as the crest of the wave splatted over the path and ran down the other side. Water ran off her. Her hair was plastered down, her clothes were lead-heavy, harsh salt was in her mouth and stinging her eyes. She was gasping with shock but she kept going, and as she reached the lighthouse straddling the pier's end, another wave shot across behind her and flooded off under the railings. It would have been hard to keep her feet if that one had hit, but the railings would stop her being washed off. Probably.

The clamour of wind and water howled around the lighthouse, but there was a sliver of partial shelter on the side of it opposite to the weather's full sound and fury. The path went right round it, on the outside, with a kerb-like wall and an iron railing where she stood for a second watching the sea. It was spectacular, rainbows dancing madly in the white towers of spray, as waves flung themselves right past her, hard and cold as hammer blows. She hung on to the rail, but the walls gave her some protection. She'd made it to the end, and she'd have a very wet time getting back. She'd have to get out of wind and water soon or exposure would set in. The sea was painfully icy. She went inside the open base of the lighthouse to catch her breath. The doorway went dark. The harbour master, come to chase her back. But it was Harold Archer, and he was right in front of her, blocking the entrance.

He was holding a golf club, raised as if to swing, but the handicap was hers. She was fitter and younger, but trapped and unarmed. She couldn't get past him and any other retreat was cut off by the storm-crazed North Sea. If the harbour master was coming, Archer could easily belt her one with the metal club before he got to them. It would be impossible for anyone to see what was happening from further along the pier, especially in these conditions. She could have 'fallen and hit her head' on the slippery wet concrete.

Could she keep him talking? She thought of the dialogues he'd had with Kingston and Chambers and the cold went to her heart.

'I knew you'd come here,' he shouted, loud enough to hear above the weather, the effort distorting his face to an animal snarl. 'It's where you always go isn't it? I saw you leave the Club, and drove down to beat you to it. You just ran right past me! I've been waiting for you just round the lighthouse.'

'Why?' Her throat was the only dry thing on the pier. 'Trouble with golfer's elbow?' She was shivering so much her voice wouldn't stop shaking. She sounded scared, which made her angry.

'Oh, no. Nothing wrong with my swing. Years of golf have left me with strong arms and shoulders.' He swished the golf club with its solid metal end back and forth. She could only get past him if she went for him, and before she could get near enough, that club could get her first.

'Blackett told me about your allegations. He doesn't believe you, or so he says, but he warned me it could affect my application for membership until it's all cleared up. After all I've been through! You have no idea! I should have known you'd be trouble, peering over fences, asking questions, butting in where you aren't wanted, even going to the Golf Club! Why did you have to interfere? And what proof have you anyway?' His voice, shrill enough to cut through the noise of the waves, almost wailed in self-pity.

'Witnesses, I found witnesses,' she lied. Without taking her eyes from the club, she thought of her neat digital recorder. A chance at least to get something on him, even if she didn't survive. She reached inside her jacket to switch it on, and remembered she'd left it, with her phone, in the saddlebag on the bike. Shit. If I ever get out of this, she promised herself, I'll superglue it to my forehead rather than risk being without it. If. Not that he'd have let her use it anyway.

'Those bloody hooligans was it? I can't believe it, you and them, ganging up on me, destroying everything I've worked for all my life, who are you to do this to me...'

'Mr Archer, *you* tried to kill *me*, remember? With a golf ball...'

'I missed, didn't I? Well nearly. But you wouldn't be put off! Bloody women, can't leave anything alone. Everyone's against me, no sooner get rid of one obstacle than another springs up.'

Her mind riffled through possibilities. Should she tell him she'd already passed her suspicions on to the police? Then what – he might feel he had nothing to lose by killing her anyway. With what he'd done already, that would be nothing to him. Except he'd never done it face to face with a conscious victim. Maybe she could keep him talking until the harbourmaster got here to check the pier was empty. (If, if, he was coming at all.) She did have a knack

424

for making people spill their guts… trying to blot out this image, 'You said I've no idea, so tell me, why did you do it?'

His face was screwed up like the butt-end of a pepper, anxiety, anger and fear shrivelling his features.

'Why?' he shrieked. 'I started with nothing, nothing! Years and years scrimping and saving, working all hours, doing night classes to get more qualifications, working my way up the housing ladder, all I wanted, dreamed of, was a nice house by the sea next to the Golf Club. Where my parents worked like peasants for members who wouldn't so much as say good morning to them. I was determined to make it, however long it took.

'That bastard Kingston conned me! Sold me a house at an inflated price, promised he'd get me straight into the club, then once I'd signed the contract, he reneged. Of course it turned out it was all up to that pompous fart of a Membership Secretary, and his precious rules! Rules to keep out riff raff, oh yes Kingston told me that, you should have seen his face! He was loving it! He'd known all along! Riff raff!'

With each adjective, and without irony, he swung the club; it sheeeshed through the salty wet air. She tried not to flinch.

'And oh,' he went on, 'how Kingston loved to keep rubbing it in! Always coming round, calling over the fence every time I went in the garden - how was the club membership going, wasn't it a long list, what a shame I had to sit and watch others play or drive fifteen miles for a game, so sorry he couldn't help, 'I'm not Jesus Christ, you know,' he'd say with that damn smug face of his, oh he loved to see me squirm. Me! Hard-headed, successful business man, pulled myself up from nothing by my own efforts and my own wit, conned by a bloody quack!'

Jesus Christ, with his crown of thorns. Or spikes. Nails in his hands. 'You're not the only one Kingston hurt.' Erica tried to dilute his paranoia. But he wasn't interested in anyone else. Like Kingston, he had tunnel vision and himself filled his field of view.

'Anyway, he's not so smug now, is he? Neither is that fool of a Membership Secretary. I always was a good shot, you know, always been a demon putter. Found a catapult, dropped by those thugs when they were running off, very powerful one I have to say. I used to fire balls I found on the course at Kingston's windows, plants, at night, just to relieve my feelings, I felt so powerless! Then one day, I saw the secretary from my window, standing on the course in broad daylight, and I just - fired. On impulse. Whack! Bang on target. Saw him go down like a sack of spuds. God it felt good... then I was worried sick. But nothing happened. Nobody knew. I even sent him a get well card!'

He laughed, swishing the club in time with his mirth. Would that harbourmaster never get here, surely the pier was dangerous enough by now...

'Then I heard that Kingston had advised Blackett to

keep the old rules until they knew if the other bloke would be coming back... that night, I heard a disturbance, those bloody young thugs out the back, high on drugs probably. I looked out my bedroom window, saw Kingston burst out of his house, sounding off at them over the golf course fence. They must have scarpered pronto, I didn't see them. I had the sadistic bastard in my sights. I didn't think I'd hit him in that light, but no! Another bullseye! Hell of a smack on the back of the head, he went down like a dead man, and did he have it coming... and you know, it felt fantastic! Then everything blurred, I don't know ... I don't remember... and still, after he's dead, still there's something in the way – you! But I had less luck with you didn't I?'

Erica wasn't feeling so lucky right then. She was shivering violently, her back pressed against the damp rough wall, Archer filling the space in front of her. He must have bashed Kingston with the stone right where the golf ball hit. To hide the tell-tale wound. To make sure he couldn't resist or taunt Archer any more.

'The lads saw you,' she improvised. 'They looked back and saw you. They didn't come forward before - they don't like the police but they told me. I've told them to tell the police.'

'Those scruffy bastards – no respect for the law! You see what you and Kingston have done? I, who have played golf with city magistrates, have been turned into a criminal, like those scum!'

427

'What about Chambers and Gupta?'

'What about them? I've no sympathy for Chambers, he was above me on the list, another stuck-up quack like Kingston. And that other bloke, the day they let his sort in the club, I'll resign. Bad enough they let them in the country. I'm not standing any trial, but I want you to know, you interfering little bitch, it's all your fault!'

'The nails, what about the nails?' She was still stalling.

'The police and those psychiatrist types can puzzle that out! My life is over!'

Suddenly he turned and went out into the storm, and stepped up onto the first railing, leaning out over the wild sea. Curtains of water fell over him, falling back to show him still there, clinging on with one hand, the other still holding onto his golf club. She darted out after him, and put out her arms to grab him. He turned towards her, his face contorted, and struck out at her. She didn't hear her wrist snap as the heavy club caught it. She barely felt it at first, numb with cold and flooded with adrenaline as she was. But she knew it was broken. There was a strange electric buzzing up her arm. At the same moment a huge wave curved up over him, and he vanished behind a smoke of grey water. When the wave fell back, he was gone.

CHAPTER THIRTY-NINE

She hung over the rail, holding on with her good hand while the water hit her like a bomb blast. She could see his golf sweater bright orange among the waves, just a glimpse… oh god. Why me?

She climbed through the rail, holding her wrist against her body, and jumped. She'd loved it all her life, but the sea doesn't love you back. That's the deal. Don't fight the sea, she clung to the thought like a life raft as she sank into darkness and surfaced. The intense cold seized her like a steel fist, keeping her ribs from expanding so she couldn't inhale but bobbed in the water, uttering shallow gasps. She forced herself not to struggle. You don't need to breathe, she told herself. Not yet. Don't fight the sea, don't ever fight the sea. Go with it. Be with it. Like fish. Small, weak, yet they can go where they want. Fish swim near the rocks, the waves pounding above. Relax, become part of the water, then you can move within it. She repeated her meditation mantra in her head, her chest slowly relaxing a little. She tried to breathe out as much as possible when her face was under water. Whenever she felt air against her mouth, she took whooping sips of breath.

She tried moving through the water, kicking her trainers off her numb feet. The water was not swimming pool water, it was opaque, dark, salty, burning her throat. She swallowed it repeatedly, retching, making breathing even harder. Using her legs, stiff with wet clothing, and her right arm, keeping her left tight against her chest, she tried to search for Archer on the surface. Except there was no surface. The waves were high, and she was often underwater, trying to see through the water left in her eyes whenever she was in a trough of the waves. She wouldn't survive long in that cold.

At least it dulled the pain caused by her attempts to wrench herself through the thick, resisting water. Where was the murderous old sod? The swinging swell of the water tried to carry her out past the piers into the worst of the storm, but she managed to keep just within the lee of the pier. Sea, sea, I love you, don't kill me, love me back, let me be part of you...

She looked up through streaming stinging eyes to where the pier wall swayed above. There was a dark figure there, waving. Something orange burned the air like a flare; a lifebelt. She swam for it, gracelessly crabbing one-armed through the water, latched onto the plastic ring with its life-saving rope, and then, freed from the fight to stay afloat and breathing, tried again to look for Archer. The figure on the pier pointed. A shape in the water....she struggled towards it. Archer was unconscious, clinging for life to that bloody club with both hands. She was glad he was out of it. She didn't fancy another swipe with that thing. She was glad she'd done a lifeguard course, but she'd never practised with one useless arm. She dropped out of the lifebelt and forced it over his head, clinging to the outside of the plastic ring. Just a pathetic man with sparse grey hair, his face bluish and calm.

OK. Now we are both in icy cold water, losing body heat fast. We are at the bottom of a high, sheer pier wall, and if we go close to it, we'll be dashed against it by the waves. For the same reason the tall dark figure on the pier wouldn't be able to do anything with the rope from up there. Just stand and watch them die. Assuming the coastguard had been notified... That was her only chance.

As if she'd spoken to him, the figure high above her, still holding the end of the rope, dived into the sea. He began to swim, not very elegantly bearing in mind he had two arms, towards them, along the rope hand over hand. It was Will, gasping, and making squealing noises as he struggled to breathe against the tight grip the cold had on his ribs. He was beginning to panic, not as used to water as Erica, unable to force his ribs to expand, unable to time any possible inbreaths and outbreaths, but they eventually met, the three of them attached to the lifebelt in water which was like chilled syrup, then more like setting cement as Erica weakened. She knew that as hypothermia set in, she'd find it hard to think clearly and to move. Her leg kicks were erratic. Most of the time her face was under sideswipes of water. She fought not to breathe except when the sea allowed it, for that way lay drowning, your blood full of seawater. She was becoming lightheaded, and a drowsy warmth was invading her body. This was when people dying of cold in the snow crawl out of their sleeping bags under the illusion they're too hot.

It all seemed like too much trouble. Timing the breaths to coincide with her mouth being above water… such hard work. It would be easier to stop breathing. She'd always wanted to do that. Be free from the drudgery of breathing, so happy in the sea like a seal… Will reached out for her, but she shrank from him, terrified he'd pull her arm, managing to gasp out, 'arm - broke' in fits and starts. He understood. He was over the first shock now and able to breathe. He had more strength left than Erica and, making sure Archer's mouth was above water as much as possible, held onto Erica as her numb hand lost the power to grip the lifebelt. 'Why bother?' she thought. 'Just let it all go.'

She thought of her mother, Jamie, her sister, her friends, her patients who needed her, but mostly she thought of Craig Anderson, Archer, Gupta; if she just gave up, she'd never know what happened. She had to know. She saw something dark ahead, heard the throb of an engine and realised the inshore lifeboat, run by volunteers now that the local coastguard station had been closed, was on its way, called by the harbourmaster presumably. Everything was being taken care of. Will was looking towards the boat. She lay back, looking up at the darkening sky and the lighthouse rising and falling, and like Ben Gunn she longed for toasted cheese, could even smell it, oily and salty.

She didn't get any cheese on toast or sympathy.

'Erica, you crazy fucking stupid idiot!'

Someone was dragging her into the inflatable lifeboat. It was Will, his hair plastered to his skull, water running off him. Hassan was there too, as was the harbourmaster, they'd dragged Will on board, and now all three men were bringing Erica and Archer onto the boat.

CHAPTER FORTY

The euphoria of incipient hypothermia, the numbness of her broken arm, not to mention all her other extremities, the peace of that little boat and all that followed seemed dream-like as she was hoisted, wheeled, moved, wrapped in silver foil like a roasting chicken, horizontal, helpless, reduced to a patient, a victim. She could hardly move or speak, her throat burned by salt, and after being taken in the ambulance to the very hospital she'd visited in search of information, she lay in Resuscitation while the nurses cut off her clothes and chatted to each other as if she wasn't there. The cold had chilled right into the core of her, and now it was chilling her again on its way out, drawn out by osmosis in the overheated hospital, and she convulsed with shivering.

'I expect Jamie Lau will want to know about this one,' said one voice knowingly. 'He is *interested* in this case, if you know what I mean.'

'So are the police,' said another. 'They're hanging about out there now, making the place look untidy. Still, that Inspector is well fit. I wouldn't mind cutting *his* clothes off and checking his vital signs.'

'He's with the old bloke they fished out.'

Archer! She tried to speak, to ask what had happened

to him.

'Just lie quiet now and we'll soon have you sorted out,' a blur of a face shouted into hers as if to a fool. They continued their conversation.

'He should be OK. But it looks like he's in big trouble with the police. Anyway, you know I'd heard Jamie was going out with some kind of alternative therapist. I expect she'll be a right pain. Probably make a fuss about meds and so on.'

'Well they've filled her full of antibiotics already, like it or not. That water is filthy. An attempted suicide they brought in here, his arm got infected, and when they analysed it, it was a bowel infection! In his arm!'

'Gross! You wouldn't get me swimming in there. Hate being a patient, me. You're no better. When that traction weight dropped on your foot, what a bleeding fuss! Even the great Kingston was a right wuss where his own health was concerned.'

'It's not as if he ever had any sympathy for anyone else.'

'Story goes, few years ago, His Godship had a minor op and came straight into work. Only fainted, didn't he! Gasping like a landed fish he was. Delayed shock. Silly sod.'

'Yeah, he'd have thought he was above human reactions. Git.'

'Dead git now.'

'Good riddance. Let's get that arm immobilised. Here's

some gas and air pet!'

This was for Erica to hear apparently. 'Just take a whiff with each breath. It's good stuff.'

'I often have a puff meself when I'm passing,' confided the other nurse. 'She's quite bonny, isn't she? I bet that hair's lovely when it's not full of mucky water and worse.'

'More bony than bonny if you ask me. Don't know what Jamie Lau sees in her. He's a cutie.'

The gas and air sent waves of anaesthesia through her. Jamie's face swam into her field of vision. She tried to smile; he would hover over her like a beautiful angel, stroking her fevered brow, not like horrible Will Bennett. No chance. He looked grim. He looked mainly at her arm instead of into her eyes, and when he did pay her any attention, it was only to say angrily, 'What the hell have you been doing to yourself?'

The nurses exchanged looks across her body. Dr Lau wasn't normally like this. She made a huge effort.

'Good thing you're so good in bed,' she croaked in an alien whisper.

Amid much giggling from the nurses, Jamie's face vanished. She heard him saying something about theatre, and then they rigged up a drip and she lost interest in the proceedings again.

She came round gradually. She still felt the swaying of the sea, she was back in the lovely little boat, heavy all over with water, her hair spread out like seaweed… she saw Archer's distorted face smoothed out by the merciful sea… golf club swishing, golf balls… she saw Kingston fall in the dark… no, she was there, bending over him, it was light, hot and stuffy, she was at the swimming pool, that's why her hair was wet of course… the lifeguard was insisting on calling an ambulance for him… he'd fainted after an operation, a little operation…. Just a little prick with a needle, I know you are, doctor, but what are you going to do…

'Erica darling!' Her mother's voice. 'That nice Inspector Bennett called me. Wasn't that kind of him with all he's got to do? And a nice young Chinese doctor was in here holding your hand when I arrived. I suppose that was Jamie? I've brought you some big tee shirts, I know you've got no nighties and that hospital one is horrible. And some flowers darling, and fruit. Don't try to talk. I've moved into your place for a bit, so I can visit you every day. They've put a wire in your arm and a plaster cast on it, that's why it's so heavy.'

Into her place? At least her skull collection would get dusted for once. It's an ill wind. There was something important she had to say, but she couldn't think what it was. Awkward lie… She went back to sleep.

She had a room to herself. That was one blessing anyway. Because of the police interest in her, or because of Jamie's, she didn't ask. The sheets were beautifully crisp thick cotton. Everything else was purgatory. The food. If food it could be called. The drugs, given out at set times whether you wanted them or not or needed more, sooner. Being woken at the crack of dawn for no obvious reason, having spent all night trying to get to sleep. She managed to sit up and do things for herself though it's surprisingly hard to give yourself a bed-bath with one arm, on a slippery bed when exhausted, black and blue and suffering from exposure. The pain in her arm was held at bay by drugs, but it was nothing compared to the muddled merry go round of thoughts that whirled in her brain.

She laboriously texted Stacey with a list of things she needed from Ivy Lodge. It was hard to hold her phone and type one-handed but this physician was going to have to heal herself. There was no reply, but next day Stacey barged in bearing Arnica, Symphitum, (made from comfrey aka 'knitbone' which has been used for centuries), her constitutional remedy, a freshly extinguished Lambert and Butler, and a sulky expression resulting from this last being enforced by staff.

'This place is a fkn prison. Aa remember havin wor Noosh in the maternity wing. Fkn nazi guards. Aalways on yer case if yer light a fag. Aa mean, they'd not have a job if we all gave up smoking and drinking, would they? Ungrateful bastards. Here's aal yer new age crap.' She dumped the remedies on the locker. 'Eee Erica, yer hair looks like something oot of a shower drain. Yer know, they pump shite and aal sorts into the sea.'

Great. Erica dropped some Arnica tablets onto her tongue. Her throat still burned from the salt water and her voice was almost gone so she texted her thanks, and Stacey automatically texted her back. 'S'OK. Lol.'

'Oh Aa nearly forgot.' Stacey pulled a large box of expensive chocolates out of a carrier bag. 'Aa browt these for yer. Course, ye'll not get much exercise in here. Very fattenin, hospital scran.' She held the box expectantly over Erica like an alien spacecraft about to land.

Erica was startled at this generosity. But Stacey was right. She could easily put weight on while helpless and out of action. She shook her head at the chocolates, and texted 'Thx a mill. u keep em.'

'Oh, right. Just for ye, Aa will. And yer'll be glad to know, since you've got nee voice, Aa'm on the case as yer intern. Gary's waiting for iz outside and Aa'm tellin yer story to him. As yer spokesperson like. It's nee bother, no need to thank iz!'

She swept out with the chocolates back in the bag, fag in mouth waiting to be lit at the first opportunity. Outside in the main ward there was some kind of uproar going on.

A nurse popped in to check on her obs and said, 'Oh, that noise is poor Mrs M, she just woke up from a nap to find someone's nicked her posh chocs right off her locker top. She's going postal. She probably ate them and forgot, poor old dear.' Yes, because patients, especially older women, were by definition stupid, vague, demented... 'I mean, who'd do such a thing! In a hospital!'

Erica felt better once she'd made some effort to take control, having more faith in her own remedies than antibiotics. Better still when her mother had washed her hair. In her privileged little room, she was alone most of the time except during doctor's rounds or the meds trolley or what were laughingly called meals.

She'd assumed with things the way they are with the NHS that she'd be patched up and slung out, and that would have suited her fine. She could recover much better at home. But Jamie arranged for her to be kept in for a few days, the combination of exposure, fracture and stress making her vulnerable. She suspected Will wanted to keep her out of the action too.

CHAPTER FORTY-ONE

Will also wanted Erica kept in hospital though the security was minimal, anyone could stroll in at any time and he didn't have the manpower or sufficient reason to have her actually guarded. Seemingly Archer was harmless enough for now, but the Operator killings put anyone believed to have evidence at risk. And they weren't sure yet exactly what Archer's involvement was as the medics hadn't let the police interrogate him. It had been touch and go if he'd live, though he was already responding to treatment better than they'd hoped.

Superintendent 'Golden Boy' George spluttered cherry scone crumbs. 'You've got not just one Operator, but two, lad, you're spoilt rotten! Archer and Anderson, both under wraps and on bedpans! They'll both keep till we can sort out who mutilated who. We're looking very good in the media just now. 'Heroic officer leaps into foaming briny to save suspect and victim.' But you'll be busy waiting for Archer to talk, won't you Will, and of course you'll be wanting to keep an unofficial eye on Erica Bruce, just in case, so don't worry, I'll handle all the press conferences for you.' And nab any credit going.

Will visited Erica as soon as Jamie would allow. His dark, clever face was drawn and scowling. Bloody little jumped up doctor! It irked Will having to ask permission from the bloke Erica was shagging. Huh. He'd like to see Jamie diving into a raging ocean to save her. Prescribing antibiotics was the most he'd manage.

Erica had been interviewing nurses and anyone else she could get at about health problems and techniques for the health page using her voice recorder. It was a mercy that, and her phone, hadn't ended up in the sea. Her voice was a lot better but she felt awkward talking to Will in a nightie. Strange, considering their past intimacy. But then she'd never worn nighties. Worse, her hair, finally washed of North Sea gunge, salt and seaweed, was still wet. She'd texted Stacey to bring the hairdryer she kept at Ivy Lodge for straight-from-swimming drying. In the meantime she was annoyed to be seen, plain, pale and pathetic and with her hair dark, wet, dragged back into a bun.

'Wow you look different. Without your hair. I'd forgotten... erm I mean I'd hardly have recognised you. How are you?' Will put a plastic bag of grapes on her locker. Typical. Grapes are full of sugar, you goon.

'Thanks. Fine. How's Archer?' She was still very husky.

'Improving. Still seems weak. We found the catapult on his bedroom windowsill.'

'So I was right about that. Oh good.'

'Though in itself it's not evidence he used it on Kingston. The wallop with the stone effectively disguised any initial fracture caused by a golf ball. There's only his partial confession to you with no witnesses, in a state of distress, and you've both had major trauma since, or so his legal team will say. I'll try and get a statement from him as soon as they'll let me. I'll try tomorrow.'

He fiddled with the things on the top of the locker, almost knocking over a jug of water. He mopped up the spills with angry dabs and a tissue, not looking at her. Erica wasn't looking at him. If he was waiting for her to thank him for saving her life, he could do one. SHE was saving Archer's life and Will helped her with that. She wasn't giving Will the satisfaction and future gloating rights of being the knight in shining, or in this case soggy, armour. Not again.

He visibly steeled himself. 'Erica, I have to say it was quite something, you jumping into the sea after him, you could easily have drowned. You should have drowned. There was no way you'd have got to any kind of land unless someone saw you, it was a mad thing to do. I know you're a good swimmer, and you've trained in life-saving, but in those waves, with your arm, well, I have to say Erica, I'm really impressed. It took real balls.'

With a massive effort, just this once she didn't say 'Ovaries.'

'Thanks Will.' She was glad he'd said it first. 'And thanks for helping me. To save Archer I mean. I just couldn't not do it. I didn't even want to! And I'm not sure I did him any favours. What's he going to face if he does get better?'

'Prison probably.'

'And he'll never achieve his dream to join Wydsand Club. It meant everything to him, shallow as it sounds.'

'I know Erica, but he can't expect to get away with it. A good lawyer might be able to get some sympathy for an impulsive act with a catapult, but the killings, the mutilations...' If they could prove any of them. '...quite apart from breaking your arm. He's not going to get into any Golf Club with that record!'

'That bastard Kingston. He's hurt so many people. A man left with serious head injuries. Tessa's years of pain, injury and fear. His own horrible death. And what of Chambers, and Gupta? And Anderson? And their families. And Archer's life ruined. He's got nothing left to lose now.'

'Well we don't know all of what happened yet, and how much of it was down to Kingston. And as for Tessa...'

'Will, you must believe by now she was abused by Kingston! After all you've learned about him! Surely now you can see she was the innocent victim here. Oh my god, you just can't bear to be wrong can you?'

'And you can't bear not to be right. Not to be in charge of how we all think...'

'You're accusing ME of being controlling? Pot, kettle...'

'We're both control freaks. Let's face it. Look, I'm sorry. I came to visit you not yell at you when you're not well.'

'I can take anything you dish out Will Bennett, well or

not.' Erica felt hot, and dizzy, and Will saw to his alarm that she'd gone an odd colour. He was appalled at himself.

'Oh my god I'm sorry, you look as if you're about to faint. Here, have some water.'

He began to pour out a glass, when Erica gasped, her eyes wide.

'Oh god, what have I done, oh god, here darling, just lie back and I'll get the nurse...'

'Bastard!'

'Look I'm sorry...'

'Not you, Kingston! Come back here, listen. I'm fine... sod the water. Listen for once. At the swimming pool one day this guy suddenly fainted... he was watching his kid have a lesson. It was hot and steamy... The lifeguard came over and asked if he was OK and the guy whispered to him. The fainting guy was so embarrassed... the lifeguard shouted right across the pool to his colleague, 'It's all right, he had a vasectomy today!' Quite funny really...'

'OK nice story. Maybe you're on too much medication?'

'Will you listen! I heard two nurses talking. Kingston fainted at work, because he'd had a minor op. Unusual because he never showed weakness.'

'Well it could have been anything. A mole removed.'

'Crap! Nobody'd faint because of a mole. But if *he*'d had a vasectomy, imagine the sadism! Torturing his wife for failing to get pregnant, when all the time he was the one who... He wouldn't want a baby. Too much competition for him. Sick, sick bastard!'

'Well he's dead now anyway. Calm down Erica. Get some rest. I can come back tomorrow to go over your official statement.' And he was gone.

Wait, what did he call me? Darling? Patronising git. Erica felt twitchy and confined, so she tried to clear her thinking with some exercises on the bed, crunches and leg lifts mainly. Then she went off to visit a lovely lady in a nearby room who had pelvic fractures and was in traction. One of the nurses, no doubt fed up with Erica, had suggested she go and talk to her. She certainly needed someone to talk to, and for her, as for all patients, the days passed slowly and the nights seemed endless hours of pain, discomfort, and boredom.

On the way back to her own room, a nurse told her that Gary Thomas was hoping to visit her the next day. Who'd have thought Gary would ever see her in bed? Fate plays strange tricks. She'd be willing to bet he'd be delighted at the latest events. The girl (petite, blonde, yadda yadda) who caught the Operator. Doctors can sleep peacefully in their beds once more. Lucky them. Operator or not, Archer might still be dangerous, if he was recovering so well. Presumably he was under police guard? It was hard to feel secure, out of her safety zone, injured, and occasionally she imagined Archer getting up, walking through the corridors, like now when there was no-one about... She sighed. It was that dead time in the afternoon, after lunch and the drugs trolley, before afternoon visiting time. Hardly anyone seemed to be on duty at this time, and everything was quiet. She tried to have a nap to make up for the wakeful nights and ludicrously early mornings, but it was difficult. She tried to meditate, hoping to drift into sleep, hoping to forget the throbbing of her wrist, though it wasn't working. Some memory was beginning to come back to her, when she heard her door opening.

She opened her eyes, relieved to see Tessa coming in, smiling. Instantly she forgot about sleep; visitors are the breath of sanity to patients, and especially at this time of day, an unexpected treat. She'd been wondering how Tessa was getting on. She looked very pretty; she was carrying a bag, and – Erica sat up in bed.

'Hi Erica. Surprise!'

'Is that a nurse's uniform you're wearing? Or am I hallucinating… it's great to see you!'

Tessa hung her bag over the chair back. 'Yes it is, and no you're not! I'm back at work, the nursing I did before I married. Agency work. I decided, to hell with computers, this is where I belong, somewhere I can be some good to people. The pay's not wonderful of course, but I'm not short of money now so I can, you know, give something back.'

'Great!' Erica had wondered if Tessa was going to look for another husband to live off, but that was better left unsaid. Though doing some agency nursing would give her access to a stream of rich and hopefully less sadistic surgeons...

'There won't be any elderly patients' call buttons hidden when I'm around, or drinks left out of reach and then taken away untasted while some poor soul suffers with thirst... But that's enough about me. What about you? I can hear you're very croaky, and your poor arm! But you look great considering. I see you got someone to wash your hair! I'll see if I can hunt up a dryer somewhere for you. That was wonderful what you did, jumping in to save Harry Archer. He'll have to go to prison I suppose, or a mental institution. So the police think he killed Robert and Mr Chambers, and Mr Gupta too – or was that the other man who cut his arm off? What a tangle it all is! I'm glad I'm a nurse and not a policewoman. Anyway, I've brought you these.'

She reached into her shoulder bag and brought out a couple of magazines. The kind that tell you how to do up your house so it looks like a house from a magazine, except there's nowhere to put a skull collection or books.

'And these facial wipes. They're hypoallergenic – I know it'll be difficult for you to really cleanse your face at night, and get all your make-up off properly. You won't want visitors to see you without your face on!'

'Er thanks.' Faceless, Erica reached across to put them in the open-sided compartment of the locker, fumbling a bit.

'Shall I do that for you?'

'No it's OK, I can manage. So what's it like, being back here?'

'Well some things are different of course. But essentially it's the same job. All those years, I was looking for someone to look after me, and all the time, I should have been looking after others! I've taken control of my own life, just as you counselled me ages ago.' Tessa looked radiant, brimming over with energy and idealism. 'And of course, the Operator has made a difference too. No-one is quite sure it's really old Archer, however mad and deluded he is. The doctors are all still jumpy, but it's a good thing really. They might think twice before throwing their weight about like Robert did… So many stories coming out. Pathologist, struck off in one area, moves to another, works as a locum, makes wrong diagnoses of women's cancer. Some die, others lose healthy breasts. He'll have been dreading someone might do a mastectomy on him. And that other chap who injected drugs into the wrong part of a young patient's spine, I bet he's scared he's on the Operator's list. If it isn't Archer, that is. Of course we may never know for sure. I heard he's not likely to recover.'

'Oh? I heard he's improving. Will Bennett's talking about getting his statement tomorrow perhaps.'

'Oh, Will's been has he? Such a shame your hair was still wet. It's so lovely. We blondes lose half our looks with wet hair. Would you like me to brush it for you? I know you've got one good hand, but it's an effort isn't it? I could trim your fringe too…. I've got some scissors here in my bag. Please let me do something for you, you've done so much for me! You helped make me what I am today, instead of the victim I was.'

She loosened and began to brush Erica's long, thick damp hair, being careful not to tug any of the snarls. Erica tried to relax; she didn't feel comfortable being this passive, but on the other hand it was soothing in a sensual way to feel the long brush strokes. She could feel soft puffs of breath on her hair and skin as Tessa stood close.

Erica could smell her perfume, alien and exotic in the disinfected air. She moved round behind Erica as far as the bed-head would allow, and then went round to the other side, brushing with hypnotic strokes.

'I hear you've got a doctor boyfriend. Hot, they say. But too soft hearted for a surgeon. Like that's a bad thing!'

Tessa took out a pair of scissors and leaned across Erica to brush her fringe down over her eyes, it really was time it was cut. She moved to kneel on the bed, at Erica's right side, settling back to keep her balance as she began to cut with one hand, the other holding the brush. Erica felt the cold steel blades against her forehead. The cutting edge, the points, against her eyelid as they snipped. She opened her eyes as they moved, light flashing on the blades and Tessa's ring.

Her face was very close, the small features, the ash-blonde hair in a flatter, neater style, brushed off her face and tied back; the carefully applied make up, English rose blusher, the pearly shine of her full lips, her light blue eyes now just inches away, a slight frown puckering the soft skin between her expertly shaped eyebrows. Little drifts of cut hair winnowed down onto the sheet. Tessa dropped the scissors into her bag, then gently brushed Erica's hair again, the length of it, all around. Time slowed down. They were close enough to kiss. Erica shifted, embarrassed by their closeness suddenly.

'Let's have a look.' Erica reached into her locker, moving the magazines aside, bringing out her hand mirror. 'Oh that's great Tessa. Thanks.'

'Hang on while I brush out your fringe again. It's nearly dry. Then you can look again.' Tessa knelt on the bed again, at Erica's right hand side, leaning across, gazing into her eyes now in an intense way, the brush in her hand gently moving over Erica's brow. 'I've never had children, but I do love to look after people.'

'Well it's not too late.'

'But...you know I can't.'

'Tessa, your husband - I think he had a vasectomy. He lied to you about your infertility. Another one of his twisted sadistic games.'

Tessa flinched, one hand pressed to her belly. 'No, he couldn't have...'

'So you can still have a family. Most likely.'

'But how do you know?'

'Listening to people. Will Bennett's checking it out right now.' If only he'd made the connection too. 'But you knew that already didn't you Tessa?'

CHAPTER FORTY-TWO

'The post-mortem report, Kingston's medical records, it's in there somewhere. You went through all those reports with a fine tooth comb. I remember admiring your stoicism when Tara told me.'

'Erica, don't. I've always admired you so much. So strong, so in control. You've been a role model for me really. A bit of a girl-crush to be honest.'

'You already knew. I could see it in your eyes, so close to mine, just a flicker before the acting kicked in. He got someone to do a cheeky little private snip for him. Wouldn't want it known. Let me guess, Paul Chambers. Doing it behind your back, when both partners are supposed to give consent and receive counselling… Chambers probably took his word for it you were on board. Tara told me how shocked you were by Kingston's reports, how you said, 'I wanted to be sure he didn't suffer too much.' He didn't, did he? He didn't suffer enough.'

'Erica, how can you say this to me? You're my friend. My therapist. You're supposed to be on my side!'

'I don't want it to be true. But I have to know. It gives you a motive to kill Chambers as well as Kingston; without that, it's less likely that you killed your husband. With it, you might have killed both of them. Two arrogant men, making decisions about your life without consulting you…'

'Erica, how can you! You know, everyone's saying Archer confessed to you that he'd killed Robert, so…'

'Archer only confessed to the catapult injuries; fracturing Kingston's skull with the golf ball. He didn't seem clear about the rest, odd don't you think in a man intent on suicide. It was almost like he was worried he'd done the mutilating, the other murders even, but didn't remember it. And if he's a stone cold serial killer, why try to kill himself, instead of just killing me? He broke my wrist yes, but only when I tried to stop him jumping. The psychology of it's all wrong. Shooting from a distance was much easier for Archer, but the Operator liked his killing to be up close and personal. If it wasn't Archer, then who? Some avenging angel self-appointed to punish doctors – but why start with Kingston? Why not some more high-profile blunderer? Chambers had no public blot on his record, why him? Gupta was the first victim who had been publicly accused, falsely in fact, of negligence. No Tessa, Kingston's death, and Chambers', they were hate crimes, and nobody had better reason to hate them than you.'

'You know my sister is a solicitor, Erica. What you are saying is libel!'

'Slander actually. Go on then, sue me!'

'You're breaking my heart Erica.' Her voice was quiet and controlled. And sad.

'Oh my god! Gupta was a heart surgeon. Was he the one, Tessa? Did Kingston tell you he'd got Gupta lined up to agree you'd died of heart failure if he decided to kill you? He probably lied about that too, by all accounts Gupta was a good man, but why stop now you'd started something so powerful? You could kid yourself you were doing it for the good of society, for the family whose child died on Gupta's table. 'Giving something back,' I think you just called it. You're dying for somebody to know the Operator is still around, aren't you? So the bad doctors keep shaking in their shoes... I bet you're conflicted about Archer taking the blame. It would mean you'd have to stop. I bet you've got a database of all those negligence cases you've been reading about. That computer course came in useful after all...'

'Look at me, Erica! Do I look like a killer?'

'No. You're a fluffy blonde, sweet as arsenic pie.' Erica's voice was straining to keep going. Her throat ached. Keep her talking... Archer's life wasn't worth a hospital sandwich if Tessa got to him before he gave his statement. If only someone would come in, but Tessa had timed her visit perfectly to hit the dead spot after lunch and before tea and visitors. The dead spot. Out of the corner of her eye, Erica saw that her phone had vanished from the locker top. Swept no doubt into Tessa's bag with the scissors. And ironically, Tessa had quietly put her call button out of reach over the back of the bed.

'I couldn't have killed Robert. I was at Tara's all night.'

'Do I really have to spell it out, or will you tell me and save my throat? It's just you and me here, after all. You went back to the marital home that night, after your afternoon visit with Tara. Somehow. Intent on getting in, I don't know why. To kill him, to inherit his money before he could change his Will? At some point Kingston went out the back door to chase off the lads. Suddenly he's flat out unconscious, whacked on the back of the head by Archer's little golf ball, shot from his catapult, but you don't know that, could have been the lads, he might have tripped, whatever. There he is at your feet, in your power, the man who hurt you and mocked you and destroyed your life and your self-esteem, helpless, injured but alive.

'This is your chance to finish him off. You grab a rock, hit him again hard over the wound to make sure. It feels good, but it's not enough though. The bastard still owes you.'

Tessa licked her lips. Her breath was coming faster, a film of sweat oiled her upper lip. Their eyes were still locked, Tessa's baby blues and Erica's sea greens.

'You drag him inside and do the rest. You're used to barrier nursing. You'd assisted in surgery, and treated patients with Ilizarov frames. You haul him onto the table, you're used to lifting patients, gym-fit and full of hell, you bang in the nails, his own surgical spikes, wearing nitrile gloves and protection from Robert's desk... risky, but you'd given way to an impulse, like Archer did, but so much more hate behind it, even more than his. Then you simply left, and went back to Tara and her children, dumping the soiled aprons and gloves in a random litter bin somewhere.

'And there he lies, dead, his hands nailed down, the hands that broke your arm, nails through the brain that thought up clever ways to torment you... but you're clever too, aren't you? Much cleverer than any of them think.'

'You're insane! Tara gave me an alibi. And as for Chambers, I was at the gym when he died, the police themselves saw me go in!'

'Easy to look different, at a gym. What did you just say, we blondes lose half our looks with wet hair? You trot in all high heels and fluffed out blonde 'do. Work out, then do a few lengths in the pool so your mates upstairs don't know whether you're still in the building or not, change into different clothes in a poolside locker, leave through the back, do the deed, go back in through the front door, with wet hair slicked back flat and in baggy sports gear and trainers, your whole look, even your walk would be different.'

'You've got some of it right. How I got out of the gym without the police spotting me. Oh those blokes notice a cute blonde strutting in and out, they don't bother to look at a dowdy, wet-haired woman in cheap sports clothes from Poundstretcher. The women in the gym didn't know, those upstairs assumed I was in the pool and vice versa.'

Actually hearing it from Tessa's own lips shocked Erica more than she'd expected. Tessa moved her left knee suddenly and quickly to kneel hard on Erica's good wrist which was lying on the bed in front of her. The other was in plaster and a lot of pain. She shifted her right leg and used her weight to pin down Erica's legs, while her right hand held down the plastered arm. She seemed to tower over Erica suddenly looking down at her almost pityingly.

'Shame you haven't much voice to call for help, and the button's out of reach. Yes, I'm the Operator. I had Robert helpless, dying, but I wanted more. I saw the pins on his desk, and remembered how when Robert hurt me he'd say, 'Don't try telling anyone. They all think I'm Jesus Christ, but you'd be the one crucified!' His little joke. He's not laughing now, that's for sure! Then I found out about the vasectomy. Chambers deserved to die too. I'd gone through hell over my supposed infertility. So I went to see him. No-one's on their guard with me, but I'm stronger than I look. Handy being a doctor's widow, access to syringes, drugs of all kinds, sterile gloves… easy to get nice and close to a man, then whack! And his own scalpel doing its work, and his hands nailed down. No more mischief from him. It felt good, better even than Robert. I realised, I'd been able to get away with it because it was meant to be. Robert was delivered to me. It was already decided before I started. The press called me the Operator. There was work to be done, people to help.'

Erica was tired, hurt, and in shock. Being right sucked. This time, for the first time, she'd much rather have been wrong.

'I…' her voice faded into a ridiculous croak.

'Oh Erica, to feel that power! It's such a rush… I *am* going to stay in nursing, I haven't lied to you. I do want to help people. I'll get to hear all the gossip about doctors. Who's under investigation, who's a bastard… I'm not a psychopath you know. The pleasure I feel is a reward for the work, a job well done. I did go back to Robert's that night. Wore jogging gear. Hair covered up in a hoodie. Got a taxi from a rank to a street the other side of the golf course. Jogged over it looking like a youth. That same trick came in handy later on.'

Erica thought of the 'youth' seen near Gupta's murder.

'I wanted to get into the house without Robert catching me. Oh I was a lot cleverer than you thought. I took some drugs from the house when Tara and I were there, gave some to her to make her sleep so she'd not know I went out. Then *I* was the lads, that night. Threw a few stones at the windows. Yelled a bit. Robert comes storming out and I hide in the bushes. Idea being, to sneak in behind him, hide in the house and leave later when I got the chance, when he was asleep or out. Big house, and I knew his routine. But I was terrified, Erica! Imagine that, terrified of him! But I just had to go back. Then suddenly, a noise, and he just fell to the ground at my feet, like magic. And my life changed just like that! But you deserve some of the credit Erica. You helped me become the woman I am. You needn't worry. The Operator won't hurt you.'

She reached down into her bag and produced a nitrile glove. 'See how useful it is to be a doctor's widow and a trained nurse. It won't hurt, I promise you.' She shook the bag almost playfully. 'I've got no nails in here!' She manoeuvred her left hand into the glove using her small white teeth to hold it.

'Tessa, how will you get away with this?'

'Why, easily, as always. Just like Robert got away with breaking my arm. No-one knows I'm here. I haven't gone back to work officially yet!'

Erica should have known. The perfume, the jewellery.

'But I know this is a quiet time, I just walked in in my old uniform – and a wig, which I whipped off just before I came in here. I really did come to visit you, bring you magazines. Before I visit Harry Archer. And that's a mercy killing you know.' She shook her bag again. 'It's high time security was stepped up here. It's not safe for patients. I'll just leave when all the visitors pile in.'

As she spoke, she pulled a syringe out of her bag.

CHAPTER FORTY-THREE

Keep her talking Erica. 'But why did you go back Tessa? If you were so scared of him? Why go back alone without Tara?'

'To get this, of course.' Tessa held up her hand, the one with the ring. 'My Tiffany ring. Tara asked for my personal things, the ones I'd left when I moved out in a hurry, but this one he said he knew nothing about. Then when Tara was out of earshot, he whispered to me that he'd still got it, but if I didn't go back to him by the end of the week, it was going down the toilet. My beautiful ring! It cost over five thousand pounds! I just had to get it back. When I'd finished with him, I found it. I told Tara a couple of days later I'd found it had been mixed up in the stuff he gave us back that afternoon. My lucky ring! It gave me Robert, and then it gave me freedom from him.

'And now,'

Keep her talking! 'So you entered and left by the back door. But the front door was unlocked when I arrived.'

'You do like your t's crossed! Yes well I knew it was the cleaner's holiday - shame really, I'd love her to have found him, the foul bitch. She worshipped Robert! Anyway, I didn't want to risk him lying dead for days. Not very nice, in my house.' An echo of Lady Macbeth. How practical

Tessa had turned out to be, when her material comfort or gain was involved.

'And it was me who was his first appointment. Lucky me.'

'Yes, I saw your name on his list. I was glad about that. I mean, knowing how strong you are, I knew you'd cope. Wouldn't want some poor old arthritis patient finding him. That would be cruel. Now I must get on. I'll just inject this where you've already got needle tracks from the antibiotic. In your left arm I think. I won't tell you what it is, but it's painless as I said. I hadn't planned this, but I can use a pillow for poor old Harry. I nicked this stuff from Robert's stash. He might have killed me with it one day.'

Erica felt sad as much as frightened. Weary. She'd fought for her life against the North Sea, against Archer, and now she'd have to do it again. This was someone she knew, someone she'd tried to protect. But she'd have to fight, if only to leave some forensic evidence. Some of Tessa's DNA had to be found somewhere on her whatever the outcome.

'Do you think I'm just going to lie here and take it? If we fight, it'll not look like natural causes, will it?' Her right arm had gone numb. Why didn't someone come in?

Tessa looked down at her, still pretty, smiling. She stroked Erica's cheek. Her hand with the nitrile skin felt smooth and dead. 'I'd really rather not do this Erica. Honestly.'

Tessa was strong. And she hadn't just fought the sea.

Her left hand would be free to plunge the syringe into Erica's injured arm just above the plaster cast, holding it still with her right hand.

'Tessa, you say you've taken control, but can't you see you're out of control? Can't you see what you've turned into? Can't you see you've turned into something worse than Robert Kingston! You're not fit to have a child!'

Anger flared in the soft blue eyes for the first time. She grabbed for Erica's neck with her free hand.

'Don't make me want to hurt you!' she grunted. Erica twisted her head down to her shoulder, and her hair, long and thick, got in Tessa's way. She grabbed a handful of it and pulled Erica's head up. She writhed under Tessa, using the momentary relaxing of pressure, spread her thighs and got her legs round her. She squeezed Tessa with her strong thighs, trying to kick the backs of her calves though with bare feet it was of limited use. She felt like she was being scalped. Giving up the neck hold, furious now at her resistance, Tessa stabbed down with the needle, and Erica jerked her left arm just enough to meet it with her plaster cast. A jarring pain shot through her, but she didn't feel the needle, as the syringe hit the floor.

'I could have done this when I was doing your hair, but I didn't think I'd have to kill you, Erica, I really, really tried not to! It's your own fault! You could have let me go on! We could both be helping people!'

She grabbed Erica's plastered arm and started smashing

it against the bed bars. Erica nearly passed out but kept holding on with her legs. Suddenly, looking across for the syringe, Tessa glanced inside the open locker compartment and froze.

'You treacherous bitch!' she yelled, and in that moment, Erica rolled them both off the bed, hoping Tessa would land underneath. She did. Hospitals have high beds and hard floors. They lay on the floor winded, Erica's broken arm was in agony, and Tessa was getting a grip on her right arm again. Someone help me, I can't manage this on my own, please, Erica prayed to anyone who'd listen.

'Fuck me!'

The door banged into the bed, painfully ringing through Erica's head which was against one of the wheels on the other side, as Stacey walked in and stared at the tangled mass of female limbs and mingled honey and ash blonde hair struggling on the floor.

'Eee, Erica man, nowt wrong with a bit of girl on girl but why bother when there's nee lads aroond to get turned on? Here's yer hairdryer then.' She dropped a carrier bag on the bed, followed by a large bunch of expensive flowers, dripping with water, and turned to go.

'The syringe...' Erica gasped, as she and Tracey wrestled.

Stacey looked and saw it. 'Hard core!' she said with respect.

'Kick it away! Tessa's the Operator!'

Tessa hit her hard across the face and started to beat

her broken arm on the floor. Stacey stood there with her mouth open for a moment, then 'Mint!'

'Stacey, please help me!'

'Nee bother!'

In one swift movement, Stacey had her phone out and was filming the struggle. 'That's the Operator attacking Erica Bruce! And me, Stacey Reed, to the rescue!' she commentated. 'Now haway ye psycho nutjob, gerroff me mate!'

Stacey reached down and hauled Tessa off Erica's limp body, pushing her violently aside. The relief of having Tessa's weight lifted from her felt like heaven to Erica. 'Be careful... she's a killer...'

Stacey put her phone in Erica's good hand. 'Hold this, man, and divven't miss owt or Aa'll kill ye meself!'

Erica was shaking too much to make an emergency call one-handed, so she just followed the action as best she could as Tessa turned and attacked Stacey, desperate and mad. This was a woman who'd killed three men, who'd pitilessly mutilated them as they died at her hands. She had nothing to lose now, desperate and at bay. She was fit, strong and insane, a screaming, biting, kicking mass of murderous intent. Stacey was an unfit, lazy smoker, but she was a Tyneside lass, veteran of years of drunken brawls and beating up abusive lads in clubs and taxi queues, used to brutal close quarters fighting, while Tessa had never faced a conscious uninjured victim. They clashed together, Tessa grabbing a lump of Stacey's puffed-up black hair, which came off in her hand.

'Ye bloody bitch, gerroff me extensions!' And Stacey launched a meaty fist which smashed into Tessa's nose. Blood spurted instantly, Tessa's hands went to her face as Stacey followed up with a vicious kick to the knee cap, and turning, an elbow to the belly before grabbing Tessa's hair, from underneath at the nape in case of hair extensions, turning her and slamming her face-first into the wall. Tessa fell to the floor whimpering, blood gushing from her nose. Stacey almost casually pinned her to the floor, her knee in Tessa's back.

'This is the Operator, dangerous serial killer, captured by me, Stacey Reed,' she announced, looking round to the camera, just as Will Bennett and Sally Banner rushed in.

'Erica!' Will sprang to lift Erica up and put her on the bed, to Sally's disgust. Sally grabbed Stacey and tried to manhandle her off Tessa.

'Come on now, that's assault,' she snapped.

'Up yours Bizzy!' snarled Stacey. 'Aa've just caught the Operator for yiz, and that's the thanks Aa get!'

Erica was still filming. Stacey, fully roused to ire, stood magnificent, solid as the Rock of Gibraltar (a local pub), bruised, bleeding, scratched, hair awry, ready to take on the world. 'That murdering bitch was trying to kill Erica who found out her true identity! Crazy fucker's been killing doctors aal ower the place, and where were ye then, man, woman!'

'Stop filming,' ordered Will, reaching for the phone. Erica tossed it feebly to Stacey. She'd earned her viral Youtube glory. 'There's no firm evidence that this is true.'

'Shurrup man! It's true, isn't it Erica?'

'Yes it's true and yes there's evidence. Full confession.' Erica reached out for her voice recorder in the locker, which she'd turned on when reaching for her hand mirror, and which Tessa had spotted during the struggle.

Stacey punched the air. 'Double fkn mint! Back of the net!'

As Will and Sally lifted Tessa from the floor, her ruined face a mass of blood and snot, Stacey took a last shot and stopped filming. 'Fag break!' and she charged out of the room. In the comparative quiet, they heard a voice shout, 'Nurse, NURSE! That's the girl who stole my flowers!' and Erica laughed until she cried, her damaged plaster leaking powder onto the flower-wetted sheets and her whole body shaking.

CHAPTER FORTY-FOUR

Erica lay on the high bed, her wounded wrist by her side, fingers curling out of the newly applied plaster like a hermit crab's legs. Will had checked up on Erica's idea, found out that Chambers had indeed done a vasectomy on Kingston, realised what a motive it gave Tessa for the first two murders, and returned to the hospital, though he'd rushed to check on Archer first, assuming he might be at risk. She tried not to think about the appalling aftermath of the struggle. Tessa's arrest. What it would mean for Tara and her family. The ongoing suffering of the victims' relatives. Craig Anderson was recovering slowly. It turned out one of his patients, who had refused conventional treatment on his advice, had died of cancer, leaving a distraught husband and a young son.

Under it all for Erica was the euphoria which goes with survival, the heartless primitive glee of knowing we'll see the next lot of daffodils. It'd been a close thing, between her and Tessa, as between her and the sea.

Six weeks, she'd have the plaster on. And she was going home tomorrow. She studied a leaflet about a plastic sleeve-type structure which formed a watertight seal over a plaster cast so she could shower, and best of all, swim. Her near-fatal immersion hadn't put her off water, not even the salty kind. And she hadn't gone off Jamie either. He'd been very proper and hands-off while she'd been a patient, and Erica was looking forward to being in her own bed again, with and without him. The thought of Will Bennett intruded itself now and again. Standing there next day without a mark on him, while there she was, a wreck, who had handed over the evidence that tied up his case for him. And how did he thank her?

'You see, Erica, I was right all along. I said it was Tessa Kingston from the start.' While Will enjoyed being right, even if for the wrong reasons, he had to admit she had supplied much of the evidence and the major jumps forward in the investigation.

They had looked at each other, and the chemistry was still there. The feel of his strong arms and the blue of his eyes had regained their appeal. Jamie's cuteness receded in her mind. Why couldn't she have both of them?

Will gazed down at her. 'Oh Erica. You're a mathematician, you have logic, if only you'd use it. You could make a fortune doing a useful job with your brain instead of this homeopathy crap.'

If only chemistry, and biology, were enough. If only Will could lose the power of speech instead of his appeal.

Erica didn't want to believe her empowering therapy had really helped to make Tessa the Operator; it was being the victim, storing up humiliation and pain, suddenly given the chance to be the one with power, that had triggered that, though perhaps it had been in her all along. But she was left to wonder how she, trained and experienced in understanding people and all their quirks, could have been so wrong about her patient. She was such a good judge of people.

Wasn't she?

ACKNOWLEDGEMENTS

Grateful thanks are due to Ann Cleeves for invaluable advice and support at an earlier stage and for a fabulous cover quote. Thank you also to authors Alex Marwood, Phoef Sutton and Chris Longmuir for pre-publication reading and reviews, to my daughter Lydia Laws for feedback and support, and to my friends of the Authors Electric blogging collective for advice on all things Amazon. Thank you also to Sheila Wakefield of Red Squirrel Press, publisher of my crime fiction and recent poetry in paperback. And finally love and thanks to Dr Allan Huggins, my long-suffering boyfriend, for computer- and image- related advice and assistance, and for listening to me ranting and despairing as well as sharing my joys.

THE OPERATOR is set on the North East coast of England, mainly in fictionalised versions of Whitley Bay and Tynemouth, and in Newcastle upon Tyne.

ABOUT THE AUTHOR

Valerie Laws is a Northumbrian crime and comedy novelist, poet, playwright and sci-art specialist. Her recent work, in new crime novel THE OPERATOR and latest poetry collection ALL THAT LIVES, is informed by funded Residencies at a London Pathology Museum, at Kings College London Medical School, and at Newcastle University's Institute for Ageing and Health, researching the science of dying with neuroscientists and pathologists. Her twelve published books (four ebooks, eleven paperback) include crime fiction, poetry collections (next due out October 2014), drama, best-selling language books and comedy. She has written twelve commissioned plays for stage and BBC radio. Many prizes and awards include: Wellcome Trust Arts Award, twice prizewinner in National Poetry competition, two Northern Writers Awards, short-listed for the McKitterick Prize. She invents new forms of kinetic poetry, devising science-themed poetry installations and commissions including world-infamous *Quantum Sheep,* an Arts Council-funded project spray-painting poetry onto live sheep. She featured in BBC2 TV's *Why Poetry Matters* with Griff Rhys Jones, with a quantum haiku on inflatable beach balls, later performed live at Royal Festival Hall London. Kinetic poetry AV installations/films such as *Slicing The Brain* have featured in public exhibitions across Europe and UK, and her embedded haiku *Window of Art* computer-controlled illuminated installation is in St Thomas Hospital London. She has had many other writers' residencies, including in Egypt in a 5* hotel, and currently at Dilston Physic Garden in Northumberland. She performs her work live and in the media worldwide.